Sunset and Steel Rails

by

Celia Hayes

Geron & Associates

San Antonio, 2015

ISBN-13 978-0-989782050
ISBN-10 0-89782050

Printed in the United States of America.

Geron & Associates
A Division of Watercress Press.
2015

Notes from the Author

Thanks and acknowledgements are due to a great number of people who contributed advice and support to the writer of this novel. I should begin with thanks to Bernadette Durbin, for her photograph of the classic 19th century locomotive, which was transformed by my clever younger brother Alex of 3iii Graphics in designing the cover elements. I would also like to thank fellow writer and blogger Andrea Downing, whose post about the Harvey Girls in January of this year inspired me to write about a heroine who took that particular route in going west.

The Fred Harvey Company was truly a novel, forward-thinking organization, particularly inspired in the way it offered respectable and well-paid employment to young women with a taste for adventure. Twelve-hour shifts, six days a week of waiting tables does seem like very hard work, but in comparison to the labor required of a woman on a farm, or in domestic service, it may have been a walk in the park by comparison – especially considering the various up-to-the-minute conveniences which Fred Harvey made available to employees.

This book is dedicated with love to Mom and my daughter Jeanne, and to the memory of Dad, the best alpha-reader ever, and to my late business partner, Alice Geron – the best editor, ever.

Celia Hayes
San Antonio, Texas
September 2015

Part 1 - 1884

Chapter 1 - The Ending of a Life, Unobserved

Under the dour painted gaze of her great-grandfather, Lycurgus Saltinstall Vining, Sophia Brewer's life ended on a mild and sunny spring afternoon, on a day when the tulips were in bloom in the Public Gardens, down the hill from Richard Brewer's fine Beacon Street mansion. The tall windows of the study stood open to the fresh spring breeze, barely stirring the curtains and bouquets of yellow tulips and blue hyacinths, which filled the tall blue and white Chinese export vases placed just so on the parlor mantel, and on the table.

"What did you say?" Sophia demanded, utterly startled out of all manners and countenance, but her upbringing and schooling was such that she quickly added, "I am sorry, Lucian – Mr. Armitage – did I hear you correctly? That you wish to break our engagement at this moment?" Sophia gazed upon Lucian Armitage with an expression which mingled disbelief and horror. *How could this be happening?* She was a Brewer, and on her mother's side a Vining. Even if her family had lately come on hard times they were of an old and respected lineage in Massachusetts. She and her affianced had pledged to each other long before the death of Sophia's mother. When the period of mourning for the widowed Sophia Vining Brewer's mortal passing was completed, it was understood and accepted; Sophia would marry Lucian Armitage with all proper ceremony. With a year and more gone by, the younger Sophia had gradually put off mourning black and donned garments of grey and lavender, as much as the sparse allowance from her brother Richard had allowed. The anniversary had passed, yet no wedding date had been suggested. With an effort, Sophia disguised her shock and disappointment; a marriage to Lucian Armitage was her only escape from her older brother's household and rule. She was not quite 21 and no reigning beauty, being slender and small in stature, with hazel-grey eyes set in a fine-boned face, and light-brown hair so tightly curling that her childhood nurse had claimed that combing it was like carding wool. But she possessed every particle of that fierce intelligence so notable in the senior ladies of her family, sharpened and refined by as an education at least the equal of any young Bostonian of means, female and male alike.

Lucian Armitage, lanky and awkward, with a brief mustache and an ambition for fashionable whiskers which nature had not favored him to fulfill with any grace, regarded Sophia with alarm. "My father has forbidden our marriage," he answered, in tones of misery. "Absolutely: He says that I cannot be allowed to marry for love unless there is a generous inheritance attached to the settlement."

"I have a small bequest from Mother," Sophia replied, although behind the tight-laced corset and grey merino bodice, her heart was breaking. She had expected so much better from Lucian. "Left to me in her will. I thought that sufficient for a marriage portion, small as it is. You are of age, and I will be by next month. We can still wed."

"My father forbids it," Lucian answered, his countenance a landscape of pure misery. "He will cast me off, if I go through with an elopement without his blessing. I am sorry. Your inheritance is insufficient for us to live in any kind of respectability. I won't ask for return of the ring with which I pledged to you, Soph. You may keep it – a gift."

He sketched an awkward bow and blundered towards the half-opened study door. Not fifteen minutes ago, he had presented his calling-card to Agnes Teague, the Brewer's maid-of-all-work. Tuesday was at-home day for the Brewer ladies. Sophia and her sister-in-law Phoebe received social calls in the parlor. On this morning, Lucian made limping conversation for some minutes with Phoebe and Great-Aunt Minnie Vining, Minnie's companion Miss Phelps, with Sophia's old school friend Emma Chase and Emma's step-mother, before asking if he might have a word in private with Sophia. How the parlor full of women had all beamed on Lucian! Sophia's mouth tasted of ashes and gall, recollecting Emma whispering, "Now he will set a date, dear Sophia – remember, we promised to be bridesmaids for each other!" and squeezing her hand.

Out in the hallway, Sophia heard the heavy front door open and the treble voice of Agnes bidding him a good morning and closing the heavy door after him. Then there was naught but his quick-fading footsteps outside in Beacon Street, and a brief pause of feminine conversation in the parlor.

Sophia's vision briefly hazed, her brother's study – the walls of books, the tall windows, the fireplace with the Chinese vases and the portrait of Great-Grandfather Vining blurred as if obscured by a veil of fog. She reached out with a shaking hand, found the back of one of the tall chairs set before the fireplace, and sat in it until the fog cleared – hands folded demurely in her lap and back as straight a posture as had ever been encouraged by the deportment mistress at Miss Phillips' Academy for Young Ladies. She sat and breathed until her vision cleared. The sweet scent of hyacinths hung in the room, overlaying the odor of her brother's pipe tobacco.

"Miss Sophia?" That was Agnes Teague's voice. Sophia lifted her head and forced a smile upon her face, more to reassure Agnes. Such a child – and an impoverished infancy in North Town made her appear even more childlike, for all that she was fifteen. The hand-me-down black maid's dress that Agnes wore when tending the parlor in the afternoon was too large for her, and made her appear even more childish, swathed in a starched white apron which hitched in the too-wide waist. Sophia was fond of Agnes, all things considered – her only intimate in the household, and certainly her only ally. "Are ye all right, noo? The gentleman left in such a rush."

"I am," Sophia breathed deeply. The last of the grey mist cleared. "Mr. Armitage has just told me that his father has forbidden our marriage on account of my impoverished situation. Our engagement has ended."

"Ohhh," Agnes Teague's eyes rounded in her peaked countenance, increasing her resemblance to a small pale owl. "Miss … what shall ye do, now?"

"I don't know, Agnes." Sophia made herself rise from the chair. "Make my excuses – but I think I shall go up to my room. This has been a horrible disappointment. I need to lie down for a while." To her secret relief, she no longer felt wobbly in her lower limbs, although she was slightly sick in the pit of her stomach. She had been counting on Lucian for so long, seeing in him an end to little-rewarded servitude in her brother's household.

"Yes, miss." Agnes bobbed a brief and proper curtsey – a gesture ruined by her owl-eyes overflowing with tears of sympathy. "Oh, miss – I am that sorry. 'Tis like that awful Captain George throwing over Miss Amelia Sedley when her own Da went bust! Oh, miss!" The tears began spilling down Agnes' cheeks in earnest. "Tell me … they won't have to sell the household goods to settle with Mr. Brewer's creditors, will they? And you and Mrs. Phoebe come to live in a boarding house on Beacon Hill?"

"Don't be silly, Agnes," Sophia answered, touched and braced by Agnes's sympathy – and diverted at how Agnes identified her own lamentable situation with the novel which Sophia was reading aloud to her, in an attempt to remedy the girl's sad lack of any education save in Papist pieties. "You live in a boarding house and Great-aunt Minnie and Miss Phelps live on Beacon Street and not far from it, either."

"Aye so – but we are poor, Da and Seamus and Declan and Siobhan. We have two small rooms and Miss Minnie may live half a mile away so we are neighbors in no small way – but she has the entire house which was your Great-grand-da's, in the day. By your counting, Miss Minnie might no' have any great estate, but compared to us, we are poor indade. Ye may have no money, Miss Sophia, but you will never be poor."

"You may be correct, Agnes," Sophia replied, touched and yet amused at the comparison. "I have that bequest in Mother's will, and our family includes connections of some influence." She sighed. Perhaps she had not been so much in love with Lucian as custom expected. It was extraordinary how calmly she accepted the withdrawal of his formal affections once the original shock had passed. From everything Sophia had been told, if she were deep in love with Lucian, she should have been incapacitated with grief, weeping helplessly and prone on the hearthrug.

Possibly it was the prospect of freedom in a small household of her own, upon which she had set her hopes; not the charms and marital attraction of Lucian himself. She was tired of dancing attendance on Phoebe, perpetually ailing, and on hers and Richards's grotesquely indulged and sickly younger son. That she had overheard Richard and Phoebe in private conversation the other evening only increased her general dissatisfaction. Going past the half-opened door of their chamber, she listened to Richard expiating at length over the fact that he was spared the cost of a governess; Sophia's presence in their household had only increased their household budget by the cost of her keep and a tiny allowance.

He had sounded terribly smug, which cut Sophia to the quick; she had admired her brother since she was a child. Father had died in the War, an officer in the 28th Massachusetts. Sophia did not remember him. Richard, fifteen years her senior had always been the man of the house. Until overhearing that conversation, Sophia had unthinkingly accepted that theirs was a family unified in temporary adversity.

Sophia had stolen up the staircase to her own little room, heartsick at this and wondering if there was a way for her to set aside the expectations of everyone in their circle of acquaintances. She would prefer living in Great-aunt Minnie's aging mansion, in the poor side of Beacon Hill, then here in the house which her father had purchased, back when the Brewers were well-to-do. If she was going to be one of those grim old bluestocking spinsters, Sophia concluded, she might as well get it over and be done.

"I'll make you some ginger-tea," Agnes promised in a whisper as Sophia moved towards the hall door. "And Mrs. Garrett kept back some of those seed-cakes she made for the ladies' tea. I'll bring them to your room, if ye have an appetite."

"Thank you, Agnes," Sophia replied with honest gratitude. Mrs. Garrett and Agnes were their only servants these days, the two women and sometimes Agnes's crippled oldest brother Declan, on those rare occasions when a task demanded manly strength. Declan might have had a wooden foot, to replace the one of flesh and bone lost to gangrene, but he was fit enough otherwise. He worked as a night-watchman at a shipping warehouse in the harbor district and was not averse to occasional additional work during the daylight hours.

Sophia climbed the stairs to her own room, resolutely ignoring the sounds of excited chatter in the parlor which hushed and then broke out again, redoubled. Agnes has delivered her message. She closed the door behind her, regarding her bedroom with a feeling of bleak despair at odds with the pretty room – papered with flower-sprigged wallpaper, and furnished with old-fashioned furniture in pale-wood finishes. A fresh spring breeze ruffled the muslin curtains on either side of the tall window which faced out into the garden behind the Brewer mansion. Dear and familiar a refuge, it might well be a prison, she thought, savagely. What was she going to do now that

Lucian had broken their engagement? They had known each other from childhood since their mothers were dearest friends.

She looked into the mirror over the washstand at her own familiar countenance; no, there was no lack in herself that she detected. She was not unpleasing to the eye, disinclined to male flirtation, or to society in general; but given the Brewer family's straitened circumstances, her opportunities to meet an eligible suitor might be fatally limited.

Sophia had no idea how to remedy that situation. Her head ached. After Phoebe's 'at home' hours were over, she was expected to walk her nephew Richie home from school. Phoebe – Richard's shadow and chorus in every way – was in a delicate state, again. Even when not ailing, she was too … Sophie searched her mind for a term of derogation sufficient to relieve her exasperation with her sister-in-law … silly and indecisive to see to the raising of her own children.

She sank into the shabby armchair before the window and leaned her head against the high upholstered back, wishing she might just sit and rest, have the leisure to think and the knowledge of what she ought to do. But there was no rest for her in Richard's house, any more than for Agnes, or Mrs. Garrett. Still – couldn't she be allowed five-ten-twenty minutes of time to meditate upon and accept what had happened. After a moment she became aware she still clenched Lucian's ring in her left hand, so tightly that her fingernails bit into her palm. Now she opened her hand and gazed incuriously at the ring – a band of yellow gold, set with a wreath of tiny diamond and pearl flowers and leaves. The inside was engraved with hers and Lucian's initials and the motto *'Amore Vincit Omnia'* – sadly inappropriate as things had turned out. She was about to rise from the chair and go place the ring in the bottom of her jewel-case, when someone tapped on the door.

"Sophie? Sophie, dear child – it's Minerva. May I come in – or do you wish to be alone?"

"No," Sophia answered around a lump in her throat. "I do not. Come in. You are the one person besides Agnes whose presence I can endure at this moment." Dear Great-aunt Minnie – the sole survivor of her generation, the last of the redoubtable sons and daughters of Judge Lycurgus Vining by his several wives. Not one of her brothers had ever succeeded in making Minnie Vining into an unpaid governess for their children, Sophia reflected, with resentment. She wondered how Great-aunt Minnie had accomplished that. Oh, never mind – any maiden lady who had faced down an anti-abolitionist mob intent on breaking up a lecture on the cruelties of that so-called 'peculiar Southern institution' would have made mincemeat of any brother reckless enough to risk such an undertaking. Now Great-Aunt Minnie closed the door softly behind her and came around the foot of the bed to sit on the footstool like a superannuated and particularly keen-eyed parrot.

She patted Sophia's hand – the one which didn't clutch the ring – saying, "I am so sorry, my dear little girl. The hope that you would be happily settled in comfortable matrimony sustained your dear mother in those final dreadful months."

"I know." Sophia sniffed and resolutely quashed those tears which only now seemed determined to fall. "That Lucian and I would be wed was a thought which also gave me comfort. I wonder now if I have not been all that in love with him, Auntie. In my mind, he was the means to an end. Is that not disgraceful? It was not him … himself … that I am deprived of, merely the honorable estate which marriage to him would have offered me. He sniffs, Auntie, and coughs in so offensively mannered a way, I believe I would have grown quite exasperated with him. As his wife, I might have endured it, becoming accustomed through long practice. Now I wonder that I had ever contemplated matrimony with a man so …" Sophia fumbled for a word, and her great-aunt supplied it.

"Spineless? There are men, and then there are men, Sophia. Dear child, I have often thought that unless one can contract a marital alliance with a man of superior character, one might as well not bother … the dirty boots, the pipes and smells … the sheer bother of all that a marriage entails." Aunt Minnie gave a small shudder.

"Exactly, Auntie – but where is such a paragon in our circle?"

"Alas," Minnie's pale grey eyes grew luminous with deep consideration. "I fear that our blood has grown thin, in these days. The late war – righteous as our cause was – took a heavy toll; not just your father, but so many men of courage and high heart! We are lessened by their loss, my dear, in ways I fear we are only now realizing. Let me think for a moment." Sophia regarded her great-aunt with fondness. Dearest Aunt Minnie: she had not been uncomely in youth. There was a portrait of herself and her youngest brother – Sophia's Grandfather Horace Vining – in the parlor of the old Vining house on Beacon Street to prove it. She was not a hag in old age either although advanced age had faded and thinned her hair and refined the flesh of her face to reveal the delicate bones. Sophia hoped that when she was Minnie's age that she would be nearly as fair … but it was never the matter of fine, heart-shaped features, or an elegant turn of figure. For Minnie it was the fierce intelligence which animated them, and drew her a wide circle of friends, some known for their towering intellects, or their wealth, but all of them interesting. "I think," Minnie ventured at last, "You should come with us to Newport for a few weeks in the summer. Phelpsie has a friend with a fine little house, and she has invited us as her guests for the summer. I would like that – the air is clean and clear, the seashore is healthful and invigorating for all, and there is a very fine and different society there.

At the very least, it will remove you from the company of that insipid Phoebe creature and her mannerless brats."

"They are not entirely mannerless," Sophia protested, more for a matter of form as affection for the Brewer boys. "I am attempting to teach them courtesy and Richie does mind me. Curgie is a horror. But he is only three and sickly."

"Phoebe cannot bring herself to exert any discipline with regard to her sickly darling," Aunt Minnie retorted. "She undermines your efforts at every turn, and as for your brother! He is not half the man that your father was."

"Richard has done his best," Sophia protested – for Richard had. Not quite of age when their father died in the trenches around Petersburg, Richard had taken up responsibility for his family – for their mother, for the household, and the investments that were the cornerstone of the family fortune. He had to put away his careless student days and ways; it was not his fault that the Marine National Bank of New York had utterly collapsed during the past year, taking a good portion of the Brewer fortune with it.

All those years since, Richard stood as a person combining the best aspects of a father and brother to Sophia; young, fun-loving and handsome, although he was capable of a particular kind of ice-cold rage when provoked by misfortune or when things met with his disapproval. Such rages had never been turned on Sophia. Her brother was rarely harsh with her although Sophia suspected that such icy rage was often turned on Fee. As a boy, he sometimes overruled Mama's strenuous objections when he took Sophia on a daring expedition to pick apples in a neighbor's orchard when they spent a summer in the country … so many fond memories, over the years, even after Richard married Phoebe. It was only upon Mama's death and the failure of the Marine Bank that Richard's moods darkened. Now he was often short-tempered and curt to the point of cruelty. It baffled Sophia, no longer enjoying that easy state of affection with her brother. She had no idea why things should have changed and wondered often if it had been her fault.

"I am certain he has," Great-aunt Minnie replied, suddenly contrite. "I did not mean to distress you, my dear child – not on top of today's disappointment. I told Phelpsie that I would come upstairs and console you. Unless you require the continued balm of my presence – which has never been described as particularly soothing – I will take my leave."

"Thank you, Auntie," Sophia replied, warmed as always by Minnie's affection. "You are a dear! I am soothed, contemplating the bliss of a time with you and Phelpsie at the seashore together with your friends. And I will hold you to it. I still don't know what to do with the ring though." Sophia added, and Great-Aunt Minnie paused in the doorway.

"The ring? You did not return it to Mr. Armitage?"

"He said it was mine as a gift." Sophia opened the hand in which she had clutched the ring so tightly that there were still corresponding red marks on her palm. She regarded the ring with more sorrow than she contemplated the loss of the man – no, not a man, just a boy – who had given it to her. It was a beautiful thing, wrought of gold with a diamond-centered flower in a wreath of pearl-studded petals and leaves. The jeweler with whom Lucian had commissioned the design was justifiably proud of his work.

"Take it back to the jeweler," Great-aunt Minnie suggested. "Ask him to make it into something pretty – a brooch, or a stick-pin."

"I'll think about it," Sophia answered, knowing she wouldn't do anything of the sort. The ring was perfect as it had been visualized and made. Remaking it would be like asking a Leonardo to desecrate his most perfect painting.

Sophie sat in her chair awhile after Great-aunt Minnie closed the door and she put Lucian's ring away. She looked into the garden below her window, that garden which Mama had taken such pleasure from – winter-burnt and unprepossessing as it was at first glance on this day. Mama had adored the garden, and the songbirds that came and cavorted in it. The tulips, daffodils and hyacinth bulbs were putting up fat green shoots. In another few weeks, lilacs would be in bloom; a brief foaming glory of purple, lavender and white lace, the tiny green lawn putting up tender green blades. The wheel of the world would turn again, and now Sophia shuddered to think how much the world might change in the next eighteen months – as surely and horribly it had changed in the last eighteen. She pressed her fingers against her eyes, hoping once again to expunge the cruel memory of Mama, in her final days – all loveliness, intellect and character ground to nothingness by the pain of the cancerous growth in her chest which first tortured and then killed her. Only the application of syrup of opium kept that agony at bay; by the end of it all, Sophia wasn't certain that Mama recognized anything; certainly not the faces of her children or grandsons.

These morbid memories were interrupted by a tap on her door, and the voice of Phoebe, Richard's wife, sounding most uncharacteristically imperious. "Sophie, dear, open this door at once! Or Richard shall send for Teague to break it down!" Phoebe knocked on the door again. "Are you there? You must open the door! What will everyone say?" That sounded more like Phoebe; querulous and uncertain. "You are in there, Sophie? You haven't done something reckless, from grief and disappointment … have you? Sophie?"

Sophia found her voice. She thought she managed to keep a tone of exasperation from her answer. "No, Fee. I have not. The door is not locked – why should it be?"

"Oh." Phoebe sounded deflated. The door opened, and Phoebe rustled in. "But you have been disappointed, in the cruelest way. Everyone assumed you would be distraught with grief. Such a shock to us, so unexpected! At least there are no plans to be un-made."

"No," Sophia said. That answer was all that Phoebe required. Phoebe usually did not require much conversation from others, being given to prattle endlessly given the slightest encouragement. Sophia regarded her sister-in-law, reminded again of how Fee resembled a sheep; a long, pale face vacant of any expression, and unfortunately protuberant blue eyes. She did possess a fine creamy complexion and very fair hair which curled bountifully of its own accord – and furthermore did not have a malicious bone in her body. Silly as Phoebe Brewer might be, most people held her in affection – exasperated, but with affection. Sophia often told herself that Richard certainly might have done worse in providing himself with a wife. Now Phoebe dropped onto the footstool where Minnie had sat and took both of Sophia's hands into hers.

"You are a dear, brave girl," She looked earnestly into Sophia's eyes. "You must think your heart is broken, but you need not try so hard to hide it. You must be distraught: do you have a handkerchief? I don't know what Richard will say when he hears of this. I suppose that he will go around and have words with Mr. Armitage. I hope that he will not demand satisfaction. You know how angry your brother can be, over insult. And this is not just an insult to you, but to us; the nerve of the Armitages as if you are not good enough for them!"

"Dueling is illegal, Fee," Sophia fought her way out of the shower of words. "You need not fear for either of us. I am only disappointed in Lucian as if an old friend had snubbed me in the street. I would like rest for a while before walking Richie home."

"Are you certain?" Phoebe's pale blue eyes still swam with sympathetic tears. Sophia resisted the temptation to snap at her.

"I am. I'm not a fragile little flower, Fee – let me be alone for a while. I'll be myself when it is time to fetch Richie from school."

Phoebe opened her mouth as if she were about to say something else – but Sophia's exasperation may have made itself plain to the dimmest of intellects "Very well," she agreed at last. "But you have given me cause for worry, Sophie."

At least, she closed the door after her, although it opened almost at once to admit Agnes, bearing a small tray with a cup of ginger-tea and a slice of seed-cake wrapped in a napkin. Agnes merely set the tray on the window sill and departed without a word, for which Sophia was inordinately grateful.

Chapter 2 – In Doctor Cotton's Care

Freed at last from the worried and fond concern of friends and relations, Sophia leaned her head back against the high chair and let her mind wander. She was rendered uneasy by uncertainty which had overtaken her life. Her future had always been set out for her in short and decorous steps; the same path that her mother, her grandmother, Phoebe even – had paced in their turn. All but Great-aunt Minnie had gone on that path. Girlhood, an education of sorts, then matrimony, motherhood, the rule of a home, good works, a constellation of children; how she longed to have children of her own, to make up for her own solitary childhood! Now that was cast into doubt. There was no room in that path for deviations, or even for uncertainty, but without any fault of her own, she had strayed and had no idea of how to return.

At half-past the hour of two o'clock, she put on her every-day bonnet and mantle, and walked to the school on Bedford Street where Richard's older son, the pride of his life attended school. No one in the house took any apparent note of her departure – not that she had expected any. This was one of her regular duties – to walk Richie home from school and attend to any small errands required by her brother and Phoebe along the way.

Richie attended the Boston Latin. Nothing would do for a Brewer than the oldest and finest Latin school in Boston, housed in a fine stone building built in the old-fashioned classical style, with four tall windows on every one of four floors and some archaic adornment on the shallow gable-end facing Bedford Street. She waited by the railings what marked off the school grounds until the flood of pupils – boys and girls alike – had emerged from every doorway and scattered like a burst milkweed pod sending threads of silk and seeds in every direction.

Richie stood out among the dispersing students for the fair hair inherited from Phoebe and the height inherited from Richard. He was well-grown for a nine-year old. Fortunately, he also had inherited Richard's features and a genial temper all his own; a good thing as Sophia reflected. Phoebe's likeness translated into small-boy form would have been bullied endlessly, even among his fellow students, who numbered among them the scions of the best Boston families.

"Hey! Auntie Soph!" Richie now shouted. Sophia winced. "Hay is for horses," she reproved her nephew, when he was close enough for her to speak without raising her voice. "You should shout like that in the street. And my proper name is Sophia."

"Yes, Auntie Soooophia," he answered, with exaggerated meekness. Sophia laughed. She was fond of Richie; in many ways more her own child than Phoebe. Now he skipped along at her side, swinging his book-bundle without a care and chattering away nine-to-the-dozen, telling of daily woes and penalties imposed by teachers, of small yet ferocious encounters and battles of wits with them and with other students; classroom triumphs and schoolyard tragedies. Sophia listened without listening, a skill she had long ago learned and practiced – the art of seeming to pay attention with part of her mind, but with much of the rest given over to her own thoughts.

Finally, even Richie noticed her distance from his conversation, and said impatiently, "Auntie Sophia, aren't you even listening? I just said that the State House dome looked as if it had crashed in, and you said, 'Yes, Richie; that's altogether possible.'"

"I did?" Sophia looked around. They had walked halfway through the Public Gardens, and she had never even noticed they had gotten to hers and Richie's favorite part of the walk home. And this was her favorite time of year in the Public Garden, with the massed plantings of bulbs in bloom, scenting the air with delicate perfume, and the young trees putting out pale green leaves. The Garden was still so new that most of the trees were young and lately planted. For Sophia, this was another reason to love Great-Aunt Minnie's residence in the old Vining mansion on Beacon Street – the front windows overlooked the Gardens and the Common.

"You did." Richie affirmed, and Sophia sighed and confessed, "I am sorry, Richie. My mind was intent on other things."

"What things?" Now he had to run to keep up with her.

Caught up in her own distress, Sophia walked faster and faster. "I am not to marry Mr. Armitage, after all," she answered at last. "He came and told me today that his promise to marry must be broken. He will not marry me since his father has forbidden it."

"Why is that, Aunt Sophia? I thought he was a … a nice chap. And that you were in love, or something." Richie's sunny countenance looked as if a sudden dark cloud had floated in.

"I suppose because we are too poor now for the high-and-mighty Armitages," Sophia answered, with wholly unexpected bitterness. Richie flung his arms around her waist in an exuberant hug. "I love you, Auntie Sophia! If you can't get a beau to marry you by the time I'm grown-up, then I will marry you myself!"

"Thank you, Richie," Sophia returned the embrace. "That is a kindly thought and I love you, too – but you can't marry your aunt, and I will be too old for you by then."

"Then I will just have to find you a beau in the meantime," Richie said, with an expression of great determination. "My quest for my own lady-fair will be to find her a proper knight and love." He suggested the name of an older brother of one of his schoolmates, in all seriousness.

"You have been reading too much Walter Scott," Sophia laughed, good humor restored. "That gentleman is a confirmed bachelor. He has spots on his complexion at the age of thirty, and has never had a good word to say to, or of a woman. Burden me not with the name of another elder brother, or uncle, Richie. I know them by family connection or by repute. None of them will suit. Of that I am certain."

"I will think of someone," Richie answered, his countenance expressing determination. "Someone brave and handsome, with deeds of derring-do on his ess—escrutchon…"

"Escutcheon," Sophia laughed, fondly. "Do you even know what an escutcheon is, Richie? It's a family banner, a shield – the good repute of the family which has one as a patent of nobility."

"And rich," her nephew added. "Rich enough not to care." They walked on, in good humor. Sophia reflected that of her family, only Richie and Great-aunt Minnie restored her soul with faith in herself; one a child and the other an octogenarian. There was an unfamiliar carriage drawn up before the Brewer townhouse, with a clearly bored coachman sitting on the box. Sophia usually recognized the carriages and horses of those of their regular callers and friends; this must be one of Richard's business associates.

"Is that one of Mama's friends?" Richie asked, as they went up the steps, pausing in the grandly pillared portico, while Sophia opened the door.

"No. She received callers earlier, and they have been gone for hours."

As soon as Sophie stepped inside the hallway, Richard called from his study. "Sophia – is that you and the lad? Come into the parlor. Dr. Cotton took the time to make a call, at my request. Fee has told me of what happened. I knew you would be distraught, so I sent for him at once. He is in the parlor with Phoebe, waiting for you."

Richard emerged from his study, and Sophia's heart warmed at the sight of him; a tall and handsome man in his early middle years. Richard Brewer was at least a decade past being in the full bloom of youth, but those years had only refined his features with an attractive burnishing of age and experience, transforming youth into sober maturity. To Sophia, he had been a father at least as much as a brother; the head of their family in all things. Mama leaned on him and the child Sophia adored him as the central sun in the family constellation just as Phoebe did. Sophia had been ten years old when Richard and Phoebe married. She supposed that she had been jealous at first: Fee was so silly! But nothing changed in the family until Mama's protracted and final illness. This occurred at the same time as the failure of the Marine National, which spelled an end to Brewer prosperity. Agnes occasionally talked of something called a *geas*; a curse upon the house. Sophia often wondered if Agnes were right. They had been happy, life had been pleasant; then Mama died and happiness fled from the Brewer house.

"I am not distraught in the least," Sophia insisted. "Just disappointed in Mr. Armitage."

"That's our brave little Sophie," Richard averred fondly. "A noble show of concealing a broken heart! I know that Mama had intended from childhood that you two ought to marry."

"I do not have a broken heart," Sophia insisted again. This was becoming an annoyance, how everyone was so certain of her feelings on the broken engagement. "I grieve at the loss of a friendship! If anything, I am angry at being cast aside after all this time because Mr. Armitage thinks we are poor."

Richard took her hands, pleading in earnest, "Dear little sister – we are not poor. We have lost some of our investments, which is quite another thing. We have this house, our affection for each other; an affection which bids me consider your health and happiness always. Allow Dr. Cotton to examine you in his capacity as a physician and relieve my mind of a burden of worry."

"Of course I will," Sophia yielded, still reluctant, but Richard bore so many cares on his shoulders. It was not fair for her to contribute to them by continuing to argue. Instead, she went to the parlor where Fee sat, jabbing an inexpert needle into her Berlin wool-work and chattering to Dr. Cotton. The good doctor himself stood before the fire, with his hands behind his back. Sophia suspected that he was doing as she had with Richie, listening to Fee without really listening, absorbed in his own thoughts while delivering an occasional noncommittal response.

He was a lean and saturnine man, a contemporary and a friend of Richard's. Sophia did not care for him although he seemed competent enough as a doctor. Old Doctor Hubbell, whose practice Dr. Cotton had inherited, had seen to her childish ailments and attended Mama in her final illness, who had her confidence and trust. But six months ago, Doctor Hubbell retired to a tiny country cottage where he communed with nature and only emerged to practice his medical arts when pressed by local necessity. While Fee sat by ignoring her embroidery, Dr. Cotton inquired into Sophia's state of mind and general health. Sophia repeated the same answers she had made to everyone else this day, thinking she sounded like a parrot. Dr. Cotton looked into her eyes, listened to her pulse with his little patent ivory and patent-rubber listening horn, and finally delivered himself of his judgement.

"You are anemic, my dear Miss Brewer. I shall prescribe a tonic which you must take every morning without fail, in order to build up your blood and your strength. I will compound it myself and send over the first bottle. I shall visit next week to assess your condition and adjust the dosage accordingly."

"We shall take every care, Dr. Cotton," Fee promised, with enthusiasm. Sophia repressed a small sigh. Fee was hopelessly enamored of potions, tonics, powders, and pills; cures for every ailment which she fancied afflicted her. Sophia refused those doses which Fee urged upon her; now Fee was backed by Dr. Cotton's authority. Unless Sophia missed her guess, Fee would redouble her efforts.

When Dr. Cotton had finally taken his leave, Sophia climbed the two flights of stairs, feeling as if she were as old and tired as Great-Aunt Minnie. "I am not heartbroken," She asserted to her reflection in her dressing table mirror. "And I am not distraught." In all this long afternoon, her reflection was the only being which did not argue with her.

Three dark-brown bottles of Dr. Cotton's prescribed tonic arrived late that afternoon, their corks sealed with bright red wax, carried in a basket by Dr. Cotton's errand-boy. Sophia thought nothing of it, save that she hoped that it was not too terribly bitter. Many of the patent nostrums which Fee urged upon her were; a reason for not relishing their consumption. Great-Aunt Minnie railed against patent-medicines, claiming they were composed of cheap brandy and other nasty ingredients. "If I wanted to be a drunkard," Great-Aunt Minnie often and forcefully observed, "I would regularly consume a finer grade of the demon alcohol!"

The next morning, at the breakfast table, Richard took one of the bottles from the antique cellaret which stood in the dining room, broke away the red wax with which it was sealed, and poured a water-glass a quarter full of that dark liquid, saying, "Sophia dear – your tonic. Let me see you drink every drop. I will see you restored to health, little sister."

Sophia took the glass, grimacing only slightly, and swallowed. It tasted as vile as she had expected. But it did have a pleasant warming effect on her, throughout that day, and those following. She was aware of heightened senses; colors appeared brighter, sunshine more brilliant, the touch of fabric on her fingers as she and Agnes sorted and refolded the family washing returned from the laundry was an intensely pleasurable sensation.

"Are you well, Miss Sophie?" Agnes did ask, with a worried expression on her owl-like little face. "Your eyes look a bit funny."

"Quite well," Sophia answered. It was not a lie; she felt very well. She could think of Lucius Armitage without a single pang of regret. "Dr. Cotton says that I am anemic and proscribed a tonic for me. Richard insists that I partake of it of every morning. I think that it has made me forget Mr. Armitage, however pleasant it would have been to marry. You were telling me that Siobhan's intended has finally asked the question, after months of shilly-shallying. How did that happen? You said last week that she had run out of patience, and wrote a letter, answering a newspaper advertisement for a position."

"Aye, that I did," Agnes nodded. "There is this grand gentleman, see – he has a business out in the West, along one of the railroads. 'Tis true, for Declan asked around, wanting to know if it were a real enterprise, an' not one making a false pretense to ensnare girls into the white-slave trade. This Mr. Harvey placed an advertisement; he has restaurants in railway stations, all the way to California, they are. And he wants proper young ladies to work as waitresses…"

"Oh, surely not," Sophia cried. "That is a low trade for a young woman – not respectable in the least…"

"Declan, he says nooo; Mr. Harvey, he's an Englishman, you see – and he wants to be running a respectable establishment, serving the finest quality to the traveling gentry. Those girls who work in his establishment, they will live in a company boarding house, with a curfew and chaperones an' all. It seemed above-board, like, and so Siobhan wrote in answer to the advertisement. This week she received a reply from Mr. Harvey. She should come to Kansas City for an interview in the next month and if she were hired, then she would go west! For at least a year, the letter said!"

"What did your sister do, then?" Agnes and Declan's sister Siobhan worked as a maid in a household in the Back Bay, but she was pretty and restless, and exasperated at her swain's inability to screw his matrimonial courage to the sticking point.

"Well, she told him she was tired of waiting for him to speak his piece, an' tired of dusting Mrs. Pottington-Potter's house and emptying her chamber-pots and unless he made a better offer, she was off to Kansas City as soon as she gave notice to Mrs. Pottington-Potter … an' fancy that! As soon as he can find a place for them both to live, they will be wed proper at St. Stephens. Da will be happy enough an' so will I, for not having to share the cot with her. Is that an evil thing to say, Miss Sophia?"

"A bed to myself? I should say not! She will be happy enough. Does he have a good trade?" Sophia's mind wandered. Suddenly, she could not recall the thread of conversation.

"Oh, aye," Agnes replied. "He is an expert stone-carver and mason. He'll never be out of employment, with all the fancy carving to be done. Miss Sophia, are you certain you are well?"

"Of course I am, Agnes," Sophia replied, annoyed. "I am under the care of Dr. Cotton."

"If you say so, Miss," Agnes still did not appear if she were completely convinced. "Here now; I'll take the Madam's things, and Sir's shirts, if you will take the sheets and the little boy's things."

"Of course," Sophia answered again, lifting the stack of neatly folded laundry. This vaguely worried her. Agnes had twice asked concerning her health. Agnes was no fool, in spite of her sketchy education. And she had worked in the Brewer household three years now; the only regular servant aside from Mrs. Garrett, whom they could afford in these reduced circumstances.

A week passed, and then another; Sophia obediently drinking her prescribed tonic every morning, under the watchful eye of Richard and Phoebe … although the curiously euphoric effect which it had on her diminished a little more on each successive day. Dr. Cotton called to examine her as he had promised. He examined her again in the parlor and under Phoebe's distracted eye, listening to her heartbeat, questioning her regarding her appetite and habits, even her dreams at night. The answers did not appear to satisfy him.

At last he said, "You are not making the progress which I had hoped for, Miss Brewer. I am going to adjust the ingredients of your daily tonic accordingly … is there a problem, Miss Brewer?"

He eyed her with sharp and suspicious attention, and Sophia answered, realizing that her brief moue of distaste had not gone unobserved, "I wish it tasted somewhat less bitter and unpleasant, Dr. Cotton. It quite puts me away from enjoyment of breakfast."

"It is medicinal," Dr. Cotton snapped the latches on his cavernous doctor's satchel closed. The sound of it was austere, disapproving. "It is supposed to be unpleasant – and serves no good purpose otherwise."

"You have exceeded yourself in that regard," Sophia murmured, while Phoebe exclaimed, "Sophia – really! I am so sorry, Dr. Cotton. My sister-in-law has not been herself since the unfortunate breaking of her engagement."

"I have so!" Sophia protested. She didn't think either of them heard a word, in the space of a moment when Dr. Cotton took his leave of the ladies in the parlor. Richard was in his study; apparently Dr. Cotton was to render his further diagnosis in a private conference there. Sophia fumed and her annoyance doubled when Phoebe set aside her wool-work as soon as the door closed on Dr. Cotton's black broadcloth back.

"Sophia! You should not contradict the Doctor in that manner! So unwomanly! He is only considering your good health and well-being! At considerable trouble to himself because he is an old friend of the family!"

"No, he is not," Sophia snapped. "Doctor Hubbell was a friend of the family. Dr. Cotton is a friend of Richards'. I do not like the taste of his potions and I am not distraught!"

"If you say so," Phoebe answered, in an uncertain tone, sounding as if she were placating the unreasonable. This irritated Sophia further. She leaped to her feet and stormed out of the parlor, intending to go to her room. If she was unwell and distraught, Sophia reasoned; why couldn't she use the same excuse which Fee used to great effect on every occasion – go to her room and lay down? Let Fee look after her own household for a while.

As she passed the door to Richard's study, Sophia was arrested by the sound of her brother's voice, conversing with Dr. Cotton. There was a tone in it which inexplicably chilled her with dread since it sounded so unlike her brother. The door was not closed all the way; she could hear both of them clearly as she paused with her foot on the first stair-tread.

"…a perilous business," Dr. Cotton was saying, in most uncharacteristic distress. "I cannot go on taking these chances, Rich. What if someone should talk?"

"What if they do?" Sophia could hardly believe that was her brother speaking, so cold, so unfeeling. "The bottles are seen to be sealed when they are delivered from your surgery. Everyone in this household can attest to that; your lad, me, my wife and sister, even our idiot housemaid. You are proof against any accusation. Don't tell me you have second thoughts at this late date."

"I … I do." That was Dr. Cotton's voice, irresolute and nervous. Sophia could picture him, fiddling with the brim of his hat, the handles of his doctor's bag; such a change from the suave assurance presented in the parlor five minutes ago. "Rich, it goes against the oath I have sworn – never knowingly do harm. I cannot …"

"Spare me your womanish hesitations," Richard snarled. Sophia shivered, as if an icy draft had blown upon her; he sounded vicious, so unlike the brother who had cherished her for as long as she could remember. "You'll do as I tell you. I want the business done within another fortnight. My sister will be twenty-one then. You know what that means. And …" his voice lowered, so that Sophia could barely hear it. "You speak of doing no harm? What of that woman in North Town? Not so much about your oath then, hey?"

"You wouldn't." Dr. Cotton sounded shaken. "You have no proof."

"But I do, Ambrose." Now Richard sounded silkily confident, assured. "I do. I've my hand around your throat. All I need do is squeeze. You'll do as I tell you: Danvers in two weeks, or I'll spill what I know and into the right ears. You won't have a practice in Boston, save perhaps among the Irish, or as a back-alley abortionist."

Sophia held her breath. *What had this to do with the Brewers?* It sounded as if her brother were forcing Dr. Cotton into something, something to do with her. Danvers? That was the state asylum for the insane. Now that draft became a gale; Sophia turned ice-cold with the realization that this was Richard, her brother saying these things, Richard whom she had trusted all of her life. It was as if a great dark pit had opened at her feet, a dark and lightless pit filled with horrors, everything in the world which she feared. Inside the study, Dr. Cotton made some remark, which Sophia barely grasped, so paralyzed with horror and disbelief. But his voice was louder as if he were moving toward the door.

He would see her if she lingered; Richard, too … she needed to think and the men must not know that she had overheard them. Sophia gathered up her skirts and fled up the stairs, walking on the carpeted stairs so that her slippers made no noise. She had reached the landing at the top of the first flight, out of sight from below, when the door to

Richard's study opened below. She heard Richard bid good-day to Dr. Cotton, as she crept soundlessly up the flight to her room, on the third floor.

Careless of the pristine coverlet on her bed, so carefully made up in the morning by Agnes, she flung herself down on top of it. The feeling that she had wandered off the proper path and that everything in her life – so secure, so orderly – had catastrophically gone wrong overwhelmed her. She looked up at the ceiling. She never had confidence in Dr. Cotton; now she had even less. What was in that tonic which he had been compounding for her, and why had it sometimes made her feel so very odd? Why was Richard so very concerned about her birthday, in two weeks? And what had changed him, so very much?

Or had Richard always been so cold, so adept at manipulating men like Dr. Cotton, and women like Phoebe, and just been able to disguise that facility? Sophia rolled over and buried her face in the sweet-smelling fresh bed-linen covering her pillow.

Chapter 3 – Potions and Portents

It was not – as she half-feared – Richard who came to her room door, and tapped on it, requesting admittance. It was Phoebe, tearful and apologetic. Sophia wondered, somewhat cynically, how much of that was due to Phoebe having to take charge of her sons herself, and to bear the brunt of Richard's displeasure at the workings of the household not going as smoothly as he had become accustomed in the last few years.

"Richard is unhappy," Fee announced, as she closed the door behind her. She shuffled into the room, the weight of the child within her body rendering her ungainly. She settled her awkward self into the bedside chair and reached for Sophia's hand. "He is so fond of you, dear. We are so worried about your condition." Sophia bit back her initial waspish response – *I had no condition until everyone began insisting that I had one!* Instead, she answered,

"Fee, I am perfectly fit. It is only that everyone insists that I am not, which puts me out of good temper. I was fond of Lucius Armitage. I do not think I loved him to any great degree, although I could have come to love him, in time. Just as you came to love Richard …"

Now, that was a startling thing, the fleeting expression in Fee's eyes and countenance – was that … could it be stark terror? Again, that cold trickle of fear ran down Sophia's spine. She looked at Fee – this time with impersonal analysis. Sophia had been ten years when Richard married his bride; all white dress and misty veil, on her father's arm, advancing in stately tread down the aisle of the ancient Christ Church. Sophia had been one of her attendants and not particularly happy because this was Richard! Fee was, as the ten-year-old Sophia saw it – an interloper: A silly and unwelcome trespasser on a happy family; Mama, Richard and herself. A ten-year-old's impatience and a touch of jealousy gave away to impatience mixed with exasperation, and to this present day, with a heavier helping of exasperation and even a degree of contempt.

How Richard had been so cold and horrible just now! Sophia wondered if she had misjudged Fee. What had Fee seen, been subjected to, in the privacy of a marital relationship? And what was Richard? Affectionate husband and brother, responsible head of a family … or something else? Sophia shook off the thought although the question continued to haunt.

A memory from her childhood came to mind; one of their close neighbors had a cat living in their stables which had kittens and Sophia had fallen in love with the prettiest of the kittens – a little smoke-grey mite with pale green eyes. She had gone to her mother and Richard, with the kitten burrowed trustfully in her arms and begged to be allowed to keep it as a pet. Richard had assented – his expression indulgent, but Mama had replied, "Oh, no, Sophia – certainly not. It wouldn't be ..." and now with the hindsight of maturity, Sophia wondered why Mama had looked at Richard, for that brief moment. "We do not make pets of animals in this house," Mama said at last, and wouldn't give any satisfactory answer when Sophia asked why. The kitten went back to its littermates. When she was a little older, Sophia had often wondered what became of it.

"Of course – he is a most loving husband and brother," Fee insisted, breathlessly. "How could I not? My dear husband is unwearied in his care and concern for us …"

"As he was from the day that Papa fell," Sophia said. She wished that she could recall Papa – see him in flesh and life. Instead, she had an image from the daguerreotype that was always at Mama's bedside and then her own; a handsome man in a dark Union uniform, one hand thrust into the front of his coat, the other resting on the sword at his side.

Fee continued, “I know that you are being brave and stoic about Mr. Armitage and everything but we cannot help but see you are unhappy, and short of temper. And we think that you might benefit from a period of quiet and rest in the countryside, under Dr. Cotton’s care.”

“I do not care for Dr. Cotton,” Sophia answered, with an edge in her voice she didn’t bother to hide. “Nor his potions, his advice, nor any else of his recommendations. I was disappointed in Lucius, for I thought he might have had sufficient spine to defy his father. This is the 19th century, Fee; what business do fathers have in absolutely forbidding a marriage when everything to do with those promised to each other has otherwise met with approval? Lucius’ father now finds me an abhorrent connection to his family because of those losses sustained in the failure of the Marine Bank! Tell me, Fee – does money now rule? Over character, affection and long-established connection?”

Phoebe regarded Sophia with bafflement in her eyes; large, cow-like eyes, Sophia thought, viciously, every bit as stupid as the cow which her sister-in-law resembled. “I suppose it does,” Phoebe admitted, as if it were the most obvious thing in the world.

Sophia could not conceal her contempt. “You had a generous dowry settled upon you when you married Richard; a very generous dowry, indeed. Was it the dowry which appealed most to my brother, or the charms of your own person and intellect?”

Phoebe colored as red as if she had been slapped, and tears started in her eyes. She sprang up from the chair, crying, “So what if there was! Richard does so love me, and we were happily wed! You have always been cruel and sarcastic, anything but a true sister; for all I have tried to be kind and affectionate!”

“Fee, I didn’t mean …” Sophia levered herself from the bed by her elbow, but was struck with a sudden fit of dizziness as she did so, and by the time she had pulled the right words of apology out of her mind, Phoebe had turned around at the doorway and launched her parting remark.

"Lucius Armitage has decided to marry – to your friend, Miss Chase! I imagine generous dowries have a recommendation after all!" Then Fee slammed the door behind her and it was too late. Sophia lay back on the coverlet, staring up at the ceiling of her room. This had the effect of a bodily blow – that Lucius chose Emma Chase within weeks of breaking their engagement; she was more disappointed in Emma than she was in Lucius Armitage. Lucius was a poor silly boy-man, still commanded by his irascible father, but Emma was her bosom-friend. She had not expected this. Was Emma so desperate for suitors, so eager for marriage at any cost? It appeared so.

The following afternoon was Phoebe's 'at home', when she and Sophia put on their afternoon best and received calls from friends and acquaintances. Sophia always looked forward to their 'at home' afternoons; a few brief hours not exhaustingly engaged in housekeeping and errands when she could sit in the parlor with her needlework and converse with those friends and kin whose company she enjoyed.

Aunt Minnie and Phelpsie appeared at once, shown into the parlor by Agnes. "My dear child, have you heard? Lucius Armitage …"

"I have," Sophia answered, curt and cold. "Fee told me last night." She darted a sideways look at her sister-in-law, who appeared to have forgotten how bitter their exchange the previous evening had been. "It matters little, Aunt Minnie. They are both my friends and I wish them well."

Great-aunt Minnie patted Sophia's hand, visibly relieved. "None the less; water under the bridge, my dear, water under the bridge. You have been spared an inevitable disappointment, given his weak and easily influenced character. Our holiday in Newport will be a welcome change of scenery, would you agree?"

"With my whole heart," Sophia answered. "Auntie, would it inconvenience you, if I were to come and stay with you and Phelpsie now? My birthday is in two weeks and I want to make decisions for myself as I will then be of age."

"But what would we do without you?" Fee interjected. "This is your home, Sophie, why …"

"No, this house is yours," Sophia returned, not without malice. "It should be your duty and pleasure to have management of it, as my brothers' wife. Being of age and a confirmed spinster, why should I not set the direction of my own life and pleasures?"

"But that is unseemly!" Fee bleated. Great-Aunt Minnie snorted. "Unseemly fiddlesticks, my girl; I am not keeping a low boarding-house. There comes a time when a woman might be expected to know her own mind and desires. Sophia shall come and live with me as she pleases, being of age and there's an end to the discussion."

"Richard won't like that," Phoebe's voice quavered. "He will be angry."

"The venting of splenetic energy will be good for him," Great-Aunt Minnie retorted, crisply. Sophia marveled at how little the prospect of Richard's anger dismayed Great-Aunt Minnie, even as it cowed Fee. Richard's anger wouldn't cow her either. Sophia thought, as she bent to her embroidery. She would go live in the old Vining mansion, cramped and dark and old-fashioned as it was, and now in a neighborhood definitely decayed. She would help Phelpsie look after Minnie, and the great silver cage in the parlor full of songbirds which were the delight of the two old ladies in the stormy winter months. She would listen to Great-Aunt Minnie's reminiscences of her brothers, and the various dramatic or mundane adventures of the various ancestors. That would prove more amusing than everyone groaning on at her over her broken engagement. She had always wondered about the adventures that her grandfather Horace was supposed to have had in his long journeys to the west; scouting for General Sam Houston and fighting in the great battle of San Jacinto. Minnie would know.

These pleasant thoughts were interrupted by Agnes, in the doorway with the silver card tray in her hand. "Oh, Marm," she said, her voice barely above a tremulous whisper. "'Tis Mrs. and Miss Chase presenting their cards."

"The nerve!" Great-Aunt Minnie snapped.

Sophia set her embroidery aside. "I don't care for what the rest of you do, but I am not at home for Miss Chase at this moment. Tell her," and Sophie took enjoyment in saying so, since it was just what everyone had been telling her for weeks, "That I am indisposed, being heartbroken and all that. I shall be upstairs in my room. Agnes, if Mrs. Brewer decides to receive their cards, wait until I have gone up the stairs, before you admit the Chase ladies."

"Yes, Marm," Agnes breathed. Sophia had no doubt that Agnes would be vociferously in sympathy with her when next the two of them were folding laundry.

As she reached the second landing, the front door opened and closed. Emma's familiar voice exclaimed, "Oh, what a shame! We had sworn to be bridesmaids to each other, for the first to marry!"

Sophia bit her tongue and hurried up the next flight of stairs to the refuge of her own room. How often would these social humiliations be delivered upon her? Likely every day, for as long as she lived in her brother's household.

The next morning at breakfast, she took what she saw as the first step towards claiming something of the independence that Great-Aunt Minnie claimed was a woman's proper birthright. Also, she hated the taste of Dr. Cotton's medicinal tonic. Richard took the familiar dark glass bottle out of the cellaret. Sophia noticed that the wax seal on it was broken, most of the blood-red wax falling away from the stopper.

"No," she said, as Richard poured the usual dose into a clean tumbler. The effect was as if someone had tossed a lit firework onto the middle of the breakfast table.

Fee and Richie looked at her with eyes rounded in surprise, and Richard scowled. "It is for your good health, little sister," he said by way of argument.

"No, I will not take it," Sophia answered, steady in conviction. She was sure that the potion was not doing her any good, and how curiously that first week of doses from Dr. Cotton had affected her. "I will not." She closed her lips, ostentatiously, and Richard appeared ever angrier. Sophia quailed – *how could Richard be angry with her?* He had never turned that icy cold rage on her before. *Was it because she had, to that moment, been always adoring and biddable?*

"You will take your dose, Sophia," Richard declared. Sophia's resolve withered within her. This was a new Richard; a horrible, unfeeling Richard. Sophia looked at her brother as if he were a person she had never seen before. His features were familiar and dear, the mature countenance a likeness of her father, stalwart in his Union Army uniform, but with a sensitive refinement in his expression which belayed the martial aspect of his sword and uniform. Richard's expression now was everything but that and his eyes were cold, as cold as grey granite pebbles.

"No," Sophia answered, although she was uncertain of where the courage and the determination to defy her brother came from, other than the conviction that Dr. Cotton's compounded potion was not doing her any good.

"Then, you may sit in the strong-room and reconsider," Richard snapped. He sprang from his own chair and caught her arm, dragging her out of her chair at the breakfast table. Her chair fell backwards, as her plate and silverware fell with a crash, while Richie and Fee gazed, open-mouthed in horror. Sophia fought against the force of his hands on her, startled and appalled at his strength. She had never expected that her brother or any other man would be able to drag her from the dining room with such apparent ease, over her strenuous physical objection. His hands were powerful, his strength inexorable; he had only to twist her arms behind her back and force her ahead of him across the hallway. Her feet could find no purchase on the floor, first the threadbare Turkey carpet, then the polished wooden parquet in the hallway. Richard tightened his grip on her arms, lifting her as he pushed her into his study.

"You're hurting me!" she cried in pained protest.

Richard replied through his teeth, "I'll do worse than that, little sister, if you don't do as you are told!" He swung her aside for a moment, as he kicked open the door to the strong-room. It was nothing more than a windowless closet with a strong door, to one side of the fireplace; windowless, airless, and with serried ranks of shelves bare of the silver it once contained. Richard shoved her into it with such force, she fell on her knees, striking her forehead on the edge of a shelf at the back. Before she might protest, he had slammed the door on her; as dark as the darkest midnight the strong-room was then. A little light leaked in underneath the door, and faintly through the key-hole, after Richard turned the key in it and took it away. Sophia huddled on the bare plank floor, stunned beyond feeling. "You'll stay there until you drink your tonic like a good girl," Richard hissed into the key-hole.

"I am not a child!" Sophia shouted. "You have no right to treat me so!"

There was no reply; Sophia thought she could hear his footsteps, and Fee's voice, muffled at least by distance as by the strong room door. The door to the study closed, the sound of a key turning in that remote lock, and she was left in silence. The living nightmare had come upon her, without warning. She struggled against belief to comprehend. One day, she had been a lady of good family, albeit an impoverished one, living a serene life of home, good works and the promise of marriage in the highest rungs of society as she knew it. At the next moment … locked into a dark and close place. She huddled on the floor – there was nothing to sit on – and thought what she might do. No use shouting for help: Richard had locked the strong-room and the study door. Even if they could hear her calling, Fee was too cowed to disobey Richard, and Mrs. Garrett and Agnes would not dare disobey the master of the house.

She was not going to drink that ghastly tonic. Why was Richard so determined that she must? Obviously he had forced Dr. Cotton to put something harmful in it, something to make her sick … or worse; make her appear fit for being sent to Danvers. Sophia shivered. How could Richard do that to her? Why? That was the true horror. Her loving and affectionate brother had been taken away by a malevolent force, replaced by a demon that looked like him. All trust, all familial consideration destroyed; everything in her life she had counted on to be as solid as the floor underneath her feet had crumbled as insubstantial as rotted wood.

Sophia arranged her skirts and petticoats underneath her, so that the layers of cloth afforded a kind of cushion against the hard floor. How long did Richard intend to leave her there? Fee would wonder; and Agnes and Mrs. Garrett, too. Great-Aunt Minnie and Phelpsie were coming for supper tonight; most certainly Aunt Minnie would note her absence and demand an accounting. Aunt Minnie. Sophia's spirits rose. Minnie would help her.

The first thing she must do when Richard unlocked the door of the strong-room – whenever he unlocked it – and run to Great-aunt Minnie's house. Without her hat or mantle, without a change of dress or a nightgown, even. Her spirits sank, momentarily deflated; she might look like a madwoman, in her plain calico morning dress, running bare-headed, disheveled and coatless through the streets of Boston. The old Vining mansion had to be her refuge if she could reach it. Sophia settled herself to endure, her back against the door. She was strong, fit, and accustomed to walking everywhere necessary in the last two years, since the Brewers could no longer afford a coach and horses. Even the last horse which had pulled the Brewer's buggy had gone to the knacker's yard, after an accident in the stable. They had never been able to purchase another. The horse … there was something curious about that. Sophia couldn't remember what it was since it happened around the same time as Mama's final illness.

The only lack now was in the occupation of her mind and hands. She was accustomed to having one or the other, to pass the time. Now, she must endure long hours in a dark locked place: the diversion which first came to mind was reciting aloud every bit of poetry she had ever had to memorize. With the strong-room door locked, and Richard's study door closed, no one could hear her anyway – but she set to work. *A Programme of Poetical Recitations by Miss Sophia Brewer* – that was what she titled it in her mind. She closed her eyes, the better to envision an audience, and herself standing before them, and began chanting. Robert Browning's "My Last Duchess" was the poem which first came to her mind. Considering the fate of that sad and silly woman, Sophia pondered on her sister-in-law. Could poor hapless Fee endure, under the strict rule of her brother, if Richard's affections turned against her, for being insufficiently agreeable to his wishes?

"I said, "Fra Pandolf" by design, for never read,
Strangers like you that pictured countenance,
The depth and passion of its earnest glance,

But to myself they turned (since none puts by, The curtain I have drawn for you, but I)
And seemed as they would ask me, if they durst,
How such a glance came there; so, not the first –
Are you to turn and ask thus."

Sophia declaimed in a loud voice to the utter darkness. She continued reciting poetry for a long time, even as she lost track of it. There was something to be said regarding an active life of the mind; it gave comfort and purpose when other lights had gone out.

Sophia had lost track of time, when she became aware of a noise – a metallic sound, in the lock of the door at her back. She scrambled aside as the door opened – just sufficiently wide that Richard could thrust in one of the upstairs chamber-pots. She was too late onto her feet, for he slammed the door closed and locked it again at once … and her chance was lost.

"Let me out of here!" She cried, beating on the door with her fists.

"When you take your tonic," Richard answered from the other side. Then he was gone, leaving Sophia in possession of herself, the darkness, the memory of poetry, and a chamber pot. She made use of the latter, having developed a dire need of it, in the recent hours, shoved it into the farthest corner of the closet, and resumed chanting poetry. Richard could not keep her in the strong-room forever, she told herself – unless he meant her to starve to death, or die of thirst. That was a real consideration; the longer that Sophia meditated on that prospect, the more it worried her, even more than the unanswered question of – why?

To quash that, she returned to reciting poetry again. This was a conflict of wills: she did not want to drink any more of Dr. Cotton's nasty tonic, yet Richard insisted that she do. Why this had become a point of contention, and why Richard was so set upon it was a mystery. No. The next time Richard opened the strong-room door, she must be ready. Now and again, she stopped in her recital, to press her ear against the keyhole, working out from the faint sounds in the rest of the house what was going on, and what time it might be. During one of these pauses, the hall clock chimed the hour of three.

Sometime in the next interval, she heard Fee's voice, raised in agitation, out in the hallway; Fee, Richie, and sickly spoiled little Curgie who was having a screaming tantrum. Not an uncommon occurrence; Fee indulged him unendingly, and he was only three. Still, Fee hardly ever took the children anywhere herself, claiming her own fragile condition. The voices and the sound of the tantrum was cut off by the heavy thud of a closing door. It sounded to Sophia as if Fee and the children had departed the house.

This was curious, with Great-Aunt Minnie coming to supper. Richard had always paid elaborate respect and consideration towards Great-Aunt Minnie, although now that Sophia thought upon it, she wondered if Great-Aunt Minnie returned the favor. Minnie regarded Richard if he were schoolboy who might revert to uncouth habits and address at any moment. Great Aunt Minnie was never openly rude to family, but she could be waspish, and she had no patience with fools, as she herself often admitted.

Sophia did not go back to reciting poetry aloud for her throat was rasped sore, and she was so dreadfully thirsty. Surely, Richard did not intend for her to remain in this closet until she died of it? She suspected that he did intend that very thing, or else wait until the torments of thirst were so great she would consent to drink that awful potion. But Great-Aunt Minnie was coming to dine soon. She would wonder where Sophia was, and why.

But Richard had doubtless had sent a message, Sophia realized, with a sinking heart. But she must be ready. Whenever next Richard opened the strong-room door, she must be alert, on her feet and ready to flee. She sat with her ear close to the keyhole, running the verses in her mind, alert for any sound; the tall hall clock chiming the hours, Richard opening the door into the study. Two or three minutes after the stroke of five – long enough for her to get through most of *Hiawatha* – the metallic sound of the lock turning in the study door came to her ears. She struggled to her feet, cramped by long hours of sitting on the floor. Heavy footsteps – a man's footsteps advanced through the room, pausing at the strong-room door. A musical jingle of keys on a ring – and she drew in a deep breath. This was her chance. The tumblers of the strong-room door turned and clicked, a crack of light opened between door and jamb – blinding to her, having sat so long in near-to-pitch darkness.

As soon as that door was wide-enough opened, she darted through it; her chance, her only chance of escaping Richard's hand – flashing across the study towards the hall door, her freedom as she knew it. She heard a startled oath from her brother, and knew that he had expected to find her whimpering and cowed as Fee, curled on the floor of the strong-room. She gained the door, grasped desperately at the knob and latch. To her horror and despair it did not open, but held fast under her hands, as unyielding as the strong-room door had, during that interminable day. In another second, Richard's iron grasp held the back of her dress and her hair, which had fallen in a tangle to her shoulders.

"Let me go!" she cried – a last appeal to affection and reason, but her brother spun her to face him and with his other hand struck her across the face so violently that she fell against the door, still somewhat upright. Richard's expression was maniacal; she could hardly recognize him, his countenance so fearfully altered. He struck her again, on her face, her breast and arms, several times more, still holding her braced against the cruel unyielding door, before flinging her to the floor with such force that the breath went in a rush from her lungs. She gasped, half-choked with the coppery-tasting burst of blood in her mouth, skirt and petticoat tangling her legs. She struggled against her own weakness and pain to rise from the harshness of the carpet underneath her, but a rain of blows from something hard and wooden drove her back again. An atavistic instinct drove her to half-curl, her arms lifted and protecting her head, while the pitiless blows continued falling. With her last dim awareness, she knew that it was Richard beating her, without mercy – although the blows which fell on her body did not hurt so much as the knowledge of cruel betrayal; the bones of her corset absorbed the worst. Just before the last vestiges of awareness fled her, she was aware of him pinching her nostrils closed, of gasping for air though her mouth. There was a weight across her body, pinning her arms to the floor. A bitter-tasting potion filled her mouth, filling it until she choked and swallowed, swallowed again, her body in desperate hope to breath.

When she could breathe again, in the last glimmer of consciousness before the darkness rose up in a great wave and pulled her down, she was was aware for just a bare moment of that weight pressing her body without mercy underneath it, and there was a new and particular pain. Then all went to darkness and she knew nothing more.

Chapter 4 – The Prisoner

Sophia returned by fits and starts to the painful and pain-filled world of the living. She had no notion of how long it had been since Richard beat her senseless, or even where she lay, although was in a comfortable bed. The first time she was even slightly aware, her head swam with pain, to the point where she feared vomiting, if she did not hold very, very still. Somewhere above, she heard Great-Aunt Minnie's voice and someone held her hand.

I must have escaped after all, Sophia thought. With so deep a relief at such a miraculous deliverance she fell gratefully back into the black darkness of not-knowing. She was safe with Great-Aunt Minnie. The next time she came up from the dark, Great-Aunt Minnie and Phelpsie were murmuring together, at a distance. Still, she was reassured yet again … wait, yet – *was that Agnes? What was she doing at Great-Aunt Minnie's?* Could Agnes have assisted in conveying her to safety in the old Vining mansion on Beacon Hill? That must be so; Sophia took grateful refuge in darkness once again.

In the next essay into communication with the living world, Sophia was able to open her eyes. It took an effort, as she was still wracked with pain, in her head and the rest of her body; every bone and every fiber of muscle still hurt. She couldn't open one eye, and her nose was clogged, so it was hard to breath. She was less inclined to vomit, even if her throat was dry and scraped, and her mouth tasted if she had bitten into something particularly vile. She struggled to interpret where she was, a room lit by a single spirit-lamp and lost in the dimness. It was a familiar room, familiar in an awful way – her own bedroom in the Brewer mansion; Sophia could have wept in frustration and terror, but she was so tired. She must have made a slight sound. Great-Aunt Minnie came rustling around the foot of the bed. This Sophia knew from the faint scent of asafetida and lavender which she had associated from earliest childhood with Great-Aunt Minnie.

"Auntie?" she croaked, hardly knowing if she had formed the words aright. Yes, that was Great-Aunt Minnie taking her own slack hand in hers. "Auntie … where am I?"

"In your own bed, my dear," Aunt Minnie replied. Moved from a spirit of deep emotion which Sophia had never associated with her great-aunt, Minnie stroked Sophia's forehead with her free hand. "Sophia, dearest … why ever did you do it? What dreadful impulse moved you to commit such an awful act?"

"Do what?" Still fogged, under whatever potion had been administered to her, Sophia regarded her great-aunt. "What did I do?"

"You took a full draught of opium, and flung yourself down the staircase," Great-aunt Sophie answered. "Suicide is a sin, child – a dreadful, mortal sin. We knew that you were in despair over Mr. Armitage, no matter how bravely and how often you denied it…"

"I didn't!" Sophia protested in utter horror and indignation – that someone might think so of her! "I cared nothing for Mr. Armitage, save as a friend of old! I would never …" She regarded her aunt – that sensible, practical Aunt Minnie could credit this!

But the old woman was shaking her head. "Dear child, we came into the house just as Richard found you, lying at the foot of the stairs. We heard a dreadful thumping noise and Richard shouting your name. Phelpsie and I let ourselves in; there you were, all crumpled at the foot of the stairs. Agnes found an empty bottle of syrup of opium the bottle halfway up the second-floor stairs. I suppose it had been prescribed for your mother in her final days. Dr. Cotton knew at once he must wash out your stomach to save your life. It was horrific, Sophia. I have not observed a scene since I volunteered as a hospital nurse in the late War!"

"I didn't do anything of the sort, Auntie!" Sophia protested. The waves of darkness threatened to overtake her again. She must make it plain to Aunt Minnie, she must. "Richard forced it down my throat!" Those words had no effect on Aunt Minnie, who patted her hand, and smoothed the covers over her. "You are over-tired, child, and you are not yourself."

"He made me drink it," Sophia whispered, with the last of her strength and conscious thought, but Great-Aunt Minnie had gone from the bedside, leaving the faint and soothing scent of asafetida and lavender. With the last awareness in her, she was aware of Minnie opening the door, saying, "Agnes, she was just awake, very briefly. Mind you go tell Richard."

There was a disputatious exchange of whispers at the door which she could not make out until Great-Aunt Minnie's was raised in indignation. "That is a vile accusation, my girl! How dare you even repeat such a thing! He is her brother!"

She was still in Hell, everyone she loved and trusted, conspiring to put and keep her there; best for her to be unaware, blissfully drink the potion and be out of this world of cruelties, until she was stronger, and could think of a means of escape. The grief of betrayal, by all whom she had thought to love her was more than she could endure for the moment. Richard, Great-aunt Minnie, Lucius Armitage, Emma Chase … everyone. But she must escape. A single tiny flame of defiance; Sophia took that with her into the dark of unknowing.

When she came up from it once again, she still was unmistakably lying in her own bed. There was a light beyond her eyelids, which she kept closed as long as possible. There was someone moving in the room; by the rustle of skirts, another woman.

"Can ye hear me, Miss?" Agnes's voice in a surreptitious whisper. "Open your eyes, if ye can. I've something t'say to ye."

"Don't upbraid me, Agnes. I can't bear it." Sophia's eyes leaked tears. Crying like a child! Such humiliation was unbearable. Now Agnes too would tell her that suicide was sinful, and she was damned to the fires of Hell.

"Why should I?" Agnes forgot to whisper. "I know the Master was putting summat in that tonic of yours. I saw him, the very day that the doctor's boy delivered those bottles the second time. I am sure he did so, ever since it was first sent for ye. If he makes ye drink it again, do not fear. I have poured out ivery drop in ivery bottle, and filled them w' molasses and water, to look like what that Dr. Cotton sent." Agnes' voice lowered. She settled herself into the chair at Sophia's bedside, and took her hand in her own tiny, work-worn one. "Make a pretense. Miss Sophia, lest he lock you in the strong-room again. I knew he did it to ye; the whole household knew. Me, Mrs. Garrett, an' Declan, too, for I told him. That's why Miss Phoebe an' the lads went to stay with her mither. She did not care to know what was happenin'."

"She did not care to prevent it," Sophia replied. Fee was a desperately silly woman, but all this time she had been Fee's sister-in-law, housekeeper and governess to her children. She owed no more loyalty to Fee since Fee had demonstrated none towards her.

"I have to get away, Agnes," Sophia's eyes overflowed again, running back into her hair and dampening the pillow which lay underneath her head. "I did not throw myself down the stairs! My brother beat me and forced me to drink that dose. No one believes me, not even my great-aunt. My brother has been telling her …"

"I know what he has been telling poor Miss Vining," Agnes' voice dropped again. "She an' Miss Phelps, they were there, y'see. Miss Phelps nearly swooned on th' doorstep an' Miss Vining turned as white as a linen sheet. She thought ye were dyin' ye see, if not dead already. Mrs. Garrett an' meself, we came from the kitchen when we heard the shoutin'. Mr. Richard carried you upstairs and went himself for Dr. Cotton; M'self an' Mrs. Garrett an' Miss Vining, we took off your things. Oh, Miss Sophia, you are all covered w' blood and bruises. Black and blue fr' head to toe, it must have hurt dreadful and Mrs. Garrett said …" Agnes hesitated, her pleasant childish face contorted with puzzlement.

"It does," Sophia replied in a whisper. She did hurt – even in places where she had never thought that one could feel pain. Her heart within her chilled; Richard's voice at a distance in the house, on the stairs by the sound of it, with Great-aunt Minnie, sounding like a furious bird, chirping at a marauding cat. "Agnes, I must escape from here. You are the only one in the household who believes me, or witnessed what my brother has done."

"Aye, ye must," Agnes bobbed her head in solemn acknowledgement. "There was a muddle o' blood left on the carpet in the study, for a' that Mr. Richard tried to sponge it away hisself … but it is he who pays m' wages, Miss Sophia. An' I do fear him, for he …" and poor terrified Agnes hurriedly crossed herself in the Papist fashion. The Irish in her voice became ever more marked as Richard's heavy tread on the stair and landing became unmistakable. "He has an evil spirit within him, ma'am. 'Tis plain to see, for those that have eyes; for a' his foine clothes an' manner, the de'il has possessed him. If he could hurt ye in the way he has, what could he ha' done to me?"

"You must leave, if you think yourself in danger from my brother," Sophia whispered, although knowing that this would leave her alone in the house. Agnes was little more than a child, a servant girl of the lowest class in Boston. She was right to fear Richard Brewer, with his friends among the rich and powerful.

But Agnes shook her head, "How could I live w' meself, knowing you were alone?"

The door to Sophia's room opened. Sophia closed her eyes, as Agnes rose from the chair, letting Sophia's had fall from hers as if lifeless; Richard's irritated voice, speaking over his shoulder to Aunt Minnie. "Cotton says that she is on the mend. The girl can look after her, better than you and that fussy old spinster companion of yours. Get back to your own household and cease disrupting mine."

"Mrs. Garrett has given her notice!" That was Great-Aunt Minnie, distant but no less indignant. Sophia's blood ran cold. "Who will keep the pantry, do the baking, prepare the meals, if Phelpsie and I leave?" Now she wished that she were still so ill that she could sink back into that blissful dark unknowing again. She closed her eyes and made a pretense, willing every fiber in her to go limp and without response. *Mrs. Garrett, gone from the Brewer household?* She had only been their cook for the last few years, a slatternly widow and not a very good cook, but cheerful, willing and agreeable to working very hard for a parsimonious wage, for which Sophia had often thought Fee and Richard should consider themselves fortunate.

"The agency has sent around a list of likely candidates," Richard's voice was bored, dismissive. "In the meantime, Agnes will cook such invalid fare as required – you will, Agnes, won't you? For myself, I'll dine at the nearest chophouse. Mrs. Brewer shall conduct interviews with them, upon her return. You presume too much on my good-will, Aunt Minnie. I insist on being allowed to conduct matters in my own household as I see fit and that includes the welfare of my sister. Your presence is no longer required, or welcomed; yours and that abominably moronic leech of a companion." The door thudded closed. With her eyes closed, Sophia guessed that Great Aunt Minnie was on the other side of it. Her brother was within the room – and the thought of his maniacal countenance in her last moments of consciousness rendered her paralyzed with horror. Desperately, she wished for the darkness of unknowingness again.

"Is she awake, Agnes?"

Sophia pressed her eyelids tight-closed, made her breathing slow and regular, but there was little she could do about the frantic pounding of her heart.

"No, she is not," Agnes' voice sounded even more childish than usual. "She moaned a bit, in her sleep as I was straightening the pillow … but she has been quiet since."

"Doctor Cotton told me that it might take a little time," Richard's voice sounded worried to anyone's ear, but to Sophia there was an undercurrent of gloating satisfaction in it which turned her blood cold. "I will sit with her for a time, while you go about your duties."

Sophia forced back the impulse to scream. Her safety lay in passivity, in the pretense of sleep. She must hold very, very still, because, if Richard wished to, he could hurt her again. She was aware of Agnes within the room, busy with her broom and dust-cloth, and Richard breathing as he settled into the bedside chair; she prayed that Agnes would remain, but in a few moments the door open and closed. The window above the garden must have been half-open. Outside, the birds squabbled in the shrubbery, and from a far distance, the rattle of wagon wheels, accompanied by the clopping of horse-hoofs on a cobbled street.

"Oh, Sophia," Richard sighed. "Why couldn't you just do as I ordered? It would have made this matter so much simpler! But you would be so willful, so stubborn; it's your own fault. I have to think of Fee and the boys and their future. Their well-being is my responsibility. Everything else is secondary. The Marine Bank business put us on such thin ice. I need to count every single penny these days. It's not as if I enjoy destroying you, Sophia – it was just that circumstances required it. You'll be happy enough at Danvers. Cotton will see to it. No decent man will marry you now, especially not that milquetoast Armitage."

She heard the rustle of his coat, the faint creak as he rose from the chair. He patted her hand, where it lay, deliberately slack outside the bedclothes. It took all of her self-control not to flinch, or cry out at that touch. “It’s for the best, then. Maybe you’ll have learned your lesson, eh, Sophia? Do as I tell you; it is your own fault when I must punish you for your defiance.”

Sophia kept command of herself until the door closed at her brother’s back. As soon as his footsteps moved away down the stairs, she willed herself to try to sit, then swing her legs to the floor and stand. Her head swam at first; she could not stand unaided and to move was an agony. She held onto the tall bedpost until her vision steadied. One step, another, until she braced herself on the heavy old-fashioned marble-top wash-stand and looked at a face she barely recognized in the mirror over it. Livid blue bruises marred one side of her face, so swollen was the flesh around her left eye that she held it open with an effort. There was a slight bend in her nose, now. She pushed up the loose sleeve of her nightgown – dark purple bruises marred the pale flesh underneath. Sophia trembled, both from the effort of standing upright and the pain that doing so cost her.

“I must get away,” she said to the distorted self in her mirror. “I must get away. Or next time he will kill me.”

A resolve easier vowed than accomplished, for the aftereffects of the forced dose, the beating and a tumble down at least a few stairs hampered her limbs and equilibrium for days. In those hours of isolation and boredom, she grasped at an understanding of why Richard was doing this.

“It must be that inheritance from my mother,” she ventured to Agnes, in one of those moments when Agnes came to her room, bringing clean sheets and to sweep out the grate. “It’s mine on my twenty-first birthday. And that is the thing I can hardly comprehend,

Agnes. It's only pocket money of my own; enough to purchase a new bonnet now and again – two or three hundred dollars per annum, from an investment in property my mother inherited from her mother and father. Richard wants to keep control of it. How perilous is his position that he must grasp at every stray penny!"

"Two or three hundred a year?" Agnes mused, wide-eyed. "'Tis a pittance to rich folk like an Astor or a Vanderbilt or such … but it would be the wages of a servant or two, even a little house in the country, I know. Little or no, Miss Sophia – 'twas supposed to be yours, by your sainted mother's word! And the Master conspiring to steal it from you! No matter if it were two pennies, and you did not care – that is still against what God commands. It is a wickedness, to be sure," and she hastily crossed herself. "It is a wickedness of my own, that I wish he be judged for his sins sooner rather than later and if what Mrs. Garrett told me …"

"What did she tell you?"

"It was nothing," Agnes replied. She gathered up the soiled linen and the chamber receptacle. "She was no better than she had a right to be, and an evil tongue to be saying such things."

But by the morning she was able to dress herself unaided in her street clothing, put on and lace up her shoes, Richard had made arrangements. There was someone outside the door, and her heart froze, although Richard had not repeated his visit to her room. Only Agnes appeared regularly bearing a tray of inexpertly prepared invalid meals – bread and broth, most days – or a heavy jug of hot water for her to wash in, setting her room to rights and taking away the chamber pot. The door opened part-way, and there was Agnes' brother Declan, a metal tool in his hand, and a padlock in the other.

"Pardon me, Miss Sophia," he exclaimed. "But himself has told me to put hasps an' a lock on your door. He said you were unwell.

'Tis for your own good, he said … t' keep ye safe an' all, in those hours when he was out an' about."

Sophia regarded him, rough Irish innocent that he was; Agnes' older brother with his wooden foot, who could get no other work than as a night watchman. An explosion in a factory nearby to the rooms that the Teague family had lived in when he was a small child had resulted in a catastrophic fire which burned that tenement to the ground. Injuries sustained in their middle-of-the-night-escape had resulted in the horrific amputation of Declan's left foot.

"I do not care for being locked in," she said, voice unsteady. She was not strong enough yet to venture very far. But her plans for an escape rested on her being able to leave the room without let or hindrance.

"Nor do I, Miss Sophia," Declan replied. His round owl-eyes, so like his sister's, were sympathetic and troubled. "But Mr. Richard, he has ordered it be done an' I dassn't refuse. He could pay another locksmith, y'see, an' then …" He broke off, at the sound of Richard's voice on the staircase below.

"Close the door, Declan," Sophia ordered, her mind galloping ahead of the present. Richard must not know that her strength had revived. In the few moments of privacy, she put off the simple day dress she had assumed, and donned her nightgown and wrapper. The dress she stuffed under the cushions of her chair, and sat upon it, giving a pretense of an ill and listless invalid, gazing out of the window by the time Richard spoke to Declan, ordering the door to be opened. She didn't bother to turn around – for one, she didn't wish to give her brother the satisfaction. For another, she was afraid that if she saw that maniacal expression in his eyes again, she might vomit or faint away from terror.

She kept her eyes fixed on the window and the garden below. The garden was sadly neglected – a ragged wilderness of what should have been tidy plots of vegetables and herbs, screened by a hedge of roses and beds of seasonal flowers. She should have been seeing to it – would have been seeing to it, but for … *Well, let Richard see to the garden,* she thought, viciously; *the flowers for the house, the vegetables for the kitchen. Either that, or let him see to paying someone to see to it.* Doubtless he was going to use her inheritance for that, or something of the same.

When the door swung open, she resolutely looked into the window and the view below, kept her face expressionless.

"I see you are up and about, Sophia!" her brother said; he sounded jovial. That was like seeing bright theatrical paint on the bare bones of a skull – an effect intended to convince the observer of life and veracity, where none existed. "That is excellent – that you are so greatly recovered – see, Agnes has brought your breakfast, and I have that tonic which Dr. Cotton so recommended. I hope you are in a different opinion about taking it – this is for your own good."

Out of the corner of her eye, Sophia saw Agnes advancing with the tray on which her simple breakfast was arrayed – and an empty glass tumbler. Agnes set the tray on the little table next to the chair, and Richard appeared, with one of Dr. Cotton's dark glass bottles in his hand. Agnes hovered at his elbow as he filled the tumbler half-full of opaque brown fluid. Sophia looked at it for a long moment. Unnoticed by Richard, Agnes nodded – a slight but reassuring gesture. Sophia took the tumbler in her hand.

"Drink it down, like a good girl," Richard commanded. "It will make you feel better."

Sophia took the tumbler. She was an automaton, a mechanical thing of bones and pulleys, without any will or thought. This was the only means of maintaining composure in the presence of her brother. Raising it to her lips, she drank it steadily. She still had the slight apprehension that Agnes might have missed a bottle, or Richard had out-foxed her but the contents tasted only of ordinary molasses mixed with water, with none of that odd medicinal flavor from before, and certainly none of that effect which the tonic had upon her previously. She set the glass aside, her gaze still fixed upon the window, and every nerve jangling with apprehension. She was not strong enough yet to walk very far. The window was on the third story, and nothing close to it which might aid an escape through it. Richard had fixed a padlock on her bedroom, so there might be no stealthy escape through the door. But her spirits rose somewhat at this realization; Agnes was her ally, Declan, too. Agnes had rendered the tonic ineffectual and baffled part of Richard's plot. She looked into the garden, calm and showing no emotion. Her brother was now a person dead to her in spirit, although he remained vexatious, if not dangerous in life. He was dead to her, and so was Fee. She couldn't bring herself to eat any of the breakfast with her brother present; certainly she would vomit.

"Go on, eat your breakfast," Richard commanded, a thread of impatience in his voice.

Agnes spoke up. "Oh, sor, she is still not very well, then. Give her a moment. Let me stay in here wi' her, while you go about your business. I'll tend to Miss Sophia an' her room, if you will come and let me out at half-past."

"Very well," Richard agreed, although to Sophia's ears it sounded grudging. Out of the corner of her eye, she saw him draw out his pocket-watch and consult it. "See if you can get her to eat and to wash. She smells of sickness."

That nearly drew a reaction from Sophia of outrage and indignation. Of course she smelled of sickness; she had not fully bathed since the day that Richard beat her. What should he expect!

"I'll bring up several jugs of hot water, sor," Agnes promised. "It is an offense in the nostrils, likely enough." She did a brief curtsy, still wide-eyed like an owl, while Sophia reflected that Agnes was likely braver than she, at venturing that brief bit of impertinence. “And sor – ye will let me in and out?”

“Certainly,” Richard answered, although he sounded as if he were bored. *Oh, he thinks me mad*, Sophia thought. *Ill, mad and biddable. I’ve never thought I was so good at acting a play-part, save that my brother wishes to think he has succeeded. Well – we’ll see about that!*

At that, Richard walked heavily through her room, out the door which closed behind him with a thud that sounded like the prison door which it was. On the outside of it, Declan Teague made some remark, to which Richard replied, short and curt.

Agnes leaned close over the breakfast tray, whispering. “Do not fear being locked in, Miss Sophia – Declan will give me the other key.”

Chapter 5 – The Escape

"That is providential," Sophia whispered, leaning her head against the back of the tall bedroom chair. The exertion of dressing, hurriedly undressing to put on a pretense of helpless invalidism, and the stress of maintaining that pretense exhausted her completely. Likely she was not as well-recovered as she assumed. When she was done with the breakfast tray, she must walk around the room for – slipper-clad so as not to make any noise – and then take a rest. "I must remember to thank your brother and make a small reward to him. Any reward within my power to give him is likely to be too little."

"Ohh, think nothing of it," Agnes assured her. She regarded Sophia with anxious eyes. "You can eat a bit, Miss Sophia? I know the bread is burnt, but I scraped off the worst bits. And the eggs are done, right enough. Ye need your strength, ye do. Declan has a crochet about being locked in. He does no' approve of it for any, after the fire when Dadda was away with the Army an' Mam was working in the laundry at night. She locked Declan an' Siobhan into their room – Siobhan was only a baby, y'see, an' Declan seven or eight. She wanted to keep them safe. Ohh, it were dreatful, to hear them tell it now! Declan can no' bear a closed room – he must keep a window open, all but the coldest nights, or he can no' sleep at a'." She peered earnestly at Sophia; so worried about the plate prepared for her. Sophia was obliged to take a bite, then another, to reassure Agnes. It wouldn't have passed muster at Delmonico's or in the meanest boarding-house in the harbor district by any means, but Sophia found her own lingering sense of hunger, and so it tasted good enough.

"He must get out, y'see," Agnes continued, speaking softly as she moved around the room, while Sophia ate her breakfast, re-making the bed with clean sheets, and gathering up those few crumpled garments that might benefit from a trip to the laundry. "So – he told me, I should have anither key, to keep w' me. He'll give it to me before he is finished. An' as soon as ye can," Agnes fixed Sophia with a particularly earnest look. "An' ye can – soon? When Mr. Richard next goes out for a long while, an' ye can walk to Miss Minerva's house … an' if the house catches fire, I will have ye' out o' this room."

"Good," Sophia took a last mouthful of scrambled egg – rubbery and weeping into the slices of toast, but she was indeed hungry. It took the taste of molasses thinned with water and vinegar out of her mouth. She had an appetite which is how she knew she was on the mend. "I can't let my brother send me to Danvers, Agnes. I imagine the only thing stopping him is that he believes I am still ill and drugged with Dr. Cotton's vile potion, although I suppose I could be carried away on a litter. The first time he leaves the house for a good length of time will be the best chance that I have."

"Aye," Agnes bobbed her head in perfect agreement. "I will set aside your clothes an' things an' hide them with the dirty things to go to the laundry, so you will have some few things w'you – no more than a single carpetbag."

"When does my brother next have an engagement away from the house?" Sophia considered the walk to Beacon Hill – not a long way, but through streets that might be busy during the day and dangerous for a woman alone at night.

"Tonight," Agnes replied. "But he has not said so straight-out. He talked of meeting with a friend for supper, so he told me. He has gone out every evening to a chop-house for a meal, but he does no' stay long. With a lock on your door, he may think he has time for a meal at leisure."

"Tonight, then," Sophia agreed. Fury and desperation might carry her when will and strength failed. She heard a distant heavy footstep on the staircase below. "There he is, come to let you out, Agnes, let me have the pillowcase." She set the tray aside, and going to her dressing table, tumbled some hastily selected contents into it. "My little bits of jewelry … my good gloves. The rest are shifts and petticoats and things. The lace-trimmed shirtwaist Emma gave me for my birthday. I might not hold her so dear a friend now – but she does have the most refined taste. There; come and let me out once that Richard has gone. I shall be ready."

"Yes, Miss Sophia!" Agnes whispered. "Into the bed w'you, so he will think you are still weak!"

Sophia flung off her wrapper and rolled herself between the fresh and crisp sheets even as Richard fumbled at the door. She closed her eyes, as if laying in a stupor, listening to Richard chiding Agnes for so neglecting the housekeeping. How hateful – when it was poor Agnes working alone, bringing in the coal and wood, and taking away the ashes and the chamber-pots, and now left seeing to the sparse meals as well! Were she Agnes, she would hate Richard with a sullen and abiding hate. She supposed it was the girl's sense of duty and personal fondness for herself which kept the downtrodden little maid-of-all-work in the house. Should Sophia escape tonight with Agnes' help, she must encourage the girl to find work elsewhere; yes, and write up a fine recommendation for her, too.

The door to her room closed with a thump, and a brief metallic rattle, as Richard padlocked it closed. Sophia listened to the voices and footsteps of her brother and Agnes fade and considered what she must do next: choose and pack those few things which she couldn't bear to leave behind … and rest. She was more exhausted from her efforts in this morning than she liked to admit, even to herself. She meant only to close her eyes and rest for a few hours, but when next she opened them, the pale golden sunshine of afternoon had painted the pattern of the window-frame on the worn Turkey rug at her bedside. A whisper at the door had roused her – Agnes' voice.

"Miss Sophia? Are ye awake? I have the key in me hand. Mr. Richard will be away at half-past five. D'ye hear me, Miss Sophia?"

Sophia threw off the bedclothes laying over her, and scrambled to the door, her heart hammering with apprehension, lest they be overheard. "Yes, Agnes – I am awake. How long is it until then?"

"The clock has just struck the hour of four, Miss Sophia," Agnes sounded immeasurably reassured. "Be ye dressed and ready. I will come and unlock the door as soon as I have seen Mr. Richard around the corner of Berkeley Street."

"I will be so, Agnes," Sophia whispered, limp with gratitude and relief. "…and bless you."

"Och," Agnes sounded embarrassed. "'Tis nothing. Ye've been good t' me, an' Declan, too, an' Father Anselm says that one should never stand by an' see injustice be done."

"I am grateful – to you and to your Father Ans…" Sophia began, but Agnes cut her off.

"No mind to that, Miss – 'e's calling for me, awa' downstairs. Be ready!"

Heedful of the danger that Richard might still choose to climb the two flights of stairs to assure himself of her helpless condition, Sophia put off donning her best street costume, and instead sorted out what she might take with her, either in her reticule, or in whatever bag Agnes might bring for the rest. She sat on the edge of the bed in her wrapper, regarding the room she had as her own, the room she had slept in since a child – every object and furnishing dear and familiar; no, she could not take any larger things, and in any case they belonged to Richard. She gathered up her ivory and silver hairbrush, the dressing set that it was a part of, several of her favorite books – to include a battered edition of *Vanity Fair*, a collection of Tennyson poems and the worn edition of the *Common Book of Prayer* that had been her mother's – a gift from her own father, who had inscribed the date and a loving message to his daughter on the inside. No, no more – too many books might make the bag too heavy for Agnes, or for herself. She added a single silver-framed daguerreotype of her parents at the time of their wedding, and the one of her father in his uniform, and the best and newest of her dresses. That was all she could carry.

Underneath the wrapper, she had on her cleanest shift, drawers, stockings and petticoat, her corset as tightly laced as she could draw the strings, and her shoes fastened up to the last and tiniest button. The minutes crawled past, as slowly as a crippled beggar working his way along the street with his crutch and tin cup, measured out every fifteen minutes by the chimes of the tall-case clock two floors below. With the windows open to the mild late-spring afternoon, Sophia could hear them clearly.

She used those minutes to consider what she must do once she achieved the sanctuary of Great-Aunt Minnie's house. She should be safe there from any effort of Richard's to pry her out; although she wouldn't put it past him to kidnap her from the street if she dared go outside. Great-Aunt Minnie would see to Sophie's safety, once within the walls. Minnie had many friends – some of them in high places indeed. The old lady had campaigned fearlessly for abolition and for the rights of women and if there was a cause she would champion to her last breath, the freedom and well-being of her dear brother's grandchild would be chief among them. But until Minnie brought her legal weaponry to bear, Sophia might yet be as much a prisoner in the old Vining mansion as she was in her brother's.

"I won't mind in the least," Sophia said aloud, more to hear a voice in the room. She had always been fond of that tall old-fashioned house, with the narrow garden and the stables – presently disused save as storage for dusty piles of crates and trunks, for the Vinings had never thrown or given away anything. When she was a child, she had loved exploring and listening to Great-Aunt Minnie's stories of the family. Her own mother had been born in the sunniest and best-fitted of the upstairs rooms – the same that her Grandfather Horace had died in, for he was a consumptive and came back to his childhood home at the last. "There is so much I will ask of her," Sophia said again, aloud. "Of my father. He was so brave, so Mama always said. And of Grandfather – he traveled, Mama told me. Traveled far, because of his bad health; Mama barely knew him when she was a child. Aunt Minnie should know of his adventures." Agreeably lost in these considerations – which passed the time, no doubt – Sophia was brought out of them by a quiet knock on her door, and the sound of someone fumbling with the padlock upon it.

"Miss Sophia?" Agnes called. "Are ye awake? Mr. Richard has gone to his supper and is away. Are ye ready no'?"

"I am," Sophia replied. She stood up as Agnes came through the door, with a limp and empty carpet bag in hand. "Let me put on my dress, my hat and mantle – oh, take this, Agnes! A minute and I will be!"

She threw her wrapper into the bag which Agnes held open for her, following it with the pillowcase stuffed full of clothing and small effects. She pulled on her plain dress, fumbling with the buttons in her desperate haste. Her mantle and hat hung ready, on their accustomed hooks in the wardrobe. She plopped the hat onto her head, skewered it with the last of the hatpins left on her dresser, and threw the coverlet off her bed.

"What are ye doin' Miss Sophia?" Agnes watched, utterly baffled, as Sophia stripped away the sheets, and knotted one to another, pulling the knots tight. During the long hour and half while she waited, she had torn each across the middle, from top to bottom.

"A false trail for my brother," Sophia gasped. "He will suspect you and Declan, but now it will look as if I escaped through the window, without any help from either of you."

Agnes's eyes went huge, in her peaked and child-like face. "Could you have done this at any time, Miss Sophia?"

"Trusted that worn-out sheets would have held my weight for a climb from the third story? I'm not an idiot, Agnes – though Richard must be convinced that I am." Sophia knotted one end of the rope of sheets around the architectural post which defined the center of the double window to her room, and dropped the loose end. As she expected, it dangled within a convincing length from the ground. "There! That should spare you and Declan from suspicion. I'm ready – remember to lock the padlock behind me."

Sophia shrugged on her well-worn mantle and buttoned it tight against the chill of an early summer evening. The wind would be blowing from the Charles River and the harbor beyond, that damp and bone-chilling cold. Agnes took up the heavy carpetbag, and they stole together out onto the landing. The house was unaccustomedly silent. Sophia contemplated that silence as she and Agnes tiptoed down the two flights of stairs. In her life to date, the Brewer household had only been as silent as this once before; that tragic time when her mother was on her deathbed. The sonorous ticking of the tall clock in the entry hall broke the present quiet. Always before there would have been the distant clamor of Mrs. Garrett clanging pots in the kitchen, Agnes going here and there with her bucket and broom, Richie and his brother making a noise in the nursery, Fee and her friends in the parlor. All that was gone now – the Brewer mansion was quiet, empty, even haunted.

Sophia couldn't depart from it swiftly enough. "I'll go through the garden," she whispered to Agnes, "And come around to the street from the alley. Mind – you have not seen me since this morning. I'll be at Miss Vining's before half an hour has passed. Thank you, Agnes – you are the dearest child, and I will swear before anyone, I owe my life and likely my sanity itself to you."

"It was only what Father Ambrose has often preached," Agnes replied. Sophia was certain that the child looked embarrassed at such gratitude. "To comfort and aid the persecuted, whatever the risk might be. 'Tis only right, Miss Sophia."

"Yes, but sometimes you'd be surprised at how many fear to do what is only right," Sophia whispered. "Miss Vining will tell you readily enough of her trials, when she was speaking at abolitionist gatherings."

The two of them stole out through the kitchen, and into the garden. As agreed, Agnes would conceal the carpet-bag in the disused stable, and bring it to Great-aunt Minnie's when she could best steal away with the excuse of an errand to run. Sophia straightened the hat on her head; this was the first time she had been out of doors in weeks. The dying sun painted the mellow brick walls of the mansion and the stables behind it with golden tints – but to Sophia, having spent the last few weeks in a room with the curtains drawn close; it was still unbearably bright.

"Don't let Mr. Richard bully you," she advised, aware of how small Agnes was. Richard could break her to pieces as if she were a china doll. "If he makes as if to talk to you, Agnes – don't allow him to stand between you and the nearest door."

"That I will not," Agnes answered with sturdy courage. "And I will give my notice in a day or so. Declan says I should not stay, and Papa has said the same. I only stayed here to help you, Miss Sophia."

"And I am more grateful than I can say." Relieved on Agnes' account, Sophia settled her hat on her head, took a firm grip on her reticule, and let herself out of the stable door into the alley beyond. The small door swung freely at her touch; the two large doors – made large enough to admit a team and carriage – had long since been bolted shut. The single-horse buggy sat in the corner, dusty and neglected. It had been two years since they could afford to keep horses, a coachman to drive and grooms to care for the animals. Their last horse … now Sophia wondered. Injured in a stable mishap; Richard had sent Declan to bring the knacker and take it away, and then he said they could not afford to buy another one suitable. So had the Brewers become poor, in everything but pride and history! But there was no need to steal out of her home like a beggar. Best to stride purposefully along, and avoid the notice of someone who might assume her a thief or a cutpurse, based on a shrinking and stealthy manner.

Still nervous and fearing that she might encounter Richard somewhere along the way before she could lose herself among the crowd, her courage revived as she walked along Beacon Street. In spite of her dread, Sophia relished the out-of-doors, the freedom to walk without fearing that her footsteps made a revealing noise. Above all, she relished the hustle-bustle of street traffic, after so many weeks of enforced quiet. People – men, and ladies, and children of every age and station – hurrying along the sidewalk! Here were carriages, drawn by sleek-groomed horses, trade wagons and teams of lesser blood but at least as well-cared for, their iron-shod hoofs ringing on the cobbles. Up ahead, by the corner of Arlington Street, there appeared to be a crowd gathering of onlookers on the sidewalk, crammed tight against the iron railings of a fine tall mansion, and a tight knot of fine carriages and teams. Sophia's footsteps quickened; this was the Chase mansion, dear and familiar but no more, just as Emma Chase had been dear and familiar, yet no more.

She approached the knot of spectators, anonymous in her plain mantle and bonnet, one more in the small crowd. It appeared that there was a grand event planned at the Chases' this evening. The portico was adorned with flowers and ribbons, with a pair of potted evergreens trimmed into ornamental shapes, the pillars framing the door twined with ribbons and garlands of flowering jasmine, a length of fine carpet unrolled from the door, across the steps and to the curb. Guests were arriving; even as she lingered on the edge of the crowd, another carriage arrived; a fine and elegant one, drawn by two teams of matched horses, hides, hoofs, brass and harness gleaming, consummate proof of the care and expense lavished on them. A footman hurried from the door of the Chase mansion, unfolding the carriage step for Emma – lovely and laughing as she looked back on her companion.

"Until tonight!" Emma exclaimed, her laughter the sound of tinkling silver bells. Sophia looked, stricken anew, at the face of the man whom she had once committed to marry, framed in the window of the coach – the Armitage carriage and team. She should have recognized them. For a moment, although it seemed an age to Sophia, then and afterwards, she met Lucian's eyes. He recognized her among the crowd at once, for his lips moved as though he said her name aloud, and made as if to unfasten the carriage door and come after her, or ask her into it. But Emma's gaze followed his, sharpening in recognition, then cold, dismissive and commanding. She said something to Lucian, who then looked between Emma and Sophia and once more at Sophia. His expression held shame and regret. Emma vanished into the house without a backward look and the Armitage's driver chirruped to the team. Sophia stood on the sidewalk, chilled and horrified by that little gesture of betrayal. They knew her; her long-time best friend, the man that Mama had arranged for her to marry since she was in short skirts – and they both turned away. The cock had not even crowed three times.

The Armitage carriage bowled away, and one of those nearest in the crowd remarked, "'Tis a grand ball they are having tonight … to celebrate the marriage to be … aye, she's pretty enough; he has the name, and they both have the money."

Sophia tried to forget that she had overheard that. She put her head down, shielding her face from observers under the brim of her hat. Now she had the sensation which she could not put aside that she had become a woman outside that well-established world which she had always known. By an unaccountable machination, she was no one, cast aside by friends and family, a person of no respect and regard. She considered that uncomfortable sensation as she strode along Beacon Street. *Who was she, indeed, if not a Brewer of Beacon Hill?* A lost particle, drifting in the wind, one of the commonality, with the yellowish marks of fading bruises still on her face; she shivered. Aunt Minnie must shelter her. She was who she was; Sophia Saltinstall Brewer, a respectable lady of Boston, of an old and much-respected family. And if her brother had conspired to take that from her … well, she would just have to see.

Strengthened by that resolve, she went on up Beacon Street, feeling the strain of exercising little-used muscles. She would be tired when she reached Great-Aunt Minnie's. The expectation of Minnie and Phelpsie's welcome warmed and encouraged her, although she did pause in one or two places to catch her breath, while the last of the dying sunset gilded the distant dome of the statehouse.

Twilight was falling on the Public Garden, shadows stealing out from under the trees. The sky glowed a rich orange and gold in the west, and the gas street-lamps began to be lit – warm and flickering small lights doing valiant battle against the dark, casting a faint gold reflection on worn brick facades. Most residents had drawn curtains against the evening, but the windows in the old Vining mansion stood open, spilling light from the first-floor windows out into the street. Sophia wondered, a trickle of unease down her spine.

That was unlike Great-Aunt Minnie … to leave the windows unshuttered after sunset and curtains not drawn. Sophia climbed the tall flight of stairs to the front door and pulled the bell. Her legs felt as if they were jelly, liable to collapse underneath her at any instant. Distant within the mansion she heard the bell chime. She wished that Great-Aunt Minnie of Phelpsie, or their single maid-of-all-work would hurry. She trembled with exhaustion; still exulting in the triumph of having made it to Great-Aunt Minnie's door. She would be safe now. Her brother must never lay violent hands on her again, or lock her into a room, or force her to drink another draught of that revolting concoction of Dr. Cotton's. With a sense of relief which nearly buckled her knees, she heard footsteps within. The door opened to reveal Phelpsie, distraught and frantic.

As soon as Phelpsie opened the door and saw who was waiting without, she cried, "Sophia! What has happened to you? You should not be here!"

"But I am," Sophia replied, the urgency of her need for refuge lending her the courage to step through the door, pushing aside Phelpsie's attempt to hold the door as it was. What was happening? Where was Great-Aunt Minnie? "Please, Phelpsie – let me in. I am exhausted – Richard locked me in and I got away!"

"Richard!" Phelpsie cried, utterly distraught. "He was here – not an hour ago. You are not safe here – you must leave at once!"

"Phelpsie, I am exhausted … there is no other shelter for me… where is Minnie? Did he do something to her?" Sophia almost burst into exhausted, childlike tears. That safe refuge was snatched from her, just when she needed it most.

Phelpsie gabbled in frantic distress. "He and Miss Vining had the most ferocious argument. I was there; Miss Vining had asked for my attendance as her companion. He shouted at her, abused her with the vilest language imaginable!" Phelpsie shuddered, in real revulsion.

Poor Phelpsie; she was such a timid rabbit of a woman; incapable of standing up against her brother or anyone with an authoritative manner. "Miss Vining … she shouted back at him. I hardly knew what to do, it was so distressing … but suddenly she put her hands to her breast and fell senseless! It is her heart affecting her – her doctor has often warned her of overexertion and strong emotion." Phelpsie wrung her hands together and Sophia fought back her own urge to break into tears. This was her only possible refuge, aside from some distant Vining cousins-by-marriage, with a house in Waltham – too far for her to walk, even if she had the strength and the cousins consent to shelter her.

"Let me stay for the night, Phelpsie," Sophia pleaded. "Bar the doors and windows – I can sit with Auntie. Richard will not dare break in …"

"He threatened the law!" Phelpsie cried. "As Miss Vining's nearest male relative – he said that he could do it, and he would … that he would see to her as he had seen to you! There is an evil spirit in him, even when he was a small boy!" Phelpsie added, piteously. "Your mother was frightened of him, then – I am certain she told only us! He is wicked, evil! What would he do to me if he finds you here with us! This is my home now, with Miss Vining. I do not have any friends of wealth and position!"

"Neither do I, it seems!" Sophia snapped, driven beyond patience with the old woman's fears. "Phelpsie – compose yourself. Great-Aunt Minnie has …"

They were interrupted by a ferocious pounding on the great door at their back. Phelpsie collapsed into renewed tears, crying, "It's Mr. Richard! You must go, at once!"

"Open the door!" a male voice called, from outside. It was not Richard, but Declan Teague. "Miss Brewer – are you there? Listen; you are in danger, now!"

"Miss Sophia?" Sophia nearly fainted from a sudden and powerful surge of relief, for it was Agnes. "You must come awa' w' us at once. We have brought your bag w' your things." Sophia reached the door in two steps; she opened it and the brother and sister fell into the hallway, Declan with his fist still raised as if to pound upon the door panels once more. "Miss Sophia!" Agnes cried, still gasping for breath. It sounded as if she had run all the way up Beacon Hill. "Mother Mary be praised! You must come away with us at once! The master returned – as soon as y' were gone! In such a temper he was! Then Dr. Cotton came to the door an' him with a closed carriage! They were intending to take you away, this very evening! They found the sheets you left, dangling from your window – an' they are searching the stable and the neighbor's gardens – in a fair swivet they are, but it is only a matter of time before Mr. Brewer comes here."

"Yes, you must go with them," Phelpsie babbled. "He must not find you here, child – he will blame Miss Vining, and she cannot bear it. It will be the death of her and I have nowhere to go!"

"Come with us now, Miss Brewer," Declan said – his voice deep and serious. Sophia hesitated a moment. No, she had no friends of wealth and importance; best to cast her fortunes with those who had been true friends.

"I will," she said. It didn't escape her, even in her exhausted condition, that Agnes, Declan and Phelpsie looked relieved. "But where to? I am so weary, I cannot go far."

"Our home," Agnes answered confidently. "It is humble indeed, Miss Sophia – but not far. Declan and I have a notion of where you can go afterwards."

"Lead thou me on," Sophia replied. "I am in desperate need of refuge." Out of the corner of her eye, she noted that Phelpsie was torn between shame and relief at this one burden and fear conveniently relieved. “Tell Auntie I am safe, and wish most fervently for her recovery,” she added, over her shoulder.

“Wait! Just one thing!” Phelpsie cried. “Miss Vining had a parcel … she was intending to bring it to you! She wrote your name on the wrapping!” Miss Phelps dived into the old front parlor and returned, gasping, with a small package the size of a book, wrapped in heavy brown paper.”

“Hurry now!” Declan commanded. Sophia gasped her thanks to Miss Phelps and dropped the little parcel into the top of her carpetbag.

“Lock the door after us, Phelpsie,” Sophia commanded, over her shoulder. “And shutter the windows. If Richard comes here tonight, you don’t know where I am. You haven’t seen us. Tell Aunt Minnie that I am safe only when she is better. Goodbye, Phelpsie; don’t open the door for anyone tonight!”

“I won’t,” Phelpsie gabbled, distraught. Sophia wondered for a moment if Phelpsie, aghast at having to face an angry Richard alone, was going to beg them to stay. But the door opened in Declan’s strong hand and closed with a thud after them, and with a distant sense of relief, Sophia heard the sound of the lock falling to. The last of her life was left behind although Sophia did not know this for a certainty for a number of hours.

Chapter 6 – A Brief Refuge

Dark had fallen entirely now, save for a pale pink smear in the western sky.

"Where are we going?" Sophia struggled for breath and against her own weariness. Declan limped ahead, a strong-wide shouldered man, her carpetbag in one hand with his stout watchman's cudgel and a small tin lantern swinging in the other. They hurried up Beacon Hill in the direction of the golden dome of the State House, still gleaming faintly in the last light of day. Agnes put her arm around Sophia's waist; an unexpectedly strong arm from her short lifetime of hard work. Sophia was grateful in equal measure for the support and that they were heading in the opposite direction of the Brewer house and unlikely to encounter Richard in the tangle of narrow old streets in the waterfront district.

"To our home," Agnes replied. "Declan an' I, we've an idea to help you escape for good."

"If you have the mettle for it, see," Declan threw over his shoulder as he hurried ahead. "'T will mean leaving Boston, so it would, Miss Brewer."

"I'd go out to the frontier and beyond, among the wild Indians," Sophia answered. "Anywhere, so I'd never have to fear my brother again."

"Out west?" Declan grinned over his shoulder. "Among the wild Indians and gunslingers? Our Seamus can't get enough of those tales, but with pluck and luck, Miss Brewer – you might have your chance."

"What do you mean?" Sophia gasped; she was being swept along by an irresistible tide. They had left the lights of Beacon Street, plunging into the depths of the old North Town, which had been abandoned by people of quality decades since, and left to the poor and recent immigrants from Ireland and elsewhere. The streets were narrow, ancient brick buildings shouldering close against each other, smells of privy, waterfront, and cooking nauseating in intensity.

"Carry this, no'," Declan passed the carpetbag to his sister. With the faint scritch of a Lucifer against the nearest wall, Declan lit his lantern. "'Tis safe enough now for a light; his bully lordship will no' be looking for us here, Miss Sophia." Declan Teague sounded most particularly satisfied.

"I cannot help fearing that there might be others in these streets," Sophia had recovered composure, after several twists and turns, each one into a street darker and narrower than the last. "Posing even more of a danger than my brother."

Declan Teague let out a rich chuckle, "So you might think, Miss Sophia. But this is where we live, among folk who know us and protect their own kin an' kind. You are safer here amongst us than you have been for a while among your kin. This is the place, above the shop of old Mendelson the Jew. Mind the steps." He held up the lantern courteously; there was a narrow alley between one tall brick tenement and the next, an alley which led to a door which once had been fine when it was the house of a merchant-prince of the last century. Declan had a key for that door. Sophia blessed him for the lantern, for the hallway inside was Stygian-dark, the flight of stairs to the next floor and the one above that darker still.

At the top there was another short hall, with a doorway on either side. Declan turned and made a short and awkward half-bow before the door on the right-hand side. "Our home, our fire an' our salt, Miss Sophia. Ye are welcome, indade. I mus' be at my place of employment. Aignéis – that is her right name here – will explain to you the solution. Sorry, I am late. There is one more thing, Miss Sophia; gi' me your hat and mantle."

"I cannot see why it I must give up my clothing," Sophia protested. At her side, Agnes whispered, "Do what he says, Miss. We have worked out a means of laying a false trail."

Declan opened the door. "Aignéis will explain, with Seamus in chorus. Y'r hat and be quick. I'll be back in t' morning."

"Gi' it to him," Agnes whispered at her side, "The mantle, too … oh, dinna fuss, Miss Sophia – I will explain, sure an' I will. Ye will be safe indade – we hae planned it out f' ye, an' ye' will ne're fear your brother again. Do ye no' trust us?" Agnes sounded so doleful that Sophia was moved instantly to reassurance.

"I have, I do, and now I trust to whatever scheme you have concocted, since I have no better choice." She pulled the pins out of her hat, holding them in her mouth as she handed it to Agnes' brother, then shrugged out of her mantle, much puzzled. The hat was new for spring and she was fond of it, but the mantle was one of her mothers', which she had altered to suit herself and to fit a more fashionable appearance.

"Good," Declan grinned again. He leaned down, not so very far, and kissed his sister on the forehead, as he deftly bundled up hat and garment into a small bundle under his arm. "No fear, Aignéis, I'll be back at sunrise. Be ready to travel at that time, Miss Brewer, y'r bag packed an' all. You an' Seamus explain our plan to her."

He was gone with his comforting cudgel and lantern, as Agnes opened the door into a dim apartment which must once have been a generously appointed room, when it was a single chamber and not sliced up into a parlor, kitchen, and sleeping quarters for a family, even one as small as that of a widower with three grown children. There was a tiny iron stove set into the hearth of a stopped-up fireplace, a stove which served as a cook-fire and to warm the premises. A single kerosene lamp provided illumination. In the corner, a length of old curtain fabric hung from a string tied between the walls, drawn back to reveal an iron bedstead where a boy a few years older than Richie sat cross-legged, reading from a book which in the dim light looked like a Wild West blood-and-thunder tome. A heap of ragged clothes and blankets was piled in the single tattered armchair, drawn close to the fire.

As the door opened and closed, the ragged pile bestirred itself; an aging and cracked voice inquired, "Aignéis - *cailín daor* – is that you?"

"'Tis, Da – and I have brought Major Brewer's daughter with me," Agnes replied.

"To this house?" the cracked voice broke with astonishment, and the pile of old clothing convulsed. "Aignéis, why? 'Tis not a fitting place for her ladyship!"

"I'm not a ladyship," Sophia protested. Agnes answered in placating tones, "Da, she had no other place to go this night. Wicked man that he is, Master Richard brought the doctor at this very hour, to carry her away to the asylum an' she is no madder than Siobhan or I."

The clothes and blankets heaved and reshaped themselves, becoming in the faint light, the figure of a man, bent with age and with one arm so crippled and shortened as to be strapped immobile in a sling on his chest, saying with the courtesy of a lord. "Ye are welcome to share our salt and shelter, Miss Brewer – little enough, but it is our honor."

So this was Declan and Agnes' father; Sophia had often heard of him, in Agnes' daily conversation – that he had been a soldier in the 28th, and crippled for life in an accident on the docks when Agnes was a baby. Now he took her hand in his good one and inclined his head in rough courtesy.

"I thank you for it, Mr. Teague," Sophia swayed, faint with exhaustion. "And I am more grateful for your hospitality than I can …" The wave of dizziness threatened to overwhelm her.

Mr. Teague chided his daughter. "Call me Tim Teague, now, will ye? Settle her in my chair now, Aignéis. The poor lady is no' well, no' well at all. Sit there, Miss Sophia – rest ye now."

So grateful for the consideration she nearly wept, she sank into old Tim Teague's chair – the only padded and comfortable chair in the room, if so shabby and broken that even thrifty Great-Aunt Minnie would have relegated it to a bonfire. Tim Teague hovered at her side, patting her hand in a way meant to be comforting, until Agnes brought another simple straight chair from the corner of the room for her father. Agnes herself settled onto a low three-legged stool at Sophie's knee, and young Seamus set aside his book – thriftily dimming the lamp-wick by which he was reading it.

"Is it true that your brother was feeding you opium and trying to drive you mad so he could steal your money?" he asked with intense interest.

"Seamus, be hushed!" his sister cried, in an agony of embarrassment, adding as an aside. "Forgive him, Miss Sophia – but 'tis true I have talked of your situation amongst the family, mind – only with Da an' Declan at the first. Siobhan an' I have always talked about folk we were in service to. It's an amusement, y'see. It's one of the only ones we have, a good gossip; sometimes like a play, or the old stories.

"No, Agnes, do not chide him," Sophia answered, around a lump of grief in her throat. Grief for the lost life she once had, grief for the illusion of a loving family, grief for herself, lost and forlorn, taking refuge in a low boarding house in old North Town. "It is true, every word that your brother said; I have nowhere to go and no friends to turn to, aside from yourselves. Isn't that as dramatic as one of your books, Seamus?"

"Oh, aye," Seamus breathed, while Agnes cleared her throat – she sounded at least as tentative and uncertain as her young brother.

"But, Miss Sophia, we have a way for ye to escape, for good an' all – if, as Declan said – ye have the mettle."

"She does, indade," Old Tim Teague assured them, patting Sophia's hand again. "Th' daughter of Major Brewer o' the 28th Massachusetts! Niver was an officer cooler under fire! Nay, he were not of my company, but all knew of him. The hotter the fire again' us, the cooler he were, striding up and down along our line, w' lead shot fallin' like hail from a summer storm! An' he'd say a few words to every man, humorous-like, as if on a stroll through the Common, w' all the time in the world, an' no other worries than a drink in the next tavern!"

"Yes, Da," Agnes interjected. "But we came away in such a hurry that Declan had no time to explain. She does no' know the plan."

"The plan?" Any plan must be Declan or perhaps Seamus' notion, Sophia knew without a doubt. Agnes was as guileless as a small child. To credit her with a stratagem of any complexity was to believe that Richie could suddenly emerge as a captain of industry.

"Aye, so," Agnes nodded, and regarded Sophia with an intent gaze, more like an owl than ever. "D'ye recall how I told ye about Siobhan, and how she answered a notice in the newspaper, to work in a respectable establishment of the railway, away out in the West?"

"I do," Sophia wracked her memory. That conversation seemed as if it had been years before, and not a matter of a mere three weeks. "She told her intended he must either offer marriage at once or she would leave Boston to wait tables."

"That was so," Agnes agreed. "She had a letter from the gentleman, offering an interview at his office in Kansas City, should she choose to make her way there and immediate employment if she were suitable. The thing is," Agnes looked embarrassed. "Siobhan wanted him to think she were a proper lady, not turn her away as a bit of shanty-Irish, so she used another given name."

"Silly girl," Tim Teague rumbled, "Putting on such airs – as if he wouldn't know the truth of it the minute she opened her mouth."

"Da, Siobhan can talk as proper as any, when she has a mind," Agnes said, and Sophia ventured, "What name did she use?"

"Yours," Agnes fixed her solemn owl-gaze on Sophia. "She wrote and called herself Sophie Teague. An' when she went to marry Tommy O'Neill, she left that letter behind. She cared nothing for the matter any more. I kept it because the envelope had such a foine picture on it and Mr. Harvey wrote in such a nice hand. Seamus wanted to practice copying it. Old Mendelson the Jew says that Seamus could go far if he writes well."

Enlightenment dawned on Sophia, not unmixed with horror. "So," she ventured, as three Teagues regarded her with varying degrees of interest or anxiety. "Your plan is that I take the letter, pretend to be Sophie Teague, and go to Kansas City to an interview with this Mr. Harvey and take up work as a waitress?"

"Aye, so," Agnes nodded and her younger brother said, "Seventeen dollars a month, <u>and</u> room and board, too."

"But I would have to work – for wages," Sophia protested, "It's just not seemly!"

Agnes sounded impatient. "An' to work as Mrs. Phoebe's housekeeper and nursemaid for nothing but your keep is seemly for a lady? 'T will be no harder, Miss Sophia, than working for wages for Mr. Harvey an' more honest-like, too. And besides, this will take ye away from Mr. Richard. They'll ne'er be able to find you, and lock you in the Danvers Insane asylum, that's for certain."

"That is true," Sophia agreed, with reluctance. "But the humiliation of wage work…"

"Work is worship," Agnes replied, as flat and stubborn as someone quoting Holy Writ. "That is what Father Anselm says. Work well done is an offering to Him. There is no matter what the work is –

only that it be well-done, perfect and with your heart. Let the ditch be the most beautiful ditch ever digged, the hearth the most perfectly swept, the dish from the kitchen as finely cooked as if the Queen of England herself were to partake of it. There is no sin in work, Miss Sophia, only in thinking you are too good to do it."

"I am chastised and rightfully so," Sophia said, upon a moment of reflection. How hard she had worked in her brother's house! And for so little reward, save the social status and some small material comfort in being one of the Brewers of Back Bay; suddenly, all of that was an intolerable burden. If she could not be as free as Great-Aunt Minnie in conducting her own life on her own terms – why couldn't she take up Siobhan's letter from this Mr. Harvey, and an identity allowing her a free life? This was a breath-taking and horrifying step – yet alluring. A life of her own; a life based upon her own talents, her own work, without the crutch of family renown and connections.

She was going to step off a high precipice, trusting on an unknown power to bear her up, lest her foot crush against a stone. She took a deep breath. Yes, this was a precipice; another world, one of which she knew little, but the alternative was the Danvers Insane Asylum and the authority of her brother. A life of captivity, of locked doors and barred windows – and she feared that Richard was not entirely sane. She considered the memory of his eyes, just before he commenced to beat her senseless, his words when he assumed she was unconscious; harsh; insensate. Even if she contrived to be freed from Danvers – there was Richard, with a false-genial manner and pebble-cold eyes, commanding the household and those who lived within it. "I consent to your plan, Agnes, whatever the rest of it entails. I am tired of my brother's plotting. Tell me what I do next. There is not enough money in my purse for a railway ticket."

"You have your rings, and brooches and things," Agnes looked to her brother. "Old Mendelson will take them for cash. He will not cheat a Teague; give the jewelry you do not value to Seamus and he will see to it."

It was not a imposing collection once unearthed from the bottom of the carpet-bag; three bracelets, a string of small pearls; things which she had been given as gifts. Only the engagement ring was of any significant value. Sophia kept back a pair of ear-bobs which Great Aunt Minnie had given her and a round gold brooch with strands of her mother and father's hair woven together. She emptied the rest into Seamus' hands. He departed, thumping down the narrow staircase with the ebullience of a boy embarking on his own adventure. She sat in Tim Teague's chair, drained and exhausted, while Agnes fussed over the fire with a battered tin kettle, and a small and chipped pottery teapot. Obviously a warm and comforting cup of tea was in order. Tim himself had shuffled into the other room.

"Why did Declan take my hat and mantle?" Sophia asked. That was a puzzle. "I'll need something to wear for the train, won't I?"

"Oh, 'twas Seamus' notion; Declan agreed. No', Mr. Richard has put about to everyone you were going to do away w' yourself, so Seamus said – leave your hat an' all on the banks o' the river where anyone will find them in the morning an' believe that you have gone and cast yourself into the water. They will be searchin' for ye in the water, an' along the banks, and never look elsewhere."

"Agnes, that is brilliant!" Sophia exclaimed, and felt shamed by her reaction; shame mixed with satisfaction that her brother would be tangled in his own web of lies! "It will serve my brother well, seeming to have his deceitful story born out! But you must contrive to tell the truth to Phelpsie and Aunt Minnie as soon as she is well enough."

"Of a certainty," Agnes replied, a wounded expression on her child-like face. "Miss Minnie is a kind lady, dear to ye an' has always been kind to us. "When ye are safe away, and she is better – an' I will burn a candle at St. Stephens for that – I will tell…"

"Found it," Tim Teague emerged from the other room with his arms full of folds of dark fabric. "'Tis an old-fashioned thing, Miss Sophia – but well-woven; Siobhan did no' want to take it, an' Aignéis wi' no' need it when she takes up her vocation." He shook out the folds, with his one good hand, and draped it over Sophia's lap; a large woolen shawl, woven in checks of rusty black, brown and natural cream-colored wool, coarse and as thick as a blanket. "An' Mendelson the Jew will not offer anything o' substance for it, y'see. Take it, Miss Sophia – for the journey. Ye are no' taking anything o' much value to us, an' the train carriage will be cold at night. Wi' wearing Siobhan's old bonnet, anyone seeing y' at a distance will take ye for Siobhan."

"Thank you," Sophia's eyes filled. She was so tired that this simple generosity was overwhelming. "I am more grateful than I can ever say – you are doing so much, when my own friends, my family turn aside!"

"Niver say that a Teague would turn away from a woman treated unjustly – an' twice niver from th' daughter of an officer of the 28th!" Tim Teague answered, with a pride and determination that almost erased his fifty years of hard life and decayed condition. He settled onto the hard chair and beamed at Sophia and his daughter impartially. "I'll have me cup o' tay now, Aignéis."

"So," Agnes poured out a measure of tea into each of three mismatched and chipped mugs, handing the least-chipped and fullest to Sophia. Lapped in the heavy shawl, and close to the fire, the bare little room, walled with cracking and stained plaster was now pleasantly warm, even comfortable. "In t' morning, Declan w' come from t' warehouse; likely he will have a ride to the South Station on Albany Street on a goods wagon w' one o' his friends. Old Mendelson w' be rapping on t' door for Seamus before that time. He likes to open early, an' he is the only man in this street to ha' a clock which strikes the hours regular. Y' must be ready when Declan comes in th' wagon. At t' station, he will see ye onto the early train f' Albany. He has a friend who is a telegraphist – an' these railway folk, they know each other. Ye must change trains in Chicago for the Central to Kansas City – but Declan, he says he w' see you are set onto the right platform. Then it's to Kansas City. I dinna know what t' tell ye when ye get there. Declan's friends will know of a place for a lady to stay f' a day … then ye will go to Mr. Harvey's offices."

"What if I am not hired – what shall I do?" Sophia's heart sank – alone in a strange city, half the country away.

"Go t' a domestic agency," Agnes replied, as if the question did not worry her overmuch. "Say ye are seeking work such as what ye were doing for Miss Phoebe. Housekeeper, a governess 'r such. Enyone w' hire you within a day, Miss Sophia – a lady, honest an' well-spoken. But no' to worry; cross that bridge when ye come upon it."

"If you say so," Sophia agreed, still apprehensive. But Agnes and Siobhan between them likely knew everything there was to know regarding domestic service, so she took comfort in that assurance. Just at that moment, Seamus returned, bounding up the stairs with Mendelson's payment for Sophia's jewelry.

"All but the ring," Seamus explained, in regret, as he gave it back to her, along with a handsome brace of notes and coin. "He said that was too rich for his business. Being from a jeweler of repute in the city, he would have trouble over it. He says to take it to a pawnbroker in another place, far from Boston an' to accept no less than …" and Seamus named a staggering sum. How much Lucius must have thought of her – and to insist that she keep it! Little did he know might buy her keep in a respectable boarding house for a while, at least; such a mordant imagining! Seamus continued, in boy-enthusiasm. "But there is enough an' more for a third class ticket, all the way to Kansas City!"

"Arright then – tomorrow, early in th' morning for ye, Miss Brewer," Tim Teague exulted. "Is supper ready, Aignéis?"

"It is indeed, Da," Agnes answered, although with a somewhat apologetic look in Sophia's direction. "It is only bread and cheese … a little extra noo – the night is still early, an' the cost of kerosene for the lamp. We retire early as we are tired of a day."

"I am tired, too," Sophia admitted with honesty – for she was exhausted to her bones. "Since I will have a long journey on the morrow … where is my bed to be, then?"

"W' me," Agnes admitted; the girl blushed with embarrassment. "T' bed here, which Siobhan an' I shared."

"Of course," Sophia made swift acknowledgement; it should have been obvious that the Teague's home was a small one. "Your hospitality may be limited by circumstances but I appreciate it none the less. I am afraid that I have become a restless sleeper and I apologize in advance. I am lately plagued by nightmares. If I have one tonight, shake my shoulder and tell me to turn over."

"Bad dreams an' a?" Old Tim Teague sounded comfortably sympathetic. "'Tis nothing new to we Teagues; I raised the thatch many a time, dreaming I were under fire at Chancellorsville. Now that was a hot fight, *cailín daor* – but I took more in bruises from the wife wakin' me, years later, by shovin' me in me ribs than I iver took in the fight itself… 'twas the fear, ye see…"

"Yes, Da," Agnes said, as if she had listened to her father on this subject many times before. "Shall I toast your bread and cheese over the fire, no?"

"I would like that, Aignéis," The old man answered, cheerfully, beaming on them in an impartial way. "But serve our guest, first."

Half asleep already, from exertion and relief of the tension which had pulled her nerves taut all the day, Sophia thought, *"He knew of my father as a soldier, and considered him very brave. I wish he had lived, so I could toast bread and cheese for him over a fire and he could console me but then, if Papa had lived, then none of this would ever have happened."*

She was three-quarters asleep, when she took off the walking dress and fell into bed. She was barely aware of Agnes folding the dress and laying it on top of her own carpet-bag before sleep and exhaustion claimed her utterly.

Chapter 7 – Walk Away and Never Look Back

Of course, the nightmare rode her that night; she cowered under Richard's blows, relieving the suffocating weight of something heavy pressing her down, down, down, the pain of that weight forcing her legs apart, a new stabbing and intimate pain that spun away as the opium took her down even further…

"Miss Sophia," a tremulous voice breathed in her ear. There was a hand on her shoulder, which she batted away until she realized it was Agnes, and that she lay in a bed in that tenement where the Teagues lived. "Miss Sophia, y'r crying out. Is it the nightmare again? O' course it is. Wake up no – ye are safe with us and soon to be far away, where he can no' harm ye again."

"I know," Sophia gulped, half-paralyzed by the ragged shadows of the dream. Her heart pounded so hard, she feared it would burst in her chest, and her shift was drenched in her own sweat. "I am awake, Agnes. I am sorry that I have disturbed your own rest."

"No," Agnes demurred, "I sleep light, Miss Sophia – and easily. Dinna regret … an' I am accustomed to being around folk with night terrors. Da an' Declan, they both awake shouting, still. Go back to sleep, Miss Sophia." Agnes's voice sounded ever more musical, with the Irish lilt to it. "I can sing a lully-bye to ye, as Ma once did, if ye believe it would help."

"Do not threaten me, Agnes," Sophia felt recalled to the present sufficient to jest. "I have heard you try to sing – you cannot carry a tune in a bucket."

"I know," at her side in the darkness, Agnes giggled. "I canno sing – it will be a cross to bear when I take the veil."

"Agnes!" Sophia was diverted from contemplating her own miseries. "You considering becoming a nun?"

"Aye," Agnes replied, in tranquil confidence. "'Tis a thing I have felt a calling for … oh, the last year or so. Da an' the boys, they say it a girlish thing, an' a matter for teasing. But I take no mind. It will be so, an' I will be guided. Just so are you guided, Miss Sophia – I have a sense of such things, y'see. But a bad dream as you had just now – there was something that Mrs. Garrett said. You cried out no, no, and Mr. Richard's name just now; it reminded me of what she said."

"What did she say, Agnes?" Sophia now felt cold, the damp shift clammy against her skin. "And when?"

"You were carried upstairs, the evening of the day when Mr. Richard locked you in the strong-room." Agnes ventured. "When Mr. Richard went for Dr. Cotton, Miss Vining and Mrs. Garrett and I took off your clothing … bruised from head to toe ye were an' soaked in blood. Oh, Miss Sophia…" and Agnes' arm tightened around Sophia in a comforting embrace. "I thought it lucky you were not in your mind, for it would have hurt something dreadful. Miss Phelps went faint, she were that distressed, but Miss Vining, she were very brave, an' sent for Miss Phelps to bring hot water and cloths. We took off your dress an' underthings. That was when Mrs. Garrett said, straight out – that it looked as if you had been …" and Agnes' voice dropped, hushed with embarrassment, "Interfered with … bruises, y'see. An' bloody matter on your under-drawers. Miss Vining, she turned white an' then red, an' said that Mrs. Garrett should shut her mouth before speaking such vileness. Mrs. Garrett, she said she may ha' been born at night, but it wasn't last night, neither an' there were no man in the house save Mr. Richard. That were when Miss Vining said that such an evil-speaking woman ought to be sacked an' Mrs. Garrett said that she wouldn't stay a minute longer in a house where such goings on were countenanced. Then Mrs. Garrett gave her notice." After a long moment, Agnes continued, "I were not certain of what they meant,

Miss Sophia. But when I asked Miss Vining later, she were angry. So I said nothing more. Was that the right thing, Miss Sophia?"

"Yes, it was. I suppose it was the start of my monthly course … yes, that must have been what it was," Sophia answered; sunk in misery and doubt, for she could not remember past a certain moment in that dreadful evening. But something awful had happened to her, which her mind quailed from contemplating, even acknowledging. "I cannot recall, after my brother forced the syrup of opium on me. That is enough for everyone to know, Agnes. Until then, I believed that he was for me as your brothers are to you. You are fortunate in your family if not in worldly things. I shall try to go to sleep now."

"You do that, Miss Sophia," Agnes embraced her again, which comforted Sophia. The Teagues were her true friends when everyone else had turned away. How very complicated her life had become! Maybe it was a good thing to go away from Boston and start anew.

Still, she could not sleep; so much to consider. Would she journey safely to Kansas City? What refuge would she find there? If this mysterious Mr. Harvey did not hire her, what should she do then? At her shoulder, Agnes breathed slow and regular, deep in slumber. At last, Sophia slithered out from under the blankets and from Agnes's light embrace. The girl obviously slept sounder than she had said, or else she was tired. There was a faint light in the room, on the other side of the makeshift curtain which sheltered the bed. By that light, Sophia rose, changed her shift for a clean one and resumed the dress she had worn that day and which she would wear when Declan came for her. That, by the distant sound of the bells from the old North Church, would not be much longer. She wrapped the coarse countrywoman's woolen shawl around her. The night was still chill, from the wind blowing off the harbor and the windows of the Teague tenement apartment leaked all the way around. She may as well sit by the fire which warmed the small place. She stepped around the edge of the curtain, and saw that Tim Teague had installed himself in his armchair – or he had never abandoned it, after allowing it to Sophia for a short while.

"Ye canna sleep, I see," he said. He was awake, his old eyes gleaming in the slight firelight. What an odd conversation; she may as well indulge him, for he was kindly and his daughter comforting, he remembered her father.

"I cannot," she replied, settling on the little three-legged stool which Agnes had sat upon the night before. The fire had had burned low, but there was still warmth in it. "I am setting out on a long journey, Mr. Teague. There are things which I cannot stop remembering."

"Tim … call me Old Tim," he answered readily, grinning as she answered, "I cannot be so familiar, Mr. Teague. You are very much my senior in age, and it is just not proper even if you were a servant. My mother was always particular regarding courtesy and respect."

"So was your father, if I remember," Tim Teague acknowledged. "He had such a way with him."

"I did not know him, and you did," Sophia asked, on impulse and suddenly shy. "He was killed before that I was born, so I never knew him. All I know is what my mother and Great-aunt Minnie said of him and they knew him as family. Not as a man – a soldier – does."

"The Major," Tim Teague settled with a reminiscent sigh deeper into his battered armchair. Sophia hugged her knees to her chest like a small child, hungry for every word. "He was not what you think of when you think of a hero," Tim Teague began. "No' at first; a quiet man, soft-spoken; in leading a charge he held his sword as if he were surprised to find such a thing in his fist. He did not give orders as if he were giving orders. He spoke as if asking a favor, but such was his manner an' intent that men obeyed on th' instant. Never over-familiar, as if he were seeking to ingratiate; always courteous. He had a notion always of when someone told him a lie; a recommendation if you came up before him on charges."

"He had trained early in law," Sophia said.

Tim Teague grinned again, relishing the memory. "An' that was my good fortune, I tell ye, Miss Sophia. It was a small matter … th' provost-sergeant – an evil man! He told a lie about me. An' so I were brought up before the Major. He, bless the man, saw how it were a lie wi' a shrewd question 'r two, an' I had my liberty at once. He was always," and Tim Teague's eyes were remote, as if peering into the far distance beyond the tiny room in an upper-floor tenement in North Town, back to a world of blue uniforms, banners floating above and before them, and grey clouds of rebel gunpowder smoke over a hard-held position, "an officer we could trust, y' see. He were a good 'un."

Sophia rested her chin on her knees, intent as old Tim recalled her father in memory, a well she could only dip into this once. She might gain a truer image of him than she had ever gleaned from her mother, whose memories of Richard Brewer were hazed by a veil of bridal silk.

After a time, Tim Teague's reminiscences went wandering, as Great-Aunt Minnie's were wont to do. Sophia listened, lulled by the musical bent of his speech. *Why was it that it sounded to her like poetry?* He talked of how he had departed starving Ireland as a young man, the misery of an immigrant ship, how he had finished up in Boston, working as a laborer on the docks, how he had met and married the mother of his children. That was before the war came, and he had enlisted … Sophia wondered if she had dozed for a while, for she wakened with a start.

Tim Teague was patting her shoulder, under the woolen shawl. "Close the door and walk away. Walk away, niver looking back. Do ye no good, *cailín daor*. There's nothing good for you, remaining. *Na deamhain* – demons will haunt ye anyway, so don't give them a chance to get their claws into you any deeper. *Faugh a Ballagh!* – That was our battle shout. 'Clear the Way!' for the 28th … We marched in the Grand Review, ye know. But for me, there were a stone in m' heart an' demons haunting m' soul for a' that I had seen. The Major was no' with us. He should ha' been but f'r a damn dirty Reb sniper at Petersburg!"

There came a quiet tap on the door to the room in which they sat, and a mumble of a voice whose words Sophia could not catch. Tim Teague lifted his head, alert as an elderly hound. "Ah, 'tis Mendelson; ye had best ready yourself, *cailín daor.* Declan will be by wi' the wagon, any moment now. Remember what I said – close the door, an' walk away, niver look back."

"I will, Mr. Teague," Sophia promised. "I can never thank you enough for the help you and Agnes and Declan have given me."

"'Tis nothing," Tim Teague shrugged her gratitude aside. "Your father did me a good turn, once: A good man, a foine officer. I could no' return the favor to him, but I can for his daughter. Go swiftly now before any o' the neighbors are awake. Take care wi' the name of Teague, for the time ye are using it."

"I will," Sophia promised. The moment came, announced by a splatter of pebbles thrown from the street against the outer window. There was a wagon in the street below, iron-shod wheels grinding and crunching on the cobbles. She gathered up her carpetbag, the heavy shawl, and put Siobhan's old bonnet on her head. Declan met her on the doorstep below, a shadow against the sky in the narrow alley-way between the tenement which housed the shop of Mendelson the Jew, and the next. Declan helped her to sit on the wagon-tail, hanging her heels like a street-urchin.

He hopped up to sit next to her, saying as the driver chirruped to his team, "We shall be in time for the first train to Albany. You shall have to change trains there and at Buffalo. I will ask the conductor to look after you. The immigrant car will take the least of your money, but there might be a rough lot in there. And it might take four days to get to Kansas City. The newsboys sell fruit, and where the train stops, you can buy sandwiches for a nickel in the station lunchrooms."

"Once arrived in Kansas City," Sophia voiced one of her chief worries, "Where shall I stay? I do not know the place and I am a woman alone."

"Aye, I considered that," Declan nodded. "Ask at the station, for directions to a respectable boarding house. Remember, now – your name is Sophie Teague. Say it to yourself, over and over until you can say it without hesitation."

"My name is Sophie Teague," Sophia recited obediently. "My name is Sophie Teague, from Boston. I am an orphan and have no brother or sister."

"Good," Declan nodded. "Remember; if you must tell a lie, make it as close to the truth as ye can and keep it simple. That way, ye don't have to remember details. And it will no' really be a lie, then – will it?" She couldn't argue with that. Declan fell into silence. The freight wagon rolled on, through the newer part of town, to the new South Station, near to the banks of the Bass River – now more of a marshy inlet than a river. All the while, Sophia repeated silently: *My name is Sophie Teague, from Boston. I am an orphan and have no brother or sister. My name is Sophie Teague, from Boston. I am an orphan and have no brother or sister.*

An orphan, from Boston – so she was now. There was no life for her here. Those bonds of affection and fond memory were severed, ruthlessly cut away as a surgeon amputated a gangrenous limb so that the patient might live.

"Declan," she asked, having been reminded of one of those small puzzles, by the regular clopping of the horses' hoofs. "Declan, you might know … what happened to the last horse we had in our stables?

Richard told us it had been injured so badly in an accident in the stable that the knackers had to come for it. But now that I pondered over the matter … how could a horse injure itself so badly? If I remember it was a gentle enough beast, with a good temper – we could have no other, to drive in the city."

"Ah, that," Declan nodded. He was silent until Sophia persisted. "Did Richard have something to do with the accident in the stable?"

"Aye," Declan replied, his voice tight with an anger which startled Sophia with the depth of it. "He did indeed, Miss Sophia, but no accident. Since that day I have hated him more than I hate the Devil for what he did to that innocent beast. The poor beastie gave annoyance or small injury to Mr. Richard, and in a fury, he took up the coaching whip and beat it around the head until the blood ran." Declan looked straight ahead, not meeting her eyes. "He beat it without mercy until he put out an eye and then kept on beating it with the butt of the whip. I was working that day, digging in the garden, and I heard … you can guess what I heard, Miss Sophia. I came into the stable and Mr. Richard, he turned around, the whip-stock and his arm bloodied to the shoulder. He says in this cold voice – the way you'd say when a dog had made a puddle on the floor – 'Go fetch the knacker, boy – tell him to bring his cart and take this mess away.' Oh, yes, he is a piece of work, Mr. Richard is. That is why I can well believe the worst of him, and happy enough I am to help you get away. He is an evil soul with a fair face," Declan shook his head. "I count it my good fortune, Miss Sophia – to thwart him, in whatever he was trying to do to you."

"I see," Sophia said, sickened to her stomach with the mental picture which Declan's words brought to her mind. Yes; Richard taking a whip to their horse – that made sense. Now she was more particularly desolate than ever. Richard was a brutal fiend in human form, she detested Phoebe; Great-Aunt Minnie was incapacitated and incapable of offering help and refuge, and all of her friends but the Teagues had deserted her. *Close the door and walk away. Walk away, never looking back. My name is Sophie Teague, from Boston. I am an orphan and have no brother or sister.*

She did not look back, once Declan had bought her a ticket as far as Albany and settled her into the immigrant coach, a simple wooden seat which likely she would have to herself for most of the day, since the coach was not very much crowded. Declan had a quiet conversation with the conductor, standing at the coach door, and came to her, twisting his plain working-man's cap in his hands.

"It's best that ye don't write to us," he said, uncomfortably. "Before I came to fetch ye, I put your hat and mantle by the shore o' t' river. Anyone findin' it will be sure that ye ha' done away wi' yourself by drowning. They <u>must</u> believe you are dead, an' nothin' to connect us to you, other thin Agnes an' I having worked for the family."

"But you should know that I am safe," Sophia replied. "Is there a way for me to send you word in secret?"

"There is no' – which will not bring suspicion on us. It's the best way, Miss Sophia."

"I understand," Sophia acknowledged. *No, not to look back.* Out on the platform, the train conductor gave a last great bellow of "All abooooord!"

"Goodbye, Miss Sophia," Declan said, breathlessly. "Best o' luck to ye, then," and he was gone. She saw him on the platform a moment later, as the passenger coach lurched with a mighty metallic clanging, and then the pillars which held up the station roof seemed to sway and crawl past the windows, faster and faster. The train slid out into the network of branching and interlaced tracks, rumbling over points, moving faster and faster. The morning was enveloped in pearly grey fog, rising from the harbor and the fingers of water which reached from it. It veiled the distant landmarks – the gold dome of the Statehouse, crowning a distant hill, the familiar forest of towers and spires – for which Sophia was grateful. Nothing remained for her here. All she had by way of material possessions was the carpetbag, stowed in rack above her seat, the clothing she stood up in and the sturdy reticule in her lap, containing the last of her money, two books, and her mother's *Book of Common Prayer* with the letter from Mr. Fred Harvey in Kansas City offering possible employment to Miss Sophie Teague tucked into it's pages. She had a luncheon of bread and cheese, bought for her by Declan from a grocery already open for business this early in the morning. The gold and diamond ring hung around her neck on a sturdy length of string, concealed under her bodice, and tucked into the top of her corset. This was on the advice of Seamus, whose devotion to blood-and-thunder adventures had given him – so he assured her – enormous insight into the minds of criminals.

Sophia had often traveled by train; most usually to Newport, in the company of Great-Aunt Minnie, or those occasions when she accompanied Phoebe and the boys to visit her parents, who lived in Cambridge. On those excursions, they had always traveled in comfort in the First Class coach and the journey was a matter of brief hours. Not so this journey. The seat and back were plain un-cushioned wood, although for many hours she enjoyed the spare luxury of no one sharing it with her. Most of the other passengers were men, young and foreign, dressed in working man's garments. She attempted reading for a good while until discovering that doing so whilst the train was in motion made her queasy. That was even before an unkempt male traveler in the seat behind her began to read over her shoulder and had the gall to chide her for turning the pages too fast.

"I am unwell," she said to him, adding, "I am sorry that your education was not the equal of mine – nor that you have not the means to purchase your own reading materiel to pass the time."

"Ohh, yer ladyship!" the man returned, in a scornful manner, and he continued being unpleasant until the conductor, overhearing the latest of his un-pleasantries, told him to move to another seat and to mind his tongue when speaking to a lady. Sophia reposed a considerable trust in the conductor who she saw ruled the various coaches under his authority with a lordly and righteous hand.

"Tell me if he continues offering offense," the conductor advised. "To yourself or any other female; I don't allow it on my train. If he continues being obstreperous, I will have him put off at the next station."

"I hope that will not be necessary," Sophia answered, for she did not want to make any trouble for anyone and cause them to take particular note of her person. She was still too near to Boston. That was one of the things which Declan had cautioned her on; she should not attract attention from anyone who might recollect her later.

"It should not," the conductor said with an air of comfortable assurance. Sophia wondered if the fading bruises on her face were still too visible; she thought the conductor had glanced at them for just a hair of a second. "I do not allow such on my trains." He hesitated for a moment and added. "You seem to be … too superior a person to ride in the immigrant car."

"My name is Sophie Teague, from Boston," Sophia replied, without hesitation. "An orphan without any close family; I am going a long way and wish to make my funds last as long as possible."

"Strange world, that," the conductor mused. The first faint tinge of alarm prickled along her spine. Sophia did not want to be noticed in any particular fashion. "Teague; that's an Irish name, but you do not sound as if you are one of them Boston Irish."

"My family has settled in Massachusetts since before the Revolution," Sophia blurted and then cringed. How should she talk her way out of suspicion? But the conductor hardly seemed to feel any such, remarking as he moved on,

"The wheel turns, Miss Teague. Some are elevated, and some brought low, only to be elevated again."

"Indeed," Sophia agreed. She was certain he would only remember her as Sophie Teague – and Declan had spoken with him before the train pulled out. Declan must have said something, either to ally suspicion or to request special attention for her.

Thereafter, for much of the journey to Albany she gazed from the window at the countryside as it unfolded, verdant with spring; shadowy woodlands patched with new-ploughed fields, orchards of fruit trees, shedding the last of their spring blossom and putting on the first of their summer leaves. Every mile, every turn of the steel wheels, took her farther from Boston, from Richard – to safety, but she wondered regret if she would ever come this way again – if she would lay eyes on those quaint small towns, and those larger ones, humming with enterprise and industry. By noon, the steel road had led into rolling uplands, with the lavender shadows of the distant Green Mountains of Vermont now and again visible in the north as the track angled up a grade, or around a curve.

She did need to change trains in Albany and purchase another coach ticket to Buffalo and Rochester. There was a long wait for that train; Sophia eased the stiffness from her limbs by walking on the train platform and her hunger after eating the simple luncheon of bread and cheese by purchasing another sandwich and an apple from the newsstand boy. Three nights and most of three more days before reaching Kansas City; she began to fear that the long journey spent sitting upright on the hard wooden seat might make her ill with exhaustion. Of the money she had for her jewelry there was sixty dollars remaining, just enough for the cheapest fare to Kansas City and a little over for meals. Well, she would have to find somewhere to sell the gold ring.

No help for it. She opened her carpetbag. She had finished *Vanity Fair*, and regretted bringing no other books of light reading with her. But that little parcel which Phelpsie had pressed upon her – that was shaped like a book. It had slipped down the side of the carpet-bag to the bottom, and she had forgotten about it. Had all that happened a mere twenty-four hours ago? Her questing fingers touched it and she drew it forth, moved nearly to tears by a pang of homesickness for the Vining mansion and Great-aunt Minnie. Yes, her name was written in ink on the little parcel: definitely a book. Upon unwrapping, she discovered a single volume of Thoreau bound in calf-leather, a philosopher whom Great-Aunt Minnie revered, having met him several times in her youth. Not as frivolous as Thackeray, Sophia thought, but opened the volume never-the-less. There was a folded paper tucked between the inside cover and flyleaf, written on the outside in Great-Aunt Minnie's careful script.

Dear child, Richard forbids me the house, so I have chosen this means to communicate. The enclosed should offer you some proof of my enduring affection for you, comfort in your time of difficulty, and a means of effecting escape. All of your dear mother's fears with regard to your brother have come to fruition, as I have come to realize with no small degree of horror. The bonds of familial affection blinded all of our eyes, especially when he was a boy and certain of his deeds could be construed as ignorant and unthinking high spirits, remedied with a stout thrashing by your father. Your mother first confessed her fears to me after the matter of the birds. You would not know of this since it occurred before you were born.

The songbirds which Phelpsie and I cherished were first and originally the pets of your mother, who took every delight from their antics and song. When your brother was about six or seven, and disciplined for some small childish naughtiness, your mother and father found him in the act of savagely tormenting her birds. Your father administered an appropriate punishment but your mother feared that Richard could not be trusted, alone in the presence of a small and helpless being. The cage and the songbirds which survived were removed to my house, in deference to her fears but she afterwards forbade the presence of pets of any kind in your house, for fear of Richard. Your mother often claimed she could see a demon in his eyes. I humored her without agreeing, for your brother seemed to be as amiable and devoted a boy as he was as a man. But I have now seen what your mother saw – and my fears for you cannot be assuaged by any reassurances. I apologize from my heart, dear niece, for not seeing the peril sooner. I fear that I have spent too many years with my eyes on the fight against greater evils and looked little upon the smaller ones among those whom I held in close affection. You are in my daily prayers, always. Come to me when you can do so in safety.

Your loving Auntie
Minerva Templeton Vining.

The paper felt thick as if there were more folded sheets inside the first. When Sophia unfolded it, to her astonishment, several banknotes fell into her lap. Hardly daring to breath, she counted them: two hundred dollars in crisp new notes. It must have been a great sacrifice for Great-aunt Minnie, as her own income had been just as much reduced by the failure of the bank. But Minnie and Phelpsie lived frugally, so such a sum was not altogether inconceivable. Sophia wished she had known about the notes from the first, instead of sacrificing those little bits of jewelry to Mendelson the pawnbroker. This changed everything. She tucked the folded notes away in her reticule, and went to the station office to exchange her ticket for a seat in a Pullman car, on the next express train, all the way through to Kansas City.

The sleeping car! She could sleep, rest her aching head on a pillow, in a starched white case. Right at this moment, a berth in the sleeping car was her notion of Paradise. Great-Aunt Minnie's notes were depleted by this expense, but on reflection, Sophia did not regret it in the least. The discomforts of the immigrant car would make her sick before very much longer. Once she got to Kansas City she would cross that bridge, Sophia decided with a calm that Thoreau himself might have envied.

She walked with her carpetbag to the correct platform for the express, the new ticket held as tight in her hand as Agnes held her popish rosary. The conductor did look at her strangely, swathed against the chill of early evening in a quaint old-fashioned shawl and a hat which had never had better days to be seen.

"Did you have any other luggage, Miss …" This conductor was a large, florid-faced man, who spoke with the indefinable accent.

"Teague. Miss Teague. No, none other than this." He was due some kind of explanation, even if only to put natural curiosity to rest. "I was provided with the ticket by a dear relative who knew of my situation. I am extraordinarily tired by traveling in the emigrant coach, which was all there was from Boston to here."

"I am certain you will find this coach more comfortable, Miss Teague," he replied. "If you will allow me." He took the bag from her and showed her into the car – a space of such comfort and quiet luxury that Sophia did not regret the expense in the least. This was so much more like the train journeys which she had undertaken with Phoebe or Great-Aunt Minnie. A black porter in a Pullman uniform straightened from his duties and the conductor said,

"George, this is Miss Teague, a lady of Boston who has paid for her passage tonight and to Kansas City. See to her comfort, there's a good lad, for she is tired from having come so far just this day."

"Of course I will, Mistah Burton, you know I dassn't do otherwise," George protested mildly. Conductor Burton grinned outright. "I know, George; just funning. I warn you that the lady travels in somewhat reduced circumstances – sorry, ma'am – so don't be looking for a big tip."

"Mistah Burton!" George sounded indignant, but more from a matter of a jest than any real anger. "As if I can't tell quality from trash! Here now, Miss Teague; it is an upper berth, but fine an' mostly private, and pardon me for saying so, but Miss Teague, you sure do look like you could use a good night's rest."

"I can – I do," Sophia answered, limp from gratitude at the kindness and consideration. "I … I will have nothing but praise for my remaining days for the kindness shown to me by New York Central, and the Pullman Company. I don't know how I can ever pay it back."

"That's all right, Miss Teague," Conductor Burton allowed. "Sometime, when you get settled, do a kindness to someone else."

Chapter 8 – Away Into the West

Now the train moved more slowly, climbing up into mountains; the Adirondacks which she knew from her schooldays edged the mighty Hudson River along the west. The sun dropped more slowly still, veiled by smoke from the tall and bulging smokestack, and taller trees pressing in first from one side and then the other.

If Heaven were not as comfortable as a soft berth made up with crisp white sheets, Sophia thought as she slid between those sheets, then she would prefer spending eternity in a Pullman berth, rather than the glorious hereafter. She ached with weariness in every limb which did not ache with barely healed bruises. To lie down in comfort was such bliss she wept with gratitude all over again. The noise of the express train clattering over the rails, the sound of the engine was muffled to a considerable degree, and the motion rocked her gently, as in a cradle. Other passengers in the Pullman car had retired, a few still awake, moving in the corridor between heavy curtains drawn for the night, but the small noise of their footsteps, conversation or snoring did not perturb Sophia in the least, or disturb her own slumber, into which she fell into at the moment she rested her head on the pillow. If she wakened during the night, startled by the motion of the train stopping, or starting again, she returned to sleep at once.

"I shall always be grateful for the invention of the steam engine," she told herself, oddly cheerful during one of those brief wakeful moments. *"And to the men who built the railways ... make them run ... all of them. The trains make an escape from Richard possible, and to get as far away from him as I can go."*

Awakening the following morning was nearly as blissful. The avuncular porter, George, tactfully guided her over those few steps towards the tiny ladies' sitting room compartment, where she was able to wash thoroughly as was possible and change into fresh clothes, as he had produced her carpetbag from the baggage car. Rested and refreshed, she was restored to her own real self; the proper and confident Miss Brewer of Beacon Street once again. When she emerged from the sitting room, it was to find the curtains drawn back, the upper berths tidily folded away, the lower transformed back into the comfortable settees which they were for the day of travel. Two ladies and a small boy dressed in a rumpled Knickerbocker suit shared the seats: cheerily introducing themselves as a Mrs. Murray, her son Bertie and her mother, Mrs. Kempton. Obviously they saw her as an agreeable companion for the remainder of the journey. Mrs. Murray was journeying out to Kansas, to join her husband at an Army post there.

"I am Sophie Teague; on my way to Kansas City," She vouchsafed nothing more than that, always recalling Declan's warning to not make herself memorable. To her relief, Mrs. Murray and her mother were most incurious regarding her reasons for traveling, and more inclined to tell her of themselves, and of Colonel Albert Murray's letters regarding what they might find at Fort Leavenworth.

"We will – if the train runs to schedule – be in Chicago tomorrow morning," the elder lady assured her. "Then another long day and night to Kansas. Tell me, dear, will you be traveling on from there?"

"I might," Sophia answered. "It depends."

Conductor Burton beamed on her with particular satisfaction, when he passed through on his rounds in mid-morning, and inquired of there were anything he could do for them. "Better traveling with the other ladies than by your lonesome," he murmured to her, when she thanked him again. "You never know what might happen, and I'd never forgive myself if it happened on my train, or to you, Miss Teague." It occurred to her that anyone observing her with Mrs. Murray and Mrs. Kempton would assume they were of one party.

Late that day Mrs. Kempton remarked on Sophia's fading bruises; Sophia explained it as the results of falling on the stairs.

Another day – this day not weighted with fear and misery – and another night passed, as the train steamed inexorably west, every minute and mile carrying her farther and farther from Boston. She dined with Mrs. Murray and Mrs. Kempton in the railway dining car, as they insisted that she share their table. She felt obliged to repay them by amusing Alfred, six and bored with the limited amusements afforded for long stretches of the journey. He reminded her of Richie; frank, fearless and affectionate. Amusing him was a pleasure rather than a duty.

"The countryside is so lovely!" exclaimed Mrs. Murray, as a long vista of lake and meadow opened before them. "A perfect picture! Mama, doesn't it remind you of those panoramic paintings displayed at the Philadelphia Exposition?"

"Store it up in your memory, dear," Mrs. Kempton advised. "I fear that Kansas will be nothing like this."

"What is Kansas like?" Sophia's ears pricked up. If she were hired by Mr. Harvey she would be going farther west than Kansas. Working in some capacity for a railway concessionaire was looking more and more appealing by the moment.

"Flat and full of dust and flies, to hear dear Albert tell it," Mrs. Kempton replied. "Or that is what he complains of in his letters."

Still, flat and full of dust and flies though it might be, Kansas was a long way from Boston and a vengeful Richard, who surely would never search for her on the wild frontier, even if he suspected that she were still alive. The farther from Boston, the safer she would be.

"My dear Miss Teague, have you ever seen such a city?" Mrs. Murray exclaimed in awe, the following morning, as they passed through Chicago, where their train was supposed to change engine and crew, and add on more passenger cars. The conductor assured them, on his most recent perambulation through the car they would arrive shortly, and there would be a wait of half an hour before proceeding. "And it was burned to the ground not … how many years ago, Mama? And look – how splendid the buildings! Such a marvelous hive of industry and commerce! If Albert's duties kept him here, I would be content, save for the smells of the stockyard!" They coughed as a sudden throat-closing miasma made itself known on the spring breeze. Mrs. Kempton raised a handkerchief to her nose, and continued, somewhat muffled. "Oh, dear; they say millions of western cattle are brought here daily to the slaughterhouses of Chicago."

"Albert wrote of seeing such droves of cattle, being brought north from Texas, so many that the hills are darkened. And the drovers who brought them! They are as wild as their cattle; just boys, most of them, without soldierly discipline."

"They seem such romantic figures," Sophia murmured. Young Seamus Teague's exploration of the Wild West contained many such personages within the pages of his dime novels.

"Those are books!" Mrs. Murray tittered. "And many such accounts of soldiers, too! Those tales are just as exaggerated. The realities of life out West are often romanticized beyond all recognition."

"I expect that I will see for myself, soon," Sophia ventured.

Another night, another day – the country unfolding before them, like the marvelous panorama paintings that Mrs. Murray described. Only this was real, and not than a painted simulacrum; meadows blowing with spring wildflowers, the trees adorned with fresh green. The land appeared flatter than what she had been familiar with for so long as if a giant had pulled the wrinkles out of a counterpane so it lay smooth. On the third day since leaving Boston, the train rumbled across a very long iron bridge. The river lay, smooth as silk and as wide as an ocean.

"That is the Missouri River down there," Mrs. Kempton observed. "We can now say we are in the west. We'll be arriving soon now. Dear Miss Teague; are you being met by friends? You have been such a boon companion; you should not be so alone and adrift, so far away from home."

"I have an appointment," Sophia assured her. "It was for such that I came to Kansas City; an offer of employment."

"Oh?" It seemed to Sophia that Mrs. Murray's attitude towards her had chilled a degree or two. She hastened to reply, feeling a sense of regret. "I was housekeeper and governess to a distant relation; a situation which did not please me. My relatives took liberties, presuming on family loyalty when asking of me what they would not have dared require of a hired employee. I preferred to seek a paid position in a similar capacity. At least, such an exchange is more honest in the exchange of work for pay, then no pay and a tenuous position as an object of charity."

"Quite right, my dear," Mrs. Kempton assured her, unexpectedly. "Being the object of charity is never comfortable for a young woman of spirit. It Everyone thought it most scandalous, when I was a girl, but times have changed. I am assured it is often quite respectable to expect a wage. Women have talents – interests and abilities outside of marriage – that condition which most assume is all we have the capability for. I believe that a woman ought to have more … choices in the world and thereby turn to our most natural role as wife and mother with a most willing heart. Have you read the writings of Mrs. Elizabeth Stanton? She is a most particularly outspoken champion of the natural rights of women."

"Mama!" Mrs. Murray exclaimed, with a touch of exasperated embarrassment.

"I know of Mrs. Stanton," Sophia answered, as if she had come upon a spring of fresh water in a barren land. "She was a particular friend of my great-aunt Minnie Vining – who lectured on the cause of abolition."

"Minnie Vining! Of course, I know her through correspondence; which reminds me; I should write to her soon. It has never ceased to amaze me," Mrs. Kempton swept over her daughter's rebuke with a magnificent display of indifference, which reminded Sophia most piercingly of Great-aunt Minnie, "How the full rights of citizens could be invested upon Negro males of suitable years, and yet be withheld from those females of every color and station, who campaigned tirelessly for those same rights. It is as if the labor of females of every station is regarded as worthy when it is expended in the cause of every other than our own. To the advantage of men, naturally."

"Mama!" Mrs. Murray protested once again, but there was no time for further discussion, for the train was slowing as it approached the station; here the reverse of departing from Boston, in a tangle of shining steel rails which reminded Sophia of strands of hair, arranged by the strokes of a comb. The came the metallic shriek of the engine wheels sliding against the rails as the brakes took hold, steam escaping everywhere.

There was a tall man in Army blue waiting on the platform; small Bertie shouted, "Papa!" as he ran ahead of his mother and grandmother. Just as the elder lady was about to follow, Sophia detained her with a touch on her arm. "If you should happen to write to Miss Vining, pray make mention of me; when next I write to her, I shall tell her you were the most amiable travel companions,"

"Of course, my dear Miss Teague," Mrs. Kempton promised, but her eyes were following her daughter and grandson. In a moment, Sophia stood by herself, with her carpetbag in her hand, watching the joyous reunion with wistful eyes. She turned, hearing a respectful cough at her side, to see George, the porter. "I never get tired of watching folk," he confessed. "Happy, or sad, eager to travel on, grateful to be home: Is there anyone meeting you today, Miss Teague?"

"No," Sophia replied. "But I have an appointment, at the office of Mr. Fred Harvey. Can you direct me to it?"

"Mr. Harvey? I don't know that Mr. Fred Harvey is in town at this moment; he's been feeling poorly of late. Mr. Benjamin most certainly is. The office is in the Annex. I'll have one of the newsboys show you." George shook his head, sadly. "This Union Depot is the largest train station outside of New York, they say, and one of the most confusing. They call it the Insane Asylum … here, did I say something wrong?" he added, for Sophia flinched. "They call it that, for the big pile it is; towers on towers and domes on domes, and ornament stuck on every which way. But it's in the West Bottoms – right handy for freight, but not such a genteel neighborhood, especially not after dark."

"It is enormous," Sophie recovered sufficiently to admire the station itself. "And very modern." What was even more entrancing to her was the sheer purposeful energy of the place, a kind of lightening which never stopped; constant motion, the near to incessant noise of trains, of barrows of luggage shouldered past by large sweating men in rough clothing, while the newsboys shouted their wares. Steam whistles, the rumble of wheels, half-heard conversations, the practiced shouting of conductors calling "All abooooord!" merged into a cacophonous symphony.

"It's the busiest station on this stretch of the river." George explained with considerable pride. "They say that if you sat in the main hall watching long enough, you'd see everyone of renown in this whole United States. Here now, Miss Teague; if you go out this door, and along to the telegraph office, you'll see the sign for the Harvey offices at the bottom of the stairs. Are you interviewing to work in one of Mr. Harvey's places?"

“I am,” Sophia nodded. To her vague surprise, George looked as though he approved. “I hope …”

“Oh, you’ll be taken on, Miss Teague,” he assured her. “I seen a lot of those Harvey girls at work, and even more who come to interview with Mr. Benjamin and Mr. Harvey. You be just the kind they hire; proper ladies, but willing to work. You’ll do fine. It’s a good job; bed and board, passes to travel for free on the railway, and fine folk to work for, if a mite persnickety. But so’s working for Mr. Pullman. You work for them. That’s something to take pride in; you know you are somebody!”

“Thank you, George,” Sophia shifted her carpetbag to her other hand. “For your encouragement and looking out for me on this journey; now I see where the telegraph office is.”

“You take care now, Miss Teague,” A broad and merry grin split his face. “See you out on the railway sometime, you hear?”

Sophia climbed the flight of stairs to the Harvey office, wondering in her heart if this wasn’t something like joining the Army. She had brushed and sponged her best walking dress in the ladies' parlor this morning and George had taken away her shoes for a good polish during the night. There was not much that she could do with Siobhan Teague’s hat, though, but she had brushed out and re-dressed her hair. The Teague shawl was rolled up and strapped to the side of the carpet-bag as though it were a travel-rug. A deep breath, a pause before she knocked on the door; timidly at first, and then because there was no answer from within, a trifle less timidly. The door opened as she were about to knock again; a small foyer, with several half-open doors leading to other rooms. A young man stood inside, his hand on the door, and looking at her, quite startled.

“Can I help you, Miss?” he said, just as Sophia said,

“Is this the office of Mr. Harvey? I am Sophie Teague. I have a letter from him concerning possible employment.”

"It is," the young man replied taking the letter that Sophia took from her reticule, as another voice asked, from farther inside, "Who is it, Ford?"

"A Miss Teague," Ford answered over his shoulder, as an older man appeared, saying, "Show her into Benjamin's office, lad. We'll be with her in a moment. ,"

Sophia obediently followed young Ford into the nearest office. Against her expectations, it was a faultlessly neat place, ledgers arrayed, and folders of correspondence stacked as if lined up with a carpenter's rule. There was a pedestal table in the middle of the room, flanked with four side chairs. The surface of the table gleamed with polish and there was a small crocus-pot filled with fresh flowers. The only disarray was a faint smell of cigar tobacco, the only noticeable noise the distant sound of trains, rumbling across the iron bridge over the Missouri River.

"Miss Teague," The door opened, admitting two men. The older of the two was tall, with a pleasant and narrow face made narrower by a receding hair-line and a beard elegantly trimmed to a point. "So pleased to make your acquaintance; I am Fred Harvey; this is my colleague, Mr. David Benjamin. So you have come all the way from Boston in answer to our advertisement; most extraordinary! Most usually, the girls who come to interview have not made so long a journey. They are most often farmer's daughters, from the locality. Do sit down, Miss Teague, sit down. Indulge my curiosity – why?"

"I have indeed come from a long distance." Sophia looked at him with honest curiosity in return. Mr. Benjamin pulled out a chair for her. Both he and Mr. Harvey sat down also, looking at her in friendly expectation. Mr. Benjamin was younger by about fifteen years, with solid square-jawed features adorned by a flowing mustache. "I am an orphan, sir, twenty-one years of age without any living close kin or income, and the prospect of being a poor relation did not appeal. I wished to travel and see more of the world than I had previously been allowed."

"You are not married?" That was Mr. Benjamin.

Sophia shook her head. "No and not entertaining any intention of being so at this time." Both men stifled smiles, but it was Mr. Benjamin who answered, "You might change your mind eventually. You are an educated woman, I presume – you speak well and pleasingly."

"I was educated in the finest school in Boston," Sophia replied.

Mr. Benjamin carefully held no expression on his countenance. "How do you regard hard work?" he asked. "It will be hard work, and that I can guarantee; nothing which a woman of superior social station would be accustomed to. It will also be among members of the public – also not anything a woman with station would aspire to."

"I am accustomed to work," Sophia replied, nettled. "I was retained as a housekeeper and governess in the household of a distant relative, for several years upon the death of my mother. The work was intricate and responsible, the duties most varied, and many of them on a menial level. The hours were long and compensation for them negligible; in reality, for nothing more than that of being accepted in society as worthy. I have since concluded that I would prefer to be open and transparent regarding such matters. Work is worship," she added, recollecting the words of Agnes. "Work well done is an offering to our Lord. It does not matter the work – only that it is well-done and with all your heart."

"Exactly, Miss Teague!" Mr. Harvey exclaimed. He thumped the table, in enthused agreement. "The worship of perfection as well as the Lord; I like that, Dave! Make a note of it, hey? Now, what you say regarding working in a railroad establishment, catering to … well, whoever comes through the door with the price of a meal in their hand? What then, Miss Teague?"

"I would be agreeable," Sophia replied, earnestly. "I have been so … so well-treated on my journey, which was by railroad, all but the very first mile. I like railways – there is such energy about them. Those people so employed whom I have met along the way have been so able and courteous. I would welcome an opportunity to be a part of a similar enterprise. And it would be so exciting!"

"If you contracted to work with us," Mr. Benjamin ventured, after a look at his associate. "It is a guarantee you would go west to work in a location very far from friends and family; indeed, for you, considerably farther. Many such towns where we have our establishments are primitive places; raw frontier, occasionally dangerous, and with a scarcity of female company save for fellow-employees. Will you have an objection to living in such a place for a year as per a signed contract with the company?"

"None," Sophia answered, firmly. "Far away from Boston and my previous connections suit me extraordinarily well."

"We have high and very strict standards," Mr. Harvey ventured, after exchanging a brief nod and a meaningful look with Mr. Benjamin. "Of service and personal conduct while under contract; one of them for our female staff is that no jewelry or personal adornments be worn while on duty." He looked significantly at her and Sophia realized that he was looking at her earrings, those small things which had been a gift from Great-aunt Minnie. With suddenly unsteady hands, she reached up and removed them from her ears, meeting Mr. Harvey's gaze with a level one of her own.

"When do I start?" she said and Mr. Benjamin barked a short laugh.

Mr. Harvey chuckled and slapped the table. "If possible, yesterday!" he exclaimed. "I like your spirit, Miss Teague! Ford!" he commanded over his shoulder. "Bring in two copies of the company contract. When you've done that, go send a telegram to the Newton house, tell them to expect Miss Teague and Miss Nyland by the next train. You can leave today, Miss Teague, I hope?"

"Yes," Sophia answered, giddy with relief. "I came directly here from the Chicago train. I have not even unpacked my bag."

"Excellent," Mr. Harvey rose from the table. "Dave will explain everything else to you … oh, good." He took a sheaf of papers from Ford, and spread them out on the table, as Mr. Benjamin took an inkwell and a steel-nibbed pen from his desk.

Mr. Harvey filled in the date at the top, signed his name with a flourish on both copies, and passed the pen to Sophia for her own signature. She was just mindful enough to sign herself as Sophia B. Teague. "Welcome to the company, Miss Teague," He shook her hand with a firm, but mercifully brief grip. "Hopefully, we'll be able to renew the contract in a year! Work is worship – remember that – you too, Dave. I shall see you in a few weeks, Miss Teague." And he was away, leaving Mr. Benjamin to go over the details of the contract and of her employment. Sophia could hardly bring her attention to bear: Mr. Benjamin was telling her that her clothing; dresses and aprons would be provided, the pay would be $17 a month, but forfeit the balance if she chose to leave employment before the year was up, and that she would train for a month without pay. To all of this she indicated she understood, and at the last Mr. Benjamin filled out her name and date on the other pieces of paper and handed them to her.

"This is your pass for travel without charge on the Atchison, Topeka and Santa Fe," he said. "And vouchers for meals at our Harvey houses along the way. Do you have any further questions, Miss Teague?"

"Just one," Sophia collected up her papers and her thoughts. "Where exactly is Newton?"

Chapter 9 – The Harvey Way

Her feet were feather-light, as Sophia sped down the stairway to the street, the load from her shoulders similarly light. Exuberant with joy and relief, she wanted to dance along the sidewalk, sing and shout. She was not tired, she was not a desperate and near to penniless fugitive. She had a pass for travel without charge on the next train … to Newton, which Mr. Benjamin had explained – with amusement – was six or seven hours journey farther west. She had just missed the most recent train west and had a few hours wait for the next. Her feet slowed … yes; there was one thing she ought to do, now she was truly in the west. If she was a woman inclined to making careless, symbolic gestures, she might have dropped the gold engagement ring into the Missouri River, but the Brewers – and the Teagues – were not given to indulge in such wastefulness.

Just as George the Pullman porter had said, the Union Depot in Kansas City was at the core of a district like old North Town in Boston; a pity in Sophia's eyes, for it was a magnificent building. It took her no little time or distance from the ornamented red-brick façade and towers to find a pawnbroker and get a hundred and fifty dollars for the gold, diamond, and pearl ring. She might have bargained for better, in accordance with the advice of Mendelson the Jew, but she cared little enough, now she was assured of employment by Harvey contract, and truly in the west … although so far, it did seem to be too much on the respectable side to be considered wild. She walked away from the pawnbroker's establishment, with an odd sense of being unburdened. The last significant physical link to her old life was cut, and she was free. She swung the carpet-bag as if it were a light thing. The railroad pass and the vouchers in her reticule crackled; the stiff paper they were written on a talisman and an assurance.

She found the proper platform for the next train after assuring herself of the correct time. It was early yet, only mid-morning. There was only one other passenger waiting, a Junoesque young woman her own age, in a plain dark traveling dress and jacket. She was a striking figure, with white-blond braids pinned in a coronet around her head, underneath the brim of her hat. She had a small trunk at her feet. Sophia wondered if she were also traveling to Newton – just as the young woman glanced in her direction and said,

"'ello – are you for Newton? The train does not leave for another hour and a half. So Mr. Harvey told me." The young woman had a faint, but pleasing accent; foreign-born, but fluent enough in English. Sophia rapidly made connections, from overheard mention.

"Miss Nyland? Yes, I am bound for Newton to work in Mr. Harvey's establishment; Sophie Teague from Boston. I am an orphan, with no living family."

"Oh!" the woman replied, instant sympathy in her face, and wide blue eyes. "Poor Sophie – how sad for you! I am Laura Nyland, from Minnesota and I have six brothers and five sisters, all older. My old papa; he cried when I said I would answer Mr. Harvey's newspaper thing. But he gave me his blessing. I did not want to work on the farm any longer. You have not worked on a farm, Sophia? A very fine farm, but … oh, the muck! And the milking of cows, the laundry and the cooking … eh! To work in a fine restaurant! I like! And save for a dowry! I want to be married, some day – but to have a dowry. My papa could not afford a dowry for any past my third sister Kristin. My brothers, they find their own way – so why not I?"

"Indeed," Sophia agreed, and settled onto the bench beside Laura Nyland. In the space of time spent waiting for the train and in spite of considerable differences between them, she and Laura became fast friends, not least because Laura possessed a sharp eye, an even sharper wit and a robust confidence in expressing it, which convulsed

Sophia with laughter many times while they waited for the train, and during the hours to Newton. Laura had been presented with a larger selection of sheets of paper, printed in different typefaces, and not a few written out by hand.

"They want everything to be just so," Laura pronounced, as they read them together, the fair head and the sandy-haired one bent together, as the midday train to Newton and points farther west rolled through Kansas. "There is a rule for everything."

"But it is logical," Sophia agreed. "This is nothing more than setting a proper table for a formal dinner party. Haven't you ever done such a thing, Laura?"

"On the farm!" Laura hooted with laughter. "With my brothers and the hired men hungry from a day of work? As if the forks and knives would even rest on the table next to the plate! And what is this … about cups and saucers?"

"A signaling code," Sophia had gone to the next page. "For what the guest has ordered to drink, so it may be provided within seconds."

"It is required to be efficient," Laura nodded. "The train stops for half an hour exactly for water and coal. In that time, they must order their meal, it must be served promptly and they must eat."

"Did they say anything about where we shall live?" Sophia asked, regretting that she had either not pressed Mr. Benjamin for this intelligence, or if he had provided it, she did not recall.

"Above the restaurant," Laura answered. "The ladies live in rooms … two sharing. This is provided as are our meals. But they are very strict with us. We must be home before a curfew at 11:00 every night, and if a gentleman wishes to pay court, he must ask permission of the manager, first. As if we were living with our very watchful papa and mama – but on one day a week, we are free to do what we wish. Is very good, Sophie – much better than the farm. And seventeen dollars a month! My brother Sven is a carpenter in town, and he earns twenty dollars a month, when there is building in the summer. We will earn almost as much as a man with a skilled trade, more than a woman teaching school! Think on that, Sophie!"

"We will have to earn it first," Sophia warned, somberly. "And prove our worth in the first month."

"Pooh! It is only work! I am not afraid of work!" Laura exclaimed; her confidence an infectious tonic. "Kansas now; the western territory – I do not know of this place, Sophie. Do you?"

They looked out of the train window, at the endless waves of grassland stretching as far as the eye could see; a sea of grass, with a faultlessly blue sky arching over it, an endless dome, unmarred by a single cloud. They had long left the Missouri River behind. It was a long way between those small towns with names which suggested high civic hopes; Osage City, Emphoria, Strong City, each a tiny island in the ocean of grasslands.

"In the books of geography in my great-grandfather's house, it used to be called the Great American Desert," Sophia said at last. "There was nothing but herds of buffalo and wild Indians, and it was perilous beyond belief to venture into it, even on the established trail … but now it is becoming settled. The soil is very rich, they say."

"No trees to clear away!" Laura giggled.

For the first time since Lucius Armitage had fumbled with his hat and his calling card in the parlor of the Brewer house, all those weeks ago, Sophia was returned to her usual good spirits. She was in the west, sufficiently far enough away from Boston, on the verge of an adventure, and had a place to go and purpose for her life. If it was not the purpose for which she had been aimed at since babyhood … well, this was the modern age, was it not?

They reached Newton as dusk fell, sweeping down on the prairie like the wings of a vast dark bird. Stars had begun to spangle the night sky, as cold, pale and distant as the lanterns which lit the platform and the station were warm, golden and close. Sophia and Laura stepped from the train.

"Where are we supposed to go?" Sophia asked. "Was there someone we should speak to? I suppose that we can ask for them."

The other passengers alighting at Newton were making in a group for the nearest doorway; a double door with large glass panes in the center of each. The doors allowed hints activity within to spill out onto the platform, and Laura sniffed appreciatively.

"Good food cooking!" she exclaimed. "This must be Mr. Harvey's place."

"I suppose we should go inside," Sophia ventured, but before they could follow the other passengers, a young woman emerged from between the doors – a young woman clad in a black dress with a narrow white collar and a starched white bibbed apron.

"Miss Teague and Miss Brewer?" she asked, with a smile. "Welcome to the Newton Harvey House! I am Miss Maitland, Jenny for short. Mr. Benjamin sent me a telegram this morning, telling me to expect you. You must be tired and hungry, too. Come inside, but this will be the last time you will ever sit when a train stops here." Jenny Maitland added with a twinkle in her eye. "May as well eat first, and have a notion of what to expect, then I will show you upstairs when the rush is over."

Sophia gasped involuntarily, on beholding the dining room; never in the world would she have expected such splendor in such a place as this – out beyond the frontier of the Missouri River; spotless white table linen, silverware that shone as splendidly as if it had just come from the hands of the silversmith, monogrammed china, laid out with superhuman precision on each table. A pair of enormous silver urns presided over the room, set on a table of their own – a table also dressed with a faultlessly white cloth. Jenny showed them to a table in the farthest corner, saying,

"What would you prefer to drink?"

"Milk for me," replied Laura, and Sophia ventured,

"Tea – orange pekoe, if you …"

"Of course," Jenny twinkled at them again, arranging one cup off the saucer, and the other with the handle pointed in a specific direction. "You both look so hungry. Let me bring you that which we have done the best with, today. Take your time in savoring it, for you do not have to get onto the train again in twenty-eight minutes."

She swirled away, her skirts and apron rustling, to be replaced in seconds with another girl in a black dress and starched pinafore apron, bearing a tray laden with carafes. Milk for Laura, orange pekoe tea for Sophia, appeared as if by magic from the carafes.

The girl grinned at them both and whispered, "I'm Emily Adams – you must be the new girls!" She also swirled away, a black-and-white clad sprite in constant motion, before either of them could reply.

"It's … marvelous," Sophia ventured. "It's a dance – like a ballet. Look at them, Laura!"

The lamp-lit dining room presented a picture of constant purposeful motion – a dozen women in nunnish black dresses and white pinafores moving between the tables. Not a minute or two had passed since the passengers had come from the station platform; now the women in black and white danced between the tables bearing plates – of soup, and salads, then bread and savory entrees, emerging from a farther door.

For once, Laura lost her previous easy assurance. "Oh, Sophie … do you suppose we will ever learn this?"

"We'd better do so," Sophia pointed out. "If we want to earn that generous living and you to obtain that dowry. Besides – they all have. Every one of these girls had to learn the system, and so can we."

Such was a daunting prospect but as Sophia told herself and whispered to Laura over their meal; sufficient unto the day were the evils thereof. Meantime, they both were ravenously hungry, the satisfying of which appetite took their immediate attention. Dinner was chops with potatoes au gratin, and fresh green beans with sauce hollandaise. They were the last to be served, which was logical. By the time that Sophia and Laura were halfway into their supper, the train whistle blew – a distant shriek – and instantly they were almost alone in the dining room. Everyone else had put down their dessert forks or spoons and rushed headlong onto the platform.

"I assume that this is the usual meal-time at Harvey?" Sophia ventured, as Jenny Maitland appeared, with a small salver bearing two dishes with a serving of apple pie – a whole quarter of a pie! She set the plates on the table and took a chair opposite.

"Yes, pretty much," Jenny Maitland answered cheerfully. "And many times a day, as the trains arrive. We have word in advance by telegraph of how many passengers are for the restaurant, and how many for the lunchroom. You will begin duty in the lunchroom, tomorrow. Enjoy your pie; Mr. Stahlmeyer is the champion of bakers. He does the bread, you know. All the cars which have restaurant service call for it and his pies and pastries!"

"Is good," Laura observed with her mouth full. "Even better than Mama's!"

"Well, he is a foreigner, too." Jenny Maitland said. Laura replied in small indignation, "I am not a foreigner! I was born here, just the same as you."

"I apologize," Jenny Maitland colored. An awkward moment; Sophia ventured, in an attempt to sooth it over, "We all began as foreigners, if not in our own selves, then in our ancestors. Mine were from England, Laura's from Sweden. It's a matter of degree. Oh, that pie <u>is</u> delicious!" It was; a delicate crust, crumbling into a savory confection of apples, sugar and spices, still delightfully warm from the oven. "I have never tasted anything better," She added with honesty, for Mrs. Garrett's pastry skills were a matter better left unexplored by the fastidious. "You say we will begin in the lunchroom? What will that involve?"

"Rising very early," Jenny replied. It appeared the awkward moment had passed. "Properly dressed, and ready to work."

"How early?" Laura had decided to allow that unintended slight to pass.

"Five of the clock," Jenny answered. Even as Sophia mentally cringed from the thought of that early hour, Laura shrugged and replied, "The time to milk the cows. So – where do we sleep tonight?"

"I'll show you," Jenny said, and eyed their empty plates. "If you are ready?"

"Yes, indeed," Sophia was tired to the point of feeling ill, although the meal had somewhat assuaged that. A good night sleep – then she would see to the next act of her life.

The rooms that would make their home were on the upper story of the Harvey establishment: the stairway to them began in an anteroom off the main restaurant kitchen, where Jenny led them. It was as if they had been led back-stage; beyond the splendid façade at the front of a theatre into the cluttered and workaday rooms and mechanical devices which assisted in making such a magnificent appearance.

As she led them through the vast kitchen and the maze of storerooms which also opened off the anteroom, Jenny paused to call to a middle-aged man working in his shirt-sleeves at a wooden-topped table. "Good night, Mr. Stahlmeyer!" He nodded, in an abstracted manner, wholly absorbed in his work; raising and thumping a great mass of pale bread-dough down with a crash which shook the room amid a rising cloud of flour. His own countenance was coated with a dusting of it, cut through with trickles of perspiration, and his flowing mustaches likewise dusted with flour, like snow on a fringe of bushes. "He's the baker," Jenny explained, somewhat unnecessarily. "That's what he does to beat the air out of the bread dough. It seems odd enough, but there's not a better loaf of bread to be found between Topeka and San Francisco."

She led them up the staircase, dimly lit by a flickering gaslight at the top of the stairs, into a long hallway with regular doors on either side, and decorated in sparse fashion by a thin arrow of plain carpet going down the middle. "My room is here," she said, as they passed the first door. "Because I have worked here the longest, I play mother hen to all of you little chickens. There is the bathroom, and the lavatory … we have running water inside, you see. And hot water at the turn of a tap which is bliss indeed. Because we are over the kitchen our rooms are warm in the winter which is delightful … not so pleasant in the summer, on the very hottest days, though. This will be your room." Jenny opened the door towards the end of the corridor. "There – you are home at last. Emily drew your work dresses and aprons from the wardrobe closet. You might want to try at least one of them on tonight, so you can be certain of the fit. But Emily is very good at this. Now, you both have black shoes and black stockings?"

"Yes, I do," Sophia answered, and Laura nodded. She sank onto the edge of one of the iron beds, exhausted to her bones. Both beds were freshly made with clean sheets and blankets, each with a chair and a nigh-stand. There was a wash-stand and a small mirror in the corner, a single chair, and shelf with a row of hooks on the wall in the other corner; intended to serve as a simple clothes press. There were a dozen shapeless black dresses and as many white bib aprons hanging there, and a pile of detachable white collars and cuffs on the shelf above.

"Very good!" Laura exclaimed, rubbing the corner of a pillowcase between thumb and finger. She sat on the other bed, yawning, while Jenny drew up a chair. "Of course! These are the same linens and bedding used at Mr. Harvey's Montezuma Palace. It saves on sorting out the laundry. All the houses send their laundry here by train weekly to be washed in the central laundry. Your dresses and aprons, too – but we always add more starch, to better the appearance."

"There are more dresses and aprons here than I and my sisters and my mother have between us," Laura exclaimed in disbelief. "How many times a day do we change clothes like a fine lady?"

"Whenever you get a spot on your dress, or cuffs or apron, no matter how small," Jenny replied. "Mr. Harvey insists that we are to be immaculate at all times. It is part of his vision. Our travelers deserve the best, he says. The best food, the best service, the best of china and linen; he believes in a civilizing mission, you see. Bad food, slovenly service and slatterns thumping down tin plates of pig-swill any old way will not do, not for Mr. Harvey. And you are tired. tomorrow you will learn the Harvey way." Jenny rose from the chair. "Good night, girls. Sleep well, but tomorrow morning? You should fix your hair in a plain bun at the back. There are white ribbons in the box with the collars and cuffs. Clean your hands with care: no dirt under your fingernails. I will hold an inspection tomorrow morning before we begin the daily work." She looked at them with a fond but assessing eye. "You both will do well – one has a sense about girls who will work out and those who won't. But tomorrow … we will see. You both might wish to take a bath tonight, for the water is hot, and before the other girls finish their duties downstairs."

Jenny departed in a starchy rustle of black and white, and Laura sighed. "I am so tired, Sophie. But the prospect of a hot bath … we are in luxury!"

"Yes, but we work for that luxury." Sophia answered. She was searching in her bag for her wrapper. Yes, a hot bath would do well.

If there were a heaven, Sophia decided, one of the annexes to it must be the upstairs bathroom of the Harvey House female staff residence. Four generously sized enameled bathtubs with screens between them filled the larger part of the room. A single enormous wicker hamper contained folded white towels; another hamper held the same, crumpled and damp. Sophia recollected what Jenny had said regarding the washing dispatched to the central laundry: this must be a part of it. This was a practical arrangement, dealing with the needs of the Harvey establishment, which – Sophia decided as she sank into a tub filled halfway to the rim with hot water emanating from a wall-tap – had a mania for personal cleanliness unmatched since the ancient Romans, as well as the practical nature and the purse sufficient to indulge it. There were hotels in the east which aspired to provide such consummate luxury to guests; but Sophia had never heard of any which saw so attentively to the needs of the staff. On the other side of the screen, she heard Laura groan.

"Are you ailing?" she called.

Laura answered, "No … *Herregud*, that feels so nice! A bath where I do not have to carry cans of hot water to heat over the stove. And it drains away, afterwards! Sophie, I like this! I would work for nothing to live in a place like this!"

"We sing for our supper," Sophia pointed out. Laura answered, over the splashing of water, "*Ja*, for this I sing like Jenny Lind. After the farm, this is nothing."

"We'll see what kind of tune you sing after tomorrow," Sophia prophesied – yes, one might rightfully be skeptical. Not that she had any doubts regarding Mr. Harvey, or Jenny Maitland – but things would be paid for, one way or another.

Chapter 10 – A Single Nickel

Morning – if not precisely dawn – arrived far too early, in Sophia's groggy estimation. The first harbinger sounded at first like a storm of blows upon the panels of the door to the room in which she and Laura had slept. She swam up out of as deep a state of sleep as she ever had had under the effect of Dr. Cotton's disgusting potions; the storm resolved into a polite tapping and Jenny Maitland's voice.

"Miss Teague, Miss Nyland? Wake up! There's a train due in Newton in half an hour, and we must be ready. We'll have our breakfast in the interval between that and the next, but you must be downstairs and inspection-ready in twenty minutes. Miss Teague!"

"I'm awake," Sophia found her voice. From the other bed, she could hear Laura grumbling; strong oaths, from the level and passion of her voice. "So is Miss Nyland. We'll be ready directly."

There was starlight seeping into their room through the thin muslin curtains over the window they had left open for fresh air. The moon was a small mother-of-pearl circle, just hovering over the buildings opposite. It shed just enough pale light to allow Sophia to light the gas fixture as Laura heaved the bedclothes aside.

"Time to see to the cows," she said, with remarkable cheer.

Sophia giggled. "Not cows, Laura," she replied, searching in her as-yet-unpacked carpet-bag for her cleanest shift. "Hungry travelers on the railway."

"They wish to be fed, and will eat of what is put in front of them," Laura replied. "Men … cows. Little difference I can see."

"Except that men don't expect to be milked, as well." Sophia said and was disconcerted by Laura's knowing chuckle.

"They want their service, just as the bull does," Laura replied, inscrutably. She had found her stockings and rolled them up around her pale shins as she sat on the bed. Sophia did not know what to say to that. She and Laura dressed in relative silence; combing out their long hair before the single mirror and pinning it into plain and serviceable buns.

"We look like nuns," Laura remarked, looking over Sophia's shoulder as they stood in front of the small square of mirror over the wash-stand. Sophia regarded herself and Laura – pale rounded faces reflected in the watery glass; Elsie collar buttoned high and close, plain black dress and narrow sleeves, with the white bibbed apron … it did appear positively nun-like. All they lacked was a coif and a black veil. "That may be the idea," Sophia replied.

She had ruminated over this since Jenny Maitland outlined the code of appearance and dress on the previous night. "You know what ordinary people think of a single woman who must work for a living, away from her family and friends. At least, I know of how they are seen in respectable Boston society; usually of the servant class and sometimes no better than they ought to be. It's very hard, Laura, for a woman alone to have any kind of respectable life, so Mr. Harvey and his strict rules are a defense, a protection, even – against vicious gossip. Like Caesar's wife, we must be above suspicion."

"You are right," Laura made a brief moue of distaste. "Still – how dull for us!"

"We may not flirt with customers, and we must not cultivate particular friendships among our fellow employees within the house, but Miss Maitland said that there was nothing in Mr. Harvey's rules for us forbidding such attachments to gentlemen employed on the railroad. The telegraphists and engineers and such; they are reputed to be daring and clever young men, prepared to move up in the world. I might like to be courted by an intelligent and ambitious young man of no particular family background … if, that is – I wanted to be courted at all."

Sophia set down the comb with which she had been taming the last rebellious curls of her hair, bidding them forcefully to go along into the modest bun at the back of her head. "The main thing for me, Laura; is that I want to work in something associated with the railroad – so new and exciting! You have no idea how boring my life in Boston was. Not a person I knew, save for my great-aunt, ever had a notion or said a word that their farthest ancestors had not already said before. I suppose that I have never felt so alive. As if I were a new woman."

"Me, I am tired of chickens and cows and slaving over a wash-tub," Laura gave one last look at herself in the mirror, an ancient Nordic goddess come to magnificent life. "Now – we go be new woman, *ja*?"

"Modern women," Sophia echoed. They turned off the gaslight as they left their room. Out in the corridor there was a bevy of girls in black dresses and white aprons, chirping excitedly or yawning. Sophia and Laura followed them down the staircase, through the kitchen. This was already a hub-bub of activity, redolent with the odor of baking bread and ham, of bacon and apple pies, muffins and sausages, clamorous with the voices of men shouting at each other in several languages besides English, and clanging iron pans on the tops of stoves – a clamor which diminished at the first appearance of the girls in black and white. The girls went around the edge of the kitchen, into that hallway which led to the larders, the ice-room, the locked liquor store, the manager's office, the telegraphist's office, and the parlor set aside for the waitresses.

This was a comfortable room, set about with chairs, settees and tables of plain and unadorned make, set against the walls. The parlor was brilliantly and mercilessly lit, the gas-lamps turned up to their highest extent so it was as bright as daylight. The girls made a circle as if for a country-dance; Sophia and Laura followed suit. Jenny

Maitland had told them the night before that they would be inspected in a most stringent manner before they went on duty today.

Now the senior waitress went around the inside of the circle; each woman holding out her hands, first palm-up and then down for inspection. Jenny looked severely at their hands, their aprons and their hair, each in turn. Just as she began this, a young man appeared in the doorway of the parlor, a piece of paper in his hand.

"Just come over the telegraph from Florence, Miss Maitland," he said, with the air of someone bearing an important message. "Thirty-five for the lunchroom, twenty-four for the dining room."

"Thank you, Mr. Boatwright," Jenny said over her shoulder, "We'll be ready." The young man vanished like a mechanical Jack-in-the-box. "You have a spot on your cuffs," she said to the girl standing next to Laura. "Run upstairs and change, quickly now." Another girl had a crumpled apron. She also made a swift departure for upstairs, both of them returning, out of breath within a few minutes. Now all of her attention was on Laura and Sophia. It appeared to Sophia that they both received a particularly exacting examination. Jenny made them turn around, lifting the hems of skirt and apron to show they had on black shoes and stockings, and their hair tied with the plain white ribbon. Was this what it might be like to join the Army, she wondered yet again, and found the comparison rather amusing.

"Miss Nyland, Miss Teague? You will start out in the lunchroom – it is sometimes rowdier than the dining room, but the menu and the arrangements are simpler."

"And the boys don't tip like they do in there, either," remarked the girl who had returned at that last minute. She had a gap between her teeth and wildly curly hair, even curlier than Sophia's, but still contained in a disciplined bun tied with a white ribbon. "But it's a start. You follow me, Miss Teague for the first round – watch what I do. I'm Selina Bennett – this's my sister Frances. New girls always start in the lunchroom. Do you know the cup code yet?"

"Not well enough to be quick about it," Sophia replied honestly, and Selina Bennett laughed, frank and honest. She and her sister both wore small round pewter brooches on their pinafores, each with an inset numeral 1.

"You'll learn. It's very tidy and orderly; a systematical method for every motion, a place for everything and everything in its proper place, just so. It's like doing counted stitch needlework," Selena added, as somewhere outside on the station platform, a whistle shrilled over the metallic shriek and clanging of a train coming into the station and applying the steam brakes. To that symphony of noise was added the ringing notes of a gong.

"Here they come, girls," Jenny Maitland swiped an invisible soot-fleck from her white apron. "The first train of the day – to work, now."

At a nod from Selina Bennett, Sophia followed her into the Newton house lunchroom – a room not as grand as the dining room, but still dominated by a set of the same large silver coffee urns which adorned the dining room. Here there were no white-covered separate tables, but one long horse-shoe shaped counter, with chairs ranked along the outside circumference. Each place was set with a cup and saucer, and place setting – as in the dining room, polished so highly they appeared as if they just had been turned out by the silversmith. A double-doorway behind the counter, to one side of the massive coffee urns led into the kitchen, the doors mounted on spring-hinges so they moved open at the slightest push and swung closed.

"Go in by the right," Selena instructed her breathlessly. "And come out of the kitchen the same way. Never by the left, or you might meet someone with a full tray coming the other way."

"I see," Sophia answered. The smell of fresh-brewing coffee hung rich on the air, reminding her of her own hunger.

The outer door to the lunchroom swung open, admitting at this early hour a stream of male travelers; plain working men by the look of them, most of them young. They joked among themselves in the manner of young men, exclaiming over how hungry they were, and how the smell of good food cooking promised a grand feed. Several of the bolder also exclaimed over the pretty waiter girls, but they were shushed by their fellows as they settled along the long counter and looked expectantly at the coffee urns and the flock of girls with their trays and platters moving forward to the counter.

Sophia's heart quailed inwardly under the breast of her black dress and starched apron. This was what being a waitress meant; a servant in an eating-house, at the beck and call of anyone, strangers with crude manners or even no manners at all. What would Mama have thought of this? Gentle, well-bred Mama would have been horrified at the lengths that her daughter had been driven to by the actions of her son. Sophia steeled her resolve and followed after Selina Bennett. She could only hope that Mama would have been equally horrified at Richard's vicious machinations. In any case, this was her life now, no longer the privileged Miss Brewer of Back Bay. Best to put Boston memories well behind, the fond ones as well as the frightful; she was Miss Teague, the aspiring waitress in a Harvey House railroad restaurant, nothing more and yet nothing less.

She hovered at Selina Bennett's elbow; the first customer was hardly more than a boy in the rough dress of a cattle drover, with a calico kerchief around his throat, rather than a proper cravat.

"Scrambled eggs, bacon and toast," he said. His eyes wandered towards Sophia. "And orange juice, Ma'am. I'd purely love some orange juice."

"Of course," Selina Bennett nodded briskly. "Miss Teague – orange juice." She whispered, "In the kitchen, now … they'll be squeezing it at the little table in the corner."

Sophia, given an order, brief and perfunctory as it was, went to the right-hand door, pushed through, and was astounded at the hive of activity in the kitchen which presented itself.

"Gi' out of th' way, ye ninny!" exclaimed the girl who came through the flapping doors at her heels.

"Orange juice," Sophia gasped, "Where do I get orange juice?"

The other girl's pewter badge had a numeral 1 embossed on it. "There!" she jerked her head towards the corner of the kitchen where a single kitchen worker stood before a strange metal contraption which looked at first glance like a water pump – a lever sticking out at the side and a basket heaped with fresh oranges at his side. The man deftly sliced each orange, putting one half and then another into the pump-like workings, and pressed down on the pump-lever. Not water, but pure orange juice came out of the spout, caught in a crystal pitcher underneath.

"A glass of orange juice," Sophia's voice quavered in her own ears, and the kitchen worker glanced from his labors, and poured from the pitcher into one of the range of tall glasses that stood on a tray at the other side.

"Here now," he said, gruffly. "Go with it now, lest it go off from being fresh-squeezed … on a tray, girl!" he seemed to note her unadorned pinafore, and his tone went from brusque impatience to one of almost kindness.

"A tray …" Sophia looked about her. No one had said anything to her about trays.

"There," the kitchen worker indicated a shelf, stacked ready with polished silver-plate salvers. Onto the salver, the glass of juice, and Sophia went out again, remembering at the last minute she should go to the right. Just in the nick of time; another black-and-white clad waitress erupted through the swinging doors from the lunchroom, calling out,

"Scrambled eggs, biscuits and ham, two eggs over easy with sausage and toast, one scrapple, fried egg and biscuit, three bacon, scrambled eggs and toast … what are you doing, just standing there like a ninny? Deliver that and take the order; the train only stops for another twenty-five minutes!"

Gasping, Sophia shot out through the other door, a single glass of orange juice held as if a prize, and on the other side of that door, Selina Bennett commanded impatiently, "What about his order then – scrambled eggs, bacon and toast?"

"I'll see to it," Sophia panted. *Oh, dear, if this is a race, I am dreadfully behind.* She set the glass of orange juice in front of the young drover, and shot off again towards the kitchen, barely hearing his thanks for it, and Selina Bennett hissing a reminder, "On the right of his plate, Miss Teague – above the knife and fork!"

"Scrambled eggs, bacon, toast!" she called, as soon as she came through the door.

"On it," replied a sweating cook, in constant activity before the nearest of the stoves. "That's it– oh, you're one of the new girls."

In the flash of an instant, he had scooped a portion of creamy yellow scrambled eggs from the mess of them coagulating on the griddle in front of his station, and three crisp strips of bacon – which were languishing with a dozen patties of sausage on the section next to them. A standing army of toast-grills stood at an open grill – in the flash of an instant, a plate of scrambled eggs, bacon and toast appeared. Sophia accepted the plate onto the tray which she unaccountably had still in her hands and ferried it out through the right-hand door. She set it before the young drover, relishing a small flash of triumph as he said,

"Thankee, ma'am," and tucked into it with a will and a good appetite that reminded her of Richie tackling his breakfast.

Work was worship. That's what Agnes said, and now Selina Bennett ordered, gimlet-eyed, "Those two next to him want eggs over easy, sausage, toast, and scrambled, scrapple and cornbread. Think left to right, Miss Teague. Order your tray as they say and commit to your memory what they have asked for."

Out through the right-hand doors, singing out the orders as the other girls did, repeating – she hoped – exactly what Selina had said. Magically, two full plates appeared; a pair of fried eggs, sausage patty and toast on one, a creamy mound of scrambled with a square of scrapple and yellow cornbread on the other. Her stomach grumbled with hunger, tormented by the odor of fresh coffee and frying bacon.

'I can do this,' Sophie told herself with a mild air of triumph, soon dashed when she set down the first plate, and the customer looked at it in distaste, saying,

"What in tarnation is that muck!"

"Left to right!" Selina whispered. Sophia fumbled an apology, certain she was all thumbs and clumsy ones at that.

"I'm so sorry – that's scrapple, it's for someone else …" She moved the plate to the second place along the counter, and set the plate of fried eggs, sausage and toast in front of the first one, just as Selina completed her humiliation by hissing,

"You've a spot of egg on your cuff! Run upstairs and change it before Jenny sees."

"Of course," Sophia replied, now so dispirited and rattled as she went towards the door, only hearing Selina's cry of, "On the right!" when it was too late. The swinging door collided with a tray in the hands of Frances Bennett, sending plates, tray and breakfasts onto the floor, encountering Frances' hitherto spotless apron in descending.

"I'm so terribly sorry!" Sophia gasped, horrified by the wreckage of food and broken crockery at their feet.

"Watch where you are going, you stupid thing!" Frances raged, and that was the farthest limit; Sophia burst into tears. She ran thorough the busy kitchen, dodging other waitresses and kitchen workers as she ran upstairs to hers and Laura's room. This humiliation was complete: she could have no particular future with Harvey after this disastrous debut in the lunchroom, and crying like a punished child in front of everyone. *Why had she even thought she could do this?*

In the refuge of the room, she sat on the edge of Laura's bed and contemplated the row of black dresses and white pinafores hanging from their pegs. No, she couldn't do this. The best thing would be to pack up the battered carpetbag, and use her dwindling funds to go … well, anywhere, and find work as Agnes had advised. Before she could do anything other than consider this, someone tapped at the door; Jenny Maitland.

"Sophie? Sophie, are you there? Put on your clean cuffs; we have a full House of customers and you are needed downstairs."

"I don't know if I can do this," Sophia gasped, between sobs. "I'm not cut out to be a waitress, I'm sorry."

"Of course you can," Jenny replied, in a chiding tone. "May I come in, then?" Without waiting for a reply, Jenny opened the door. Sophia was too overwrought to protest. Jenny sat next to her and brought a clean handkerchief out from beneath the bib of her perfectly starched white apron. "It's your first time – you were rattled. It happens. Don't be a silly goose and give up before you have given it a try."

"Frances is angry with me," Sophia wept into the handkerchief, "And Selina corrects everything I do, as if I cannot get anything right!"

"Of course you can't get everything right," Jenny replied, calm and remorselessly patient. "You only started doing something you had never in your life before, seven minutes ago. Did I have a girl come to work in the House on her first day and do everything perfectly from the moment of her first shift, I'd suspect that Mr. Harvey had sent a spy among us, to ensure that we work ever more efficiently and perfectly. He will do that someday, I am certain," Jenny added as a knowing aside. "He and Mr. Benjamin go on random expeditions, on the pretense of being ordinary travelers …"

"The plates were broken, and there was a horrible mess on the floor," Sophia refused to be consoled. "Right in front of the lunchroom customers! It was a humiliation, not to be borne. I shall go away and find work elsewhere …"

"Run away?" Now Jenny sounded impatient. "Like a silly little school-girl, scolded by the teacher? Listen, Sophie. Don't be a goose. This happens all the time. Do you know what happened to me, the first time I set a table in the dining room? I took such care with it! And Mr. Harvey, on one of his inspection tours – came into the dining room with the passengers from the afternoon train. He took one look at it, and whipped out the tablecloth from underneath. Glass, china, silverware – all went crashing to the ground. Humiliation? You've no notion. And I had been working in a House for months and my family are friends with his wife. Listen, Sophie – you are a clever girl, you see what needs to be done and why, which many new girls do not grasp.. Dry your tears and change your cuffs; go downstairs and do it, this instant. Listen to Selina, she knows the Harvey method. And," Jenny added, with an air of cheery cynicism, "Going through the wrong side on your first-ever day? I wish I had a nickel tip for every time that has happened. If you were at the end of your probationary month, then I'd judge you were not suited to be a Harvey girl and say so to Mr. Benjamin. But on the first day?"

Sophia sniffled and wiped her eyes with Jenny's handkerchief, wondering if she had been as much of a hysterical fool as Fee ever was. Now Jenny smiled – with a sense of relief that Sophia did not realize until many months later. "Change your cuffs, Sophie. Do not worry over Frances or the dishes. And if you can take any comfort from this as a lesson learned the hard way – you will never, ever go through the wrong side, for the rest of however long you will work for Mr. Harvey."

"That is likely true," Sophia hiccupped, seeing the truth and humor in it. "I'll be down directly, Miss Maitland."

"We have fifteen minutes until the train leaves," Jenny briskly consulted the tiny gold ladies' watch she pulled from a pocket under her apron. "And then we will have our breakfast."

All the men in the lunchroom had been served by the time Sophia emerged from the kitchen again, so there was little for her to do save to carry the heavy tray of pitchers and carafes along the counter, refreshing drinks. There was little of the sense of urgency which had so rattled her in taking orders at first. The young drover who had asked for orange juice shyly requested another, just as the train whistle blew a single blast outside.

"Five minutes," Selina Bennett enlightened Sophia. "Until their train departs." To Sophia's relief there was no hint of rancor in her voice or expression. Almost to a man, those in the lunchroom bolted the last few mouthfuls of sausage, or scrambled egg, cramming in the last bite of toast, and a final swig of coffee before heading towards the cashier desk out in the hallway, leaving behind a litter of dirty plates and empty cups.

"Jus' like after breakfast at the farm," Laura grumbled, as she and Sophia worked from one end of the counter, gathering plates and scattered silverware. She looked keenly "You are all right, Sophie?"

"I am, now." Sophia answered. "It seems that perfection is not immediately expected at once from us, not on our first day."

"Lucky, that." Laura's grumble turned to amusement. "Look, Sophie, this must be for you. This is where your first customer was sitting." She took up the plate and the tall glass which still held a puddle of orange juice in the bottom. A little to the side of where the plate had been was a small silver coin – a single nickel. "Your first tip … and a generous one, considering."

"I will keep it for good luck," Sophia replied, touched and at the same time a little shocked. How low this would have seemed in Boston, in that life which she was now categorizing as her old one – and yet how completely acceptable in the here and now. *Close the door and walk away, never looking back.*

"Is good omen, yes?" Laura said. "And now we have breakfast! Better than home, for we do not have to cook it ourselves!"

Chapter 11 – Chance Met in Newton

Their probationary time passed as if in a dream for Sophia, the hours of the day marked by the whistles of arriving trains, and mindfulness taken up with memorizing the minutiae of the Harvey system, of threading her way between lunchroom and kitchen, bearing trays throughout the daylight hours and into the evening. On one particular morning, she looked up from pouring a cup of coffee at the lunchroom counter to meet the eyes of Mr. Harvey, thinly disguised in a lamentable overcoat and a hat which was the masculine equal of Siobhan Teague's forlorn and unfashionable bonnet.

"Good morning, Mr. Harvey," she retained enough self-possession to say, as if every morning she brought coffee to the head of the company. "What may I bring to you? Mr. Stahlmeyer's bread and pastries always delight and he has baked a prodigious number of them this morning."

"I know," Mr. Harvey grinned, for a moment wholly and uninhibitedly boyish. "I know everything about my enterprise and of what I have forgotten, Dave and Ford remind me. So you are content in our house, Miss Teague?"

"I am, sir." Sophia replied, truthfully. As she accustomed herself to the work, and the system behind it, her movements became swift, assured; now she skimmed through the lunchroom with the dance-like grace which she had envied in the other girls on the night of hers and Laura's arrival. The cup codes, the way of setting a place, and taking an order swiftly and accurately became as much a second nature as breathing in a short time. Jenny Maitland was correct: she could do this.

"Good," Mr. Harvey appeared pleased. "Dave and I were certain you were a girl who would work out – consider yourself a part of the company for the term of your contract; Miss Maitland has given a good report of you Do you prefer to remain in Newton for now, or would you be willing to accept an assignment elsewhere as needed? Next year, if you renew your contract, you may request an assignment in any of our Houses along the AT&SA."

"Newton for now, sir," Sophia replied. "I have so many friends here already; I should dislike to be parted from them. There is still much for me to learn – and I would prefer to consider where I might go next at leisure. As far from Boston as possible, I am certain."

"New Mexico is a coming place," Mr. Harvey agreed. "And the weather in California is mild in comparison to Kansas. Take your time, Miss Teague. I understand that you are an orphan – consider the company to be your family at large."

"I will, sir," Sophia was as light with relief as a balloon on a windy day – as light as she had on the day In Kansas City when Mr. Harvey said that she was hired. She was safe here from Richard, having friends, allies, gainful and respectable employment. She slept well on most nights, being exhausted after a day of work. As a precaution, though, she kept the hair brooch and the money she got for Lucius' engagement ring sewed into a tiny pouch sewed the inside of her corset. Her fear of Richard, and Dr. Cotton and their allies springing on her, and packing her off back east to Danvers never entirely faded from her mind, even as the last of her bruises healed.

But the sheer excitement of being at the crossroads of the west never palled; one spring day, three trains bearing the company and horses of Buffalo Bill Cody's Wild West extravaganza, passed through on their way east. On another day it was a great party of Army officers, hung with gold braid. The girls working in the dining room insisted that General Phil Sheridan, the highest-ranking general in the whole Army of the West, was among them.

Sophia's later memories of that summer in Newton – her first year as a Harvey Girl were a rapid-fire series of stereograph images;

of ferrying trays from kitchen to lunchroom, the faces of travelers there, mostly young but not always, the screech of brakes on metal wheels and the shrilling of a steam whistle. The sun burned golden in a hot blue sky, and where the streets of Newton raveled out into the countryside, fields of wheat, corn, and hay rippled in the summer breezes, the waves of a leafy ocean, while the scent of dust and new-cut hay hung in the air. At night, after a soak in one of the bathroom tubs, she fell into the dreamless sleep of exhaustion. Three or four times Laura woke her, claiming that she was talking in her sleep, but Sophia never remembered what she had dreamed of, only that she was left with the memory of imprisonment in the strong-room, and of a hideous weight pressing on her so she could not breathe. But weeks passed between these occurrences; by the turn of summer, she had gone for weeks without Laura wakening her from a bad dream. But she always kept the brooch and money secreted in her corset and a change of clothing folded in the old carpetbag, along with the Irish-woven plaid shawl,

In mid-summer, she discovered by chance that the station newsstand often had issues of the *Boston Daily Advertiser.* She bought a copy now and again, to read on her one day off, feeling sometimes as if she were reading of a place incomprehensibly far away, but now and again jolted by mention of a familiar name. Lucius Armitage and Emma Chase married at the end of summer, in rites which were so elaborate they merited several columns of breathless description. The writer added, in disapproving tones, a list of the costs; flowers, dresses for the bridal party and such. Sophia shook her head at that. She might just as well been reading about the marriage of European nobility, in a place far, far away, for all it had to do with her own life in the here and now. That old life; childhood and school-days, the term of servitude in Richard's house – that was a small memory-boat, adrift in the Charles and floating farther and farther downstream, until only a pale speck in the distance. But she might as well keep on reading the Boston newspaper, for news of Great-aunt Minnie and the Teagues, if nothing else.

To her mild amusement, she was courted by Billy Boatwright, the young telegraphist who took the precaution of asking for permission of the House manager if he could walk out with Miss Teague.

"Be sweet to him," Jenny Maitland advised. "He is a nice lad, he has lovely manners, the sole support of a widowed mother, but he will never go so far as to give your mother or his, the least worry regarding his intentions. Walking out with him is as perilous as walking out with a very obedient lapdog. He will talk about telegraphy to the point of tedium, so be warned."

"How unexciting," Sophia remarked. Jenny raised her eyebrow. "I was courted in Boston by a man like that. His father might just as well have kept him in leading-strings all of his life."

Jenny's prediction proved correct: walking out with Billy Boatwright was like going for a turn around the park with an obedient lapdog, but Sophia did not mind. Laura was walking out with another telegraphist and the four of them together made a nice party for picnics and the occasional buggy-ride out into the country, especially as the two men fell deep into conversation regarding doings on the telegraph line of which they had knowledge, and left Laura and Sophia to giggle over gossip of the House and of the peculiar things they saw in the lunchroom.

Sophia opened a bank account with the last of Great-aunt Minnie's notes and faithfully deposited her monthly wages and the sometimes astoundingly generous tips. It was well into the autumn before she felt secure enough to spend on herself, ordering a new winter coat of heavy wool, a good dress for Sundays and three heavy flannel petticoats from the tattered Ward Company wish-book which sat on the sparsely furnished bookshelf in the parlor. Everyone told her that Kansas winters were bitter cold; the few clothes she brought with her would not be enough for a prairie winter. Laura told her of deep winter snows in Minnesota, and Jenny Maitland described how the furious winter storms might cut off the sight of the storefronts opposite the station, and snow drifting so deep over the rails that the trains might stop running.

Laura also opened a bank account, for what she called her dowry fund – but splurged more of her tips more on fashionable clothes. She took great pleasure in wearing them, which amused Sophia considerably.

"What are you going to do with your savings, then?" Laura asked her, the evening after the two of them had scampered across the street to the bank to make their weekly deposit of collected tips. They were sitting at that table in the kitchen where the kitchen workers and waitresses took their meals, industriously polishing high-piled trays loaded with silverware.

"I haven't considered it," Sophia answered. "Save I want an independent life, an income of my own."

"You could homestead," Laura suggested. "They allow single women to homestead, and since your father was a Union veteran." Sophia turned that notion over in her mind; a claim on a quarter-section of good land … a tempting consideration. "I don't know if I could settle happily away out in the country. But a claim near a small town where I could have a house of my own, and a garden … Likely, I will just save until I can buy land and build a house outright."

Laura nodded, in agreement. "Land is good … and it is the only thing there is being made no more of."

One cold and blustery day which presaged that coming winter, the last scheduled train of the day came and went, bringing the usual rush of hungry passengers into the dining room and the lunchroom, and bearing them away again a brisk half-hour later. There remained only a special train, sitting on a side spur away past the end of the platform; engine, coal car and a single ornate palace car, with light seeping from behind closed curtains. The sides of the car were hung with dark fabric; she had not paid it much attention although every aspect of her world was now ruled by the railway and Fred Harvey between them. She had been promoted from the lunchroom into the dining-room proper and run off her feet with the rush to serve the regular passenger train travelers. One of the busboys brought supper to the engineer and the firemen and returned with the intelligence that the palace car belonged to a wealthy rancher. On a journey to Colorado, the rancher, a man of some years, fell ill and died. They were bringing him back to Texas to be buried in his home acres, the busboy reported. The palace car had a kitchen and staff, so the passengers on it had no need of coming to the Harvey House.

Sophia wondered why the special still waited as dusk swept over the prairie; a vast dark wing, bringing with it a chill breeze that threatened frost before sunrise. Outside the stars in the eastern half of the sky began twinkling faintly, but mellow golden lamplight bathed the dining room, reflecting off the spotless white tablecloths, the twinkle of silverware, and the great silver coffee urns. She polished away a nearly invisible splatter from the surface underneath the spout and regarded her station with anxious pride. It was ordinary work; those whom she once had associated with in Boston considered it demeaning, a step above from being a common housemaid. But out here – this was good and useful work, in which one could take pride. Ever at the back of her mind was Agnes's girlish voice, saying in all earnestness that well-done work was worship.

She was almost at the end of her shift; twelve hours on her feet, in more or less constant motion; everything about her person, actions, words and demeanor a living demonstration and testament to the Harvey ideal. She stifled a yawn behind her hand. The dining room was empty; a handful of diners with time and leisure to enjoy their meal. Footsteps resounded along the station platform, and a pair of men came through the nearest door; the younger as tall as a tree, and very fair. He looked to be in his late thirties, with pleasant features marred by a long scar across one cheek to the corner of his eye. The other man appeared fifteen years older; wiry, fit, and weathered by a lifetime in the out-of-doors. They both were in dark suits, with a band of black crepe on their coat sleeves; Sophia assumed they were from the special train. No need to lend them a coat to sit in the restaurant. She put away her polishing cloth and showed them to the end of a table, noting as she did so they were speaking German to each other.

"Would you prefer coffee, milk, iced or hot tea?" she asked courteously in that language and the younger gentleman's eyebrows rose. If the older gentleman was surprised, he concealed it well.

"*Milch, bitte*," he replied and the younger man nodded. Sophia arranged the cups, upside down and apart from the saucer; she could see Laura with the tray of jugs and carafes coming across the dining room. Laura poured out the milk; fresh, sweet and cold from the cool-room where it had been stored until just a few minutes before.

The young man's eyebrows rose again. "How did she know?" he asked. "You never said a word!"

The older gentleman laughed. "It's magic," he said, cheerfully. "Don't ask the magician – these Harvey *Mädchen* – how it is done, Peter."

Sophia recited the dinner menu for the day. The gentlemen both decided on fresh trout from Lake Michigan, with duchesse potatoes, and fresh green peas, with cheese, water-crackers and fresh fruit for afters. Before Sophia even took their order to the kitchen, Letty appeared with the salad course; fresh oranges, sliced into rounds, dressed with fresh onions and olives and set them in front of the two gentlemen.

The older gentleman took out his napkin, saying, "The first time I crossed from Texas to California, I'd have thought myself in heaven to have sat at a meal such as this."

"Times change, Onkel Fredi," the younger said. "Now and again for the better. Not even Absalom could have contrived fresh lake trout in the middle of Kansas."

"And Hansi's palace car beats sleeping under the wagon, not so?" Sophia heard Uncle Fredi answer. Her apron rustled with the stiffness of many layers of starch applied. How pleasant to continue speaking German to Uncle Fredi and his tall nephew, Peter. She had learned the language because Great-Aunt Minnie claimed that so many interesting things were written only in German; poetry and belles-lettres and matters of scientific interest. She had practiced assiduously in her schooldays with those native speakers of that tongue, but any conversation with diners save of the most brief was frowned upon – yea, discouraged.

When their main course emerged, piping-hot and savory, Sophia ferried them back to her station. She had removed the empty soup plates and set out the entrée course with the care that Mr. Harvey had always insisted upon. It gratified her that Uncle Fredi and Peter both looked at their supper with delighted good appetite, but Peter stayed her as she would have rustled away.

"May we ask for a serving of this for my wife, taken to our coach? More of that fine soup and that good bread as well? My mother-in-law may be coaxed by the doctor to take in some nourishment. You see, we are in something of an emergency. Miss…"

"Teague," Sophia answered, not noticing that he had switched over to English. "Miss Teague. I am certain this will be allowed – it is Mr. Fred Harvey's dictate that every reasonable indulgence be taken for the satisfaction of our guests, but I must first ask permission of our manager."

"Thank you," Peter looked at his exquisitely arranged plate; fine bone china, silverware polished until it gleamed like glass. "You encounter us at an unfortunate moment in our lives, Miss Teague. My father-in-law, Hansi Richter, who has always guided our enterprises, was suddenly gathered to his ancestors, when we were in Colorado examining the possibilities of expanding our holdings there. We are returning to Texas without any warning to our regular staff and my mother-in-law is prostrated with grief. Here we await a visit from a doctor to attend on her, but in the meantime …"

"I couldn't endure the megrims any longer, myself," Uncle Fredi remarked in somewhat acerbic tones. "Up on the highest tower, or having fits of weeping in the cellar; that's always been my sister."

"They were married forty years, Onkel," Peter sounded reproving. "You should be more understanding."

"Understanding? Bosh, Peter lad; I've been understanding all the way from Raton. I'm not the doctor in the family – it's never been my nature to oblige female hysterics."

"It will be our honor and pleasure," Sophia assured them, her spirits rising at this challenge. This was out of the ordinary and an opportunity to sooth a fraught situation. It had been her personal experience that the aftermath of a death, even an expected one, brought out familial tensions. "My sincere condolences regarding your untimely loss."

"Thank you, Miss Teague." Peter looked genuinely grieved. "Put the extras on our bill." Suddenly, his gaze sharpened. "Pardon me for asking, but you do not speak as if you are from around here."

"I am from Boston," Sophia replied, the customary refrain. "I am an orphan, without any brothers or sisters."

"Boston?" He replied with brightening interest. "My father was from Boston! He came out to Texas for his health in the earlies. Taught school and fought at San Jacinto. He had the biggest library there was in Austin, back then. Horace Vining; might you have heard of him?"

"No," Sophia answered, her heart jumping in her chest at the sound of the name. "My grandfather was named Horace Vining, but it was a common name among my older male relations; I know of at least five or six of them."

"Among ours, too," Peter Vining agreed, with a grin. "My brother and his son were named Horace, too, although I was given to know that my father disdained the formal and preferred to be called Race. We might be distant cousins, or something such," Peter Vining turned his attention to his plate. Sophia took that as a hint and rustled away to find Jenny Maitland and let her know about a supper tray for the ladies.

"Bring them a loaf of Mr. Stahlmeyer's good bread, and some fresh fruit to go with it," Jenny Maitland approved enthusiastically, as Sophia had known she would. "You are off duty as soon as you carry it out to the special," she added, in a tone approaching deepest envy. "Sophie dear, take note of what their car looks like on the inside, for we shall be eaten up with curiosity. They call them palace cars, you know. I've seen pictures in the rotogravure, but I've never been inside one, in all this time of working for Mr. Harvey."

This would be something out of the ordinary, so Sophia took care in assembling it in the kitchen. A small boule of fresh-baked bread, still warm from the oven, and Mr. Stahlmeyer paused from his labors at beating the air out of tomorrow morning's batch of dough to ask what she wanted with the tray of cooling pastries, from which she was selecting four of the choicest.

"It's for a client on the special train," she said, and cunningly added. "They speak German, Mr. Stahlmeyer. They say that their regular servants have been caught unawares by the suddenness of the journey on the death of the head of the family."

"Ja?" His own interest brightened. "For them indeed, some of my pastries! I listened to the boys talk – this is the special train of Richter the cattle baron, is it not?"

"I think so," Sophia agreed.

Mr. Stahlmeyer sighed, disturbing the flour settled upon his generous mustache. "Of him, I have heard much, little Miss Teague. A poor farmer's son; came with his family from Bavaria through the auspices of the Society to Texas as a young man and finished up with more lands and riches than most of the noblemen who invested in the *Verein* to begin with."

"Irony indeed," Sophia agreed, wondering – *The Verein?* No, this was another thing about the west she had never heard of. Her education in the world had not begun until she took her fate in her own hands and went west. She went into the cool-room to see what was best and most succulent of the fresh fruit left to the House before the next refrigerated shipment arrived in the midnight hours and settled on a small bunch of California grapes and some oranges. When she emerged from the cool-room, Mr. Stahlmeyer had assembled a small pasteboard box of his most delicious pastries, and the last of the cooks on duty sought out the smallest covered cook pot, ladled it full of the daily soup, and assembled another plate of trout, duchesse potatoes and fresh green peas. All fit onto the largest covered salver in the kitchen and made a burden not much more than the usual. When she emerged from the kitchen bearing it, Peter Vining had gone to settle the bill with the cashier and return to the train. Onkel Fredi waited by the door, with his hat in hand and warm scarf around his neck.

"I am bidden to take you out to the train," he said, as jaunty as if he were a man half his age. "You are sure you don't want me to carry that? It looks heavy, and it's a good walk to our train."

"It is no heavier than what I am accustomed to carry," Sophia replied. He opened the doors for her, which was appreciated, although she looked at the long trudge along the platform to the side-spur where the parlor-car waited and stifled a sigh. She wished then she had allowed him to carry the tray, and that she had on some kind of outer garment herself, for the chill in the evening air bit through the thin cotton of her pinafore and dress.

Two men waited, in the dim light of lanterns hung on the rear platform of the parlor car – a kind of balcony, set with a pair of comfortable wicker chairs. Peter lounged in one of them, his pipe already alight.

"I've told my wife about the bountiful supper," he called to them, getting to his feet. "And Absalom has come to take it in charge, as is his right and duty." Absalom came halfway down the iron steps, holding out his hands for the tray – a tall, middle-aged Negro porter, in a smart uniform adorned with a double row of brass buttons as highly polished as anything in the Harvey House.

"If you will allow me, miss, I will take that now," he said. Sophia yielded it up with gratitude. There was no way she could clamber up the steep iron steps from ground to train with her hands full, even after a summer of managing full trays

"There is a plate set with a full supper on it," she gasped, as Onkel Fredi's strong grip from below on her elbows boosted her up the steps. "And a loaf of bread and a box of pastries, fresh from the ovens; Mr. Vining asked for our soup as well, so I have brought a pot of that."

"It is the custom hereabouts to bring food to the house where folk be in mourning," Absalom replied, with immense dignity. "We are grateful to Mr. Fred Harvey an' all."

"The doctor has been and gone," Peter Vining spoke across the balcony to his uncle. "Mrs. Liesel is inconsolable. He has administered a dose of opium spirits so she may sleep and the remainder of us get some rest tonight. Ma'am Becker is with her now."

"Miss Teague, is there something the matter?" Onkel Fredi spoke unexpectedly. Doubtless he had sensed her start and shudder at the mention of syrup of opium.

"No, nothing," she replied, intending to reassure him, for he did sound concerned. Perhaps he was not as unsympathetic to female megrims as he had sounded. "Should I wait here to take back the plate when Mrs. Vining is finished?"

"Of course not," Onkel Fredi answered. "Peter and I will have a quiet evening smoke out here. Go inside and keep Anna company where it's nice and warm."

"My wife was terribly interested to hear of Mr. Harvey's girl waitresses," Peter added. "She has always had a head for business herself."

"Go on," Onkel Fredi urged her to follow Absalom, who had vanished with the laden tray though the door which led into the palace car's interior. "Likely she'd relish any distraction in suppertime conversation, after the last three days we have had." He held the door open for her – a plain and undeniable suggestion, which Sophia obeyed with alacrity. After the warmth inside the dining room and kitchen, it was bone-chillingly cold outside, and she was shivering.

She entered such a splendidly appointed and decorated apartment she could hardly believe that it was a train carriage, save that the room was much longer than wide and with curtained windows along the long sides – a room decorated as a parlor with fine and comfortably upholstered chairs and small tables set here and there. The room was well-lit, with hanging lanterns in the higher ceiling which ran along the center portion of the room. Light gleamed on expensively finished wood – paneling and tabletops alike. A fine woolen carpet with a design of interlocking initials covered the floor and deadened the sound of her footsteps as the door to the platform outside closed behind her.

Absalom, resplendent in his brass-buttoned livery was just now setting out the supper plate on one of the tables, with a degree of solicitous care and precision which would have given him credit in a Harvey House. There was a setting of silverware on the table, a green bottle with an elegant label, and a pair of tall cut-crystal wineglasses. An elegantly clad woman sat in the chair before it, eyeing the dish with sincere appreciation. She looked up as Sophia moved cautiously into the parlor-car.

"Come in, come in – Miss Teague is it? I am Anna Vining and I am grateful beyond words for this. It has been a most difficult day. My husband wonders if you might be a distant cousin of his – amazing, but not so, on consideration. I have cousins everywhere. Do sit down. I cannot eat, looking up at you. Have a glass of wine with me." With a note of command in her voice, Anna Vining filled the second glass and gestured towards the comfortable armchair across the table. Sophia obeyed authority, both tired and insatiably curious. Anna Vining was tinier than her presence suggested, with dark hair in which a thread or two of gray barely showed. The lines and shadows around her coffee-dark eyes suggested exhaustion rather than any age, for her complexion was as smooth and pale as cream. "Excuse me," she added, wolfing down the first few forkfuls of trout, "but I am ravenous! This is most excellent. You have eaten, I trust, yes? Such a day as this has been, you have no idea. My poor mama is prostrated with grief."

"I understand that she and your father were married for a long time," Sophia ventured. It seemed safe enough. Anna Vining nodded, her mouth full.

When she had swallowed, she said, "It happened so suddenly, I still do not comprehend. He had a simple chill, from the mountain air, everyone said. Then pneumonia the next day, and the day after that, they say there is no hope for change in his condition … and then…" Anna Vining blinked back tears and defiantly sipped from her wineglass. "Are your parents yet living, Miss Teague? If so, you are blessed."

"No, I am an orphan," Sophia replied, over the tightness in her throat. "My father was killed before Peterborough with the 28th Massachusetts. I never knew him."

"That is so sad for you," Anna replied. "And a rebuke – I was fortunate to know my Papa well. I worked in his store, from before I was the age you are. And then I was his secretary when the family did business. It is good for a family to work together."

"I had a brother," Sophia was emboldened by the wine, for it was rich and sweet – the best she had tasted in a long time. "And he made me work as his housekeeper, because his wife was a fool. It was <u>not</u> good. So I came west."

"So now you work for Mr. Harvey? I had read of this … is it better than family business?"

"Much better than my brother's house." Sophia replied.

"Tell me," Anna Vining asked, and to Sophia she sounded genuinely curious – not disapproving. For twenty minutes, she related a carefully edited version, of answering a newspaper advertisement, how she came to Kansas City and then to Newton. She even made Anna Vining laugh, relating accounts of incidents in the dining room, or in the kitchen, and repeating some of Laura's pointed observations. When Anna set down her fork, both hers and Sophia's wine-glasses were drained. Before Sophia could even recall herself to the present, Absalom appeared like a cat-footed ghost and whisked plate and silverware aside.

"I have your tray and pot ready to return, Miss Teague," he said, clearing his throat. "As soon as I wash up this last plate."

"I'll take a turn with Mama so that Auntie Magda can eat something." Anna sighed and rose from the table. "You have been looking around at Papa's palace car, little Sophia – would you like to see a little of the rest, while Absalom washes up?"

"I would love to," Sophia exclaimed. "Miss Maitland said that I should tell them what it looked like on the inside. We have seen many palace cars, here in Newton – but always from the outside."

Chapter 12– East and West

"It was marvelous!" Sophia exclaimed to the waiting Jenny Maitland, on her return to the sleeping Harvey House, with the salver, pot and plate which had borne the special meal. Yawning, Sophia carried them through into the kitchen. "Mrs. Vining showed me a stateroom and the offices! There was a dining room, too – but that was where Mr. Richter's coffin was in state. There is a tiny kitchen, and a little cabin for the staff, and everything so cunningly contrived! So luxurious – the best beds, the most comfortable chairs, the finest wood paneling you can imagine on a train car. She was kind, and wanted to hear ever so much more, about the Harvey House, and how they are managed. I have not been indiscreet; everything about us is public knowledge, and she asked intelligent questions! I would have not expected the daughter of a rich cattle baron to be so down-to-earth. But she told me that when she first married, she and her husband would go up the trail between Texas and Kansas with cattle herds and she the only woman among them!"

"You were there for such a long time," Jenny said, laughing. "I might have worried – but then I knew you would have to bring back the china before their train departed Newton."

"They so appreciated the meal so much," Sophia assured her. "Mrs. Vining promised to send a letter of thanks to Mr. Harvey. Mr. Steinmetz said it was so late at night he must accompany me to the door. He was pleasant and considerate. It has been such a long time since I was able to speak German."

"Mr. Fred Harvey doubtless will be pleased," Jenny agreed, yawning. "Oh, my, am I tired! This will be almost like being mentioned in dispatches, for us. Tell me all about the parlor car tomorrow. I am sure the other girls will have a thousand questions." She yawned again, and turned to lock the door at the top of the stairs behind them, as they passed through. “Sleep well, Sophie – and bundle up the quilts on your bed tonight, for winter is on us and tonight is supposed to be freezing-cold. Mr. Boatwright had a message from the telegraphist in La Junta. There is a storm blowing east. They have had snow falling there all day. Likely we will have it tonight.”

“I hate to see summer go,” Sophia mused. “I’ve always hated being cold.”

“The benefits of having our rooms over the kitchens,” Jenny agreed. “Unpleasant in summer, but welcome in the winter. Good night, Sophia.”

“Good night, Miss Maitland.” Sophia went to her own room, made a hasty preparation for bed, her feet already cold once she removed her shoes. Laura was asleep, her breathing the only sound within the room. An icy wind rattled the panes of glass, and in the distance, before she fell into her own sleep, Sophia heard the whistle of a steam engine, heavy wheels grinding against the rails; the special train on its way, returning to Texas. The passage of it vibrated the station building slightly, and then it was gone, leaving winter behind, with the soft rustle of the first heavy flakes of snow falling and brushing against the windows.

By the following morning, it was obvious that winter had arrived in Kansas, and Sophia was more than grateful for her new coat, the warmth of those flannel petticoats, and the old-fashioned hood which Laura had knitted for her out of heavy wool in an ornate geometric pattern she said was a traditional one from Sweden that her mother had taught her. The cold was a dry cold, not as damp and miserable as winters were prone to be in Boston, but the winds were merciless. Most mornings, the windowsill was dusted with a layer of snow which had sifted through the cracks around the window-frames and the glass itself covered thick in the geometrical scrawls of frost. Not for the west a gentle veil of falling snow, whispering and rustling as it fell; here the wind propelled the snow in hard, gritty pellets that felt like small hail and stung the exposed flesh. The air sometimes was so cold it scorched like icy fire and stung in her nose and throat – no, there were days when to walk across to the bank, Sophia must wrap her muffler twice around her face, because it would hurt to take a deep breath.

No more the excursions out to the countryside for picnics with Bill Boatwright, and Laura and her young swain, Andrew Belton. Sophia's one day off was more likely spent in the parlor, sewing and reading, or sometimes playing children's card games with the other girls. Nothing stopped the regular train schedule although there were storms which came close to doing so. Passengers, supplies, mail and newspapers arrived from east and west without fail. On a Sunday morning in December, Sophia rewarded herself with a copy of the latest *Boston Herald*, and settled in for a leisurely read of it. Her feelings, on leafing through the pages of newsprint were an odd mixture of nostalgia at the news of familiar places, the scattering of familiar names as welcome as having caught sight of them in the street or walking in the Public Garden, and satisfaction she was doing so from far, far away – as if she stood outside the bars of a cage and watched a dangerous tiger pace back and forth.

She turned the page, and her eyes fell on a familiar name – one which leapt at her like that tiger.

Miss Minerva Templeton Vining, late of this City.

Great-Aunt Minnie. There was a chill in her heart, which had nothing to do with the icy draft from the closest window. She was reading the social pages, a collection of short paragraphs on the travels and doings of various prominent or near-to-prominent citizens.

She found the start of the item and read it carefully as if to distill the import of every word.

"We have lately received word from a correspondent in Newport that Miss Minerva Templeton Vining, late of this City, has passed to her final heavenly reward at a private residence in Newport, attended devotedly in her final decline by her dearest friends. Our Readers of a certain age will fondly recall that dauntless lady as a stalwart speaker on behalf of the Abolitionist cause, her volunteer service with the Sanitary Commission nursing the wounded in the Late Conflict, and her devotion to and support of many other worthy and charitable causes in our City such as Temperance, Female Suffrage and the education of the Poor. Miss Vining was the last surviving offspring of Judge Lycurgus Saltinstall Vining, a magnate in the China trade, who's many descendants still inhabit this city. We offer up our most sincere consolation to her friends, associates and family, who – we are certain – will miss her lively presence on the social and charitable scene immensely. Her obituary and notice of memorial services will be published as soon as they are available to us."

I wish I could have been able to write to her, Sophia thought, as she laid aside the *Herald. Let her know that I was safe – she believed me at the last. But I couldn't – a letter, a careless word – would have put both of us in danger, and the Teagues, too. I put nothing past Richard – he would have found a way, I know he would have. His vicious humor was something only the readers of the worst kind of dime novels might have credited. Old Tim, Declan, Seamus and Agnes – yes, he would have done his worst on them in revenge. Richard's malice and cunning posed all too real a danger since he was a man from an old and respected family. I hope that Mrs. Kempton wrote to her and remembered to say she had encountered a girl named Sophia in Kansas. That news might have lightened her grief and provided comfort. Dear Great-aunt Minnie ...*

The door to the parlor swung open, admitting Laura, dressed for the outdoors, and carrying Sophia's coat and winter things. "There you are, Sophie! You simply must come sleigh-riding with us – the day is so fine and clear, and the snow is packed! Mr. Belton has a sleigh and team…"

"I ..." It was in her mind to refuse, but Laura cried impatiently,

"You cannot stay in the parlor all day, reading your silly newspaper – you will have cobwebs in your head. Let fresh air blow them away!"

"All right," Sophia agreed. She folded up the newspaper and left it for anyone else, although first she tore out the page with the society notes in it, and tucked it into her pocket. Laura was right. Fresh air would do her good, and if winter so far was any indication, the next fair day might not fall on a Sunday. She donned her coat and warmest hood, thrust mittens onto her hands, and followed Laura out through the House: before the Newton station, a team of horses waited in harness to an open two-seat cutter. The bells on their harness jingled sweetly as they tossed their heads and shifted in their traces. Andrew Belton – the telegraphist walking out with Laura hopped down from the driver's seat.

Bill Boatwright sat with the reins in his gloved hands – he grinned at the girls, saying, "About time! I thought you would take all morning." Andrew kissed Laura on one cheek. "Get in, girls – time is passing and the horses are impatient!" He handed them up to the back seat, piled high with a pair of heavy buffalo robes. "There's a foot-stove, at the bottom, and more blankets under the robes!"

"This is fun!" Laura bounced up into the cutter, pulling aside the robes and blankets. "My brothers and their friends, they used to race on winter days! As fast as the trains!"

"Settled?" Bill Boatwright asked over his shoulder, as Sophia burrowed under the robes and blankets. There was a puddle of warmth at her feet – the foot-stove, fully charged with fresh hot coals. "Then let 'er rip!" He slapped the reins on the horses' backs, and they set off at a lively trot. The runners made little but a faint rasp on the new snow, and the horses' hooves were muffled by it – the loudest thing by far the jingling bells on the horse harness. The air blew ice-water cold on Sophia's cheeks: she and Laura had the buffalo robes pulled up to their shoulders, for there was no shelter from the biting winter wind in an open sleigh. The men were talking together as was their custom.

"Something has made you sad, Sophia," Laura asked, most unexpectedly. "I will listen, if you wish to tell me what it is. Was it something in your newspaper?"

"Yes," Sophia acknowledged, at last. This was something she had kept to herself for more than half a year. The sound of the horses' hoofs crunching on snow, their harness bells chiming provided a cover for quiet conversation. "The death of someone close to me. And I am sad not just because I will miss her very much, but I couldn't tell her where I was. In the west. Working for Mr. Harvey. She would have approved, I think."

"Why could you not write to her?" Laura sounded puzzled.

"Two can keep a secret if one of them is dead," Sophia replied with a bitter laugh. "There was a man who threatened our lives. He was cruel and stopped at nothing when thwarted. I had to get away, you see. I could not tell anyone where I was going. I was afraid that this man – if he found out that my friends among the servants had helped me – if he even knew I was alive, he could hurt them, somehow. And then he would hunt me down. I had to let everyone assume I was dead, for their safety and mine."

"So," Laura mused. "Your name is not Teague? And everyone where you came from believes you dead?"

"I call myself Teague," Sophia insisted. "A family of that name were kind and loyal to me. Not my family – to me. I suppose that the person I used to be is dead. At least, I am sure that Richard thinks so."

"Richard?" Laura's blue eyes widened. "You have said that name, sometimes in your sleep. Your husband?"

"No," Sophia laughed, curt and bitter. "I was never married. Richard is my older brother. I used to adore him when I was a child. But I wonder now, if he was ever what he appeared to be. My great-aunt's companion hated and feared him. She said he was evil."

"A brother?" Laura exclaimed. "But you always say you are orphan, with no brother or sister."

"He treated me so abominably," Sophia answered, "That I doubt he ever held me in mind as a sister – I was just a stranger in the way of something he wanted. My great-aunt said in her last letter, that sometimes my mother said she could see a demon in his eyes. He carried out a lifelong pretense of being an amiable and well-mannered gentleman, but I am certain that his wife feared him. And I came to realize that he would kill me, as he had killed the birds."

"Oh, Sophie!" Laura fumbled for Sophie's mitten-clad hands underneath the robe, and took them into hers. "How horrid – unbelievable!"

"I know he took pleasure in tormenting animals. People, too. When I was a small child, I wanted a kitten. My mother forbade it. I thought she was unreasonable but now I know she was afraid Richard would harm it." Sophia's voice dropped as she considered her childhood memories. "When I was a small girl, my mother feared that Richard might do the same with me. He never did … well, not until the last. Then I also saw the demon in his eyes. But he fooled nearly everyone, Laura. And he is a … a well-respected man in Boston; a man of power and position. I could not risk the lives of my friends. I sent a message by round-about means, to tell my great-aunt I was alive and safe. But I cannot be sure she ever received it." The two girls sat, huddled together against the cold, warm under the buffalo robes. Now they were out at the edge of town, into snow-clad fields and meadows unrolling on either side, broken here and there with a line of leafless brush or scrub-trees casting long blue shadows on the pure white snow.

"I wouldn't be surprised if you did not credit a word of this," Sophia said at last. "It must seem quite … melodramatic to you – a brother like mine."

"No," Laura shook her head. "Not at all; there was a boy once – the age of my oldest brothers, from the other side of town. Only son, only child. His parents farmed … and he was odd. So my brothers always said. They did not like him, much, although his mother and father were friends to all, and they were schoolboys together. But there was something strange about him. They said that he liked to do cruel things to the animals, but sneaky in doing so … bungle killing a chicken, so he could watch it running around and laugh as it died slowly. Trap a rabbit in the field, watch as it writhed in agony. The other children teased him, for he wet the bed at night. His poor mama – who must wash the sheets and nightshirt always! And he liked setting fires. Of this my brothers said, often, when this was spoken of. He loved to start a fire – and watch it with a gloating expression. My brothers," Laura drew in her breath with a hiss. "They said the same as you – there was a demon in his eyes at such times. I have not thought of this for many years, Sophie – this was when I was a little girl and much has happened since then."

"What happened to this boy?" Sophia asked, hardly daring to draw a breath. This sounded dreadfully similar to Richard. Laura shrugged.

"There was a fire one night, which burned up the farmhouse and killed his parents together. He lost the farm and went to work as a hired man in the next town. One night, he killed the farmer for whom he worked with a shotgun. He was tried and convicted, but everyone said he was insane. He was sent to the St. Peter State Hospital. They say he died in a fire there. My brothers wondered if he had a hand in setting it."

When they returned from the sleigh-ride, exhilarated and laughing from the speed and adventure, Sophia took out the single page from the Herald and clipped it close around the item about Great-aunt Minnie with the scissors from her sewing basket. She folded it small, and tucked it inside the front cover of the volume of Thoreau which was Great-aunt Minnie's life-saving gift, along with the note which had enclosed the money. At least, Sophia reflected, with a touch of grim satisfaction – Minnie was gone far beyond any machination of Richard's to do her harm. There was one less person to fear for; doubtless Miss Phelps would find refuge with another employer. Could she might risk writing to Old Tim, and Seamus? No, Declan had advised against that. *Close the door and walk away,* his father had advised. She ought to just do that.

But she still bought a copy of the *Advertiser* once a week. Just to assure herself that Richard was not persecuting the Teagues.

Spring came later to the prairies than to Boston, Sophia realized. The last rags of snow vanished by late March and a thin haze of green began to color the prairies by April. Clean white clouds scudded across a sky so deep and purely blue that Sophia wondered if she had ever seen a sky that blue. When the grass grew higher, it was starred with wildflowers, and the wind ruffled it, again like the wind on the ocean waves, while cloud-shadows moved swiftly, as if chasing the flocks of birds returning north. With spring came her 22nd birthday, and shortly thereafter, a renewal of her contract with Fred Harvey Company.

"Do you want to stay here, or go farther west?" she asked Laura one Sunday evening, as they prepared for bed in their room. Laura had gone for a drive that day, alone with Andrew Belton. There was a week left before the renewal of their contracts; Sophia was considering where she might go for the next year. Newton was pleasant, the dining room, and the lunchroom were lively enough with all the trains passing through of a day, but Sophia couldn't help wondering about those other places; surely there was more to the west than Kansas. "I am considering New Mexico. Jenny says there will be an opening at the house in La Junta. There are mountains there – and it would make a change. Kansas is well and good, but it is too flat. Mountains make a landscape interesting. What do you think?"

"There were mountains in Sweden," Laura replied, from in front of the mirror where she was combing out her hair and weaving it into a long flaxen braid for the night. "Mama and Papa were tired of mountains. So many rocks! Easier to plough on the flat land … Sophie, I will renew. Andrew Belton has asked me to marry. I have such a fine dowry now, I am decided on saying I will. Andrew wrote to Papa and has his blessing."

"You are decided on this?" Sophia sat up in her bed. She had been so certain she and Laura would go on to another Harvey House together since they had been such firm friends from the moment of their meeting. The fleeting and pro-forma attentions of Bill Boatwright were such a casual thing to her; she had been unaware of Andrew and Laura's attentions becoming serious and profound.

"You sound disappointed, Sophie. I am sorry. But this is a thing I did not mean to do for long. We have been fine friends, *ja?* But I am certain of Andrew. This is what I meant to do. You are the modern woman, as you say and Mr. Boatwright, he is not serious." Laura tied a single ribbon around the end of her braid and came to sit on the edge of Sophia's bed. "So in a week, Andrew and I will go to Minnesota to meet my Mama and Papa, and to be married. Then he wants to go to Texas, to Galveston on the coast. He will be the senior telegraphist for the railway there. With this, he can support a family."

"You should have told me sooner," Sophia said around the lump in her throat, and Laura shrugged.

"I had not made up my mind … and it was only today he told me of Galveston and a higher position. Wish us well, Sophie – please?"

"I do," Sophia replied, although her sense of loss pierced her through and through. "You have what you want, through working for Mr. Harvey – and you are happy and Mr. Belton is happy. I am just sad for myself, that you will be in Texas and I will be somewhere else, where we cannot do the things that friends do together."

"I know," Laura blue eyes filled momentarily. "For that I am sorry, too. But we will write to each other, *ja?* You have never had letters before, in all the time you have been in Newton – and now you will have them from me. So you see; I will have a husband, and you will have letters!"

"That's a look at the sunny side of things," Sophia agreed, and in spite of it all, she giggled. "That's what I will miss the most, Laura – you don't ever let me feel sorry for myself."

"So, will you go to La Junta?" Laura got up, and quenched the gaslight. In the quiet darkness, broken by the thin moonlight shining around the edge of the curtain, Sophia heard the rustle of bedclothes and springs, as Laura got into bed.

"I will ask for that House," Sophia replied. She pulled the bedcovers over herself, and turned to one side, so she faced Laura, unseen in the darkness.

"Will you find what you want there, Sophie?" Laura's voice came from across the room. "They say that everyone goes to the west, looking for something – what are you looking for, then?"

"I am not altogether sure," Sophia replied. "But I am certain that not depending on the charity of relations is a goodly portion of it. I will know when I find it … I hope."

Part 2 – 1890

Chapter 13 – Arrival in Deming

"We'll be in Deming in ten minutes," the Pullman porter said, as he passed by Sophia's seat in the regular train from Albuquerque to Guaymas in Mexico. "You all ready for the wild west, Miss Teague?"

"Don't be funning with me, George," Sophia replied, closing the book she had been reading and slipping it into her reticule. "I've been working for Fred Harvey Company six years now. I have been singularly disappointed with the actual wildness of every place I have been, for all the sensational newspaper stories and dime novels. Wild west indeed – I consider the wildness vastly overrated."

George (whose name wasn't George, but all Pullman porters were called George) was a casual acquaintance of several years standing, an association farther tightened by their mutual service to the railway. "Shush yourself, Miss Teague," he replied, with a conspiratorial wink. "Them writer fellas mus' have something to write about. And sometimes those range wars get to be pretty intense. I used to ride trail for the RB outfit in the Panhandle country, til' they got sideways of a bunch of cattle thieves – it was no game for a man who wanted to live long enough to have grey hair."

"Did you indeed?" Sophia asked, suddenly interested. She had always assumed that he had always worked for the Pullman Company. "You were a cowboy, then?"

"For a time, Miss Teague. But it's hard work; only a young man can endure it. Had me some fine times though." He grinned, in reminiscence. "I might write up an account of them, someday."

"You ought to do that," Sophia replied, as she stood up, reaching for the trusty old carpet-bag in the rack over her head. "I'd most definitely read it."

"Allow me, Miss Teague," George said. He lifted it down easily. "So are you going to work in the Deming Harvey house or jus' stopping for a visit?"

"Work," Sophia sighed, in happy appreciation. "One of the girls from when I started in Newton is here – Selina Burnett. She wrote and told me that there was an opening and Deming sounded interesting, so I requested a new posting."

"You been all over the Atchison-Topeka Harvey Houses, haven't you?"

"I have," Sophia replied. She could sense the train beginning to slow. She and George stood by the end of the car, closest to the door. "La Junta, after Newton. Then a couple of months at the Montezuma Palace, in the dining room. That was boring – no trains. And all the way out to California, to Barstow; there were trains, but it was sand and desert; even more boring. And then to Albuquerque … I substituted from there, to other Houses which were short-handed. I liked that. Having once learned the Harvey method, I could go anywhere, and I had friends in every other house after the first few years. George, can you arrange with a porter to take my trunk from the baggage car to the House lodgings? I expect that they will need me to help out today. There was a message yesterday morning before I left, saying that two girls were sick in bed and couldn't work."

"Mos' certainly, Miss Teague. No rest fo' the righteous, so it says in the Good Book," George replied.

"Indeed," Sophia said, although there was no real reply for that. The train slowed even more; as it curved around a bend in the track, Sophia could look out and see the tops of tall trees, and a metal daisy-field of idly spinning windmills, with the railway water and coal towers thrusting up at the heart of Deming. Her heart lifted in happy anticipation.

Six years as a Harvey girl; she would not have traded the experience of that for anything in the world. She had a substantial nest egg saved from her wages, a small but elegant wardrobe, bought new and to her own taste, and she had traveled! Oh, how she had traveled, confidently and alone, for the most part; mostly for the business of the Harvey Company, which provided a train pass on the AT&SA for every one of their employees. The little pewter pin for her work pinafore now bore a number 6 on it, which made her senior in most Houses. With seniority came responsibility and increased authority, which Sophia relished. She might even rise far enough to manage a Harvey House. Great-aunt Minnie would be amazed and proud, if she could see that!

Boston was so far behind her now. She had even stopped reading the *Boston Daily Advertiser* so assiduously. It did not seem so urgent a matter, viewing the activities of those whom she had once known so well at such a distance. It was long ago and far away, and of decreasing importance in her life. For a long time there had been that fear in the back of her mind that Richard and Dr. Cotton, or some men working for him might step from a train brandishing warrants and papers, apprehend her as a fugitive, and pack her back to Danvers. It had never happened; she never set eyes on any acquaintance from Boston again. She was now Miss Teague, a valued employee of Fred Harvey Company. No one west of the Mississippi would have dared lay hands on her, wild and lawless or not.

She took her carpetbag from George, with a word of thanks – for he was caught up in attending those passengers debarking at Deming – and was down from the train before it even stopped moving. She swung the carpetbag, feeling the joy of a child released from school; she knew the Deming station from having stopped there several times, and because the Harvey Houses were often arranged on similar principles; everything just so. If you knew one or two of them well, then you knew them all. Just ahead of the surge of other passengers, she walked into the Harvey House, past the busboy standing ready at the gong.

"Is Miss Bennet in the dining room, or the lunch room," she paused to ask.

"Dining room," he replied, looking beyond her at the scattered passengers making a purposeful way towards the house. "Miss Teague? You were expected on this train!"

"And now I'm here," Sophia strode into the house and stepped into the dining room, where a harassed-appearing Selina was overseeing the last few preparations. "Selina, I'll put my bag upstairs and change. Where do you need me?"

"Thank heavens," Selina brightened. "Second room along on the right is yours. The laundry sent along your work things. The lunch room if you don't mind."

"Not at all," Sophia replied. "I'll be down in two shakes."

She had become accustomed to performing swift changes in her toilettes in the past five years. Off came her travel dress and the plain flat straw boater pinned at a daring angle on her hair, arranged in a plain bun. She wore black shoes and stockings as a matter of habit. She was fastening her white cuffs as she ran down stairs, and through the kitchen. One of the cooks waved to her from behind the stove. The kitchen melt of good food excellently cooked.

"Not wasting a moment, Miss T., are you?" He had worked at the Montezuma Palace.

"Never," she called back, moving through the doors into the lunchroom just as the first customers emerged from the other side.

"Miss T.!" chorused the duty waitresses, in relief and gratitude. She recognized all three; in fact, she had trained two of them in the Harvey method, although in separate places and the third had worked with her at the Montezuma – a circumstance which relieved her mind no end. Today was no time to be training a new girl when they were short-handed.

"Remember," she whispered, bringing an answering smile to those three faces. "Left to right – and always go by the right-hand door!"

Late that night, when she finally reached the end of the shift, and climbed the stairs, she found her trunk sitting in the middle of her new room. Yes; when you worked for Fred Harvey Company on the railway you were a member of the tribe, that tribe who looked after other members.

Before she had been in Deming a week – not even long enough to have a day off on Sundays, that distant past was recalled to her in an unexpected manner, through an overheard conversation between a pair of customers in the lunchroom. Two travelling drummers in city-cut suits and lamentably garish waistcoats came in together amongst the usual crowd, taking seats side by side and continuing their conversation – a conversation focused on headlines in a newspaper which one carried. They were interested in that story, for a reason which Sophia could not fathom. They asked for coffee and ordered the cheapest meal possible: she ordered their cups and bustled away towards the kitchen.

As she went, she heard one say, in tones which combined a degree of gruesome relish with sanctimonious disapproval, "… ruined in the bust-up of the Marine National Bank, but went on living like a lord in a big house on Beacon Street…"

Her ears pricked up: Beacon Street? The Marine National Bank? There must be many once-wealthy men ruined in the collapse of the Marine National Bank of New York, and there must be Beacon Streets in other towns than Boston? When she returned with a tray of plates, she cast her eyes on the newspaper, lying carelessly between the two drummers. Judging by what she could see of the banner across the top page, it was a newspaper called the *New York World.* She could read the garish headlines up-side down, the letters big and black: **Wife and Children Drugged in Fatal Fire**, and in smaller letters, **Accused in Horrific North Town Murder**.

"… thought it was an accident, 'o course," the first drummer said. "And the house burned so hot, it wasn't certain for days."

"Shocking," the second man tucked into his lunch, hardly looking at it. He had more of an appetite for nourishment than for scandal. "So when did they see something was amiss about it all?"

"He'd been cut in the street by friends, after he was brought in to be questioned the first time. People thought there was something odd going on. Miss, may I have more coffee?"

"Certainly," Sophia replied, and signaled the girl with the tray of jugs and carafes. Curiosity did not in the least overwhelm her sense of devotion to Harvey strictures on unnecessary conversation with customers, during a stop by a train. She continued taking orders from other customers, ferrying trays from kitchen to lunch counter, contriving to pass by the two drummers with the intent of overhearing their conversation. To her disappointment, they were now talking about the trials of their journey, and the eccentricities of the customers they encountered. When the train whistle sounded the alert for departure, they both gobbled the last few bites of generous quarter-slices of apple pie, flung a few coins on the counter where they had sat, and made as if to depart for the cashier's desk.

"Excuse me, sir," Sophia called after them. "You have forgotten your newspaper!"

"Already read it," the drummer in the loudest suit called back, over his shoulder. "It's yours, if you want it."

"Thank you, sir!" she said, as the door closed behind them. She claimed the newspaper, rolled it under her arm. No time to read at any length, although she sneaked a look when the lunch counter was clean and fresh-laid, awaiting customers from the next train.

Mr. Richard Brewer, of Beacon Street in Boston's most prosperous neighborhood of Back Bay, was found dead by his own hand in the burned remains of his family home on Tuesday last ... the remains of his wife and two young sons were also discovered among the wreckage of what had been the ancestral mansion of one of Boston's most prominent families ...

Sophia folded up the newspaper into a small square. "I need to go up to my room," she said to the closest of the young waitresses in the lunchroom. "Just for a moment. I will return to help with laying out for the next train."

She ran up the back stairs to the House quarters: she had to read of this in private, lest she betray herself by an unguarded word or tear. At the moment, she had a bedroom to herself, since the Deming house was still short-handed. She read the article; the words and what she deduced of that left unsaid. The Brewer house caught fire early in the morning and was well-alight before the nearest neighbors were made aware by the roar of flames well along in the second-floor bedroom and in the stairway which burned as if in a flue. Two brave firemen broke down the front door, searching for residents of the house and got as far as the foot of the stairs, by which Sophia knew they must have gotten to the door to Richard's study. They had a glimpse, as if in the heart of a furnace, of a man sitting slumped in an armchair, a long revolver lying on the floor by his slack hand. They could not reach him; at the moment of that seeing, something crashed down from the third story, above their heads and the firemen escaped in a shower of sparks and falling beams and joists.

Despite all efforts of the fire brigade, the roofs of houses one either side also caught … Sophia skipped the breathless accounts of how their occupants escaped; it appeared they all had been wakened by the clamor in time to snatch up clothing and small valuables and make their way to safety. When the embers cooled sufficiently to be searched, five days later, Richard was identified by his engraved pocket-watch and cravat stick-pin, the fire-blackened remains of a revolver by his side, while the charred bones of Fee, Curgie and the youngest boy were recognized by Fee's wedding ring and for their bones being the right size for a woman and two children known to be residents of the house. Richie had escaped the carnage by being away at school. He was now, the newspaper noted in nearly the last line, in the care of a trusted guardian.

Sophia set aside the newspaper with shaking hands. Poor silly Fee and sickly, bad-tempered Curgie; it was for their benefit that Richard had claimed to do what he did to secure the use of her small inheritance. She wondered if he had stupefied them with drugs first and hoped that he had. The newspaper account gave no hint of why Richard had chosen this action although the conversation of the two drummers hinted at him being under suspicion for some awful crime – which suspicion led to him being snubbed in the street by his friends. She folded up the copy of the *New York World* and laid it carefully away in the trunk at the foot of her bed.

Richard dead; and an end to fearing that his malice following her, Javert-like, over river and plain. There was now a line drawn under that mistreatment and brutality he had served to her, and the long misery of flight, of becoming known by a name not her own and family not of her own blood. Might the shadow of the Danvers Insane Asylum be banished for good? Was it safe for her to reclaim her proper name since there was no reason to fear someone stepping off a train with a warrant from back east? She realized with a shudder of horror; there were excellent reasons to fear far, far worse; a reporter from a one of the Eastern sensational news-sheets, panting like a hungry dog after scraps of scandal, a new and scandalous aspect to the fire in Beacon Street. Her new life would be ruined. What sickeningly prurient details might be added or created out of whole cloth if required? No; best to keep on calling herself Sophia Teague. Besides, she recollected with another trickle of unease down her spine; there was Richie, in the care of a guardian entrusted to look after his interests. If Richard's friends, like Doctor Cotton, were anything like Richard, likely they would also stop at nothing. *Close the door and walk away*, as old Tim Teague had advised.

Enough of this; there was another train due in Deming, in fifteen minutes. Before she took up her station in the lunchroom, she stopped at the newsstand.

"Do you have any copies of the *Boston Daily Advertiser*? I'd like the latest issue and any old ones you have saved."

"Eh, Miss T. – I have only what came in today," the newsstand manager replied. "I'll set a copy aside for you, at the end of the day."

"Thank you," Sophia made as if to return to the lunchroom, but the newsstand manager asked, with sudden concern, "Are you well, Miss T.? Is there something wrong?"

"No, only that I have news of some old acquaintances back east," She replied, and escaped before she had to lie regarding her reasons for wanting the *Advertiser*. To her good fortune, the remainder of her shift in the lunch room was too busy for her to think much about Richard, and what had happened in Boston so many weeks ago – and it was too busy for any of the other girls to take particular notice of her own mood. She perused the current issue of the *Advertiser* when she was alone in her room, but it offered little more to what she had read already. The house had burned, deliberately set afire by its owner, and the writer for the *Advertiser* was even less inclined to speculate on his motivations.

More than anything, she wished that she still shared a room with Laura Nyland – Laura who was shrewd and blunt, the only one of her friends among the Harvey girls who knew about Richard and what Sophia had been escaping from. Now Laura a small son, named Andrew after his father and wrote happy letters from her yellow-painted cottage in Galveston, not far from the white-sand beaches along the Gulf. She should write to Laura the next morning. Sunday was her day off work. There was, so she had been told, a proper Episcopalian church in Deming. That was it – she ought to go to church the next day.

She dressed with care the following morning; not in her absolute best, but in a modest brown poplin walking costume trimmed with slightly darker brown passementerie braid in an elaborate pattern at hem, lapels and cuffs. The dress, otherwise plain in cut had fashionably large leg-o-mutton sleeves, and the hat which she pinned at a coquettish angle was a cream and brown confection, trimmed with a bunch of bright red artificial cherries. It was so awkward, sometimes, when the Harvey girls mixed with local society. Laura often observed with cheerful cynicism on those few occasions back in Newton that it was because they were not fish nor fowl; not quite the respectable maidens from good families because they were working far away from the authority of their families – the good papa and the mama-hen mother, the fierce brothers – but many degrees above the women who worked in low dance-halls, saloons and chop-houses. The solution to the conundrum was to be more tastefully arrayed for the occasion than the dance-hall and pretty waiter-girls but not so fashionably turned out as any of the local merchants' wives and daughters. That would excite envy and scorn. Sophia regarded herself in the mirror with anxiety, considering if her toilette had achieved the desired effect, and concluded that she had – not for nothing had been her upbringing in Boston when it came to judging the strictures of society. She took up her reticule; her mother's cherished copy of the *Common Book of Prayer* and sallied forth through the door which led from the kitchen onto the lower end of the platform.

The hour was early yet, for Sunday was a day of rest, but there was a gentleman in a well-cut dark suit sitting on a bench, under the shade of the awning. His hat – of the wide-brimmed sort favored by Westerners, lay on the bench next to him – but his attention was bent on a small saucer, placed at the edge of the silent platform six or seven feet distant. The plate held finely minced chicken, and a small grey cat gobbled it with ferocious intensity. The sound of the door closing behind Sophia startled the cat which looked over her flank with fear-widened eyes and fled underneath the platform, abandoning the meal half-eaten, as the gentleman rose from his ease on the bench. Sophia could not help seeing that a long-barreled revolver hung from a wide leather belt at his waist – the only unexpected accessory to what was otherwise the perfect representation of gentility.

"You startled her," the gentleman remarked, without reproof. "Never mind – she'll be back. Poor little Miss Kitten may be timid, but she is always hungry."

"I am sorry," Sophia began; the gentleman seemed familiar. Wiry and weathered by sun, clean-shaven save for a looming mustache and light brown hair thinning a little, he spoke with a faint but decided accent.

"I am taming her, by fits and starts," the gentleman replied, and looked at Sophia for the first time. "I have a property which soon will require a good mouse-hunting cat. None have been forthcoming in response to my advertising the position, so I am recruiting volunteers.

I know you from somewhere – are you employed by the Harvey House?"

"I am," Sophia answered, still baffled. Six years and the customers who had come and gone, eaten a meal with honest appreciation all merged in her mind. She had waited on him, but when and where was a momentary bafflement.

"Miss Teague, from Newton!" the gentleman exclaimed, the light of dawning comprehension on his pleasant countenance. "I recall now – you brought us a meal to our car … some five years ago."

"Mr. Steinmetz!" The light of recognition dawned on Sophia. This was the man addressed as Onkel Fredi by the man who claimed the same surname as her grandfather, Horace Vining of Beacon Hill in Boston. Mr. Steinmetz had claimed nothing like that familiarity, but he had been courteous and even attentive to her, if somewhat acid towards his family. "How extraordinary to meet you again! Your niece Mrs. Vining was so amenable. I do remember the parlor car and that she was such a charming hostess; we talked for days afterwards in the House of what she had shown to me."

"I haven't got a parlor car to show to you today, Miss Teague," Fredi Steinmetz replied with the asperity which Sophia recalled so well when she recollected him. "Only a poor shy kitten and a pile of adobe bricks where my ranch house will be, one day."

"I have seen the kitten, Mr. Steinmetz, and I do not have a moment for the bricks, since worship begins at St. Luke's in twenty minutes."

"Permit me to escort you, Miss Teague. Deming is a rough place in spots, still, and I don't like to see a lady come to harm." He offered his elbow, and Sophia was still so astonished to meet him again that she accepted it.

"Thank you kindly, Mr. Steinmetz. I am most grateful. I have only just arrived and do not know the town."

"Can't say I know it that well myself," he replied. "I've been trying to sort out the ranch since I bought the property, a year ago … not much time to spend in town. But I'm having a new house built, and some wells drilled. I started living at the station hotel and taking meals at the Harvey House while the work is going on. I didn't know that you were here in Deming too, Miss Teague."

"I've been working in the lunchroom," Sophia explained. They strolled the length of the platform and crossed over the tracks. As soon as they had gone a distance, Sophia looked back, and saw the tiny grey cat applying herself to the saucer of chicken once more. She thought how companionable, even comfortable – she felt, walking next to him. They were about the same height and matched strides easily.

"So you've been working for Fred Harvey Company, all this time," Mr. Steinmetz mused, and Sophia nodded. "I am certain I have been everywhere in the west. I even spent a year in California."

Mr. Steinmetz chuckled. "Spent a couple of years there myself, before the War, when I was a feckless young pup looking for gold."

"Did you find any?" Sophia was intrigued.

"Not so much," he confessed. "It turned out that the availability of gold in the diggings had been vastly exaggerated. I finished up doing a lot else, to keep myself in grub, and finally came home to Texas. Trailing cattle wasn't near as much of a back-breaker."

"What kind of things have you done for a living, then?"

"Anything I could turn a hand to," Mr. Steinmetz sounded reminiscent. "Trailing cattle, of course; to California that time and many times to Kansas after the War. Ordinary hand at first, trail boss and ranch manager for my brother-in-law later on. Drove freight wagons; hired out to wash glasses in a saloon for a time when I was partners with a crazy old piano-playing Fenian. Sold newspapers on the streets of San Francisco, rode for a pony express mail … not <u>the</u>

Pony Express," he added hastily. "Just between camps in the diggings before the War. My partner and I went on tour with Miss Lotta Crabtree after that, up and down the diggings. My friend played accompaniment for her, I drove the wagon and set up stage. Funny little bit of a thing, she was then; my pal swore she had the soul of stubborn old lady in the body of a little girl. Then he got himself knifed, trying to break up a fight in a saloon between two friends. I chucked it then and came home to Texas just in time for the War."

"Did you serve in the Army?" Sophia ventured, recalling too late that Mr. Steinmetz must have served in the Confederate and not the Union Army.

"A trooper in the Frontier Regiment … mostly protecting against Indians, although I went as far as the expedition into New Mexico Territory. When it was over, I figured that I'd best stick to ranching and trailing cattle and leave politics to my brother Johann … he's my twin, and I guess he got most of the brains intended for the two of us." Mr. Steinmetz grinned, unrepentantly. "He trained as a doctor and had the sense to pick the winning side. He joined the Union Army rather than take the loyalty oath. What about you, Miss Teague; why did you come west to work for Fred Harvey?"

"I'm an orphan, without any close family," Sophia answered. "We had money once, then we didn't, and I didn't wish to be an object of charity for those relations who did still have money."

"Sensible woman," Mr. Steinmetz approved so warmly that Sophia was charmed into forgetting for the moment that he was nearly old enough to be her father.

Chapter 14 – Lottie

The streets of Deming were filled with ruts, the occasional puddle and mound of horse-dung, and flanked with unadorned frame and adobe-brick buildings, but at least the city fathers had lined a few of the main streets with wooden sidewalks. Ahead of them, Sophia could see a plain white-washed steeple which must mark the sanctuary of St. Luke's. This was not anything like the spires of churches back in Boston – tall stone or brick, ornamented with carvings and iron-work, from which the chiming of bells rang out the hours and events. But this was the West, and Sophia had over the last six years become accustomed to it.

"I adore looking out of a window and seeing mountains," she remarked, for such mountains rose all around Deming, dark-blue, tan, or rose-colored, depending on the time of day and angle of the sun. "There were none to speak of around Newton, but there were splendid ones at La Junta. *Flee as a bird to the mountain* … I always liked that verse, even though there were no mountains around Boston – only hills."

"There were hills where I was raised as a boy," Mr. Steinmetz said, and Sophia looked sideways at him – an easy undertaking for their heads were much on the same level.

"I thought you came from Germany," she ventured, and he nodded. "I did. From a tiny village in Bavaria that no one has ever heard of or likely will. But when my father and my sister Liesel's husband decided that we should take up the offer of the Verein and come to Texas, my brother and I were seven. My mother … it was very sad. She died on the ship coming over. You remind me of her, Miss Teague, or so I can remember. My father was an unworldly sort; he made clocks and read books. We finished up in the hill country of Texas, two or three days' journey north of San Antonio. What with one thing and another, Johann and I were too much for him to handle, so Vati sent Johann and I to live with my oldest sister Magda and her husband. They had a fine little ranch on the Guadalupe River. My sister is formidable, you see. Magda's husband was born American, and he was formidable in his own way. Then Johann went back to Germany to study medicine, and I got the gold fever. In between times, I came back to to live at their place. Magda's son owns it now, and he has a family." He grinned at her, "So, I had to settle on my own place."

"Was that the cattle baron?" Sophia frowned in deep puzzlement. "The man who owned the cattle and ranches, and the parlor car?"

"That was Hansi – my other sister Liesel's husband. Magda's husband Carl was murdered by the hanging band during the War. He was a Unionist, you see. A long time since then, but she still wears black for him. May I ask the favor of sitting with you for the services, Miss Teague? I have been so long and unremitting in my absence from such observances that the roof may fall in on me, so I beg the pleasure of your company."

"Certainly," Sophia replied, with as demure a manner as Fee had always urged upon her. "Although of late I confess that I have not always been observant either."

"The days sometimes just run away from you," Mr. Steinmetz commented wryly, as they approached the church, with its brave little tower lifted up into the faultlessly blue sky. There were other churchgoers ahead of them, lingering by the door greeting arriving friends before the service began. Most were men, stiff and formal in dark town suits which they donned once a week, but there were two or three women among them – plainly wives or daughters. Sophia was glad to be with Mr. Steinmetz; men outnumbered women in the west, and if she had come alone to church, she would have been the focus of interest – wistful on the part of single men and censorious on the part of women, single and married alike.

"*Gott in Himmel,*" Mr. Steinmetz exclaimed, reverting into German in his surprise. "As I live and breathe, Lottie Deno! With Frank Thurmond; she married him at last! Good for them both, I say!"

"Who is Lottie Deno? Was she someone you knew in California?" Sophia assumed that he meant the handsome woman dressed in the height of fashion, standing at the church doorway. The woman had flaming red-gold hair, piled high under a fashionable hat, and she leaned on the arm of a tall man in a well-cut suit that was equally the match to her elaborate day-dress. Mr. Steinmetz grinned like a mischievous boy.

"No. San Antonio, when I used to amuse myself playing cards at the University Club; I confess, Miss Teague, it was a gambling den, but one of the honest ones. She dealt poker there. She didn't allow bad language or liquor at her table, neither; the most lady-like dealer you ever laid eyes upon … that is, if you set foot in a gambling den at all, Miss Teague. Her right name is Charlotte Thomkins, but one night a cowboy with too much liquor in him looked at her pile of winnings and said, *'Darlin', with winnings like that, you outta call yourself Lotta Dinero,'* and after that, everyone began calling her Lottie Deno." He looked sideways at her, and added. "She's a good 'un and a lady as well but don't ever bet money against her when she's flipping those pasteboards. Might just as well give her your poke straight-out, and save time and trouble. I'll tell you the one story about her I saw with my own eyes …"

He was interrupted, by that handsome woman exclaiming, "Fred! Darlin' Dutch! I knew you were in Deming, Frank relays the suitable gossip to me, but I never in all my days expected to see you here!" She came down the steps toward them, a white swan among ducks, a sailing yacht among scows, parting from her path like commoners before royalty. Her accent was Southern, as sweet and slow as honey dripping from a comb, and she embraced Mr. Steinmetz with as much affection as if she were a kinswoman.

"Lottie, *liebling* – you are a spring of cool fresh water in the desert," He kissed her hand with gallant affection. "I had no idea you were in Deming until this moment. Have you and Frank re-opened the University Club without telling me? I shall have to come and sit for a game."

"La, you are naughty, Dutch!" Lottie struck him lightly on the arm, with mock-anger. "We have given that up, being respectable citizens now. Frank is a banker – can you imagine?"

"He banked enough of my money, over time," Mr. Steinmetz answered, laughing. Lottie struck him – again, lightly.

"And you have not introduced me to your lady! Were you born in a barn, Dutch?"

"Close to it," Mr. Steinmetz replied, much amused, although he covered Sophia's hand with his own in a reassuring way. "Lottie, may I present Miss Sophia Teague; a young lady of good family from Boston who has lately arrived as an employee at the Harvey House. We are acquainted from the time she worked at a Kansas Harvey house and have just this moment renewed the acquaintance. Miss Teague; Mrs. Charlotte Thurmond, likewise of a family most suffocatingly respectable yet afflicted with an equally impetuous spirit of adventure."

"Isn't he the naughtiest," Lottie Thurmond replied, although her brown eyes sparkled with merriment. "How can you endure him, Miss Teague?"

"With the same composure which was my family habit in any emergency," Sophia replied. Lottie Thurmond giggled in delight.

"Yours too, Miss Teague? We must become friends, then." To her vague surprise, Lottie Thurmond embraced her, in a froth of sweet-smelling ruffles and lace, whispering, "The Harvey House – how tremendously exciting! I will want to hear all about it! Our little outpost of civilization in a far and desolate land … oh dear – there is the bell. Come and speak to me after the service. This is our highest social occasion of the week, you see. Attention must be paid!"

The bell in the steeple above rang once, twice and once more – the last of those latecomers catching a hasty greeting from their friends on the steps before the door recalled the purpose for which they had assembled themselves on an early morning. Sophia and Mr. Steinmetz found themselves sitting in pew, side by side.

"You said that you could tell me a true story about Mrs. Thurmond," Sophia whispered, under the murmur of other parishioners settling themselves into their own favored pews. "It's not improper, is it? I hate to hear something rude when she has been so welcoming."

"No, it's not improper," Mr. Steinmetz whispered in return. "There was this one evening at the University Club when she was dealing, and two men quarreled and drew on each other. Every man jack of us hit the floor or ducked behind the bar at the first shot. When they were done exchanging lead civilities, there was Lottie, sitting as prim and calm as you please, and she said, 'Gentlemen, I came here tonight to play poker, not roll around on the floor!' Cool as a cucumber, she was." Mr. Steinmetz shook his head, obviously still in awe.

The familiar words of the service were as a balm to a troubled soul; Sophia found herself comforted, recalling as they did her happiest childhood days in Boston, sitting between Mama and Great-Aunt Minnie in the Vining family pew. *Why, oh why had such happy contentment not continued on as it had?* If she had married Lucian Armitage as had been intended, they would have undoubtedly been blessed by children by now. When she was a little girl, she had pretended that her dolls were children – her own family. She envied Laura her little boy and the home she had with her telegraphist.

Sitting next to Mr. Steinmetz, sharing her prayer book with him, silently pointed out the order of service and the readings was a balm, too. He sang well; a light and pleasant tenor, although he whispered to her at the end of the service, "Doesn't seem right being in English; back in Texas when I was a boy, our church was in German, but I always fell asleep during the sermon."

"That was very naughty of you," Sophia replied. "What did your father say, then?"

"Nothing much – he was a free-thinker. My sisters would pinch me though. I always thought it was just because I was a boy and Pastor Altmueller's sermons bored me. Then I grew up … and he was still boring. He'd say five sentences together, and I'd start to snore."

"Sermons are supposed to be improving to one's character," Sophia reproved him.

"I always wondered about that," he admitted. "But as I said before, my brother Johann got most of the brains intended for the pair of us. You should be warned, Miss Teague – I see that Lottie is waiting for you by the door."

So she was; as soon as Sophia and Mr. Steinmetz approached, Lottie Thurmond exclaimed, "Miss Teague, Fred – you simply must join us for Sunday dinner. I must insist on it. Frank wishes to catch up on old times, and I am perishing for lack of stimulating conversation. If I listen to one more conversation between two females comparing the cleverness of their children and recipes for jam, I vow to you that I will scream … say you will indulge me, Miss Teague. We will talk about books, or the diseases plaguing cattle, the difficulties in digging wells in this country, or Indian depredations, and you may tell me all about your adventures … whatever you wish."

"Why yes, certainly," Sophia replied, charmed and overwhelmed by the intensity of Lottie Thurmond's interest.

"Splendid! Frank is bringing around the buggy – although it is a short way to our house, we could walk, but the day becomes so warm. Fred, you are building a new house, are you not?"

"Yes, ma'am, I will be doing that," Mr. Steinmetz explained. "As soon as the wells are dug; can't have the cattle dying of thirst, you know."

Swept along in Lottie Thurmond's enthusiasm and Mr. Steinmetz' friendly interest, Sophia spent the remainder of the day most enjoyably, much more so than she had expected. The ghastly report in the New York scandal sheet, which still had the power to horrify, somehow did not matter to her as much as it had when she first read of it. Boston and the events surrounding her departure from it had again receded into the past. Richard and Fee – everyone who had turned their faces away from her in those dreadful weeks – ceased to matter much at all, on this pleasant Sunday.

The Thurmond house was still new, but beautifully appointed with furniture from the east. Lottie's parlor would have fitted in superbly well in Boston, she was the most gracious of hostesses, and her husband was lean and saturnine and possessed of a particular dry wit which Sophia found most appealing. Late in the afternoon, Mr. Steinmetz walked with her back to the railroad station and the Harvey house, replete with good food, and an afternoon spent in the Thurmond's congenial company. As they approached the station, with the late afternoon sun painting long blue shadows across the dusty street where the water towers and the telegraph poles stood against the sky, he cleared his throat and ventured,

"If I might be permitted, Miss Teague – may I accompany you to St. Luke's next Sunday, if you are inclined on regular attendance?"

"I welcome your company, Mr. Steinmetz – and yes, I do so intend. You will have to make your intentions known to Mr. Loftus the House manager. Mr. Fred Harvey has always taken the position they should see themselves as standing in the place of parents when it came to protecting the honor and good name of the girls – but Mr. Loftus could have no objection to you, when I do not."

"Next Sunday at the same time?" Mr. Steinmetz grinned and kissed Sophia's hand. "And we shall see each other now and again during the week. I am as likely to take meals here as I am at the ranch. If you are interested, I might take you to see it … yes, you and Miss Lottie, of course. She is interested as well."

"I will find much enjoyment in such an excursion," Sophia answered. "Mrs. Thurmond's company has been delightful, this day! I had forgotten what it was like, to sit in a comfortable private parlor," she added, with a touch of wistful envy. "I have lived in Harvey company rooms since the day that came to work for them, and they are comfortable and tasteful in the main but they are not individual, as Mrs. Thurmond's parlor is."

"When I come to fitting out the ranch quarters," Mr. Steinmetz offered, "Once it is finished, of course; I shall ask you both for a consultation. I'm afraid one place is like to any other to me, and I care little and notice even less of such details. I only see the end effect, not the thought going into it."

"I shall be happy to do so," Sophia answered, thinking of how much she had enjoyed his company and that of the Thurmonds for this afternoon. There was not the awkwardness of those excursions with Laura during the year in Newton, where the gentlemen had talked to each other exclusively, while she and Laura were left to their own conversation.

As they approached the kitchen door, a small grey shadow appeared from underneath the platform, eyeing Mr. Steinmetz reproachfully.

"Miss Kitten looks as if she is unhappy with you," Sophia said, remembering the grey kitten which she had begged permission from Mama to make a pet of, so long ago.

"I have neglected her supper, but she will forgive me," Mr. Steinmetz saw Sophia to the door. "Thank you, Miss Teague – I value the pleasure of your companionship far above Miss Kitten's temporary unhappiness."

"I have enjoyed myself likewise," Sophia regretted the ending to the afternoon. "I look forward to next Sunday." To her vague astonishment, he kissed her hand with a flourish that was entirely foreign, saying, "*Auf wiedersehen*, Miss Teague, until we meet again."

In the twilight that evening, she lit the lamp in her room and wrote a letter to Laura by its light, the window open to the panorama of the mountains to the east of town, as the setting sun painted them in fading hues of rose and gold, while moths flitted in and out through the window, attracted by lamplight. *"I have made new friends in town,"* she wrote, *"And I think that I have a new admirer, although there is no hint or breath of scandal likely in our attachment, since he is very much older than I am, and intent on escorting me to church services every Sunday ... My dear friend, I had intelligence from the East this week which at first distressed me considerably, and I ask your sympathy and advice ... it seems that my brother chose to end his own life ..."*

Before she received any answer from Laura, the Deming Harvey house had a demonstration of what Mr. Steinmetz had remarked upon

– it was still a rough town, in patches. Late in the afternoon of the Thursday following on her arrival, Sophia emerged from the lunchroom into the main hallway which led to the platform, her mind on the process of setting everything to rights after an influx of diners. Both the lunchroom and the restaurant had been busy all the day long, with trains arriving and departing. Sophia and the other waitresses had been in a whirl of constant activity since the first train arrived. Because the Deming station served both the Southern Pacific line and the AT & SF, it was as busy as Newton had ever been, extraordinary for a small town in the middle of the desert. The House was also the focus of much public life in town and from the ranches and mines in the locality, so the restaurant and lunchroom were never entirely empty. They were at this moment though; a good time for Sophia to ask Mr. Loftus the House manager for leave to send the duty lunchroom waitresses for their own meal.

She noted a handful of customers remaining in the hallway, most of them waiting at the cashier's desk to pay for their meal, where Mr. Loftus presided over the cashbox. A travel-worn gentleman with a long duster over his suit and the brim of his hat pulled over his forehead stood second in line, his eyes darting warily here and there, as previous customers paid and took their leave. The travel-worn man in the long duster appeared to take an inordinate interest in prolonging his presence in the hallway – he even stepped aside, allowing a woman ahead of him. Sophia stopped short; there was something odd about that woman, which she couldn't put her finger on at first. She was young, but tall, with shoulders that would have looked well on a man, hair cropped to a length just short of them, and her skirts were indecently short. Why, her dress was short enough to show she was wearing men's boots – which Sophia noted without disapproving. Certain of the western women she had seen pass through stations served by Harvey Houses wore men's boots, especially if they need deal with the muck of a farm-yard or a cattle herd.

Now the young woman stepped up to the cashier and opened her reticule. But instead of bringing out money to pay for a meal, she had a small derringer in her fist – even as Sophia realized with a start what had struck her as being odd. The young woman's throat wasn't straight from chin to collar-bone, but had a decided Adams' apple … not a woman, but a young man in women's clothing.

"Give up the cashbox!" the man-as-woman demanded in a treble boy's voice, as both Mr. Loftus and Sophia stared in shock. The man in the duster likewise produced a long revolver, and snarled, "Don't either of you move! You there, give my friend the cashbox and keep your hands where I can see them!"

Overtaken by the conviction that this couldn't possibly be real, Sophia stood frozen to the spot. In a blink of time, she stood before her brother, in his study in the Beacon Street house, he with the cold-pebble look in his eyes, she cringing helpless before the blow to fall. Mr. Loftus had no such hesitations.

"That is Fred Harvey Company property!" He answered, with indignation. "Who do you think you are, sir!"

"It's our property now," the older robber replied. "Give it over or you're a dead man."

Instead, Mr. Loftus slammed the cash box shut, and held fast, shouting, "Put away that peashooter and get the hell out of here, both of you! Robbery! We're being robbed!"

The boy with the derringer hesitated. The snub-nose barrel wavered between Sophia and Mr. Loftus. It was obvious he expected Mr. Loftus to yield up the cashbox at once, and failing that, had no notion of what to do.

"Shoot him, Bill!" the older man commanded; at that, Sophia found her voice and screamed. Several things happened at once, yet at the same time slowly, as if in pantomime. Mr. Loftus seized the cashbox in both hands and cast it with all his strength at the young robber in woman's clothes. The cashbox hit his chest with considerable force, knocking the derringer out of his hand, and fell to the ground, spilling notes and coin, while the young robber cried out in pain. The older robber cursed viciously and aimed his own revolver at Mr. Loftus. The shot crashed like a cannon in the small hallway, and Sophia screamed again.

It was not Mr. Loftus crumpling to the ground, with his dark lifeblood spurting out of a hole in his throat and his weapon spinning uselessly at Sophia's feet but the older robber. Framed in the doorway to the restaurant dining room, Fred Steinmetz lowered his own revolver; the calmest man in the room, as House staff members and a handful of guests erupted from every door, drawn by the sound of that shot.

"You – stay on the floor and keep your hands where I can see them," he ordered the younger robber, who was scrabbling on the floor after his derringer much impeded by the skirts of his unconvincing disguise. He sounded calm and conversational. "Are you folks all right?" he added. "Miss Teague, you have not come to any hurt?"

"No," Sophia replied, although her voice quivered. Fred Steinmetz holstered his own weapon and scooped up the derringer. "I thought I told you to stay on the floor," he added, in a dispassionate tone, and deftly kicked the young robber on the hip, so he fell flat, moaning on the floor. "You want to send one of of your lads for the sheriff?" he suggested, as he took Sophia's arm. "Miss Teague, you'd best sit down, you look shaken. Sorry about the mess, Loftus – he was drawing a bead on you, for sure."

"Don't worry," Mr. Loftus had recovered his composure, if only a small portion of the spilled cashbox contents. Sophia was more grateful than she could express for Mr. Steinmetz' quiet strength. Not that it was over, she found herself trembling – and if it were not for his arm around her, she feared that she would have fallen. For a horrible moment, she was not in the hallway of the Deming House, but in Richard's study. And then she was back in the present, sagging against Mr. Steinmetz, who was talking to her in German; calm, steady, comforting talk, as if he were a father comforting a small child, although it took her a few moments to make them out.

"*Sopherl*, little Sophie, you are safe now; it's all over. The Sheriff is coming. Those bandits will be taken away, soon now."

"I am all right," She felt confident enough to say, although she couldn't help thinking she would have liked to go on leaning on him for longer. She was safe with him, protected, even cherished. But then, he was a man of the world who had been everywhere, and likely faced down worse than a pair of singularly inept robbers in his time.

Chapter 15 – Haunted

The attempted robbery of the Deming Harvey House proved to be a nine-day wonder, long-remembered and recalled by everyone who had been present, every detail discussed and agreed upon. All agreed Mr. Loftus had been stalwart beyond belief; faced with two armed men and a demand for the takings for the day, and Mr. Steinmetz acted the part of the hero in so realizing the gravity of the situation and taking swift action in dispatching the most threatening of the two robbers.

"Miss Teague might have been harmed as well!" Selina Burnett exclaimed with much indignation. "Sophia dear, you look so dreadfully pale, as if you would faint away – do you want us to call for the doctor? He will attend on you at once …"

"No!" The vehemence in her own voice startled her; she shook off Selina's concern and Mr. Steinmetz arm. It was as if she were being slowly strangled in the cotton-wool of everyone's insistence she must be distraught. This was too much like how everyone had talked to her when Lucius Armitage had broken their engagement, insisting she was upset, ill, or sad when she was nothing in the least. "No, I don't need the doctor, or to go upstairs and lie down. I am perfectly well."

"You are sure?" Selina and Mr. Steinmetz both regarded her with doubt. The sheriff's deputies had just removed the body of the dead robber and taken away the live one in handcuffs, commanding Mr. Steinmetz himself to follow shortly, to answer questions. "I still think you…"

"I am fine, Selina. There is a train due. I prefer to be working."

"It's the best thing, getting on the horse that threw you," Mr. Steinmetz agreed. "But may I come and speak with you later? If you choose, come and sit with me on the platform when I bring Miss Kitten her late supper."

"I would relish that," Sophia agreed and gratefully escaped to her regular duties. The day might have been disrupted for a time by the robbery attempt, but hungry passengers cared little for that, only for a good meal, well and attentively served.

That evening, her shift completed, she slipped out of the kitchen door, saying she needed fresh air. A little light sifted onto the platform through the station and Harvey House windows. Not much to her surprise, Mr. Steinmetz sat on the same bench where he had sat on Sunday morning, watching Miss Kitten eating minced cooked chicken from the same saucer. This time, the dish was moved from the edge of the platform to the center. Beyond the overhanging station roof, the dark sky stretched to infinity, spangled with stars. A cool breeze fanned her cheeks, bringing with it the scent of dust, of sagebrush dampened by a brief wandering rain shower earlier in the day.

Miss Kitten, startled by the opening door and Sophia's quiet footsteps, looked up from the saucer, hesitating on the brink of diving for safety under the platform. But since Sophia did nothing more than sit on the bench, a little apart from Mr. Steinmetz, the cat returned to eating.

"She is tamer today," Sophia commented. "Are you moving her dish closer, each day?"

Mr. Steinmetz nodded. "When she eats from the dish at my feet, and lets me scratch behind her ears, I will find a covered basket, and put her dish into that. Once she is accustomed to the basket, and being petted, then I will take her to the ranch. She will have the time of her life, hunting for mice."

"Will your house be finished, then?"

"Perhaps. Or perhaps not. The workmen have only begun making mud-brick this week, now that the first well is finished. There is always grain where there are horses. Where there is grain, there are rats and mice."

"She looks so much like a beautiful grey kitten I wanted to keep when I was a girl," Sophia sighed. "My mother didn't permit me to have pets. She was afraid … well, afraid that I might be scratched, or something like that," she added hastily.

"You didn't live on a farm," Mr. Steinmetz replied. "There are cats enough on a farm … dogs, too; always dogs. My old pard in California had a little terrier that went everywhere with him. Good to have something in your place that's glad to see you, when you return. How was the remainder of your day, Miss Teague, after all the excitement over the robbers?"

"About the same as every other day in the Harvey House," Sophia leaned her back against the hard bench, grateful for being able to sit down, the wandering cool breeze, and Mr. Steinmetz' undemanding company. "Very long and very tiring; did you satisfy the Sheriff with your answers to his questions?"

"I believe so; the dead man is a known desperado in the Territory, with a long, long list of offenses against his name. Escaped from a couple of jails suspected or convicted for robbery, stock thieving, house-breaking, assault, arson, claim-jumping … everything except forgery, which the sheriff says requires a modicum of education. This one just had just crazy-mean in him, like a rabid dog. The young chap in a dress and bonnet was just one of those fools who drifted into bad company. He'll do a term in the territorial prison, and if he learns a lesson from it – he might yet make something better of himself."

"Such as not to disguise himself as a woman or go about in the company of human mad dogs?" Sophia couldn't repress a shudder.

"He had such a hateful look to him … eyes like pebbles, with no expression in them. He would have thought no more of shooting Mr. Loftus than of squashing a bug. I could not believe what I was seeing at first, and then that I would see eyes like…" she closed her mouth, just barely escaping mention of Richard, and the horror renewed. That momentary vision of him from six years before, superimposed over the presence of the robber in the hallway that day, had shaken her deeply. Now she wondered if she would awake tonight from that dream of Richard beating her, throwing her to the ground and choking her. She had not been ridden by that nightmare in months. "I fear I will dream about this matter, tonight."

But Mr. Steinmetz remarked, in casual sympathy, "Ah – then you have seen such before, *hein*? I did, as a boy, when Vati had sent me to live with my sister and her husband. All I could think was that I saw a man, with the evil eyes of a wolf. He was a horse-thief and certainly a murderer, which I know for certain. One had only to look at his eyes when he was on a spree for killing to know that. Mutti had told us fairy tales of such, back in Bavaria. The comfort of tales as she told us is that those creatures receive their just reward though it might take years to bring such about."

"What happened to that man, whom you knew?" Sophia asked. Yes, it was an obscure comfort to think that there was a shred of divine justice in the world; that evil men with the eyes of wild wolves, or the look of cold stone in their eyes might eventually have justice meted out to them.

"Someone shot him," Mr. Steinmetz answered. "Dead in the streets of Fredericksburg, two years after the War was over. And no one ever knew who pulled the trigger, yet everyone agreed privily that whoever had done that deed had performed a generous public service. Me, I'm a straightforward man; what I do, I'll own to doing in the face of anyone who asks. So, Miss Teague – where had you seen such a man and has justice ever been properly done to him?"

"In Boston," Sophie answered, warmed by his sympathy but guarded against saying too much; was there anyone whom she could trust since leaving Boston? Maybe Laura, in those early days with Fred Harvey Company. *Walk away and close the door. I am an orphan, without any brothers or sisters.* "He was a near relation," she confessed after a long silence in which they both watched Miss Kitten gobble the last of her meal, and scamper cat-like, under the edge of the platform, into whatever safe burrow she had. "Closer than a cousin, and raised in the same household, but … he had the same look, the same expression in his eyes, when it came to savaging the powerless. He was a well-respected man in Boston society, with wealth and many friends, so he continued in his habits for many years. Eventually, I think it came out, and he was snubbed in the streets. I read in the newspapers long afterwards he killed himself after setting the house on fire to burn around him."

"You see, Miss Teague? Given time, the devil claims his own."

"Yes, but he took his wife and two sons with him in the burning house," Sophia replied. "Sometimes I wonder if there is a taint in the blood and that his sons or other relative show the same taint in time."

"Men are not like cows or dogs," Mr. Steinmetz shook his head. "Neither are women. Oh, maybe in a small way, as far as an appearance goes, for light hair or dark, or their features. That will carry on, generation after generation. You have only to look at my sister's children or their Vining cousins to see the family likenesses. But I have known too many brothers, or sons of fathers whose character and temperaments were completely dissimilar; improvident wastrels with worthy sons, and sensible men with shiftless and quarrelsome brothers to wholly believe in inheritable character. We are each our own man, or woman."

Sophia considered his words for a long moment, vaguely comforted by his assurance. Richard's character was an anxiety which had begun to haunt her. With all the advantages of family and position, how was he capable of such horrific deeds; from earliest childhood at that, according to Great-Aunt Minnie's account of how Richard had savaged Mama's cage of songbirds.

"I hope you are correct," she said, at long last. "You are terribly wise – experienced in the practical things of life. Mr. Steinmetz, I believe that you must have received a fairer portion of that capacity between your twin and yourself than you believe."

"Then will you sleep soundly tonight, Miss Teague?"

"I hope I shall," Sophia replied, as she stood. She had best not linger. Selina would be closing and locking the upstairs door into their quarters in another five minutes. Mr. Steinmetz rose, just as she did. "Thank you for so kindly indulging my megrims. It seems little to you, I am sure, but I am grateful for your understanding. Today was extremely distressing."

"Always a pleasure to be of service to you, Miss Teague," he replied, and although his tone was light, Sophia sensed that there was a strong emotion underlying it. But he did nothing more than take her hand and kiss it with Continental gallantry. "You are not altogether unexperienced in practical matters of life yourself. We shall meet here on Sunday, at the appropriate hour, so I may escort you to services at St. Lukes'?"

"If course," she replied, with demure good humor. "It appears that you were correct – that Deming is still a very rough frontier town."

In spite of her apprehensions, she slept soundly that night, and in the morning the only recollection she had of her dreams was that in them, Mr. Steinmetz was accompanying her on a journey, and on that account she was perfectly secure. On Sunday morning, she dressed for church and emerged at the same hour as the previous Sunday to find him sitting on the same bench, observing Miss Kitten, whose dish was six inches closer to his position.

"Patience is the key," he replied, when she remarked on this. "She's near to a wild thing and not inclined to be trusting."

"You sound as if you have experience in taming wild things," Sophia put her hand into the crook of his elbow as he offered it, and he grinned like a mischievous schoolboy. "A little; you should be warned, Miss Teague – Lottie has extended an invitation to dinner after the service. I have accepted for myself. Will you dine with us?"

"I most certainly will accept her kind invitation," Sophia exclaimed, joyful anticipation springing up in her heart. "Last Sunday was such a happy experience, and hers and Mr. Thurmond's hospitality was so enjoyable – yes, I relish the prospect!"

"That is good," Mr. Steinmetz patted her hand, in the crook of his elbow. "Lottie is a good sort, a good friend; if it were not for her, Frank, and you, I'd not have any social life in this place."

"Everyone in Deming comes to the Harvey House," Sophia remarked, as they set off on their walk towards St. Luke's. She had a parasol which she unfurled as they set out from under the sheltering shade of the station platform. "I have seen Lottie – Mrs. Thurmond – several times in the restaurant this week. She and some of the other ladies of town come in for coffee in the morning or tea in the late afternoon."

"It is the place to see, and be seen," Mr. Steinmetz agreed, with a reminiscent sigh. "A Demonicos of the distant territory. When I was a boy, our center of social life was the casino-ballroom of the grandest hotel in Fredericksburg, and the beer-garden in the garden next to it. Captain Nimitz kept a grand state and knew everyone of importance. We had concerts and theatrical performances in the hotel ballroom –

and that in a town not much larger than this. No railway then, you see. The Hill Country was then the back of beyond though there were many people of culture living there at the time."

"It sounds as if it were pleasant and civilized, in spite of the hardships of the western frontier," Sophia answered, considering her memories of Boston. "Not all bandits and gunfights in the streets and Indians raiding!"

"Little of that," Mr. Steinmetz agreed. "Not to say it doesn't happen, but you should tell me of Boston, Miss Teague. Surely you had family – schooldays – excursions which you recall with pleasure. I cannot believe that you sprang into being in a single day at the Newton Harvey House; a Venus on a shell, drifting into shore."

"Certainly not!" Sophia's mild indignation gave way to giggles, at such a mental image. "I had a pleasant childhood, I believe as such things go. My father died in the War before I was born. But he left my mother well-off until the failure of the Marine Bank. I believe that we lived happily enough; I went to school, had many dear friends; a quiet secure life, with many simple pleasures and amusements. My great-aunt was a treasure, and fond of me." She immersed herself in those fond and untroubled memories, pouring them out to Mr. Steinmetz, the sympathetic listener, as they walked along towards St. Luke's. Only when they approached the modest spire, did she wind them up and tuck in the inconvenient ends, having omitted mention of Richard. "My dear mother died when I was in my nineteenth year, and it turned out I had to accept the charity of close kin and work in their household; work hard and for little reward. As arduous as the hours are for us in the Fred Harvey Company, I consider that we are well-paid and generously compensated with other privileges. I came out West as soon as I was twenty-one, and have been pleased with my decision to do so ever since."

"And so are we all, who frequent the Harvey Houses," Mr. Steinmetz replied, with the gallantry which he displayed in brief flashes. "There is Lottie and Frank waiting for us on the steps. Miss Teague," he added in a low voice. "It would please me no end, if you developed a firm friendship with Lottie. She is a good sort, a lady by any lights and completely blameless but she spent years dealing cards in gambling hells across Texas. There are none among the ladies of Deming who have kicked over the traces as you both have. Indeed, there are some – who if they knew of it, might be inclined to hold that against her, or so my reading of things such as society in a small Western town advises."

"The curse of respectability," Sophia sighed, in amused sympathy. "As my great-aunt termed it; she gave abolition and temperance lectures in public when doing such things was held to be as much of a disgrace for a lady of good family as it was to deal cards in western saloons. I would say to Mrs. Thurmond to do as my great-aunt did, saying often, 'Make of it what you will, my conscience is clean. The time, occasion and the cause demanded it!'"

"That's the spirit," Mr. Steinmetz smiled in approval. "She sounds like a firecracker, your great-aunt. You and Lottie are of the same kind of womanhood, so I think you will get on well."

That last was said in a murmur as they approached the lower steps of St. Luke. In a moment, Lottie Thurmond swept down the steps, a white swan in a waterless world, and embraced Sophia in a sweet-smelling embrace.

"Dear Miss Teague!" She exclaimed, "You have returned! We so enjoyed your company last week, pray Mr. Steinmetz has told you of our standing invitation for supper this afternoon? How marvelous – he has! Come and sit with us? You cannot be a stranger, pleading the press of your duties…"

"Sunday is my day of rest," Sophia replied, and Lottie beamed upon her in fond approval.

"And rightfully so, Miss Teague!" Just then, the bell above their heads chimed sweetly for services, and Lottie Thurmond whispered,

"At supper, then!" and embraced Sophia again. "Afterwards – a game of whist? The good reverend Lloyd shall join us in a friendly game. Poor man, he must return to his home this afternoon in order to conduct services there, so he cannot remain for long."

"That is not a game I play," Sophia whispered in protest, and Lottie replied, "Then I shall teach you – amusements are so infrequent here, you see. And Fred enjoys a good game – don't you, Fred?"

"Shush, Lottie," Mr. Steinmetz hissed, sounding most particularly severe.

"I will not shush," Lottie Thurmond replied. "But if you have lately discovered a disapproval of playing cards, we should take a ride into the country instead, and see the beginnings of this house of yours. You have told us of that lovely spring, back in the hills above your property … I know," she exclaimed, in a whisper as they went into the sanctuary. "We shall have a picnic out there, instead!"

"Lottie, sweeting, your supper menu is decided upon and guests invited," Frank Thurmond whispered.

"Next Sunday, then," Lottie replied, and they went into church and settled into a single pew, all in a row. The familiar words of the service and the music of the hymns gave such unexpected comfort to Sophia at least as much as the presence of Mr. Steinmetz on one side, and Lottie Thurmond on the other. She felt herself doubly fortunate, in having come to Deming after a long series of wanderings across the west.

And that next week, after services at St. Luke's – they did go on a long drive from the huddle of buildings, the shining steel tangle of rails, and the turning silver wheels that pumped up water, sprouting in and around Deming like some exotic breed of metal daisy. They went in company with neighbors of the Thurmond's; a young couple named Woods and their two children.

"You have not said anything regarding your ranch!" Lottie called to Mr. Steinmetz, as the road out of town towards the south began to rise gradually into the tumbled foothills at the base of a range of mountains as ragged as broken glass. Frank Thurmont sat in the driver's seat of the resplendently stylish buggy; Mr. Steinmetz, in his town suit, no less, rode one of his own ranch horses. His chosen mount for this excursion and Sophia intuited that was his accustomed habit, was a mere and scrawny cow-pony of no appearance and no good breeding, but well-fed and well-mannered, obedient to every command.

"Not much to say at this time, Lottie – Miss Teague, Mrs. Woods – two corrals, a well and barn and a great pile of drying adobe bricks."

"But full of potential," Frank Thurmond pointed out. "Any potential for a copper or silver strike."

"Haven't looked for color," Mr. Steinmetz admitted. "I had enough of that kind of game when I was a young feller in California."

"Ellie, you mind your manners with Miss Teague," Eleanor Woods chided her daughter, who leaned confidingly against Sophia, at the expense of crushing the ruffles of her walking dress. "Sit up straight, like a lady."

"I don't mind," Sophia answered. Truly she didn't. Ellie was eight and full of artless worship. Her company reminded Sophia of Richie. She thought wistfully of how pleasant it would be, a life with children in it. The only children she had anything to do with since departing from Boston were the occasional family traveling together. Richie had been such a good little boy. He must be eighteen by now, she realized with something of a start. Entirely grown-up, and likely altogether too much like his father.

She adjusted the angle of her parasol to cast some shade on Ellie as well as herself. The wheels of the buggy cast up a small cloud of dust in their wake.

"The old Butterfield stages used to run this way, before the railroad came through," Frank Thurmond explained. "Because of the water. I know it doesn't look all that much like a garden but there is water to be found if you know where to look for it."

"I came past this place with the Fabreaux herd in '55," Mr. Steinmetz called, from the saddle of his pony. "Near enough, or close to it. We saw a flash-flood come roaring out of the mountains from a storm that happened miles away, and not a drop on us. Never set up camp in one of these dry riverbeds, our trail-boss told us."

"Wouldn't you be afraid, building your house too close to the mountains?" Eleanor Woods asked, and Mr. Steinmetz laughed.

"On a patch above the arroyo – the only water I'll have at the home-place is the rain on the roof and from the well … we're nearly there, ladies – but in plain fact, there isn't much to see as yet."

Mr. Steinmetz' ranch was not a terribly impressive sight, with little to differentiate it from acres of desert sagebrush on either side, save only a tall metal tower with a windmill endlessly turning, and a scattering of spindly bushes large enough to consider as small trees, which cast a few patches of shade. There was evidence of work started in the way of a crude plank-built stable nearby, and row upon row of large oblongs set on end, the color of the desert earth.

"It is a good thing, Fred, that you have not raised our expectations terribly high," Lottie said. "I can't think what drove you to select this particular place."

"Old habits of thinking of defensibility and a good water well," Mr. Steinmetz replied, with wry amusement. "And a liking to see the mountains; there's open land to the edge of the arroyo. It'll take some doing for some bandito to sneak up on me. By the end of summer, the lads say they'll have the walls up and the roof-beams in. Come back then, you'll see another aspect of it entirely. You will come back again, won't you, ladies?"

"I will," Sophia heard herself replying. Really, she could tell that Mr. Steinmetz was embarrassed by the poor showing of his place. To cheer him up in that regard was the least she could do.

"I'll take that as a promise then," he said, but light and casual, as if he had no means of binding her to that.

Chapter 16 – Summer in Deming

Frank Thurmond, at the reins of the buggy, followed Mr. Steinmetz' horse up a narrow and dusty track which first crossed the arroyo and then re-crossed it so many times that Sophia lost track. A thin trickle of water ran from pool to pool somewhere in the center of a stretch of tumbled rock and gravel as the narrow worn track mounted gradually into the foothills. The abrupt and jagged slopes of a brief mountain range frowned upon them from the near horizon – hard blue shapes, as craggy as if chipped from slabs of glass. Almost imperceptibly, their party had mounted into the foothills; still gently rounded hills, hardly worth the name, but the horses were put to an effort to pull. By this Sophia knew they were going up. They came around to the top of a low knoll where appeared a distant aspect of Deming, spread before their eyes as if in a life-sized bird's-eye view map. The sun struck distant silver glints from the turning windmill wheels – that and a few birds wheeling on motionless wings high in the sky above being the only sign of life.

"Only a little farther," Mr. Steinmetz reined in, and spoke over his shoulder. "See the top of that tree? There are a couple of cottonwoods up there, by the only year-round spring I can find. I've come up sometimes of an early morning, hunting venison, but haven't bagged one yet. I always change my mind about shooting them when all they want is a nice cool drink of water."

"You're disgustingly sentimental, Fred," Frank Thurmond said, in slight disparagement. "Animals were put on earth so we could make use of 'em."

"I make use of them," Mr. Steinmetz responded, without heat. "It gives me a mighty pleasure, to sit and watch them, fine and strong and proud, going about their business."

"You'll go hungry in winter, Fred," Frank Thurmond replied, and Mr. Steinmetz laughed. "What use is it to gut and dress a whole deer, and smoke the meat over a fire, since it is more than I can eat in a month myself, when I can just go into town and get a good meal at Fred Harvey's without a tenth of the trouble? Priorities, Frank. Priorities; now I have the luxury, I might as well take full advantage." He grinned at Sophia. Moved by sympathy for small and large wild things and approval of Mr. Steinmetz' sensibilities, she said, "I think it noble of you, to do so. There are wise old philosophers who believed that it is healthier and even morally superior to abstain from meat in any form."

"I won't say I take it that far, Miss Teague!" Mr. Steinmetz laughed so heartily that Sophia might have taken offense; save that there was not a hint of insult in his words or tone. "I am in the cattle ranching business. I relish a good bit if beefsteak, or a pork cutlet as well as any man, especially when it is cooked in a Fred Harvey kitchen and brought by one of his pretty waiter girls!"

"It is always a pleasure to set a meal before a man who appreciates good cooking," Sophia replied, only realizing when the words were out of her mouth she did sound terribly flirtatious. But it was not Mr. Steinmetz who took another meaning from that, but Eleanor Woods, who blurted, in tones over which a slight touch of frost hovered,

"I did not realize, Miss Teague – that you were employed by the Harvey House. You seem like such a respectable person."

"Miss Teague is a respectable person, Ellie," Lottie Thurmond leaped into the conversation with a tinkling little laugh, turning her head from the front seat of the buggy where she sat next to her husband. "And I relish her company. She is one of these New Women you read so much about in the magazines."

"I suppose so," Eleanor Wood's voice thawed, although she still sounded dubious. "It doesn't seem quite right to go away from your family, and work for wages."

"I'm an orphan, with no close living relatives," Sophia replied, as if by rote. "I consider Fred Harvey Company as my family."

"But still," Eleanor Wood persisted. "It still seems strange – even if for family, doing work in the public sphere. A woman's proper place is in the home."

Mr. Steinmetz snorted in derision. "Tell that to my sister and niece. They worked in the family general store while my brother-in-law and I drove freight wagons. Later, when my niece married, she took to trailing cattle north with her husband. As for the Vining boys – <u>their</u> mother kept a boarding house, and by all accounts she was a fine woman indeed. You'd meet the most important men in Texas at her table. No angel of the hearthside business for them. There was too much to do."

"That was in the West, before everything was settled as it should be," Eleanor Wood argued. "Conditions were different than in the east, then…"

"So they are still," Lottie Thurmond agreed. "And long may continue to be, for I favor such a wider degree of freedom, and I am certain so does Miss Teague. Is this your darling little spring, Fred?"

During that conversation, the buggy had come around another turn in the rough track, and now they looked full on a steep rock hillside, with a pool of water at its base, rimmed by smaller rocks, and stands of water-loving reeds. A narrow white thread of water fell through a ragged cleft between two rock faces, which were painted with small blotches of velvety green moss. The sound of the water, splashing and chuckling to itself was musical, entrancing as the scent of cool fresh water – cool water and a patch of green grass. Poplar leaves rustled in the light breeze over their heads, and small insects hovered over the water's surface, their wings catching brief glints of gold in the spotty sunlight. The air in the little dell felt deliciously damp after the aridity of the open desert around town. The wagon track went no farther than here, for the hillsides closing in all around were too precipitous for any but a single man on foot. The little dell was adorned with bright green vines, spotted with red and blue flowers, hanging along the steep rock slope, and a few straggly bushes covered with yellow blooms which looked like daisies – as lovely a wild garden as could be wished for in the west.

"It's beautiful!" Sophia's breath caught in her throat, overwhelmed by a sudden longing for the verdant green landscapes and gardens of the east. Mr. Steinmetz hastily tied up his pony and reached up to help Sophia from the buggy.

"Do you think so?" he asked, and Lottie Thurmond replied,

"A more perfect place for a picnic luncheon can hardly be imagined than your little paradise, Fred."

"It is the most perfect place," Sophia echoed. Mr. Steinmetz was most ridiculously pleased by her approval. Lottie, looking on them both with a benevolent expression, continued briskly, "Fetch us the basket, Fred, and the rugs. Frank wishes to try his hand with his new fishing rod."

"There aren't any fish there save minnows," Mr. Steinmetz warned and Frank Thurmond hissed, "Not another word from you, spoil-sport!"

Mr. Steinmetz shook his head in pity and handed down little Ellie from the buggy. "There are some tiny little frogs, though," he added. "And one morning, I saw a wild jaguar-cat come to drink."

Ellie gave a small squeak of dismay, and her mother exclaimed, "Surely there is not any danger to us, Mr. Steinmetz!"

"Only if it diverts you to imagine so, Mrs. Wood; they are nocturnal creatures and normally shy of humans." He sounded exasperated; Sophia recalled his impatience with what he called female megrims. Of course, as a man of the world and long experience of the west, he would have encountered many more ferocious and dangerous animals.

"I'd love to see such a beautiful creature as a jaguar," she said, slightly breathless. "Not as in a zoo, as in Boston, but wild and free; here – just as you watched the deer."

"He won't come today, that I can assure you, Miss Teague." He smiled at her, the corners of his eyes crinkling in a most endearing way. "Wish I could whistle him up for a visit here, just for you. Another time?"

"Perhaps, Fred," Lottie replied, just as briskly. "Sophie and Eleanor, my dears – can you assist me with setting up our feast? The gentlemen are hungry – there should not be any great labor involved, for my cook has packed every kind of delicious food, and it will not take any time at all."

"Miss Teague is well acquainted with the method of serving food in a small amount of time," Eleanor Wood purred, in a tone of lazy malice, but there was no sting in it. Sophia, overtaken by a sudden fit of school-girl emotion, stuck her tongue out at her, behind Lottie's back. Eleanor Wood's expression went through a brisk series from startled, through pique, and finally to rueful humor. She stuck out her own tongue, and then both of them burst into giggles.

"If you are both finished with being childish," Lottie replied, without turning around, "The gentlemen are hungry. And so am I."

"The schoolmistress has eyes in the back of her head, so she has!" Eleanor whispered, Lottie stated, without turning around, "No – only one which works properly to the front, but my hearing is extraordinarily acute," whereupon all three women dissolved into giggles. Young Ellie and the two men regarded them, baffled as if they had gone quite mad.

Before Frank Thurmond assembled his fishing rod or Mr. Steinmetz lighted his pipe, the gentlemen helped unfold and spread several heavy horse blankets onto the ground, and unfolded a number of camp chairs. There was a hammock, strung between two cottonwood trees, from which Frank Thurmond lazily cast his line over the pond. Lottie's cook provided a huge wicker hamper filled with all manner of good things packed on top of a small block of ice wrapped in a length of waterproof canvas at the bottom of the basket to keep them chilled; sandwiches of chicken and ham salad, wrapped in paper tied with a ribbon, hard-boiled eggs, plain bread and butter, cheese, and two kinds of cake, to be washed down with cold tea and lemonade.

"Pure bliss," Lottie sighed, reclined like a fashionably clad odalisque on several cushions, with a glass of iced lemonade in hand and a plate of cake at her side. "A divine way to spend the remainder of the Sabbath; the only thing lacking is a small orchestra, just out of sight, playing tasteful music for our entertainment."

"I could become fond of this place," Sophia said, to no one in particular. Meanwhile, Ellie hunted for those little frogs, and minnows, who flicked their way across the shallows, after having removed her shoes and stockings at Eleanor's bidding. Lottie, Eleanor and Sophie took their ease; a breath of relaxation, of relishing good food, cool peace and shade, the engaging sound of falling water in the little dell.

"I am certain she will fall into the water," Eleanor sighed in resignation. "And I will have to repair her dress, after sending it to the laundry. She is such the tom-boy; I do not know how to discipline her to ladylike demeanor when my husband is so indulgent!"

"She is a spirited girl," Mr. Steinmetz took his pipe from his mouth. "And Mr. Wood is wise. It's a pity to hamper high spirits in any child – boy or girl – such quality being rare enough as it is."

"I'd agree with Fred," Lottie said, her sweet southern drawl sounding particularly pronounced. "To crush the spirit of a girl – not knowing what the future may hold, and that her fate might require that she may have need of every ounce. Your Ellie is a charming child. Little dresses are easily mended."

"But he encourages her to such unseemly behavior!" Eleanor was not comforted. Lottie replied, "Your husband is a respectable merchant, and in a good and stable trade. Now <u>my</u> father taught me to play cut-throat poker, which in general opinion today is far, far more unseemly than forgetting lady-like demeanor. We are now at peace in this land, and can afford our children every indulgence. The old Puritans are long-gone – let Ellie play as she wishes."

"Yes, do," Sophia echoed, wistfully. "So many were the times, Eleanor – I wish my dear mama would have permitted me to do the same. Only … Boston, where poor children went without shoes, and we could not be thought poor! My great-aunt allowed me to go barefoot at the beach at Newport, and build sand-castles, and I so enjoyed that brief liberty. And it is such a lovely day, today!"

"Then we will do this again this summer," Lottie said, with the decisive air of someone giving an order. "As often as Mr. Steinmetz's duties permit."

"My house is yours," Mr. Steinmetz sketched a brief salute from his own chair. "In it's current and future condition alike. And my little paradise garden as well. As often as you wish."

As often as you wish; over the summer, the Thurmonds, with Sophia and Mr. Steinmetz, and the Woods – occasionally other friends and their families from St. Luke's – picnicked at the spring every two or three weeks. No matter how the fierce sun blazed upon them, the spring falling from the cleft in the rocks never faltered, although towards the end of summer the water flow lessened by half, and the pool diminished in size, edged by a band of dried water-weeds. Still, it remained cool, the breeze fanned their cheeks and the water-loving dragon-flies hovered like marvelous, gem-eyed brooches wrought of bronze. To Mr. Steinmetz's obvious pride, and the ladies' interest, the walls of his house began to rise from the leveled site upon which it was to stand, first waist-high, then, head-high and above, until there came the day in autumn when he invited them to pause and walk around between the walls and explore the rooms and open verandah which would surround them – as it now was close enough to completion that the interior spaces – parlor, dining room, a kitchen, a small office and three other rooms on either side of a long hallway which went the entire length of the structure – could be imagined easily in their finished condition.

"They're bringing in lumber for the roof-beams next week," he said, on that particular Sunday. "I've two wagons of shakes for the roof on hand. Next week, they fit the windows and doors. It must be completed before winter begins, lest the rain reduce it all to mud again."

"Why didn't you not build in lumber from the beginning, Fred. It would have saved time and trouble," Lottie commented. "You'd have a house finished and ready to move into!"

Mr. Steinmetz shook his head. "No, this is best suited to this country, for the trouble of construction – warm in winter, cool in the summer. It's in my nature to think stone or brick are more secure for building a comfortable house, although it might not be so pretty as one of your adorned wooden beauties – even once inside and out are plastered over."

"I think it will be a charming a house," Sophia spoke up in agreement. With walls two feet thick, the Steinmetz establishment was as solid as a fortress of old. By some consideration of builder and designer – Mr. Steinmetz himself? Every tall window or doorway looked out upon a marvelous view; towards the jagged heights of the mountain-ranges, the wandering and green-fringed line of the arroyo, or the distant view of Deming, a smudge of wood-smoke, bright-metal or split-shake roofs, and the ever-turning windmills. "Even newly finished, I want it to appear as if it has been here since the beginning of time."

"How are you going to furnish this palace of yours, Fred?" Frank Thurmond enquired, as they returned to the buggy and continued their journey across the arroyo towards the spring.

"With the usual sort of things, I expect," Mr. Steinmetz replied, candidly. "I was hoping for ladies to assist me with advice. I have catalogues from the east. I brought them with me today, 'smatter of fact. Perfectly fine things they have in them, but I'm blessed if I have any idea of what would suit, and be most useful. I've never set up a household for myself – it's always been bachelor rooms, boarding houses, my sisters' houses or sleeping on the ground under a wagon. I know as much about setting up a comfortable household as I know about building a railroad which is to say, nothing more than buying a ticked and boarding."

"You should have asked us before, silly man," Lottie exclaimed. "We would be happy to look at your catalogs and make up lists of what is best required."

"Just mark the catalogue and how many of each," Mr. Steinmetz untied his horse from the wheel of the buggy, as Frank Thurmond and Mr. Wood – who had come with his wife and daughter today – helped the ladies from the buggy. Sophia couldn't help noticing that Mr. Steinmetz looked to be inordinately pleased with himself.

"Like Tom Sawyer, after having persuaded his friends to whitewash the fence for him," Sophia murmured to Eleanor Wood, who began giggling.

Once arrived at the spring, Mr. Steinmetz produced a thick sheaf of catalogues and circulars from his saddlebags and presented them, saying, “Into your hands, my dear ladies, I present every hope for the future comfort of my house. Treat me kindly, I beg – and my pocketbook, too. This will be a simple ranch residence and not a palace – but I want it to be a place where I can invite family and guests without feeling apologetic for fear they think they might have to rough it.”

“Our pleasure, Fred; our most very enjoyable pleasure,” Lottie embraced him. “Now, set out the chairs and the hammock, and we shall begin our review of your household needs.”

“One question, then?” Sophia ventured. “How many sleeping chambers?”

“Three; one for me, two for … guests. The little room at the end of the hall is meant to be an office for ranch business.”

“Well, they are all of a good size, but that one,” Lottie said.

That afternoon was most happily spent, in drawing up a list of required furniture; both Lottie and Eleanor had decided notions on that, but Sophia’s bent toward simplicity and utility better matched with Mr. Steinmetz’ preference, on those instances when they simply had to appeal to him.

“Great heavens, it looks like something from the better sort of parlor … parlor gambling house,” he exclaimed, when shown the page picturing an elaborately carved suite of parlor furniture. “No, I prefer Miss Teague’s choice in this regard … although,” he added, “Yes to that large model kitchen stove.” He read the description with close attention. “Hot water boiler, five burners, bread-warming oven; if there were any more fanciful bits added to that stove, it might cook supper by itself.”

"For a kitchen stove, the bigger, and the fancier, the better," Lottie turned the page. "Fred, will you have any books requiring accommodation?"

"I might," Mr. Steinmetz replied, after a sideways glance at Sophia.

"Well, you'll have ledgers in your office," Lottie ticked a particular page in the catalogue. "So one shelf at least; that kind with the glass doors to protect the books."

"I think books look well in a parlor," Sophia ventured hesitantly. "Or any room where it is comfortable to sit and read."

Lottie made a note on the page. "Three bookshelves then," she said. Mr. Steinmetz winced comically.

The list of household furnishings lengthened; tables for the parlor and kitchen, a stove, patent ice-box cupboard, dresser and stove for the kitchen, a settee and armchairs, bookshelves, chairs both plain and upholstered, bedsteads, washstands and armoires for each bedroom, a coat-rack for the hallway. Mr. Steinmetz possessed a desk and other oddments, but little else in the way of household necessities.

Lottie sighed, upon hearing this. "Give me a pencil and a piece of paper, Fred – I shall begin making a list. Sheets, blankets, towels; I suppose that you have no kitchen things or china and silverware…"

"Oh, I'll ask my sister to make up a list of those," Mr. Steinmetz answered. "I daresay that she and my nephew George can pull them from the warehouse and send them along. It is just the main furnishings I needed you ladies' expert opinion on. I have to get everything settled and moved in by spring round-up. That's when I'll move in."

"I will …" Sophia began, and then stopped, suddenly hesitant.

"Will what?" Mr. Steinmetz asked, with apparent casualness.

"I will miss seeing you in the restaurant, every day," Sophia confessed. Mr. Steinmetz replied, grinning with his usual boyish air,

"Oh, I will be in and out, and I will faithfully escort you to services every Sunday. Do you know what? Miss Teague, I think you should learn to ride. If you are going to be a Westerner, you should be able to sit a horse, properly."

"I do not have a side-saddle!" Sophia protested. Lottie said, "Much less trouble to wear a split-skirt and ride astride, as men do – it's safer out here."

"We can go farther up into the hills for picnics," Mr. Steinmetz suggested, "Farther than we can go in a buggy … and there are prettier springs and waterfalls farther up into the mountains than this one here."

"I wouldn't have thought it possible," Lottie exclaimed. "Do say that you will, Sophia dear. It will be wonderful. Nothing is as invigorating as a good ride."

"I'm afraid I should fall off," Sophia quailed.

"Nonsense; show her, Fred. Show her how easy it is. Put Sophia up on your horse …"

"I'm wearing my best dress, Lottie!" Sophia protested, and Lottie relented. "Very well then – bring a shirtwaist with you next week, and I'll loan you one of my riding skirts."

Sophia yielded gracefully; in point of fact, she did want to learn to ride. The Brewer income was too reduced to afford a ladies' riding horse and saddle when she became of an age to learn. She had envied Emma Chase's possession of a pony and series of fashionable riding habits; now was her chance to sample those experiences which had never been permitted to her, back in Boston.

Chapter 17 – The Man from Pinkerton

The following Sunday morning, Sophia folded her oldest shirtwaist into the largest of her reticules and went to meet Mr. Steinmetz for the walk to church. It was the end of summer, and Miss Kitten had advanced in domesticated friendliness to the point where she ate from the saucer, a mere ten inches from Mr. Steinmetz's booted feet, and only look up for a single wary moment when Sophia opened the door.

"She is tame," Sophia remarked. She would miss tiny, smoke-grey Miss Kitten, now so domesticated that she could endure the brief touch of a human hand, scratching behind her delicate grey and pink-silk ears. "When are you going to take her to your house?"

"As soon as the roof is done, and the doors and windows installed," Mr. Steinmetz stood, offering Sophia his elbow. "Next week, I shall begin the task of accustoming her to the basket. Once the carpenters are done, and the place is quiet. I would not want her to be frightened by noise and run away. The coyotes are dreadful bold – I believe they would take a poor little cat in broad daylight."

"Wait until your furniture is delivered," Sophia advised. "For that will be another great festival of noise and disruption."

"Excellent suggestion, Miss Teague." Mr. Steinmetz patted her hand, where it lay in the crook of his elbow. "Now – are you ready for a riding lesson, this afternoon?"

"I believe so," Sophia replied. She must have sounded apprehensive, for Mr. Steinmetz chuckled. "Don't worry; I have brought the gentlest and most well-mannered of our ponies for your first lesson."

"I fear I may be too old to really learn a new skill," Sophia worried, and Mr. Steinmetz chuckled again. "I did not learn properly until I was the age of eleven or twelve, but I was hardly out of the saddle from that time on. I am not half the teacher that my brother-in-law was, but I won't be trying to teach you some of the trick-riding stunts he did! It's practice, to accustom you to the saddle, Miss Teague – that's all."

To her vague surprise – no, it was neither particularly difficult nor especially frightening, when she came from having changed her dress in Lottie's guest bedroom for her old shirtwaist and the split riding skirt which Lottie provided as she said she would. Mr. Steinmetz led the pony from the stable behind the Thurmond's house, saddled and bridled – as he had promised, a gentle and well-mannered beast. In the absence of a mounting block, Mr. Steinmetz made a stirrup-step of his hands and boosted her up into the saddle – where she felt faintly dizzy at first, sitting so far above the ground, tiny movements of the horse shifting underneath her reminding at every moment she was sitting on the back of a live creature. Mr. Steinmetz then set each of her feet properly into the stirrups, and showed her how to hold the reins in her left hand and at the proper length, while Frank and Lottie Thurmond hovered like protective parents over a much-loved child.

"Hold your hand palm-up," Mr. Steinmetz instructed her. "One rein on either side of your first finger … that's it. Now, close your fist. This little girl is neck-trained in the western fashion – so if you will have her go to the right, touch the rein against the left side of her neck. If you will have her go left – touch the rein to the right side of her neck. To have her stop, pull back evenly … gently now!" he added as Sophia attempted to follow his instructions. "Like that – and she will back up! No – just a gentle pull on the bit as she is moving."

"How do I make her move?" Sophia asked; this was going to be a flat failure – riding a horse! Then she remembered that first day in the Newton Harvey House. After that, she could do anything. Everyone rode horses in the west! Indians rode horses, boys who couldn't spell their names rode horses, men rode horses everywhere and all over the country! Now she attempted it, perhaps it would come to her easily. She was one of these New Women.

"You nudge her ribs with your heels," Mr. Steinmetz answered, "But be careful in this, for the more emphatically you do so, the faster she will go. If you would like, I will take her on a leading-rein until you become used to the balance and feel."

"No – I shall start as I mean to go on," Sophia replied, the example and memory of Great-Aunt Minnie telling her about the feelings she had, before her first Abolitionist lecture; a mere woman, speaking in public – no, if Minnie had the nerve for that, then her niece must also for the simpler challenge of riding a horse astride. She nudged the small and gentle cow-pony with her heels, and to her secret relief, the pony stepped forward.

"Good!" Mr. Steinmetz exclaimed, and in relieved triumph, Sophia directed the obedient pony to walk around, and around the Thurmond's stable-yard.

"May I ride out with her to our lovely spring?" Sophia asked, wondering if she really glowed like an electric lantern from that small success.

"Yes, of course," Mr. Steinmetz replied. "But as soon as you feel the slightest ache – ride in the buggy. You will feel the unaccustomed position and exercise … probably in the next few hours, rather than right away, but it will be painful."

"I don't care," Sophia was enjoying this too much. She and Mr. Steinmetz rode ahead of the buggy, elbow to elbow. As always, she relished the short journey itself, the angular and jagged aspect of the mountains, the breeze in her face, and in a small way, the mastery of her previous apprehension.

"You have a natural seat," Mr. Steinmetz observed, with approval. "Are you up to a short canter? That's a smooth enough gait for a beginner."

"I do!" Sophia exclaimed. She nudged the pony's flanks. To her exhilaration, the pony leaped forward – and it was like a bird flying on the edge of the wind, soaring and wheeling effortlessly. Mr. Steinmetz was at her side in a moment, looking between them, and laughing like a boy.

"What do you think?" He called, and Sophia answered, gasping,

"It's marvelous – I could go on like this forever!"

They came up on the turn in the track which led to the spring, and slowed the horses to a walk again, Mr. Steinmetz still laughing.

"You don't want to push too hard on the first day, Miss Teague – for you will know it in the morning for sure."

"I might at that," Sophia admitted, flushed pink with the excitement of the brief canter, and her hair sliding from its pins. "But I'm having so much fun now, that I don't care."

"That's the spirit!" He replied. Though he was correct, and Sophia did begin to feel the effects of unaccustomed exercise almost at once – no, she really didn't care.

"Miss T., There's a man asking for you by name," Elsie Watkins said, breathlessly. "He didn't say why; just it was urgent that he speak to you. Life and death, he said." The mid-morning train had just pulled out, leaving relative silence behind, a swift-dissipating streak of grey coal-smoke from the smokestack and the usual disorder in the dining room – a disorder being banished even as Elsie spoke. It was several weeks after Sophia's first riding lesson, and the first cool weather of autumn had come on Deming.

"You have a smudge on your apron, Elsie," Sophia reproved her, her eye sweeping the abandoned dining room. She couldn't imagine who Elsie could mean. The room was empty of customers, even if only for the moment. "As soon as you have the last table cleared, go and change it at once. I don't see anyone."

"He's in the office," Elsie looked abashed. "Not in the parlor. He said it was a private matter an' told me to be discreet. Miss T., there ain't been trouble at home for one o' the girls!"

"No, he'd have asked for Mr. Loftus, as manager and he would have sent for me," Sophia answered. Her heart skipped a beat. Life and death; what could that mean unless this man was being melodramatic. "Since he has asked for me, it must be a personal matter."

"Miss T.," Elsie's eyes rounded. "Is there trouble at your home, maybe?"

"I don't see how there could be," Sophia answered with a brisk assurance covering inward apprehension. "I am an orphan, with no close living kin. Did this man give a name? Is he from Boston? Perhaps he was a friend of my family."

"A Mr. Siringo," Elsie replied. "He doesn't sound like a Yankee; not like you, Miss. T. I's say he's a Southerner, a Texan, maybe."

"I'd best not keep him waiting," Sophia patted her hair. "I hope he does not have lengthy business. We have an hour until the next train."

The man waiting for her in Mr. Loftus's office turned, as she opened the door. He had been looking out of the window, his gaze fixed on the endless sweep of desert beyond the station platform, and the mountains blue-violet in the distance, a ragged edge of torn blotting-paper against the sky.

"Mr. Siringo, Elsie said that you had a matter of importance to discuss with me," Sophia closed the door behind her and the man turned around. He reminded her of Fred Steinmetz at first glance; a wiry fellow, of middle age, with regular, even refined features, adorned with a drooping mustache gone quite grey. "I pray that you will be brief since we are always busy, as you might have noted."

Mr. Siringo swept off his plain city bowler hat and inclined his head most politely towards Sophia. She had long become accustomed to sizing up customers. Her assumption was that he was a gentleman of sorts; well but not flashily dressed. A lawyer; discreet, professional, soft-spoken. "I am pleased to make your acquaintance at last, Miss Brewer," he answered.

Everything around Sophia had shattered into splinters. She blinked, certain that nothing in her expression revealed nothing but polite bafflement. "I beg your pardon, Mr. Siringo – I was told you wished to speak to Miss Teague. I am Miss Teague. If this is a joke, I am not amused."

Under the mustache, Mr. Siringo smiled; a kindly and fatherly smile. "I am sure you are not, Miss Brewer. You took considerable trouble to hide yourself these last few years. I'm an agent for Pinkerton, working for a private client. I'm not blaming you for your actions, although they have put me to a lot of work! Eight months it's been," Mr. Siringo added, feelingly.

"I can't think why anyone might search for me," Sophia held tight to her composure. *A Pinkerton! A private detective – what reason could someone have to go to that trouble and expense, after all this time? Great Aunt Minnie was dead, Richard dead by his own hand, if that newspaper account of the fire in the Beacon Street mansion was anything to go by.* "There's no law I have broken, other than going by another name. Explain your business, Mr. Siringo; who is this client?"

"Your nephew, Richard Eaton Brewer," Mr. Siringo answered, earnestly. "Should we go for a stroll along the platform outside, Miss Brewer? We can talk without being overheard." He offered her his arm, and Sophie accepted it in silence, although she realized as soon as they were outside that her silence implied assent. She looked out at the desert – so familiar to her now. Boston, Beacon Hill, Aunt Minnie; far away and long ago. She once had been that person, Miss

Brewer, but not now, not in this year of 1880. They walked the length of the empty platform, out beyond earshot of anyone else.

"Richie was only nine," She remarked presently. "I'm surprised that he remembers me."

"He does," Mr. Siringo assured her. "And with fondness. There were things which he overheard as a boy which disturbed him, although he did not realize the full import until much, much later. He's a fine young man. He came into a small inheritance and decided to use them to clear his father's name."

"Clear his name of what?" Sophia demanded. Those memories of her last weeks in Boston curdled her blood and haunted nights when she was especially tired or distressed.

"Of a suspicion of murder," Mr. Siringo explained. "There was talk in Boston at the time of your departure; quiet talk, as most thought well of your brother and sympathized over his misfortunes. But folk began to think that it was altogether too convenient that you do away with yourself in a fit of insanity and leave him in charge of an inheritance which would otherwise have been yours. Miss Minerva Vining said so, and others took note of suspicious coincidences. Your brother developed an unsavory reputation. He had a taste for …" Mr. Siringo seemed embarrassed. "Women of the lower sort, and conduct which may have led to the death of one of them. Not that there was any prosecution at first. The influence of powerful friends, you see."

"I see," Sophia nodded. "That never got into the Boston newspaper although the New York scandal sheets hinted at it. I never came forward after his death. I … I am content in my life. I wished to continue unmolested by the interest of the vulgar press. I also feared Richie's guardian; I had the tenor of my brother's friends, Mr. Siringo. I was certain Richie's guardian was of the same ilk."

"You had nothing to fear," Mr. Siringo answered. "His guardian is the headmaster of his school; as disinterested and charitable a gentleman as could be found anywhere. The one thing which spared your brother from charges of having murdered you was that there was no body to be found. Only your bonnet and mantle, pulled from the water's edge."

"I see," Sophia nodded. "When I desperately needed help, the family of our housemaid came to my aid. Her brother Declan threw my bonnet and mantle into the Charles, to set a false trail."

"Agnes Teague, who worked as a maid and Declan Teague, who did odd jobs?" Mr. Siringo nodded. "A common name among the Boston Irish; I could have spent years there, fruitlessly searching for those Teagues who worked in your household. I had reason to believe you were alive, but only they knew where you had gone. All I had was a statement at third-hand that Declan Teague saw you onto the early morning train to Albany, the day after you had vanished from your brother's house."

"The Teagues lived in rooms in Old North Town, upstairs from a pawnbroker named Mendelson," Sophia began, "They should have been easy enough to find!"

Mr. Siringo nodded, patiently. "They had been gone from there for years. Old Teague's mind began to wander, and he was living with his daughter, Mrs. O'Neill, and her family in Cambridge. The boys followed the silver boom to Colorado within a year or two of you leaving Boston. That muddied your trail almost without a chance of following, Miss Brewer. Old Mendelson put me on the right track. I had a drawing of your gold engagement ring, so I thought – nothing ventured, nothing gained. I'd hit a cold trail as far as locating the Teagues, so I surmised that you must have had pawned your valuables. There weren't as many pawnbrokers in Boston as there were Teagues. I think I only talked to a third of them before I hit on Mendelson. My first lucky break; he recognized the ring, told me how it was brought to him, and he didn't want to touch it. He liked young

Seamus, and Declan, thought anyone they wanted to help must be worthwhile, but the ring was too rich and too identifiable for his blood. He readily told me that Siobhan Teague married a stonemason named O'Neill. Easy enough from then on, tracing her through church records."

"But why on earth did you begin searching for me in the first place?" Sophia demanded, in distress. "What did Richie want of me?"

Mr. Siringo cleared his throat, an expression of mild reproach on his countenance. "Young Mr. Brewer thought for years you were dead. One of those alarming incidents he witnessed was his mother, angry at his father, saying he was putting 'too much' into that tonic you were told to take. 'You'll kill her!' was what his mother kept saying; she was frightened, his father angry. He was frightened, too, believing that his father was poisoning you and nothing he could do about it; he was a child and no one would believe him."

"Richard was poisoning me," Sophia confessed. "With syrup of opium; we had it in the house for my mother when she was dying of a growth in her chest. Richard fed it in a tonic prescribed by the doctor, either to make me an addict, or to make me sick. It doesn't matter, Mr. Siringo. When did Richie come to believe he could clear his father's name?"

"After a conversation with Mrs. Leticia Phelps; they met by chance at the sea-side and renewed old acquaintance."

"Phelpsie? Great-aunt Minnie's companion? I hope she is well." Sophia had not considered Phelpsie in years and felt remorseful on that account.

"She is," Mr. Siringo had one of those mild smiles, half-concealed under his mustache again. "I can provide you with her current address in Newport. She lives in retirement, sharing a cottage with another older lady. At first, Mrs. Phelps intended only to reassure young Mr. Brewer that you had not been murdered. When I came to interview her at the beginning of this case, I asked how she could be so certain, as she had never laid eyes on you since the night you came to Miss Vinings' house and then went away at once. Miss Phelps replied that she had Miss Vining's word for it. 'But,' she told me, 'Their serving man assured Miss Minnie that he saw Sophia onto the Third Class coach early the following morning and he is a trustworthy man!' So then I had to search out any of your old servants … I believe I talked to every Irish domestic in Back Bay, until I gave it up as a bad job and concentrated on tracing the ring."

"They were so kind." Sophia mused. "And my brother could have done so much harm to them, if he ever suspected them. We agreed that for safety of all, that I must never write, or seek them out, once I got away. But they were in my prayers, always. You have told me you found Old Tim and Siobhan – what of Agnes and Declan?"

"Agnes Teague is in a cloistered order of nuns," Mr. Siringo answered. "I was not able to speak with her directly. In a written communication, she said that she would pray for the repose of your soul … leaving it a matter of conjecture if she believed your soul was located in this world or in the next. She was remarkably cagy on that score. I believe she would have endured the worst tortures devised by the Inquisition without betraying you by a single word. Considering her profession, she would have considered that an honorable martyrdom."

Sophia laughed, with the fondness of memory. "She would be glad to hear of your good opinion. She was the first to suspect what was going on, with the tonic and the opium syrup. What of Declan and Seamus?"

"Declan Teague," Mr. Siringo coughed and cleared his throat. "This is the embarrassing part. He is a Pinkerton agent, too. The wooden foot hampers him but little – he cannot do undercover work. His specialty is railway work; organized robbery gangs, targeting the railways. He recognized your ring in a secondary market in Kansas City four years ago and purchased it himself. He wrote to me – a carefully phrased letter, after I distributed copies of the design and notice of my search for Miss Sophia Brewer, gone from Boston under mysterious circumstances in the spring of 1884. He insisted on meeting personally, and assuring himself that my client, the younger Mr. Brewer intended no harm towards you."

"And did Declan satisfy your questions?" Sophia demanded.

"He did. When we conversed, he assured me he wished to take it from circulation, to further protect you."

"How did you come to have a drawing of that ring – I do not see how anyone now could recall its appearance in any detail." Sophia mused, in wonder. Mr. Siringo extended his elbow, and they went at a decorous pace, the length of the platform.

"I had the jeweler's drawings from your former fiancée," He answered. "I questioned Lucius Armitage regarding your state of mind, after he broke your engagement, on instructions from his father. He assured me, over and over again that you had not been overly distraught. Just my own feelings as a man, though, Miss Brewer; I believe he regretted it. Mr. Armitage also swore that he caught a brief glimpse of you, in the crowd by the Chase residence on the night of the engagement ball. He is haunted by that memory, Miss Brewer."

"He turned around and married my best friend," Sophia observed, acidly. "At his father's bidding. There are women in this west who would have gone after him with a knife if they did not already believe he was gelded at the start."

"Likely," Mr. Siringo displayed another of those brief mustache-veiled smiles. "The inheritance which started this farrago should have been administered by your husband. I came to believe your brother deliberately confabulated with old Mr. Armitage to wreck the possibility of your marriage with young Mr. Armitage. I cannot prove this since the senior Mr. Armitage has gone to his reward. The younger Mr. Armitage is alive and well, although not ungelded, in a manner of speaking."

Sophia laughed outright at that although briefly. "Lucius was a kind person, and not incapable of finer feelings. But he had none of hardy interior strength. I think that I might have been the making of him. Married to me, he might have have become a better person. What is he now?"

"Likely enough, he might have been," Mr. Siringo agreed with a certain degree of respect. "He is still married to Emma Chase-that-was; they have three children. She is noted in Society for going with a very fast set. I have it on good authority she cuckolds her husband with every handsome gallant who takes her fancy."

"She was always a dreadful flirt," Sophia mused. "Even as a girl, her parents indulged her every whim; their fault, not my brothers. Breaking my engagement with Lucius was not the worst part of what my brother did to us."

"And what was that worst part?" Mr. Siringo's voice was especially gentle, and Sophia swallowed. She had tried her best for ten years to put that memory away. Mostly she had succeeded, save for nightmares now and again, especially after the attempted robbery of the Deming Harvey House. "Tell me; what happened that day when you refused to drink the drugged tonic?"

"I was tired of being ruled by my brother. I determined that when I became of legal age, I preferred to live with my great aunt. He was infuriated at this and locked me in the strong-room in his study. I had never seen anyone so angry, Mr. Siringo; he was demonic. When he opened the door later – I am sure he was certain I would be cowed – I tried to escape. He is … was a large man, quite strong. He beat me to insensibility and forced the dose down my throat. I don't remember anything after that." Sophia shuddered; yes, she had a brief memory of one more thing, the memory-ghost of something horrific; she had never been sure if that had been real, or an opium-dream. She fervently hoped that it had been an opium nightmare.

"What then, Miss Brewer. What do you recall after that?"

"Nothing. I came into myself days later. Everyone told me how shamed I should be, that it was a wicked thing I had done. I could not make them see I had not. Richard put on the pretense of being a fond and loving brother, insisting I was not myself but his eyes were always cold. As if there was nothing behind them but an empty room." She shuddered again.

"And yet, you escaped?" Mr. Siringo asked, after a long silence. Sophia willed herself back to the present. "Declan Teague had two keys. Little liking what he saw and having good reason to distrust my brother – he told you of the horse, when you spoke? He gave the second key to Agnes."

"So Mr. Teague confirmed. And as soon as you could rise from your sickbed, Agnes helped you escape from the house?" Mr. Siringo prompted her, and Sophia nodded.

"It went according to plan, except that Richard had frightened Great Aunt Minnie into a heart-spasm. It was obvious I couldn't stay there. But the Teagues planned that I should take the letter that Siobhan had from the Harvey company."

Mr. Siringo nodded. "Mr. Benjamin at the Fred Harvey company confirmed this when I spoke to him in Kansas City. He said that you have been an exemplary employee; those who have worked with you have spoken well … although he confessed that he always suspected that there was a small mystery in how you came to apply to Fred Harvey. Nothing that would have prevented your employment; just that you appeared to have come from such a superior background he has always wondered. I did not enlighten him in any fashion – save you were blameless for your situation – as it was not my position to reveal specifics of my client's interest in you."

"And what are you going to do now, Mr. Siringo?" Sophia demanded. What was she to do, now? Not return to Boston; that she had never contemplated. Return to a cage, living in genteel poverty and inaction, among strangers, without a purpose? Never!

"Turn in my report to Mr. Brewer." Another of those mild and gentle smiles, half-veiled under the drooping mustache. "I will tell him you are alive and well and appear to be in the best of spirits – and in fortunate circumstances. Do you wish to write to him yourself? I can provide you with his address. Or do you prefer continuing to continue in this … estrangement."

"I don't think so," Sophia answered, after careful consideration. "The circumstances of my leaving Boston were so distressing. I have put aside most of the unfortunate memories associated with it behind me. Walk away, old Tim Teague advised me; walk away, lest I be haunted forever and ever."

"Do you wish for me to tell Mr. Brewer where you are?" Mr. Siringo pressed, and finally Sophia nodded. "I suppose it will do no harm, but impress upon him I have no intention of ever returning East and a life of hapless dependence. I am a spinster of independent means and intend to remain that way, just as Great-Aunt Minnie did."

"I will so inform Mr. Brewer." Mr. Siringo nodded. "Will there be anything more that I may do for you, Miss Brewer?"

"There is one thing," Sophia considered carefully. "I read that my brother killed himself and his wife and sons, but there was something unsavory hinted at in the newspaper stories which I read after it occurred … suspicion and condemnation, which high social position could no longer deflect. Since you have made a study of my brother and our family, do you have a notion of what led to him to destroy himself, his wife and the two boys?"

"I do," Mr. Siringo hesitated, and looked sideways at Sophia. "But it is as you suggest, an ugly, unsavory story, Miss Brewer."

"You may as well tell me straight-out," Sophia felt as old as Great-Aunt Minnie. "Can it be any uglier than what Richard attempted to do to me?"

"No, perhaps not," Mr. Siringo agreed and sighed. "You will recall, I mentioned that your brother had a taste for the company of a lower class of woman? As part of his customary congress with them, he was in the habit of administering savage beatings. He appears to have derived perverse satisfaction from this activity. I am trying to be delicate regarding this, Miss Brewer, but it is in the nature of unnatural vices to require more and more of the stimulant to achieve satisfaction."

"So the beatings became worse and worse," Sophia wondered if she would throw up. Yet she had to know.

Mr. Siringo nodded, relieved. "Exactly; those women who colluded with him in these entertainments were not always undertaking it voluntarily. Eventually, your brother could not pay sufficient to stop the women from complaining over their treatment and when at least one of them died from it, her friends among the demimondaine, as they call them … went to the police. Your brother was interviewed at length. I was privy to a number of the affidavits by those women and statements your brother made, under questioning. It is vile and sickening stuff, Miss Brewer, and I speak as a man of the world not unaccustomed to the seamier side of life. At any rate," Mr. Siringo sighed again. "It became common gossip, not just among the lower sort of people, but your brother's intimates and associates. They looked at him askance in the streets at first and then began snubbing him and Mrs. Brewer socially. People who had suspicions voiced them. As the uglier parts of the investigation came out, it was obvious he would be charged and tried, likely convicted. The old scandal regarding your disappearance was revived. It was suggested openly that you had been murdered by your brother. He was advised by those acquaintances still speaking to him he should consult a lawyer. On the evening of the day he spoke with the lawyer, he dismissed the cook to her home after supper. He sent a telegram to young Mr. Brewer at his boarding school, requesting his presence at home that day. By good fortune, the telegram went astray, or else young Mr. Brewer would have perished, too."

"The newspapers suggested that Richard drugged his wife and the two boys before starting the fire," Sophia remarked. "I hoped so – I have an absolute horror of burning to death in a fire."

"Those reports are likely true. Even if smoke stupefies after a time, from the position of the bodies of Mrs. Brewer and the two boys on the bed, they made no move after being placed on it. The fire took a long while to get going. You'd have thought that at least one of them might have been aware."

"There is something pagan about it all," Sophia remarked, after a moment. "One of the ancient gods, immolating himself and all his family and possessions, out of a terrible sense of pride. Perhaps they were right – in thinking that fire cleanses the wickedness out of the world. Thank you for your persistence and understanding, Mr. Siringo. I suppose that I will be as grateful to you as Richie will be. When you see him in Boston, to report your findings to him … tell him I have always recalled him with affection."

"I will," Mr. Siringo bowed over her hand and took his leave of her. She looked out at the mountains – those mountains which rose to the southeast, with Fredi Steinmetz' magical little spring, tucked into that cleft of the hills at their feet, and wished that she could be there, this very moment. She wondered if she should tell Lottie and Mr. Steinmetz of this.

But there was a train due in fifteen minutes.

Chapter 18 – Coming Home

Mr. Siringo's conversation with Sophia brought her a sense of composure, a sense of a new lightness of heart. She had not realized, until that afternoon, how her fears – even inchoate and unspoken – had haunted her, that dark and hovering dark cloud, even after reading of the fire which destroyed the Brewer house. She had been so accustomed to guard her words, to edit her memories – and had lived with those apprehensions for so long they had become wholly a part of her, as her eyes were grey-blue and her hair curled in tight ringlets. Now it was as if a veil of black cloud were away, revealing a clear blue sky and bright sunshine. She could tell her name to anyone, and not have to fear that somehow, somewhere, Richard and Dr. Cotton appearing with a closed coach to carry her away and lock her up in the insane asylum. She had practiced an odd vigilance which had become a second nature – always having a that little purse of money and the hair-brooch in her corset, the bank books for her accounts at hand, having the old carpet-bag in a corner of the close-press, packed with a change of clothing and some books, of keeping her ears always attuned for the accents of Boston and the east. Now that threat was utterly gone – although, she knew that a chance of the worst kind of yellow newspaper taking an interest in her still remained. Best keep the Teague name a while longer although she could now let herself be known as Sophia Brewer Teague.

"What did that gentleman want of you, Miss T?" Elsie did ask, that afternoon, as they sat in the corner of the kitchen, polishing silverware. Sophia had considered how she ought to answer – for certainly Mr. Siringo's visit did not go unnoticed.

"He was a private detective, actually," Sophia replied, as sedate as if this manner of occurrence happened all the time. "Hired by a distant relation in Boston, who had been close to my late mother, but had lost track of the family connection when I came out west. That relation of mine chose to make use of a private inquiry agent to locate me." *'If you have to tell a lie,' Declan Teague's advice whispered in her memory, 'Make it as close to the truth as ye can, and keep it simple. That way, ye don't have to remember details. And it will no' really be a lie, then – will it?'*

"Ohh, Miss T.!" Gasped Elsie, awed and impressed. "Is your relation … is he very rich?"

"Likely not, after paying the wages and expenses of a private agent," Sophia replied.

"I suppose that you will write to your relation, Miss T?" Elsie ventured.

"I don't think that I will," Sophia replied, after a thoughtful moment, during which she polished several spoons. "Since I barely recall that relation and have no real reason to maintain a connection."

And that was the last said, or at least the last said to Sophia, or within her hearing. She silently blessed Mr. Siringo's tact and consideration, for she had no other necessity of making an explanation to anyone within the Harvey House.

On the following Sunday afternoon, she had an appointment to ride with Mr. Steinmetz – another of her lessons in riding. The two of them set out from the Thurmonds, for rain had fallen heavily over the previous days, and even now in a constant light drizzle – not a good day for a picnic, everyone agreed. Better a good supper and a fire built up against the first autumn chill.

"Supper is at six," Lottie reminded them, as Mr. Steinmetz helped Sophia into her own saddle. "Are you sure you won't change your minds and stay in a nice warm parlor, playing cards with Frank and I?"

"I've been looking forward all week," Sophia replied, "And this would hardly count as bad weather at all, back East."

"If you say so," Lottie sighed, in resignation.

"If it begins to come down hard, we'll come straight back." Fredi Steinmetz promised. He had thoughtfully provided Sophia with a waxed cotton overcoat, which he assured her would shed water, for the most part. Once away from town, their horses' hooves falling with a wet squelch with every step along the muddy track, Mr. Steinmetz looked across at her, and asked, "Where to, Miss Teague?"

"The waterfall where we always picnic," Sophia replied.

"The water will be running strong, after this rain," he replied, "But yes – that's a favorite place of mine."

"It will be perfect," Sophia took in a deep breath of fresh air. "I love how the air smells, after the first rain settles the dust … and the raindrops have bruised sage leaves and pine needles, just a little."

"Very fine," he agreed, and they continued in companionable silence for a good way. "They delivered the last shipment of furniture for the ranch house this week," he remarked, after a while. "So, night before last night, I took Miss Kitten home with me."

"How did she like that?" Sophia asked. "And is she settling in?" The little grey catling had become increasingly tame over the last month, but still skittish and inclined to hiss at strangers who came too close to her and flee into whatever refuge there was at hand. "A little bit of complaint at not being let out of the basket right away," Mr. Steinmetz grinned. "But I left her in the kitchen, with a bowl of cream and cooked chicken. I expect that I will be forgiven."

"She is a cat," Sophia pointed out. "They carry their grudges for a long time."

"I wouldn't be surprised to find she has made a privy out of my boots," Mr. Steinmetz agreed. "But this morning, I saw she had finished off the food I put for her, and she made a bed on a pile of horse-blankets in the corner."

"I have a friend raised on a farm who said that they way to make a cat stay in a new place was to put butter on their paws … by the time they licked it off, they have decided to stay."

"Messy," Mr. Steinmetz said, and they rode on, content to be in the open air, with the fresh smell of the rain in their faces. Sophia hoped that being a house and barn cat was an improvement for Miss Kitten over a space underneath the railway station platform. Soon their chosen path passed by Mr. Steinmetz' ranch property, with the silver daisy of the windmill turning in the lightest of breezes.

"You finished putting on the roof just in time," Sophia remarked, seeing how the recent rains had carved shallow trenches along the near side where water had dripped off the roof.

"That we did," Mr. Steinmetz agreed. "Right and tight, and only one small leak; there is nothing like sitting inside a well-built house on a stormy day. I shall have to have you and the Thurmonds and my other friends come for a visit, soon – having seen the place when it was nothing but a couple of acres of drying bricks, you may appreciate the improvement."

Soon the path dipped down, paralleling the streambed which ran out of the mountains. Today the splashing sound of water running swiftly between its banks came to meet them. The stands of rushes which grew along the margins of the stream were bowed over, and there was a wrack of sticks and small branches piled up wherever the water had deposited them. Sophia had never seen the stream as more than a knee-deep meander, easily forded by horse and buggy, but this looked to be waist-deep to a man, belly-deep to a horse.

"I'm afraid that the water will be too high to cross," Mr. Steinmetz ventured at last. "I mean – I'd cross over, if there were a serious purpose but I do not want to risk your safety, Miss Teague, on what is supposed to be a mere pleasure jaunt."

"I am agreeable to turning back, if there is even a small danger," Sophia sighed. Yes, she wanted to visit the little dell with the waterfall – but on the other hand, she was damp enough from where the waterproof overcoat did not cover. A sound caught her ear, a sound not the gentle pattering of rain on leaves and ground, nor the chuckle of water running around rocks and small boulders in the creek-bed. "Do you hear that?"

Mr. Steinmetz reined in his horse, listening intently. "No, your ears are younger than mine. What does it sound like?"

"A very unhappy cow," Sophia replied. "It sounds as if … it's coming from that direction. Upstream."

"There's a good-sized pond up that way," Mr. Steinmetz looked annoyed. "I've had the boys put in a dam to make a stock tank … I'm betting that a cow-critter got stuck in the mud. And me in my good church suit, too."

"I'm sorry …" Sophia said, and Mr. Steinmetz shrugged.

"Not your fault. We'd better see how bad the critter is stuck."

Another two or three bends in the creek-bed brought them to the pond; just as Mr. Steinmetz feared, a small yearling stood in the middle of it, water washing against its flanks, and loudly protesting. A small knot of cattle, three or four, stood on the banks, regarding the stuck yearling with mild curiosity. It sounded, Sophia thought, more unhappy than distressed, and looked at them with rolling eyes.

"First things first," Mr. Steinmetz took his coiled lariat from the back of his saddle. He deftly spun it into a larger and larger loop, then dropped the final loop over the yearling's head.

"Come on, then," he called to the cow and tightened the lariat. The yearling bawled again – for the first time sounding as if it were really in discomfort. Mr. Steinmetz dallied the lariat end over his saddle horn, and with his pony's help, pulled harder. The yearling bawled again.

"You're hurting it," Sophia exclaimed and Mr. Steinmetz replied, "If the water rises tonight, it'll be more than hurt. Here, Miss Teague – when I say to, back up Little Bucky, nice and gentle." He tied the end of the lariat around the horn of Sophia's saddle. "Little Bucky's a well-trained cattle-working horse, she'll know what to do, as soon as you tell her."

"What are you going to do?" Sophia was apprehensive. This was far beyond anything she had ever dealt with in the Harvey House. Mr. Steinmetz stripped off his own waterproof and the coat underneath it, laying them across his own saddle. He looped the gun-belt and pistol, as much a proper Western item of attire as a gentleman's watch and watch chain anywhere else, over the saddle horn. After a moment, he added his waistcoat, and hat. His pony stood obedient, watching without any particular emotion as Mr. Steinmetz in his shirtsleeves waded into the murky water.

"Keep the rope taut," he said over his shoulder. Sophia – completely rattled by now – answered, "What are you doing? The water is … is it deep? Deep enough to be dangerous?"

"Only the mud," he replied. "And only if this wretched ungrateful beast kicks me in the head." He was now waist-deep in the water, close enough to the cow to reach it with an outstretched arm.

Sophia gasped, her nerves shredding to their last fiber. "Oughtn't I go for help?"

Mr. Steinmetz appeared to take a deep breath. "Dear Miss Teague, we are the help. Take care to keep the rope taut." And with that, he vanished under the surface of the water, although agitation of the water itself, and the rolling eyes and agitation on the part of the yearling hinted at something of significance going on, unseen. In a moment, Mr. Steinmetz appeared, gasping for breath and applying himself with vigor against the yearlings' hind quarters. "Pull!" he shouted, and Sophia kneed her pony, who took one step and then another backwards. Mr. Steinmetz vanished underneath the water again, this time having moved around to the yearling's forequarters.

The yearling bawled, most piteously, and all of a moment, came unstuck with the sound of a messy cork coming away from a slushy bottle-neck. In another space, the yearling came surging up onto the bank of the pond, bawling as if it had been skinned while living, dripping with water and fresh mud. Mr. Steinmetz appeared, similarly covered, and laughing in triumph.

"You provide the most interesting amusements, on our rides," Sophia remarked, when she recovered her composure. Mr. Steinmetz, still laughing, took his lariat from off the horns of the yearling, and sent it off at a gallop with a hearty thwack across its flanks. The other cattle followed.

"That's a cattle ranch for you," he replied. "The amusement of it never ends. Miss Teague, I will have to change into dry things, before we return to Lottie and Frank's place. Do you mind if we delayed a short time at the ranch? I had meant to invite you for a visit in any case."

"I would enjoy that," Sophia answered, without a moment's consideration of the proprieties, there being no doubt in her mind that Mr. Steinmetz was the most considerate gentleman of her acquaintance. "It cannot be good, to continue for long in wet clothing. I am eaten up with curiosity as to how the furniture appears."

"Quite nicely, I think – for whatever my opinion counts for in such matters," Mr. Steinmetz agreed. "But I'd be pleased if you make a quick scout and then report to Lottie and Mrs. Woods on their choices for a poor lonely bachelor establishment."

"I will, most certainly," Sophia agreed, her heart rising at the prospect. Curiosity had not eaten at her, but taken small nibbles, ever since those varied crates directed for Mr. F. Steinmetz, Deming, New Mexico Territory, began arriving at the station.

"It's not a patch on Lottie's house," he warned, as they approached the ranch, with the sheltering verandas spread out on every side. "But it suits. We'll just be a moment. Go on in by that door – I'll take the horses into the barn for now."

They had come up on the side of the house. He helped Sophia dismount and step up onto the verandah. Relieved to be out of the rain, and regretting her previous insistence on going for a ride, she looked around. The verandah was bare, but swept clean. The door was one in the French style, set with glass as a window, and it stood half open. She stepped through and found herself in what was supposed to be a parlor; the settee, chairs and bookshelves set against the walls, and a round table with a fancy kerosene lamp in the center stood marooned in the middle of the room. Yes, they looked well, better than they had appeared in the catalogue – neither too large nor too small, and well-suited to the room. A fine oil painting hung over the settee; of rolling green grass and a river beyond, threaded by a line of cows with enormous spreading horns and men on horseback; a trail drive, and painted from life, she thought.

"My sister Magda's boy did that," Mr. Steinmetz said, from behind her. "Of our first drive from Texas in '67; he wasn't with us that time, but he painted in all the boys and the horses that were, every single one. Sam Becker – he's gotten to be right famous, now."

"He's most marvelously good," Sophia replied, with honest appreciation, for the pictured horses and men were painted with verve and in lively colors.

"He makes a living at it, too, which not a one of us expected at the start." Mr. Steinmetz had his coats and waistcoat bundled in his arms. He had left a trail of wet footprints behind him. "I'll just be a moment, Miss Teague. Miss Kitten is in the room at the end of the hall if you want to pay your respects."

He vanished through another door – this one led into the interior of the house, and an unseen door closed behind him. Sophia followed, after a moment. Yes, the ornate carved hat and coat rack sat in this hallway, the only ornament. She looked into the other rooms, taking her time. All the doors but one stood open; yes, bedrooms. Only the last room looked as if anyone lived in it at all; Mr. Steinmetz' office, presided over by a massive mounted head of another longhorn, this one with one horn shortened by eight inches. "Old Blue" said the little metal engraved label underneath the head, and its glass eyes regarded Sophia with vague disapproval. There must be a sentimental attachment, Sophia assumed – else, why have such a grotesque object hanging from the wall?

The kitchen was dominated by the monumental stove – brand-new and barely used and an equally massive cold closet made of golden-gleaming wood, with polished brass hinges and latches. Even if Mr. Steinmetz had just taken up habitation this week, it appeared as if he had already made arrangements for regular ice delivery. It also looked as if he were taking his meals in there, for there was still a dirty plate and a used tin mug sitting at one end of the kitchen table. Miss Kitten's basket sat in a corner – as Mr. Steinmetz had said, the cat slept on a pile of folded horse-blankets next to it, looking like nothing so much as a small puddle of pale grey fur. A saucer sat next to the basket, with a little skim of milk in the center.

Sophia looked around. This could be such a pleasant kitchen if properly run and ornamented! The tall windows in the outside wall looked out towards the mountains, their jagged tops veiled in grey clouds. Were this hers, she would have a garden just outside, of vegetables and cooking herbs, perhaps a fruit tree or two … pretty china, lined up on the kitchen dresser shelves, and a fist-full of bright canyon daisies in that blue pottery jug, which now sat forlorn on top of the cold closet.

"What do you think of it, so far?" Mr. Steinmetz appeared noiselessly in the doorway, clad in dry clothing, but still in shirtsleeves.

"It's a lovely situation," Sophia confessed. "And the furniture ordered for it looks very fine, set within the rooms, but …"

"You speak as if there is something lacking," Mr. Steinmetz completed the thought.

"You have a cat for your house," she replied; light and casual, without thinking. "But I think that it lacks a proper housewife to make it most perfectly complete, and beautifully comfortable … it's a lovely house, any woman will come to treasure it."

"Ah, then, you see," Mr. Steinmetz seemed at a loss for words, for a moment. "I have had … do have, a candidate in mind. For a proper housewife … if she … if you would do me the honor. All this would be yours; if you would consent to marry me. I have always had the greatest respect and admiration for you, Miss Teague. Please consider my proposal."

"Of course," Sophia spoke, without consideration beyond the briefest impulse. The path she had strayed from when Lucius Armitage broke their engagement so long ago in Boston had miraculously reopened before her feet. Her affection towards Mr. Steinmetz – whom his friends called Fred – was deeper, more honest, and more profound than any she had ever felt for Lucius; poor bullied Lucius. "Yes; I have considered it and consent in the affirmative. I am agreeable to marriage with you."

"Oh, good." Mr. Steinmetz – Fred – looked as if sunrise had broken in the east, with relief and happiness. He felt the outside of his trouser pockets. "I hoped that you'd say yes. I have a ring. Damn – sorry Miss Teague – it's in my waistcoat pocket. I'll go get it."

"There's no hurry," Sophia said, her heart overflowing with affection.

"Yes, there is," he answered. "You might change your mind."

"No, I won't." Sophia was utterly calm, serene. There was rightness to this, a solid comfort in his embrace of her, as if she were coming home to a place she had never been, after so many years of wandering like a refugee from place to place. This was where she belonged, where she had been meant to be. She fit into the circle of his arms as if the two of them were fashioned for each other. There was a little awkwardness in the way that he kissed her – shyly at first, as if he were young lad kissing a girl for the first time.

"Ah, *Sopherl* – little Sophie – you have no idea of how happy this makes me," he said at last.

"It makes me happy, too," she replied, for the certainty he would be her husband and her life would be here, lived in the stoutly built ranch house with a view of the mountains rising to the west like a jagged wall. "You planned it this way, didn't you? Asking Lottie and Eleanor and I to choose the furniture for you?"

"Well yes. But I intended making more of a show of asking you, though," he confessed. "You know, down on one knee, with the ring in my hand. You're still sure?"

"Certainly. I suppose that I may call you Fred, now." Sophia ventured.

"Whatever you please, as long as it's not Rumpelstiltskin, or honey-cheeks or something embarrassing in front of people like Frank and Lottie."

"Never. Honey-cheeks," Sophia whispered, and knew that he was laughing. More than anything, she liked the sensation of his laughter, of feeling his heart beating against hers. "Not in front of Lottie and Frank then. Do you think they will be surprised?"

"Never," Fred kissed her again. "I suppose we had better be going, before she thinks that we have decided to run away together, or fallen in the creek!"

Chapter 19 – The Uncharted Frontier

As neither of them were in that first bloom or youth, or blessed with large families resident in the vicinity, Sophia and Fred did not want their wedding celebration to be a one of those impractically lavish ones; there was no society or distant cousins and aunts to impress. Sophia hoped for a modest number of friends and a small ceremony performed by Reverend Lloyd in the parlor of Lottie's house, or a larger gathering of friends in the chancel of St. Luke's.

Lottie would not hear of that. "No, Sophie, dear – you will have it done in the church, and then we will have a party at our house. I shall arrange with Mr. Loftus to cater it – I know the other girls will be as pleased as anything to support you. You and Fred have so many friends hereabouts. Since there is little of amusement here, save for weddings and funerals, and now and again an infamous robbery, you must not deprive Deming of a celebratory occasion. And think of St. Luke's – this may be the first wedding of note in the parish!"

"As long as you do not insist that I wear a white silk dress and a long veil," Sophia protested.

"Why not? With luck, one is only married once; you may as well have a grand fling," Lottie answered.

"It's impractical – a dress I can wear once!"

"Order yourself a new one – something pale and pretty, and a new bonnet," Lottie insisted. "I shall write to my clever dressmaker in New Orleans – I will have her collect up some Godey fashion-plates and samples of fabrics and trim for a quiet ensemble suitable for a lady of mature years – and it will be my wedding gift to you! You will not dare deprive me of my amusement, will you?"

Sophia protested, but not very energetically; once Lottie had the bit in her teeth, she was away with it at a gallop. And besides, Sophia admitted to herself: Lottie was right. This would be a notable occasion in Deming, with Fredi Steinmetz being one of the established local ranchers. As it turned out, with the press of daily work at the House, and overseeing the lunchroom, the coming nuptials slid more or less to the back of her mind. Two days before the day set for the Reverend Lloyd to perform the wedding rites, Sophia packed away most of the possessions which had adorned her room into a steamer trunk, keeping back a few black uniform dresses and aprons, and a nightgown. One of Fredi's hands came in a wagon for it late in the afternoon; and when the wagon had rattled away from the station, Sophia sat on her bed and looked around at the newly bare room, with the flush of the sun sliding down in the western sky, painting the plain whitewashed walls a warm and rosy pink. It was real, it was happening – she was to be married. So far from Boston, so far from the circumstances into which she had been born and expected to live out her life. They were all gone, those closest of kin – only Richie left among the living, and a handful of second and third cousins, far, far away, most of whom she recognized as names, but not faces.

She would work one more shift, then tomorrow evening, take the rest of her things in a small carpetbag and walk the few blocks to Lottie and Frank's house, and spend the night. The wedding dress awaited her there, arriving as Lottie had ordered it, packed in a huge paste-board dress box in layer after layer of tissue paper. In two days she would put it on, go to the church and be married. Tomorrow and tomorrow, and tomorrow, all the rest of her life, Sophia mused; for seven years her life was ruled by the railway and Harvey, as familiar to her as the Brewer mansion had once been, and a much more secure refuge. She was more than the daughter of her father, the sister of Richard: she was her own woman, succeeding by her own labor, her own dedication to perfection. Work was worship – that's what little Agnes had said earnestly, those years ago, on that night she had comforted Sophia, cuddled under those thin harsh-textured blankets in the front room of the meagre two where the Teagues lived – that home from which Agnes and Seamus and Declan sallied every day … to work. They had succeeded in their own ways and lights, judging what Mr. Siringo had said of them in the years since she had parted from them.

Work was worship – not metered out by convent bells, but by the whistle of a locomotive, the chime of the alarm signaling hungry passengers. Sophia had found fulfillment and reward in that work; pleasure and pride, too. Could she find the same fulfillment and pleasure in marriage? Meditating upon it, Sophia was certain she would. It was, so she had always been told, the path designated for her and for most women. As for Mr. Steinmetz –Fred – theirs was not a connection so much of overpowering passions that which might soon fade, but one of friendship, respect, trust, and true affection. Overheated romance was for silly schoolgirls and trashy novels read by maids and shop-girls. She and Fred were responsible, steady, having seen and experienced much, although Sophia admitted to herself in honesty, her intended had seen far more of it than she had. Still, it would be a change; the rule of her own household. She feared that she might miss the constant bustle and rush of the House, both upstairs and down; no longer the frantic rush to complete a toilette at the beginning of the shift, the comradery of the other girls, the constant comings and goings and the excitement of the trains arriving, which never palled.

Just as she recalled Agnes's words, about work being worship, so did old Tim Teague's advice came to mind: "Close the door and walk away," he said, rheumy eyes near to overflowing as he talked of Ireland and his youth, of his service in the War, and his memories of Sophia's father, in that haunted last night before she left Boston. "Walk away, niver looking back. Do ye no good, *cailín daor*. There's nothing good for you, remaining. " Then he had maundered a while, recollecting what he remembered of Major Brewer, and how the regiment had marched in the Grand Review at the end of the War … *Close the door and walk away, walk away niver looking back…*

Yes – she could close the door and walk away; but the memories would always be there. Perhaps it was different for men. With some effort, she had closed the door on Boston but never on those months and years since.

On the morning of Sophia's wedding, Lottie came to the guest room where she had spent the previous night, with folds of heavy fabric spilling from her arms; she had warned Sophia the night before that she would supervise her donning the dress and bonnet she would wear as was proper for a bride. Sophia had already tried it on several times, so that Lottie could adjust the fit and drape; heavy cream-color silk, with a walking-dress length to the skirt and a tight high-collared basque with fashionably large sleeves. The bonnet was a brief thing of blue in accordance with custom, trimmed with cream lace and a spray of silk and wax lemon blossoms.

Bright sunlight poured through the tall window, made misty by the thin lace curtains drawn before the glass. Sophia sat on the edge of the bed, irresolute, a single white stocking in her hand. She had on her shift and corset, and a single petticoat. Lottie exclaimed,

"My dear, you haven't even done up your stockings! Do them now, and I'll pin up your hair for you. If you are late, poor Fred and the Reverend Lloyd will think that you have had cold feet and decided not to go through with it at the last minute."

"I have cold feet," Sophia confessed, in misery – although it was not her feet, but an icy lump of terror in the pit of her stomach, a terror which she had not felt in the waking world for a long time. "I'm afraid of what will happen…" she couldn't finish the thought.

"Dear silly Sophia," Lottie draped the dress over the foot of the bedstead and sat down, drawing Sophia into an embrace. "You mean the wedding night? Dear girl, it is a delight to embrace and kiss the one you love and yes, there is more than that. You're a woman of the world, you must know about…" and she ventured a brief indelicate description, which made Sophia laugh, although it was a tearful laugh.

"Oh, I knew that – women talk, and some girls had been married before, or were quite awfully bold. I just this morning realized that won't Mr. Steinmetz be expecting … that is, he will be able to tell the difference, won't he, the first time that he …"

"He what?" Lottie was struck to momentary silence. "The first time? He hasn't been a monk all those years but I don't believe that he's been a notorious libertine, either. He will be considerate, Sophie – there's nothing for you to fear."

"The first time that …" a hot blush rose in Sophia's face – she wondered if she were burning red all over from the shame and embarrassment of this confession. "Lottie, there was something awful that happened a long time ago, in Boston. I am not certain I am a virgin."

Lottie's arm around her tightened in reassurance. "Good heavens, Sophie – how can you be in doubt? If there is one thing that a woman can be sure of in this world, it would be …" and she repeated the same indelicacy. Sophie shook her head.

"My older brother was poisoning me with opium, to secure the use of my inheritance after I turned twenty-one. It wasn't even that large an inheritance which adds insult to injury! He and the doctor – a friend of his – were plotting to lock me up in the insane asylum. I began to see that there was something wrong in the tonic and one morning, I refused to drink it." Sophia steadied her voice with an effort. This was something she had never spoken of, save to Mr. Siringo, who knew the worst – or all but the very worst. "My brother beat me, viciously. When I was insensible, he forced a large quantity of opium syrup down my throat. I remembered nothing after that. When I came to myself, I was in my bed and everyone telling me I had drunk a near-fatal dose and thrown myself down the staircase. But I had bruises all over me. I … hurt on my insides and I found out I had bled onto my under-drawers as if it was my monthly course although I am not altogether certain of that."

"Oh, my dear Sophie!" Now Lottie flung both her arms around her, drawing Sophie's head onto her comforting and elegant shoulder. "How vile – how horrible! But listen to me. Listen; I suppose your brother arranged with some ruffian, the doctor, even, to dishonor you. Were there any other men in the house at the time, I wonder?"

"I don't know," Sophia hiccupped, reassured by Lottie's worldly indignation. "I can't remember. I've never been able to remember. I'm sure I can't marry Mr. Steinmetz, though."

"Yes, you can," Lottie answered, stern and fierce as an avenging angel. She put her hands on Sophia's shoulders, and shook her, as if reprimanding an unruly child. "You can, my dear Sophie and you will. Listen to me as if I were your mother, loving you dearly and knowing what is best. There will be no more shillyshallying. I won't have it, you cannot inconvenience the Reverend Lloyd since he came all this way, and you can't disappoint Fred. Sophie – I am going to tell you something straight: you did not consent to what happened, hmm? And you have no memory of any such thing? Then you cannot go on thinking yourself guilty. And besides," Lottie lifted Sophia's chin with one finger, so they could look into each other's eyes. "He knows that you were escaping from something horrible. He doesn't care what it was, Sophie. It doesn't matter to him. Nor to me, either," although Lottie added in an aside, "I didn't think it would be turn out to be anything as wickedly melodramatic as a brother scheming to steal your inheritance and send you to a madhouse."

"What did you think?" Sophia hiccupped again, and Lottie brought out an immaculate handkerchief from her sleeve and blotted up the tears on Sophia's cheeks.

"The usual story," Lottie answered, "An ill-considered marriage to a man with a bad temper and a heavy hand and you running away from him; sensible of you, we both thought. The west," she added, meditatively, "Is full of men – women too – running away from something. I ran away from my widowed mother's desperate wish for me to contract marriage to a man rich enough to revive our family fortunes. Frank ran away from angry kin after killing another man in a knife-fight. Not his fault; the other man picked the fight to start with. Fred is not running away; he is merely a stone rolling hither and yon, looking for something. You would be good for him, Sophie. He will settle down, for you, just give him the chance. He built the house on the chance it would to tempt you to stay, you know."

"You have been conspiring, behind my back!" Sophia exclaimed, torn between affection and mild indignation.

"Yes, of course we have, dear girl; that's what friends do. Fred is at least as much my friend as you are and he came asking for my advice."

"And what did you tell him?" Now she considered it in hindsight, Fred had been wooing her with such gentle care; Lottie's masterful touch was all over it.

"I told him to go slowly, never make a sudden move, and now and again offer you a small delicacy."

"As if he were taming Miss Kitten," Sophia realized with a giggle.

"Exactly the same," Lottie consulted the tiny watch pinned to the lapel of her bodice. "There we are. Now wash your face, and get dressed, or we shall be late."

Under Lottie's dictatorial hand, the wedding and celebratory party afterwards went as if by well-maintained clockwork. All that Sophia needed to do was what Lottie told her, clucking like a mother hen with one chick. Her misery and apprehension melted away, as if by magic, at the moment she came into the church, on Frank Thurmond's arm, and met Fred's eyes. He grinned at her, as merry as if they were chance-met in the street, or at the Harvey House. Lottie was right, Sophia realized. Whatever had driven her from Boston, Fred didn't care, and that she trusted him more than any other man in the world, except possibly Mr. Harvey.

The familiar words spoken which made them man and wife, the plain gold ring slipped onto her finger, a gentle kiss on her cheek and it was done in hardly any time at all. So did the celebratory luncheon at Lottie and Frank's – it passed in a mellow daze for Sophia, anchored to the real world by the gentle hand under her elbow. Fred; not young, nor handsome, well-to-do only in terms of land, cattle, and friends – now he was more than just her good friend, he was her husband. For the remainder of their lives, they were linked in the eyes of the world, each a half which together made a whole. Sophia wondered if this was as much a change for him as it was for her. Likely not; out here, a wife was as much a partner in her husband's business, be it ranching, mercantile or professional, as if she had signed a legal contract. Which she had, come to think on it.

"*Sopherl,*" he whispered to her in German, when the merriment in Lottie's parlor and dining room showed no signs of diminishing by late afternoon. "Let's go home. Frank has the buggy around in front."

"Yes, let's!" she replied. He winked at her as conspiratorial as a schoolboy with a prank aimed at the schoolmaster.

Lottie appeared at that moment, laughing, with a plate of cake in her hand. "I heard that!" she exclaimed. "Go on, the both of you; don't forget to throw your bouquet at the door."

"Thank you for everything," Sophie whispered, and kissed Lottie on her flawless cheek. "You are the best friend in the world!"

"Go!" If it were possible, Lottie blushed at least under her powder. "And be happy, both of you – and fruitful and multiply!"

"I am sure we will," Fred answered, confidently, taking Sophia's hand in his. "Ready on the count of three! One, two, three!"

They hurried through the parlor, accompanied by startled exclamations from the other guests, but they had taken everyone by surprise.

"They're getting away!" someone cried. Hand in hand like a pair of children, Fred and Sophia raced through the hall and down the stairs. Frank stood by the buggy, and handed Sophia up to the seat as Fred ran around to the other side, and took up the reins. Sophia flung her bouquet from the seat into the gathering, and they were away in a cloud of dust and flying rice.

The streets of Deming being so limited, they were out in the country before they were even out of hearing of the calls of good wishes from the wedding guests, out on the familiar road to the Steinmetz ranch at a brisk trot. Sophia leaned against the buggy seat back as tired as she was after a day in the House. Fred looked at her sideways, in sympathetic commiseration.

"Done, and off-stage at last," he said. "A grand performance, for a full house!"

Sophia giggled, recollecting what he had told her of his youthful days in California; his adventures there had included a stint as a stage hand for the glorious Miss Crabtree. "That was most wonderful timing, Fred. I love Lottie as a dear friend but I am convinced that I was enduring this day for the fondness I hold towards her, and the friends we have. She insisted that when I first told her of our engagement that the party would be at least as much for our friends as it was for you and I."

"Too true," Fred agreed. "But she's a fine noble woman and knows these things." He transferred the reins into one hand and embraced her with the other arm. "Ah, *Sopherl* – I have never been married before, or started a family, but I have seen it done, time and time again. Well, not the actual starting of it, although," he added, in a tone of scrupulous honesty, "When I was a small boy back in the Old Country, I did often see my sister Liesel come from the hayloft, brushing straw out of her hair, and not two minutes later, her soon-to-be husband also come from the hayloft, buttoning up his trousers and fastening his braces. They were starting their family … or perhaps trying it out. We lived on a small farm then, you see. Not much goes past, unobserved in a place like that." Now he looked sideways at Sophia, his expression questioning. "You know about … that which is involved, starting a family?"

Sophia sighed. "I do, Fred. If I had not gained a sense of that natural process from observing Miss Kitten, I have from the conversation of the other Harvey House girls. Some of them came from farms, and others had been married. Or as your sister did – trying it out. I have been assured it is a most pleasurable experience, given an affectionate and considerate lover."

"So it is rumored," Fred agreed in a wry tone, and his arm around her tightened. "I won't hurry you, *Sopherl* – you know that. I treasure you too deeply to rush things."

"I know that." Sophia answered. She nestled into his side, feeling as safe and as sheltered as she always had with Fred. "So … do you want a large family?"

"Of course; but how many is 'large'? Liesel and her husband had nine. Three girls and six boys although two of them died as children and another ran off to live with the Indians."

"Eight at least." Sophia replied, confidently. Anything seemed possible, now. "When I was a little girl, I so wished that I could have had many brothers and sisters to play with. Eight. Ten. Twelve. A bounty of children; I love children, Fred and I know that I could manage."

"Seeing you manage a dining room full of hungry travelers, who could doubt it?" Fred brushed her cheek with a brief kiss, and the rest of the journey to the ranch house passed in companionable silence.

She had visited the ranch house often enough, but until the day he proposed marriage she had always considered the place as his; a comfortable bachelor establishment. Now they came from the last of the low hills which sheltered the house, stable, barn and corrals, and Sophie regarded the place with new eyes. This was now her home. She gloried in the feeling of proud possession: the thick walls, newly plastered and the color of rich cream, the sheltering roof of the veranda which went all the way around the central cluster of rooms, the new shakes which covered the roof, the faded rust-red tiles of the floor. It was not the least bit like the Brewer mansion, or even a Harvey House, with those modern splendors afforded by the newest and best, but it was hers, hers and Fred's – every stick, stone, tile and brick.

"I put your trunk in the bedroom," Fred said, as they drew up to the front. "And there's a crate or two of things from the East to be unpacked in the veranda. I had the lads open it but I figured you'd know best where to put the things in it."

"What kind of things?" Sophia asked, as one of the hands came around from the stable, to take the horse and buggy away.

"Wedding present sorts of things," Fred replied, inscrutably. "For the house; bits of china, linens, glass. I wrote to Mr. Ford Harvey and asked where to get the household fittings you'd be accustomed to. And my sister Magda, she sent a crate. I wrote and told her I was getting married. She knows me well. She was convinced that I'd be bringing my bride to an empty shack." They stepped up onto the veranda, Fred with his hand under Sophia's elbow again. He looked at her – not down, as their heads were much on a level, and he cleared his throat. "I know that I should carry you over the doorstep – it's one of those things – but …"

"No," Sophia replied, decisively, as they paused at the door leading into the parlor. "I'm not a helpless little maiden and this is our house. We step over the threshold together."

They linked their arms around each other, and Fred counted softly, as he opened the door. "One, two, three, on your right foot advance, *Sopherl*!" They stepped in unison over the wooden beam of the threshold in a single step, and Sophia gave herself up, laughing, in a fond embrace, just inside the open doorway. "Welcome home, Mrs. Steinmetz!" Fred exclaimed, and they kissed, somewhat less shyly as they had in the church, since here there were no eyes upon them. "No hurry then," he added as Sophia drew back. It was still daylight after all. Someone called for Fred, around at the back of the house, and he sighed. "Something about a cow with calf, *Sopherl* – I have to go."

"I'll unpack my trunk and arrange the house," Sophia promised, although in part of herself, she longed to embrace him again. Tonight, then. He kissed her again, and departed through the door with a purposeful stride, to attend to whatever matter he had been called for. Sophia was not resentful, even on her wedding-day. The ranch was a business, it was their business, and Fred had been seeing to cows for a considerable number of years.

Well, she had the house to attend to; her own house. She savored the taste of the words in her mouth. Her house; not poor Fee's house, or the various establishments of Mr. Harvey, but hers, and hers alone, to rule and to see to the comfort of everyone who lived within its walls. At present, that was just herself and Fred, but when that changed … Sophia resolutely put that thought aside, for now.

She changed out of her good satin wedding dress, opening her trunk to pull out and don one of the plain black dresses which was her own, putting the new gown and bonnet away with her other clothes in the standing wardrobe in the main bedroom.

The crates stood under the shelter of the verandah, with the wooden tops levered off, leaving the excelsior that had protected the contents undisturbed. Sophia delved into the first, as happy as a child at Christmas unwrapping a bounty of presents: *ohh*! – linens, china and glass, of the make and quality provided to Harvey establishments, and a set of excellent pots and pans, too! She emptied the crate, running back and forth among the rooms, with armfuls of things. Was this like being a child with the grandest and most marvelous dollhouse in the world? The contents went into their appointed places, Sophia thinking of what a marvelous house Fred had caused to be built. There was a place for everything, and now everything was in a proper place at last. She pulled from her trunk a few framed prints, found places for them along the walls – they would have to be hung from the picture rail, so she left them leaning against the wall. Her books. The pieced quilt in the wedding-ring pattern, a gift from the ladies of St. Luke's went on the bed. The crate from Fred's sister contained fine linen bedding, pillows and a vast feather-bed. Buried underneath were three smaller items; a lovely English painted washstand ewer and bowl, and a mantel clock with a wooden case which showed signs of having once broken and expertly mended. There was a note in an envelope laid on top of the clock, addressed in spidery and somewhat foreign-appearing handwriting to Mrs. Friedrich Steinmetz.

Yes, that was her name now. Sophia opened the envelope, feeling trepidation – which she ought not to have done, for the note inside was as affectionate in tone as it was brief:

To my new sister – I wish for you all the happiness in the world upon the occasion of your marriage. I would never have thought that my little brother Fredi was inclined toward matrimony, but I rejoice that he has now settled upon it with you. You must be an extraordinary person, to achieve this condition with a man who for so long has given every indication of being a confirmed bachelor. The sister of my own beloved husband sent me a bowl and ewer like this, on the occasion of my own marriage – a useful and pretty thing, which I present with every wish of happiness for you both. The clock is one made by our beloved father, Christian Friedrich Steinmetz of Ulm in Bavaria. It adorned my own house for many happy years, and I pass it to you, in the hope that it may do so in yours for many years to come.

Your loving sister,
Margaretha Vogel Becker

The clock went on the narrow mantel-shelf in the parlor. Sophia wound it up and set the hands, and it ticked away as smoothly as silk. The bowl and ewer ought to go onto the bedroom wash-stand. When she carried them into that room, she saw that the long French glass door which opened onto the veranda stood open; while she unpacked the trunk and crates, late afternoon had turned into early evening. Outside, beyond the edge of the veranda roof, the sky had turned to a dark and glowing red, and the single long and violet-hued cloud on the horizon had edges of molten gold.

"*Sopherl*? Is that you?" Fred's voice came from the verandah. "Come out with me and watch the sunset. It's a good one, better than any painting."

That was why there was a wicker settee and three chairs out on the west-facing verandah. Fred made room for her, and she sat beside him, blissfully tired and happy that this day was nearly over. Fred obviously was. He had exchanged his boots for carpet-slippers, unfastened the collar of his shirt and abandoned his cravat. He put an arm around her waist, and she leaned against him, her cheek resting on his shoulder.

"It's good to be home, at last." She signed. The color of the sky intensified. Now the red-gold sun dropped from behind the cloud and touched the edge of the far hills. The hills had darkened to frozen waves of blue, blue-violet, dark grey. "I think that I never saw sunsets as spectacular as this in Boston, not until I came west."

"One thing we have over the east," Fred agreed. There was a bottle and a glass on a small table next to the settee. "I'm having a brandy. D'you want one? It's good stuff, none of the usual saloon rot-gut. M' nephew George in Galveston gets it straight from France. He's the buyer for the family general stores, y'see."

"No, but I'll take a sip from yours," Sophia replied, curled up on the settee. There was only the one glass, and this was their moment together. She had left Boston and convention behind many miles and years since. The sky darkened imperceptibly; in the beam of lantern light falling through the open door, Miss Kitten stalked an errant luckless moth, herself nearly invisible in the twilight. Sophia could not imagine any degree of higher happiness and contentment.

"So you are set on a large family?" Fred asked, as the last shreds of red and molten gold faded along the horizon. The level of brandy in the single glass had diminished by small sips over the last half-hour, and Sophia felt the slight but heady effects.

"I am," she replied. "I am not in any doubt … but can we afford a large family, Fred? Is there enough space on the ranch for them all? That is my single worry. I once knew a poor family – they lived in two rented rooms and loved their children dearly but …"

Fred kissed her, with gentle affection. "Of course we can, *Sopherl*. We can add to the house. And – expert wranglers and cow-hands are always in demand. Good we can raise them from scratch, as it were."

"I name the girls," Sophia insisted. The brandy had made her feel warm and especially affectionate; this was Fred, who loved her, had carefully plotted his courtship; a man of the world, so Lottie affirmed. There was nothing bad that could happen in Fred's embrace, or in the marital bed. She kissed him, or he kissed her – Sophia was not entirely certain of the sequence of things at that moment.

"Certainly, dearest little *Sopherl*," he murmured. "Now – let us go start that family, shall we?"

Part 3 – 1900

Chapter 20 – A Man of Family

"Sophie, my dear," said Lottie Thurmond on the occasion of the baptism of the Steinmetz' sixth child and third son, "When I suggested after your wedding – and it was only a suggestion, mind you, although based on Scriptural authority – that you and Fred should go fourth and multiply, I did not for a moment think that you should take me so literally. It's as if you are attempting to fill the children's Sunday school single-handed."

"We love children," Sophia replied, serenely. She settled baby Christian to a more comfortable position in her lap. "And we agreed that we would try and have a large family."

"Yes, but it must seem as if every time Fred throws his trousers on the foot of the bed, you are in the family way again. Six children in ten years! At this rate, you will never get your figure back."

"I don't care," Sophia smiled at her friend. They were sitting in the parlor of Lottie's house. "Looking after the children and the house keeps me thin, and I never was plump to begin with."

"At least, motherhood suits you," Lottie acknowledged in humorous resignation. "And you are happy in it. Fatherhood suits Fred – who would have ever thought it!"

Out in the garden, Fred was throwing horses-shoes with the older children, while Frank Thurmond smoked a cigar in the shade of the one cottonwood tree in the Thurmond's garden. Lottie despaired of ever having grass grow and had settled on raked gravel and pots of shrubs and flowers. Now the children romped with happy energy, little constrained by their good Sunday clothes, for Sophia had long resolved on practicality. Minnie – called Min within the family – Carlotta and Annabelle wore sailor dresses of stout broadcloth, in the same general cut, and handed from sister to sister, as they grew. Their brothers Charles Henry and Fred Harvey would follow the same pattern as far as hand-me-down clothing went. They were stair-step children, from Min to the toddler Fred, although Annabelle and Charles Henry were twins, and otherwise identical. This had pleased Fred Steinmetz no end. He reminded Sophia that he was a twin himself, and there was a pair of twins in his sister's family as well. Sophia loved them with fierce affection, although if pressed, she would have to confess that she was especially fond of Minnie, grave and intelligent beyond her nine years. Her oldest daughter had inherited Great Aunt Minnie's intellectual leanings along with the name.

"So, this journey to Galveston is still in your plans?" Lottie asked.

"Oh, yes. It's an occasion for all of Fred's relations; the wedding of his oldest nephew's daughter. It will be the first time I'll meet most of them. His sister and her son- and daughter-in-law came out to Deming four years ago, so I have met <u>them</u>. Her son is Samuel Becker, the artist; he painted those perfectly splendid pictures which you admired so much in our parlor."

"I remember," Lottie nodded. "Such a charming man, and quite renowned in artistic circles, so I hear."

"Yes; Sam and Jane and the children were such fascinating company," Sophia nodded. "I am eager to see them again, and my friend Laura Belton, whom I shared a room with the first year I worked for the Harvey House? She lives in Galveston now. In her letters, she says such wonderful things – so modern and fine! The seashore there is marvelous, and it is the richest town in Texas. I am so looking forward to visiting. It's been forever since I saw an ocean."

"You still don't sound as if you are looking forward to it," Lottie observed, acutely, and Sophia sighed. "Is it the thought of a long train journey?"

"No – I still adore traveling by train, and I have friends in so many places! The children will love the excursion, I am certain …"

"Fred's family, then?"

"No, although it will be daunting for me; Fred married me so late. His sisters and his brothers' children are grown, much older than our little gaggle. I imagine that I will be the object of intense curiosity, but his sister is quite the queenly matriarch. She approves of me, at any rate. It's my nephew, Richie. He's coming to Galveston with the intention of seeing me."

"Oh, dear." Lottie sat back in her chair, entirely sympathetic. "So that is it. This will be the son of your brother? He went to a great deal of trouble to locate you, and assure himself that you were still alive, my dear Sophie. Do you have reason to fear his interest, in some way?"

"I don't know," Sophia answered, bleak and miserable. She was glad that Fred and the other children were outside. "He was a pleasant and charming boy, the age of Minnie when I last saw him. My brother also appeared to everyone to be a pleasant and charming boy … but he was a monster. Once that one has been fooled in so significant a manner, one will always have doubts regarding one's judgement of character, you see. And it is not just me, but our children. He is a grown man himself, now. I fear he will have turned out like his father."

"Fred will be there," Lottie spoke with stout assurance. "And all of his family; he won't permit anyone to harm to you – or the little ones, either."

"I suppose," Sophia acknowledged, for that was a comfortable consideration. "Fifteen years, nearly sixteen, is a long time, time in which I have put aside so much of the girl I used to be. Now, I hate any reminder of how persecuted and desperate I was. Lottie, my best friends and dearest kin turned their backs on me, and I was helpless! I had nowhere to go, no means of throwing back the calumnies they heaped upon me!" Distressed and agitated, she wrung her hands together. It had been so long since she had been able to speak of her fears to an understanding person. "I do not like being reminded of that person I once was, Lottie. I fear I might be thrown back into that helpless state of mind. That is why I declined to correspond with my nephew – he wrote only once, when Fred and I were new-married. I was unwilling to enter into correspondence. Walk away, someone told me. Walk away, before the demons get their claws dug in. I had Fred to consider … and our first child."

"But you are not that helpless girl any more," Lottie reached out her hands and captured Sophia's in hers. "You became a strong and independent woman, with a darling family and friends who would not consider for a moment, turning their back on you in distress. We become many people in our lives as we pass through the stages of womanhood. I am no longer the sweet obedient belle that my mother sent out to snag a rich husband and you are no longer that desperate girl, escaping your brother's machinations. Nothing in our lives can no put us back to what we were, not after so long a time has passed."

"I suppose so," Sophia confessed, somewhat comforted by Lottie's vehemence. "And I will do my best to recall your words."

"Do, my dear. When are you leaving for Galveston?"

"A week from tomorrow; we'll go as far as San Antonio on the regular Pullman coach. The family has a most splendid parlor car of their own, and we'll go on to Galveston together with those relations who live there."

"It sounds as if it will be a wonderful excursion," Lottie assured her. "You must write me of every detail."

San Antonio
August 21, 1900

My dear Lottie:

Here we are safely arrived in San Antonio after our tiring journey. The dear children and I are all well, as is darling F. He sends his best wishes, and says that you and Frank would likely not recognize your old haunts! The old city is much changed – as have many cities – most especially by the arrival of the railroad. Little remains of the old Spanish citadel save the original chapel, now that the Army has established their new post in the hills to the north of town. There are splendid new buildings along wide new avenues, a lovely park with gardens and fountains, and streetcars everywhere. The children have enjoyed the journey so far. They have been almost angelic in their behavior, and Min has asked me the most searching questions – such a solemn little Miss!

Here we have met with the closer portion of F.'s family; his older sister Magda Becker, her two sons with their wives and children, and her daughter with her husband and family. There is a certain consistency in appearance, by which we discern that branch of the family – a tendency to be tall, with very fair straight hair and blue eyes. The family of F.'s other sister, the Richters, (both she and her husband are deceased, alas) are also uniformly recognizable by appearance: stocky, with dark hair and eyes of a brown hue. This is all complicated somewhat by intermarriage. To my astonishment, there is also a portion of the family with the surname of Vining – the same name as my maternal grandfather – and I was first assumed on the basis of my own appearance to be a connection of theirs.

On the morrow, we depart in a large party for Galveston …

* * *

Sophia omitted from her letter to Lottie one or two of the most awkward moments; the first occurring when she overheard Magda Becker's daughter Charlotte Bertrand remark in astonishment to her sister-in-law, "She is so young, Jane, so much younger than he is – half his age at least! Where on earth did Onkel Fredi meet up with her? I sincerely hope it was not a low dance-hall!"

"No, dear, she was working at a Harvey house." Jane answered, comfortably. "Her family was most respectable, but they fell on hard times. She keeps a lovely house and as far as I can see, they are as happy as newlyweds."

"Oh, I see." Sophia was about to tiptoe away from the doorway out to the terrace of the Richter mansion, before her presence was noted, but her departure was arrested when Charlotte Bertrand commented, "It is curious, though; she resembles Cousin Horrie in every particular. They could be brother and sister. Have you noticed?"

"I can't say I have," Jane replied. Shaken, Sophia slipped away. Was there a much closer connection to these Texas Vinings? The question weighed on her, especially when the Vinings, connected by marriage to both families, arrived from Austin within days. Peter Vining, the patriarch of that branch with his wife Anna, whom Sophia recalled with particular fondness from that brief meeting in Newton at the start of her time in Fred Harvey company. Peter Vining brought his daughter Rose and his nephew, that Horrie Vining whom she was herself said to resemble. Horrie's wife, Grete was also Fred's niece, which amused Sophia. "Your family is as complicated as mine is, only with two hundred years of marrying each other, right and left!" she complained merrily to Fred, upon learning this.

As Horrie and Grete were the same age as Sophia herself, their children were of an age to be playmates with Fred and Sophia's children. Indeed, their oldest son, Robert Lee, was exactly the same age as Min. Sophia had to admit, the likeness between herself and

Horrie was more than a little unsettling; of the same light frame physically, but his cast in a masculine mold, the same shape to their faces, eyes of the same blue-grey color, and the same tightly curling light brown hair. Horrie Vining was the speaking image of young Grandfather Vining, in that antique portrait of he and Great-Aunt Minnie, which once had hung in the old Vining mansion on Beacon Hill. Now and again, she thought she caught him looking at her, in a speculative fashion, and knew – somehow – that he was wondering the same thing.

* * *

August 24, 1900
Galveston

My dear Lottie:

Here we are all safely arrived, after a crowded but comfortable journey from San Antonio, with F.'s relations in every degree. The gentlemen of the family were put to the trouble of borrowing another parlor car for the excursion so we might travel in palatial comfort. The children are enjoying themselves in the society of their cousins, and I find the company of the ladies in the family to be congenial, especially Jane and Isobel Becker. They came out from England in the Centennial year and married brothers – the sons of F.'s older sister, if you are able to keep all this straight in your mind.

We are now comfortably accommodated in the splendid mansion of F.'s nephew, George Steinmetz and his wife Amelie, parents of the young lady whose marriage we are gathered from the far corners of Texas to celebrate. George is a considerable magnate in these parts. He caused to be built a splendid mansion of thirty rooms with every modern convenience – including electric lights and a telephone – can you imagine? It is in the Romanesque style, two tall stories on elevated foundations – to prevent damage from what the local residents call 'the overflow', crowned with a most magnificent square tower, with windows all around, from which may be seen practically the entire island, from the harbor on one side to the Gulf on the other. There is a wonderful garden surrounding, at the intersection of two of Galveston's most stately avenues. This noble mansion replaced one with a more seaside aspect which, because of the increase in commerce, became a less prestigious address, and increasingly somewhat less salubrious.

How sweetly the church bells sound on a Sunday! Such a lovely chorus as I have not heard since leaving Boston. As well as being the kindliest and most considerate of hosts, George is also singularly well-traveled. His father made a large fortune in cattle and settled each of his sons and those husbands of his daughters in profitable commerce and ranching. Cousin G., as he insists that I call him, sees to purchasing and importing all manner of goods for the general mercantile trade operated by the family. He began as a wagon teamster, while still in his youth during the War, and had ever so many stories of his adventures to regale us with …"

"So, it was good sense relocating to Galveston," George Steinmetz remarked, expansively, early in the evening of their arrival. He and Fred's sister Magda, and Horrie, and Peter Vining sat with Sophia in comfortable willow-wicker chairs in the open loggia overlooking a stretch of garden, planted with orange trees and tall palms. Sophia rejoiced in the cool, salt-smelling breeze that fanned her cheeks. Below in the garden, the children were playing – hers and Fred's with smallest Vinings, while little Fred Harvey and the baby napped in the center of the large bed in the suite allotted to his parents. George's wife Amelie, with Anna Vining and the other ladies were upstairs – something to do with the young bride's trousseau. Since Sophia did not know the bride, she had gracefully excused herself from participation. Fred and his Becker nephews had gone for a walk, saying they wished to see how the town had fared since their last visit.

"I suppose this is why your house is built on such a high foundation?" Sophia ventured, for it was so; the sprawling brick mansion sat six feet from the ground, as stout-built as a fortress, with tall and sturdy shutters which could be latched tightly against storm winds to protect its many windows.

"That is so," George nodded. He was a burly man of fifty, with dark hair cut short like a brush and lightly touched with grey. Like Fred, he retained the slight accent of his German forebears. "Galveston has weathered many storms; it is the expected thing here. There was no future in Indianola, after the first storm, when Morgan moved his steamships away. He did not rebuild the dock there, you see. I cannot blame him."

"You were there during that storm, weren't you?" Peter asked, and George shook his head. "No, but Jacob and Elias were, with two of Papa's freight wagons. Fortunately, the boarding house where they sheltered was on higher ground, but the lower town was swept out to sea, once the wind turned. You remember, how there was a wide bayou behind the town? Jacob said later – a wall of water, pushing everything before it out into the ocean – houses turned to matchsticks and swept like toys. And that is why this house is built strong. We have been through many storms – maybe some roof-tiles loosened, and a leak in the attic. That is all."

"It's a splendid house," Sophia made an honest compliment, and George beamed with appreciation. The voices of the children momentarily drew her attention; a child shrieked, and she could not help but rise from the chair and move to the railing. No, only excitement, not in pain; they were having such fun, their energy undiminished, although her solemn little Min and Horrie's oldest son,

Robert Lee, sat together on a garden bench, their heads bent over a book. Annabelle and Charles Henry, as inseparable as two peas in a pod were chasing after a ball across the lawn, relevant to a game of catch. Sophia watched them, distracted by motherly affection from the conversation behind her. She hardly noticed when Horrie Vining came to stand next to her, likewise watching the children romp.

"They look like twins," he remarked, after a moment.

"They are twins," Sophia replied, assuming he meant Annabelle and Charles Henry.

Horrie shook his head. "No – Robbie and Minerva; they look like they were born twins. It doesn't come from Onkel Fred and Grete's side of the family, either." He took a deep breath. It came to Sophia that he was as nervous about broaching the subject as she was. "Uncle Peter remarked on it, too. He recalled you said that you were from Boston, and your grandfather was named Horace Vining. That was curious, he thought – because his father was also named Horace Vining."

"I remember," Sophia's voice shook. "At the time, I thought we might have been distant kin. Vining is a common name in Boston; and it was not unknown for Vining cousins to be named Horace."

"And did many of those Horace Vining cousins lived on Beacon Hill, the youngest of four sons with a bluestocking sister named Minerva Templeton Vining?" Horrie looked deliberately out at the garden. Sophia felt as if she did, on that long-ago day when her brother stuck her; stunned, horrified and disbelieving.

"You can't be serious! How could you know …" she gasped, and Horrie Vining kept his eyes on the garden, but his voice was relentless. "Who died there of consumption in 1841, leaving a wife in Boston named Annabelle Saltinstall, and a daughter named Sophia … and another wife in Austin, who bore him four sons. Uncle Peter was one of them, my father the oldest."

"This cannot possibly be true," Sophia gasped. No, this was worse than Richard's dastardly plot. Her grandfather a bigamist! How shaming, how horrible! It couldn't be true. "It's outrageous – I will not stand for this insult! We won't stay under this roof a minute longer!"

Over his shoulder, Horrie said, sounding as resigned as if he had expected this, "George, you'd better fetch Onkel Fred. Mrs. Sophie is that upset."

"It's a lie!" Sophia raged, on the edge of tears. "My family … my family doesn't do things …" She stopped, as if she had walked into the edge of a door in pitch darkness.

"I believe that they do," Horrie said, sounding infinitely compassionate. "Look, Mrs. Sophie; come sit. It's true, every word, but it's a family matter; we haven't breathed a word to anyone, save the three of us here, and George. Uncle Peter."

"Come and sit," Uncle Peter echoed Horrie's words. Magda Becker looked as implacable as a carved stone goddess, or a saint on a pillar in a Catholic church, in her plain black dress, her hair braided underneath the old-fashioned white house-bonnet. Sophia wondered again how much of this the older woman understood. But she took Sophia's hands into hers, as Horrie guided her to sit beside the older woman on the settee. He pulled up one of the tuffets and sat in front of her, so intently earnest she was moved to trust him, almost against her own will. Unbidden came the thought – *Why couldn't he have been her brother, and not Richard?*

"Mrs. Sophie, I'm the family historian, everyone says so. I was close to my grandmother; Gran'mere, I called her. She died when I was little, but she talked to me when she was dying and I remembered more of what she said than most people would have thought. She talked about her husband. I'm named after him, you see. She said that I was like him, with the books and all. Perhaps she said more than she meant to, but I loved her very much and I took what she said and remembered. Everything I said just now was true; what she told me. His name was Horace Vining, from Boston. He came to Texas in the early days, for his health, taught school in San Felipe – that's the town that was the main one in the Austin Colony, back in the early days. He came to Gonzales and taught school there, and married Gran'mere; before the J.P., not in a church. Then he was a scout for Houston's army and fought at San Jacinto. Uncle Peter, show her … you know."

Peter Vining silently drew a small velvet-covered box from his waistcoat, and opened it, revealing an old-fashioned miniature portrait on ivory; a young man with curly hair and a tall collar and old-fashioned stock. He was the image of Horrie Vining and the same young man in that portrait of the younger Great Aunt Minnie and her brother. Sophia gulped, still disbelieving, even with the likeness before her. What Horrie had revealed matched Great Aunt Minnie's story of her brother fighting in a battle in Texas against the Mexicans. "There's no proof of this," she insisted – one last speck of defiance. "Nothing that might be recognized in a court of law!"

Horrie exchanged a long look with Peter Vining.

"A letter signed by Minerva Vining would be considered and recognized," Peter Vining conceded with reluctance, as he closed the velvet box and returned it to his waistcoat pocket. "In any court of law, together with another communication from the Vining family lawyers in Boston. Such a letter was sent to my mother, acknowledging the situation in every detail, and enclosing a bank draft. I don't think that my mother ever called it in. She was a proud woman, and she had the means to see to our upbringing."

"Then she should have burned it," Sophia exclaimed, in indignation. "And removed any proof of a connection!"

"I think that she intended that at the end," Horrie confessed. "But she was paralyzed and incapable by then. She entrusted the papers in her desk, her most private papers, to Miss Hetty. Miss Hetty ruled the household; Gran'mere's most trusted confidante. I think that Gran'mere meant for Miss Hetty to burn the lot, but Miss Hetty kept them secure and gave them to me in turn, at the end of her own life. She did not read them, but she sensed they were important. Mrs. Sophie, please believe me; we never had any intent of reviving an old scandal like this. It was over and done with a long time ago."

"But for my mistake in marrying into your family!" Sophia cried, distraught, and Horrie replied, stung to the quick.

"Never a mistake, Mrs. Sophie! Onkel Fredi never thought anything of it and you have made him very, very happy. It's just that … you look too much like one of us Vinings for it to go unnoticed – your children, too, especially Minnie. You couldn't help but wonder, I'll be bound; don't tell me you haven't been thinking about it, all the same. Uncle Peter and I thought that perhaps it was best for you to know for certain; I … well, I didn't think it would distress you so. I'm sorry. Truth is," Horrie smiled, self-consciously. "The truth is that we Vinings were getting thin on the ground; just Uncle Peter and I left at the end of the War. Having cousins or a sister would have suited me, fine."

What Sophia meant to say was lost on a sob, and Magda Becker said in German to the men, "Leave us, if you will. I will talk to her." Sophia was barely aware of Horrie and Peter Vining's departure into the house. Out on the lawn the children continued playing as if nothing had happened in the last five minutes. Magda waited for Sophia to compose herself and pressed a handkerchief in her hand.

"I don't know why I am crying," she confessed, sunk in misery, as she dried her eyes. "This is not something I thought any of us were capable of."

The older woman snorted, scornfully. Her accent was heavier than Fred's but her voice was kind, gentle as a mother's when she spoke. "You think? It is something in the past, *Sopherl*. Men … people … often take actions which seem sensible at the time. It is only later, and knowing only a little of why they did so, that we are baffled. There is a thing which I will tell you; perhaps it will help you to understand. To understand is to forgive, I think." Sophia nodded, touched by the formidable Magda's consideration. But the next words did not seem at first to make any sense. "Many years ago in San Antonio, in the oldest quarter of the city, there was the house of an old family, of the pure blood of Spain, as they said then. The house is long gone. The husband was older, much older than his wife – even older," Magda Becker added with a wintery smile, "Than Fredi is to you. They had no children for many years. In time, my husband who was then a young man, hardly more than a boy, became friends with them; often a guest in their house, at their table, a companion to both husband and wife. I knew of this friendship much, much later, *Sopherl*. This was before I even came to this country and made acquaintance with him. In time, the wife bore a son, a fine healthy boy to carry on the name of this family of the old blood."

"I don't see what this has to do …" Sophia began.

Magda Becker lifted her hand against the interruption. "Much later, my husband and I met. We had for a time, our own house, our own dear children. That is a long story, *Sopherl*, how it came to be, and how I came to live in San Antonio. But some years ago, a friend pointed out the house of that family. The husband had died, of course, but his wife still lived, as did her son. A fine man, with his own wife and family; I saw them on many occasions, and I always thought how much that he resembled my own oldest son. Not so much in the color of his hair, but in his features, the way he sat on a horse. I have never remarked on this likeness to anyone. It was none of my business, how a man and wife ensured the continuance of their blood, or if my husband was willingly complicit …"

"But that's adulterous – an immoral connection …"

"I suppose that it is," Magda Becker shrugged. "But it is for God to judge. Since my husband, the nobleman of old family and his wife are now dead, He has likely rendered his decision on the matter. This is the thing you should understand, *Sopherl*. My husband and your grandfather; they were young men in a dangerous time. My husband was a Ranger, a soldier. At that time, I know that he believed that he had no life, no future to live for; he was fated to die in battle with the Comanche or perhaps the Mexicans. Already a dead man, yet still in the world for a time on sufferance; he took comfort in the moment, never thinking farther ahead than the next day. Your grandfather; a consumptive, was he not? Likely he was in the same frame of mind. Forgive the dead; allow them their motivations, and their secrets. They can only hurt the living if we allow them." Sophia hiccupped; done with tears and oddly comforted by Magda's words. "You are an orphan, not so? Fredi wrote me once, saying that your father was dead in the War, your mother some years afterwards, and you had no close living family. *Sopherl*, dear child – accept that you do now; a family in one by blood and by marriage."

Chapter 21 – Between the Living and the Dead

"What did you know of this, Fred?" Sophia waited until the household had dispersed for the night to reproach her husband in private. The suite of rooms allotted to them was at the top of the house, and well-fitted to a large family. The largest room boasted a small covered porch from which one could see the stretch of water dividing Galveston from the mainland. On clear nights, one could see lights twinkling on the mainland, far, far away. Sophia appreciated it most particularly as it allowed them to resume their habit of sitting together and watching the evening fall. "That my grandfather had availed himself of two wives – my grandmother being one, and Peter Vining's mother the other?"

Fred and his nephews had finally been run to ground at the splendid Garten Verein – the landscaped beer-garden a few blocks from the Richter mansion. By the time he returned Sophia had composed herself, and then the household had gathered for supper. She could not bear to speak of this before anyone else. Magda Becker, Horrie and Peter Vining assured her of their silence and discretion – but how could Fred not have known or suspected?

"I didn't know for sure," Fred answered, slowly. "But I wondered if it weren't something of the sort. I heard plenty of stories in the earlies about men having one wife back in the East, or in San Francisco, and another one in the gold-camps. It's almost a joke – sailors who have a wife in every port – that kind of understanding, especially when you go hundreds of miles from where anyone knows who you are." Unconsciously, he echoed his sister's words. "Young bucks, thinking only of the day … they don't consider anything or anyone else, much. Stupid and unthinking, I know, but that's the long and short of it. *Sopherl*, darling," he took her hand and brought it to his lips. "That your grandfather couldn't keep his trousers properly buttoned in the presence of a pretty girl is none of my business, and not a speck of a reflection on you. I don't care and never did. Not about this, or your swine of a brother. It's only yourself and the dear little ones I have a duty and a right to care for." He kept her hand prisoner in his, for a long while, as they sat silent together. The last apricot of sunset had long faded in the west, and now the pale stars winked into view. The distant roar of the surf, rolling in against the shoreline blocks away was louder than the sound of someone playing a piano in the parlor on the other side of the house. Sophia, unexpectedly comforted, leaned her head on Fred's shoulder.

"They do look enough like another set of twins," she said, "Min and Robbie – don't they?"

"They do, indeed." Fred drew Sophia closer to him. "All of our darlings asleep, then?"

"Min is reading by candle-light," Sophia replied. "But the others are asleep. Even Baby is asleep, for the moment, at least."

"Tomorrow," Fred suggested after a moment, "Let's take them to the Midway – on the streetcar. Let them wade in the water, build sand-castles, and eat salt-water taffy and ice cream until they are sick of it. Make it a perfect holiday, umm?"

"Yes," Sophia agreed. It seemed a lovely prospect, a day at the seashore with the children. The prospect of meeting with Richie again – all of that had unexpectedly diminished, into a matter so minor it wasn't worth troubling her mind over.

Galveston
3 September, 1900

Dear Lottie:

At last I have a few moments to write to you! I know that you must have been wondering how we have fared during our stay in

Galveston, and I apologize for not being able to write sooner than today. F.'s family have been so gracious and welcoming, in spite of some initial awkwardness. Dear F. has been so long a bachelor and a rolling stone; with the exception of his sister and younger nephew, all have been astounded to see him newly reborn as a devoted family man. We have discovered new ties of affection, and older ties of blood which seem to have been closer than first was assumed. More of this on our return. I have met several times with my old friend Laura B. and her children, at her dear little yellow-painted cottage, and once for a luncheon together at the Harvey House, where we laughed and laughed over being guests instead of attending to the tables. Such wonderful conversations and reminiscences!

The wedding was a most splendid one, celebrated in the sanctuary of one of the oldest and most notable churches in Galveston, one founded primarily by German immigrants – indeed, the ceremony was in German entirely, as both the bride and groom's families are of that nation, and have long been members. The sanctuary was decorated with ivy, orange blossoms, and white jasmine mixed with roses, which gloriously perfumed the air; the bride and her attendants carried bouquets of those same flowers, and the smallest attendants wore garlands of the same in their hair. The bridal gown was perfection itself – in the latest fashion, but adorned with inset panels of antique French brocade which came from a cherished but unfortunately disintegrating heirloom; a gown first worn by her grandmother, and then by many thrifty female relations for their own nuptials. There was one somewhat startling incident. Just before ceremonies began, a pair of nuns entered the church, quietly, and sat in the last pew. I noticed this, and made mention to F. – and he said that one of the nuns was Magda Becker's eldest daughter – his niece, who had converted to the Catholic faith as a young woman and entered the Ursuline sisterhood! How astonishing –

I wished to meet and converse with her, as I had a dear friend in Boston who also became a nun, but she slipped away from the gathering before I could do so. She is a teacher at the Catholic orphanage, at the easternmost edge of the island.

The ceremonies were followed by a lavish ball at Cousin G.'s residence, where a dance floor was laid out over part of the lawn, and a tuneful orchestra played for most of the evening. Even the older children had their fun, being permitted to remain up and dance until the middle of the evening, and to nibble as they pleased from a sumptuous buffet laid out in the dining room. Oh, I cannot tell you how marvelous the sight of a constellation of paper Japanese lanterns was, swaying in the cool autumn breeze, under the brilliant stars – the music and the colors of the ladies' gowns, swirling across the dance floor! I danced many times with dear F. and then with other gentleman, while he danced with the ladies! Such occasions are what I most longed for as a girl; splendid balls, handsome beaux and music – always music!

Of course, I needed to excuse myself now and again to tend to the children, especially Baby Christian, who did demand his usual meals, regardless of the occasion! Mrs. Jane and I were similar in our absences from the ball, to tend to our infants, but I vow that the exhilaration of the day and the quietude of our own daily lives in comparison lent us sufficient energy. As dawn came, we saw the bride and groom off at the docks to begin their honeymoon journey – a sizable party throwing confetti and rice and cheering them as the steamship departed. They are traveling to their ancestral country, to spend three months among the magnificent castles and quaint villages. I do not consider myself to be envious; do not mistake my enthusiasm for description for any envy on my part, dear Lottie. My wedding was most perfect, in itself. Dear F. and I, when recovered from the day's exertions, took the children by streetcar, across the

Island to the outer shore, for a day which I relished just as much as the evening.

We were planning to begin our return journey on Friday but I have just received a telegram from Richie; he is delayed until the following day. This presents the necessity of an adjustment to our plans. The train and the parlor cars for our party is scheduled, and at this late date there is no possibility of amendment. The children were so looking forward to continued association with their cousins, and the pleasures of the family palace car! We cannot bear to disappoint them in this, for it may be some considerable time before they have a similar opportunity. So – F. departs as planned on Friday, with the children, save Min and Baby Christian and I. I will meet Richie on Saturday and depart on Monday, taking a Pullman berth as far as San Antonio, there to catch up to F. and the children. We will remain for a few days in San Antonio and then return to Deming and home. As pleasant as this excursion has been, I long for the quiet of our home, and the regular routine.

Until then, my best to you and to Frank
Sophia

* * *

On Thursday, Sophia and Fred made a last excursion to the shore with the children, relishing the cooler temperatures which autumn brought; the sky was the purest of blue, and the fresh salt-smelling breeze touched the sea with sparkling whitecaps, although the water itself was as warm as bathwater. It was the most perfect of days; Sophia thought with sentimental regret of how it would be their last day in Galveston, now that all the excitement and celebration of the wedding was over. Now the return journey – and that face-to-face encounter with Richie, at long last. She was glad it would be a relatively private meeting, well-apart from the family. There would be too much to explain; to Richie about Horace Vining's second family in Texas, and to Fred's family about Richard.

At the last minute as Fred and the children, with the Beckers and Vinings prepared to board the parlor cars at the foursquare brick tower of Galveston's Union station, he looked at her with sudden sharp attention, as he stood just beyond the gate to the parlor car's observation porch..

"*Sopherl*, do you want me to remain here with you until Monday? Magda and Anna can see to the children…"

"No – dearest Fred, they are our children; your sister is tired, and Cousin Anna has done so much. Min and Baby and I will be along on Monday's train." Sophia spoke with confidence. She had often parted from Fred in time of their marriage and never felt the slightest worry. He had business to do with the ranch which sometimes took him weeks and days. A niggling little voice reminded her that on those previous occasions, she had been home at the ranch, among folk she trusted, and who looked to her as the wife of the ranch-owner; the patron, as the Mexican drovers called Fred

"You're certain?" he still looked doubtful, even as he kissed her with especial tenderness. "Even traveling all that way by yourself?"

"As if I have never traveled alone on a train before!" she said. He leaned down to embrace her one last time, laughing. "Wednesday, then; if you aren't on the first train from Galveston, I'll come back all the way and fetch you myself. But George and Amelie – they'll look after you and Min and Baby, whatever happens."

"They are the kindest and most considerate hosts," Sophia agreed, "But I cannot help thinking they will be relieved when their house at last empties of guests and they can return to their own routine of days. I know that I would be – as happy as I am to extend our hospitality."

"Very likely, but they'd never admit that by a word or gesture," Fred scooped up Min for a kiss, and setting her down, dropped another on Baby Christian's forehead. "Goodbye my little chicks! I will see you soon." Far ahead, the train's steam whistle blew, and the cars lurched – and they were away, her children waving from behind the windows of the parlor; Carlotta, the twins and little Fred Harvey. Sophie followed the departing train for a few steps along the platform, and then in her mind's eye, seeing it roll out across the long trestle which crossed the bay.

No doubt the Richter's grand red-brick mansion did seem funereally quiet after the last guests had departed; leaving only George and Amelie and their two youngest sons, Henry and Ambrose in an empty house by comparison. The day had turned hot again, although as evening came on, clouds blotted out the stars. It was too hot to sleep; after supper Sophia sat with George and Amelie in the outdoor parlor which overlooked the garden.

"There's a storm out in the Gulf," George remarked. "I saw the flag on top of the Levy building this afternoon, and the surf is coming in pretty hard. Most of the ships in port left this afternoon – better to be out at sea than battered to pieces. I wouldn't worry, Mrs. Sophie – we've weathered storms here before without as much as a broken shingle."

"I wouldn't mind a storm, as long as it brings us more rain," Amelie remarked, fanning herself with a wide palm-frond fan. "My poor garden – everything is wilting from lack of water. If there was any rain from that lightening storm this week, it wouldn't have filled up a thimble."

"When is your nephew expected to arrive tomorrow?" George drew on his pipe, which glowed briefly red.

"On the morning train from Houston," Sophia replied. "Around noon, I believe. I think that he expects to stay at the Tremont with his traveling companions."

"I have business at the office in the morning," George nodded, in satisfaction. "But when I come home for lunch – I will take you in the coach to the station."

"I hope it does not put you to any inconvenience…" Sophia began, but George demurred, "Not in the least, my dear Sophie."

Amelie fanned herself with renewed energy. "Oh, how I wish it would rain!"

And in the morning – it rained. The clouds overhead pressed closer together, blotting out the last of the sky, turning darker and darker, matching Sophia's mood as the wind strengthened – now from the north, and strong enough to flatten out the water in the gulf as if an immense plasterer's trowel swept over it. But Min and George's sons were exhilarated; over breakfast they proposed to see the surf crashing against the outer shore which Amelie allowed, in the spirit of indulgence. Min wanted to go with them, but Sophia forbade it. Ambrose and Henry were nearly the age of men, but Min was still only nine.

"We will need to be ready to go to the station to meet your cousin," Sophia said. Min, curious rather than rebellious, asked, "Why, Mama?"

"Because he is your cousin," Sophia replied, desperately fishing for a reason other than she wanted a kind of ally at her side, even such a small one. "When I last saw him, he was the same age you are now."

Min – such a clever little girl – accepted that as a logical reason. Amelie suggested, "Leave the little one here with me. I would be quite pleased to have a baby in the house to look after again. Children," and she sighed heavily, "They grow so fast!"

"They do," Sophia answered, with a twinge at her heart. Richie had been a dear little boy, such a long time ago in Boston! What was he now; still a dear little boy, or grown to be a monstrous creature like Richard his father? Today she would know for certain although Sophia was also sure she didn't want to know one way or the other. Better to go on with fond memories of a day long past, then have to face them. Although that was not what Great-aunt Minnie had done, and Sophia took renewed courage from the memories. Great-aunt Minnie faced all manner of enemies, no matter how brutal or ignorant. She had given abolitionist lectures in public, campaigned for the rights of women against every kind of danger or public derision. Meeting Richie in a public place … why should that be such a frightful prospect?

All morning the rain poured down, and the wind strengthened. George's man of all work went around fastening storm-shutters over the windows, making the house as dark as a cave. The electric power flickered and faded. With a sigh, Amelie sought out a number of old kerosene lamps.

"Ugh," she said, sneezing. "I had forgotten how dim and smelly these lamps are. They say that one should be careful of what one asks Divine providence for, as you might well receive it!" The lower part of Amelie's garden vanished under a foot of water, all but the tallest shrubs, and a veritable torrent of water ran in the streets, carrying with it all manner of floating trash, including the wooden blocks which paved the streets and floated like corks. Neighborhood children were playing in the street, making boats out of lengths of board, barrel staves and wooden boxes.

"Divine Providence is being more than generous as regards the rain," Sophia agreed. "It has never flooded like this in Deming, not even when the creek was full to the top of the banks."

"We are accustomed to this kind of thing here," Amelie agreed. "Still … it does seem as if the wind is blowing even harder. I should not like to be in a house on the outward side of the Island."

At that moment, Ambrose, a lanky youth of sixteen came running into the house, the rainwater which had drenched every shred of clothing and plastered his hair to his head leaving a trail of drips and splashes across the floor, followed by his older brother Henry. The wind banged the door closed behind them with a crash that shook the house.

"Mama, the waves are smashing into the Midway and the streetcar line along the beach is so undermined that they have stopped the cars from running. The bathhouses are falling into the sea!"

"You should not pass on such rumors," Amelie replied, but Ambrose insisted. "We saw with our own eyes. And people are leaving their houses by the sea and going to higher ground."

"We'll see what your Papa says," Amelie said. "This street always floods when there has been this much rain."

"It's not rainwater," Henry ventured. He looked between his mother and Sophia, hesitating. "It's salt … saltwater from the sea coming up."

"Ridiculous," Amelie said. "We're on one of the highest parts of the Island." the front door opened and shut again, and in a moment, George appeared in the hallway, soaked to the skin, but jovial and laughing.

"Is supper ready?" he asked. "I'm starving." He sounded so utterly normal that Sophia was reassured; George had been through many storms in Galveston; there was nothing to worry about;

everyone was carrying on as if all was normal if wetter than usual. Still, she had little appetite for the meal.

When she and Min set out with George in the carriage, the wind was blowing so violently that the carriage swayed on its springs, all the way down 25th Street to the tall brick-built station, with its single splendid Romanesque tower. The rubber curtains to keep out the rain were rendered useless. Sophia thought she would hardly have been wetter if she and Min had walked, or taken the street-car. But George taking such consideration of his guests – such courtesy could not be refused. She was grateful to enter the shelter of the station, out of the wind and the drenching rain, for the journey had been slow, and sometimes treacherous, for water ran in the streets up to the horse's knees in some places, and to withers in others.

"There's the station brake for the Tremont, waiting for passengers, I'd reckon. Likely the train has been delayed by rough weather," George allowed, as he assisted Sophie from the carriage, and lifted Min down to her. "You're meeting your nephew and then visit for a while in the Harvey House … excellent." George squinted against the rain, and the battering wind, and looked towards one of the tallest of those buildings along the waterfront, from which a dark banner flew. "Look, Mrs. Sophie – I will come back for you in … two hours, say? Or sooner; this storm might get even worse before nightfall. I'd sooner be under my own roof by then and I promised Onkel Fredi I'd see you safe." For the first time that day, his pleasant rugged countenance reflected worry. "I'll be at my office in the Levy Building. If you want to leave before then, the telephone exchange can put a call through to me."

"I am positive I will not be in any danger," Sophia tried to sound light, unworried, more to reassure Min, who in the way of a child, was still excited by the heavy and persistent rain, the torrents of water in the streets, and the sight of other people being amused by the floods. Halfway between the Steinmetz house and the station, they had seen a young man slip and fall in the street, and carried laughing and splashing all the way into the middle of the next block.

"Good," George replied, with a smile that did not reach to his eyes; with that, Sophia felt her heart sink to the toes of her sensible black high-buttoned shoes. If he were worried – then there must be real cause for concern regarding this storm, no matter how much that chivalrous and gallant men tried to conceal it.

Chapter 22 – Storm

The morning train from Houston was delayed, but the passengers on it were arriving momentarily – so Sophia was informed, by a harassed and distracted inquiry-desk agent. The train from Houston itself was stranded a mile away, by rising water washing out the shore-side track. He hastened to reassure them that a relief train was on the way to collect the passengers, who would be there shortly. The station – so busy, so active and full of life on the previous day – was today almost empty. The thunder of rain beat down on the tracks outside, and the ferocious wind howled around the walls, sending sudden drafts and gusts of rain far into the sheltered ends of the platform. Like the streets outside, water had already invaded the tracks between the raised platforms. Sophia waited, Min at her side in the waiting room, waiting for the sound of a locomotive, the shriek of steel wheels scraping on rails, the sequential metallic clang of each car's undercarriage as the train came to a halt. No, only the increasing shrieks of the wind, and something which sounded intermittently like thunder. The waiting area was empty; a few nervous men and the tall potted palms, looking forlorn and abandoned. The hour hand on the main station clock crawled to half-past one, then uphill towards the hour of two with even more painful slowness.

"I wish we had gone with Papa yesterday," Min said once. "We'd be almost home, wouldn't we, Mama?"

"Only halfway between Houston and San Antonio," Sophia replied. "But yes, I wish so too, Min."

Without fanfare, people began arriving on the platform; soaked to their skins and wading along the track: men carrying children and assisting women to walk in water that was now waist-deep. The arrivals from Houston – it appeared so. Sophia took Min by the hand, and walked out towards them. It appeared the engine pulling the relief train had its firebox doused on the return journey, just within reach of the station.

"What does that mean, Mama?" Min whispered, hearing several of the men talking about this as they made their dripping way past.

"It means that the water was rising high enough to put out the fire that runs the steam boiler," Sophia replied. She was looking among the straggle of passengers for a familiar face, or at any rate, someone who resembled Richie. She thought it more likely that Richie would recognize her first, so she stood at small distance, with Min's hand in hers.

To her astonishment, she did see a familiar face, at once. Mr. Benjamin, from the Fred Harvey company; a little stouter from that day when he and Mr. Harvey had interviewed her in Kansas City, more than fifteen years before. She did not mean to speak and recall herself to him, but his own face lit up with pleasure. "I know you – Miss Teague, is it!" he exclaimed, "Or some married name now, as I recall? A pleasure indeed to see a familiar face; a pleasure to make up for a wet welcome to Galveston!"

"Mrs. Frederick Steinmetz," Sophia replied, heartened beyond words; they used to say that Mr. Harvey and Mr. Benjamin never forgot the name or the face of anyone who worked for Fred Harvey Company. Mr. Benjamin even recalled those who had formerly worked for the company. He grinned, cheerful as ever in spite of being drenched to the skin and absent any but hand luggage.

"I remember; an early hire and one of our most cultured and reliable girls. A loss to the Fred Harvey Company – but a great gain for you and for Mr. Steinmetz, I am certain."

"This is our oldest daughter, Minnie." Sophia said, blushing slightly. "Minnie, say hello to Mr. Benjamin." Min, always bashful with strangers, whispered, "Hello."

"I am afraid the weather has spoiled our holiday, as well as yours," Sophia ventured, and Mr. Benjamin shook his head.

"No holiday – but business, of course."

"Of course," Sophia suppressed a smile. "Always; I trust that Mr. Harvey is well?" It was a conventional courtesy, but at those words a slight shadow appeared on Mr. Benjamin's face. "Young Mr. Ford Harvey is well … but Mr. Fred has been in uncertain health for some time. He is retired from taking an active part in the company."

"I am sorry to hear of that," Sophia replied, with genuine concern. "He is one of the finest men I know of in this part of the world." Mr. Benjamin nodded in agreement, and Sophia wondered if he would have said more, but just at that moment, someone at her back said, tentatively,

"Auntie Sophia?"

Startled, Sophia whirled – like Miss Kitten in her skittish and wild days.

Richie. No, she would not have recognized him.

Mr. Benjamin said something courteous, nodded, and took his leave. Sophia did not hear a single word.

Richie. No – not a boisterous schoolboy; this tall and diffident stranger with Richard's features and Fee's blue eyes. He looked more like … Sophia struggled to recall. Yes, he looked more like her father; the officer of the 28th, who stood in Sophia's cherished daguerreotype with his hand on the hilt of his sword – the sword that old Tim Teague averred he seemed always surprised to find in his fist, leading a charge.

"Hello, Richie," Sophia recovered control of her voice and was obscurely pleased that she sounded so calm, and level. At her side, Min looked between the two of them, gazed at Richie with silent curiosity, pressing press close as if seeking reassurance. "It has been so long. I'd not have known you."

"Too long. I'd have known you anywhere," Richie replied. He blinked once or twice. When he spoke again, Sophia was certain he tried to keep a note of reproach out of his voice. "I thought for years you were dead."

"It was for the best," Sophia answered. An unaccountable sense of panic choked her breathing. The nightmare overwhelmed her; that nightmare of Richard holding her nose and forcing her mouth open. "Your father …" Suddenly she could not speak, overwhelmed with that old sense of fear and horror. She knew that Richie's arm was around her waist, holding her up as if she were fainting, of Min's uncertain voice, saying, "Mama?"

"Is there a place where we may sit and talk?" She was barely aware of Richie leading her into the waiting room. "I … my friends are going on to the Tremont. My father's … what he did to you and to Mama and my brothers is not yet something I wanted to speak of, in front of them. They are friends, stout-hearted chaps. But there are limits."

"Yes, there are," Sophia sank onto one of the padded benches in the deserted waiting room. Unaccountably she began to laugh until the tears came. Finally she gasped. "Min, darling, go sit on that rocking chair … yes, by that potted palm tree. This is a conversation that is not fit for childish ears." When Min obeyed, good obedient girl which she was, Sophia continued, "Murdering your wife and family, burning down the family house, and robbing your sister of an inheritance must come pretty close to those limits, Richie."

"Exactly," her nephew agreed, with a wry twist to his lips. "Gentlemen have standards, which my late and unlamented Papa often transgressed, I am afraid." Sophia laughed again, heedless of what Min would think of this, watching from the far end of the waiting room. Richie – dear little Richie, grown to manhood but not materially changed as to his character. She had been a fool to fear so

… but considering what basis she had for those fears, she only regretted having kept him at such a distance for so long, and the curt tone of the letter she had written in response to his; *'I am happily settled in my life and do not wish to encourage any continuing correspondence.'* There was so much that could not be said through ink and paper.

"It was best that no one know where I was, or even alive while your father lived," Sophia confessed. "I considered him as a monster. I knew his temper, and how viciously he avenged himself on those who slighted or defied him. I could not bring harm to anyone who aided me – you know their names. After I knew that he was dead, there was the risk of exposure of our connection. The newspapers would have made hay of it, you know."

"I know – Siringo assured me on that point. He said you were well-situated and happy. You ought to be left alone, he told me. After what you suffered at Papa's hands you deserved a measure of happiness. Nothing I could do to ensure that end, so I took his advice. Though I wish you had written." he added, almost shyly.

"I had reasons, Richie," Sophia sighed. "And children with my husband. It seemed best, at the time."

"Children?" Richie's handsome face brightened. "More than that one little miss?"

"Four more and a baby," Sophia replied.

Richie laughed in delight. "Auntie – how wonderful! Everything I wished for you after that awful spotty what-was-his-name broke your engagement. Is your husband tall, handsome, and impossibly, respectably rich?"

"Not very tall," Sophia giggled, remembering that walk through the Public Gardens on the afternoon that her engagement was broken, the last normal day of her old life. "Or so handsome, considering that which is said to be the beau idéal. He is a dear sweet gentleman, as tall as I am, and owns a moderately prosperous ranch in New Mexico, where we have raised our children. Although his family is … they are well-thought of, in this part of the world," Sophia floundered – how to explain this to Richie. Just at that moment, Min appeared at her elbow.

"Mama," she said, her serious little face apprehensive. "Mama – the water is coming in."

"What?" Sophia turned, horrified to see that a pool of water was spreading above the level of the platform, across the floor of the station, rising inexorably, without a ripple. The station itself was raised above street level; how deep was it now outside?

Richie took her elbow and Min by the hand. "We should go up to the mezzanine level," He suggested. "Or … to higher ground … if there is any higher ground, in the geographical sense."

Before they reached the staircase – now being converged on by others besides themselves, the water was up to the second step. With relief, Sophia saw that Cousin George was there, with Henry at his heels. Both were as drenched as Richie and hatless.

"We must go home now, Mrs. Sophie." George commanded. The expression on his face upon seeing her was a mixture of worry and relief. He nodded to Richie, a hasty courtesy, and took Sophia's other elbow. "The storm is getting bad now, but my house is safer, being far from the shore. I sent the carriage with my assistant to bring his family as soon as I heard what happened at the Ritter-Café. Their house is a flimsy place, too close to the beach. We must walk, I am afraid."

"Getting to be a habit," Richie said, under his breath.

"What has happened at Ritters?" Sophia asked, baffled. Just an hour ago, George had been insouciant regarding the storm, even as the streets flooded. Storms were nothing to worry about in Galveston – that was everyone's cheerful attitude, so Sophia had quelled her own apprehensions. Now, George was not even trying to put on a pretense of normality.

"The roof blew off – poof! And then everything in the upstairs fell down upon the café. Like a house of cards. Five are dead, maybe more. Then I see Mr. Cline, the weather bureau man coming from his office – he told me to go home at once, the storm is very bad. He is a sober and careful man, not one given to exaggerate."

All this time, he was leading them out of the station, Henry running ahead to open the door for them. The boy had to throw his whole weight, and brace with all his might to hold it open against the wind and water. Sophia gasped, horrified. The omnibus for the Tremont was gone halfway down the street, water up to the bellies of the horses that pulled it. The water itself was full of floating scraps – crates, scraps of wood, whole planks, barrels in part and whole, the blocks of wooden street paving – anything that would float in water. It was as if those wide avenues had become part of the bay, inundated in water and every kind of floating trash. The winds howled, pressing against her with such violence she could walk against it only with difficulty. If she stepped from the sidewalk, the water would come to her waist. Sidewalk and street alike were also filled with sodden refugees, men and women bent against the force of the wind. There was none of that amusement and cheer she had observed on going to the station, not two hours before. All good humor had evaporated. In the streets horses, their eyes showing white all the way around in a way she meant near to panic, drew their burdens against the mighty current.

"Up on my back, then," Richie sang out, bending his knees so that Minnie could reach up to his shoulders. He stood, with Minnie pick-a-back, and clinging to him like a baby monkey. "Good girl," he said to her, and grinned to Sophia. "Now – how far is this house of yours?" he shouted to Cousin George, who shouted in reply,

"Eight blocks distant on 25th at Broadway … it's higher ground, so the water won't be as deep."

The clouds pressed overhead, darker and darker; it looked more like early evening as they struggled across the Strand. There was a current in the water. Sophia felt it, wrapping her skirts and petticoats around her legs, hampering her steps at every moment. George and his son put her between them, and glad she was of their support and strength, for she feared that if she fell, she might not be able to get up again.

As they boosted her to the sidewalk on the other side, she gasped. The body of a small child went floating past in the Strand, a boy the age of Fred Harvey. Three years old or thereabouts; motionless and just underneath the surface of the water, his pale face looking up at the dark-bruised sky with unseeing eyes. She hoped that Min didn't see, but George did, and his grip on her arm tightened. The wind howled, with redoubled fury, and a skein of slate tiles from a roof opposite went winging into the sky like birds. To her horror, a tile struck a man on the opposite sidewalk with incredible force; he toppled without a cry into the deeper water of the street. A brief red cloud bloomed around him, and his body went spinning away like that of the little boy.

"Can't you help him?" she gasped. Cousin George replied grimly, "No, Mrs. Sophie, it's as much as we can do to help ourselves."

On they waded, up to the next street, assailed by wind and the horrific noise which seemed a physical thing, as of a mighty smith with an enormous hammer were pounding away … pounding on an anvil the size of an island. Not only could she hear it, she could feel it, too. One block farther towards the safety of higher ground, and Cousin George's fortress of a house, across the next street – in which the water, true to Cousin George's gasped encouragement, really shallower. Richie strode fearlessly ahead, bearing little Min on his back. The dark sky pressed closer and closer; so much for Galveston being impervious to storms; Sophia wished more than ever that she and Min and Baby had gone home on Friday. So much for the most prosperous city in Texas – now there were corpses floating in the streets and floodwater over the level of sidewalks and flowing into the ground floors of houses and stores!

Another street to be crossed, and then another; now it felt as if the wind had redoubled as well as the energy of the rain which felt as if they were being pelted with pebbles. Little Min buried her face in Richie's shoulder. The wind peeled more and more tiles from roofs as they passed; heavy slate tiles which flew like sheets of paper, cut like knives, and kicked up great gouts of water when they fell into the flooded streets below. A tree in the garden of a house they passed suddenly bent over to the ground, under the force of an intense gust of wind, and snapped with a crack like a cannon firing. Sophia cried out from shock and surprise.

"Almost there," Cousin George gasped, his face reddened with exertion. He was not a young man, but he had strength equal to that of Richie, half his age, and that strength carried her willy-nilly across the next street. Now Sophia saw the tall conical towers, the red-brick walls of the Richter house, through the drenching veil of rain, the water that swirled at her legs. "Through the garden, *hein*?" he shouted, and their path diverted into the narrow street at the back of the half-block behind the Richter establishment. They splashed through a back gate at the stables, and across the wide lawn – in a cruel mimicking of a day at the seaside, with water sloshing to their knees. It had not reached the main floor, Sophia noted as they arrived, slogging around the side of the red-brick walls, which sheltered them from the worst of the wind. The wedding and the grand ball in the gardens now seemed as if it had happened an age ago, instead of barely a week. Sophia thought she would never for the remainder of her life be so happy to come under the shelter of a sturdy and sheltering roof again.

Even though water now came to the top of the stairs, the four of them scrambled up that staircase to the front door with joyous relief. A pair of unharnessed horses stood on the porch with their halters tied to a porch pillar – an incongruous sight indeed. Amelie met them inside the front door as they stood gasping and dripping just inside. Several kitchen chairs and piles of provisions lay in the hallway, where the carpets had been rolled up. She flung herself into her husband's arms, murmuring broken exclamations of relief interspersed with endearments. Richie let Min slide from his back, and Min flung herself on Sophia, as she burst into tears.

"I said there was no cause to worry," George exclaimed in German to his wife. "It was only down the street to the station, and we are returned safe and sound. Ambrose and young Arpel and his family – they are safe, I see the horses, safe too. Now … we wait out the storm."

The voices of other people came from the parlor. Quite a few families were sheltering in the Richter house; with good reason, comparing the sturdy solidity of brick and stone to the plank-framed houses they passed along the way. Those houses were showing effects of the storm, teetering on foundations washed away, slates peeled from roofs, and roofs themselves wrenched away from walls.

"Your nephew?" Amelie embraced Sophia with relief, urging her to go upstairs and change into dry clothing. "Good … see to the little one! I put him in the cradle in our room; it is the safest, I think – most sheltered from the wind. Come and help me move things upstairs. I am afraid that the water will come to this floor and spoil my nice Persian rugs."

Some of the refugees had busied themselves in carrying armfuls of furniture and groceries up the stairs. Sophia took Min by the hand and followed them. They changed, in that guest room on the upper floor, where the noise of raindrops pelting on the bare wood of the de-shingled roof sounded like hard hail. The plaster ceiling was saturated with spreading patches of water; in places it bubbled in huge blisters. The windows opening onto the little sheltered porch were far enough under shelter as to need no shutters over them. Sophia stripped off her wet clothing with a shudder of revulsion for the street-filth doubtless soaked into them, especially around the hems.

Clothed in dry petticoats and plain dress, she stood for a minute looking out at the amazing sight of the city below, a city transformed under darkening skies from regular blocks of streets lined with gardens and houses into a sea irregularly studded with islands and the remains of trees. She was struck by a sudden memory of the drowned lands of Lyonesse, in Tennyson's *Idylls of the King*, where the church bells still rang in abandoned towers under the waves, stirred by the current, and wondered if there were a real Lyonesse and if it had been sunk forever underneath the sea by a mighty storm such as this. Even as she watched, horrified, the water rose. Two streets away down 25th Street, a row of six or seven small cottages suddenly collapsed, sliding like a falling house of cards, dissolving into the rising water in a scattering of planks.

Chapter 23 – Sunrise in Lyonesse

With Min clinging to her side, Sophia went to tend to Baby – relieved to find little Christian no more than moderately fussy, laying in a cradle moved to the corner of the elder Richter's palatial bedroom. She cuddled him close her, nearly crying in relief, for now they were all three safe, dry and together. Christian nursed with vigor and fell asleep in her arms. Outside the wind howled like a wolf, striking the side of the house in fury at being balked and refused admittance. The few candles that relieved the darkness flickered and smoked behind glass chimneys – a careful housekeeper like Amelie would worry about a lit candle falling and setting a fire. The bedroom door stood partway open, to the tramping of feet on the stairs and in the hallway as the men carried furniture, and rolled-up rugs upstairs.

"The water is still rising, *Sopherl*," Amelie said, when she brought in a mantel clock and an elaborate arrangement of wax flowers under a dome which had formerly adorned the parlor. "We have sent everyone to shelter on the second floor, on the side away from the wind." The house, with windows closed and shutters fastened over them, was not only dark, but close and hot. Amelie's face shone with perspiration.

"Let me help you," Sophia blurted, overcome with housewifely sympathy. Amelie was a year or two younger than Mama had been when she died – and had been a gracious hostess all this time. "Min … stay with Baby, and look after him."

"Mama," Min protested with a single word, but her grave little face reflected fear and desolation.

"I will be within the house," Sophia detached Min's frantic hand from the skirt of her dress. "There is nothing to fear, darling. We are safe within these walls. Cousin George's house is the biggest and strongest there is in Galveston."

"Those houses fell down, Mama," Min replied. "And the people in them thought they were safe within their walls."

"Min, dear – I must help Amelie," Sophia kissed her daughter, and her son, and put on an expression of resolution. "Be brave for me – and for your dear Papa, and for your little brother."

Min gulped and nodded, her eyes filling. Sophia felt her own eyes welling up with tears she dare not let fall. It would frighten Min, who was frightened enough. She followed Amelie; the upstairs was crowded – with friends and neighbors of the Richters and their sons, soaking wet, frightened and yet grateful for refuge between sturdy walls. For a wonder, the dreadful howling wind had ceased, and the silence itself was as deafening as the noise had been. Sophia looked into the front hall from the broad landing halfway down. The downstairs rooms were stripped of their rugs; just in time, for there was a pool of water seeping from under the front door, and spreading from other rooms, ink-dark in the light of a single lantern. She caught up to Amelie, looking with horror on the invading water. George stood with his arm close around her.

"We have fifty-six people in our house," she overheard heard him murmur to his wife, in German, in that silence. "Old Mr. Pascoe with his wife and her niece are coming from their house, which is falling to bits. Ambrose and Young Pascoe have gone to help them across the way. They tell me that wind has dropped."

"Does it mean that the storm has passed over?" Amelie asked. George shook his head. "No … it means we are now in the center of it." The knocking on the front door sounded loud in the silence. George sprang down the staircase with an energy which belied his age and the weariness piled on him by this dreadful day and unbarred the door to admit the new party; Ambrose, another young man, and the three refugees; the oldest carried among them. "The water is rising," George shouted. He made as if to close and bar the door on the darkness and the driving rain outside, but before he did so, the tide went in one smooth motion from a puddle at his feet to his chest, flowing into the hallway, the parlor and the other rooms. "Upstairs, everyone!" he shouted, as there came the crash of breaking glass and wood from within. Sophia fled up stairs, stumbling in her panic. The storm had breached the final fortress. And now the wind howled around its walls with renewed energy.

She sat at the foot of the Richter's bedstead, with Christian in her lap, and Min leaning against her side, with the Teague's old plaid woolen shawl wrapped around them all. Min had always treasured it as a blanket, since her own babyhood, for some inexplicable reason, and now sought comfort in those rough and scratchy folds. George and Amelie sat at the head of the bed, with Henry and Ambrose beside them, or pacing the crowded room; other refugees from the storm lay on the floor, or leaned against the walls. Candlelight flickered over their tense faces. The invalid Mrs. Pascoe lay on Amelie's chaise longue, her lips moving in a silent desperate prayer. The atmosphere in the room was hot, humid with the scent of terror and desperation, waiting for the storm to break open the brick walls as though breaking an eggshell. Richie sat on the floor at their feet; he alone appeared at ease. The noise of the wind was such that words could not be heard across the room unless shouted. Time stood still, as still as the hands of Amelie's parlor clock … and yet, the walls of George Richter's house held; battered by rain, by flying slates and timbers which crashed against the windward walls. A queer thumping came from under their feet. Sophia realized that it must be the remaining furniture downstairs, driven to and fro, dashed against interior walls by the high tide within.

Min fell asleep at last, exhausted; without disturbing the child's slumber, Sophia laid her daughter across the middle of the bed with

Baby Christian and covered them both with the plaid shawl. Silently, Richie took Min's place. It was comforting to lean against him, to have the support of a man's shoulder on this terrifying day. Sophia wished that it was Fred's – but Richie's would do.

Presently, Sophia ventured, "We wouldn't have been here, but for the delay in your travel plans. We'd have been on our way home by now."

"I know," Richie answered. "I'm sorry for that, Auntie … we have been nothing but trouble and danger for you, in every way."

"Never you, Richie. This storm is just a terrible coincidence. I might just as soon blame myself. I should have been agreeable to corresponding with you. You and I are the only two left. I should not have been so afraid … but I had just married Fred. I wanted to leave it in the past where it belonged … but it's not possible, is it? The past is not so easily abandoned as that."

Richie sighed. "That is what Rosy said, when I asked him for advice. I thought you'd be happy to hear from me, you see. Professor Rosemont … he was the headmaster at school. Dear old Rosy was my guardian after Papa did what he did. A decent old stick; he called me into his office and broke the news. About Papa and Mama; I suppose that I blubbed, and asked him where I should go when the term was over, and Rosy handed me a handkerchief and said, 'To me and Mrs. Rosemont, of course.' And that was the end of it. Rosy settled it with the lawyers. I did have to say to a judge I preferred them to be my guardians over any other, but Rosy and Mrs. Rosy turned out to be as fair and good as any parent might have been. Fairer than Papa, I have to say – and more generous-tempered. Although Rosy was irate when I enlisted in the Colonel Wood's volunteer cavalry to fight in Cuba."

"You were in the Rough Riders?" Sophia exclaimed, in astonishment, and Richie laughed.

"More like the Weary Walkers," he answered. "It was a bit of an adventure, I made friends among them; stout fellows, every one. When we were mustered out, I didn't want to go back to Boston and spend my days looking at the walls of an insurance office. I liked the looks of what I saw of the West, so," he shrugged. "I decided to chance it. Coming to see you was just a part of it. My pal – his family has a spread in Arizona … and a pretty sister I have an understanding with. I met her once, in San Antonio, and she wrote when we shipped out of Tampa. She's a clever woman – you'd like her. Especially since she worked as a Harvey Girl too. Likely I'm going to settle down with her, once I've built up enough of a stake." The wind dealt the side of the Richter house an especially violent blow, which silenced conversation for a moment. "You see, Auntie Soph; I can't possibly die in this storm tonight. I have plans. I just wanted to square things with you. To make it right, in a small way."

"You have made it right, now," Sophia clasped his hand in hers. "I should not have been so afraid."

"You had good reason, once, Auntie Soph," Richie kissed her cheek gently. "It just takes pluck to face up to them, once and for all."

"And then to see they weren't that fearsome," Sophia felt a sense of calm peace overtake her, as if she and Richie sat together with the sleeping children in that quiet place in the heart of the storm. As time passed, she dozed, waking with a start now and again, her head on Richie's shoulder in that candle-lit room, surprised at each wakening that the walls still held, as solidly as the castle and refuge that the Richter house had first appeared to be.

"There is something I need to tell you," Sophia ventured, at one of these awakenings, when the wind had diminished. "It's about Grandfather Vining. Great-Aunt Minnie's brother – there was a portrait of them both in the old house on Beacon Hill. We may yet have closer kin here in Texas than we thought."

Richie listened without interruption, a particularly thoughtful expression on his face. When she had finished, he mused, "I never considered that, but it makes sense of a sort. He went out West as a young man, spent most of his life here … what are they like, these half-cousins of ours?"

"Pleasant and worthy people, and at least as embarrassed by the connection as I was."

"In the past, Auntie Soph," Richie answered, with an air of finality. "Considering what is happening outside this very minute, it's not a matter I'm going to trouble myself with, over much – tonight or tomorrow, should we live to see it."

At that final awakening, Sophia discovered that she had slept for a considerable time; that Richie had moved her onto the bed and she lay next to Min and Baby. Amelie slept, fully clothed – and dim daylight leaked through the cracks and edges of the storm shutters. Mrs. Pascoe snored gently on the chaise longue. Sophia, still feeling as if she had just finished an exhausting shift at a Harvey House, slid from the bed without disturbing the children. She tiptoed to the hallway and the staircase up to Cousin George's marvelous tower. Pearlescent sunshine poured down the staircase – blindingly bright after the darkness in the Richter's bedroom. Most of the windows were smashed and broken glass littered the floor. The wicker chairs and settee were tumbled to one side, their cushions soaked with water.

Cousin George stood at the north-facing window with Ambrose and Richie; a mild breeze stirred the bedraggled curtains, a breeze that smelt of the familiar salt sea … and a wisp of something else, something less savory.

"Oh, my dear lord," she exclaimed. There was nothing outside resembling in the least what had been there, a mere twenty-four hours before. The Richters' garden, the lawn where the children had played, was a wilderness of shattered lengths of lumber, of whole small structures – outhouses and chicken coops tumbled together, trunks of palm trees like limp feather-dusters, and the bodies of dead horses. Not the two which had been left tethered on the front porch the night before; they were grazing moodily on those stretches of lawn now left exposed between the debris. Sophia saw what she first thought to be bundles of clothes or bedding, and realized gradually that they were bodies … bodies entangled in the rose-bushes, and in the hedges which enclosed Amelie's garden. The water which had been up to the second story of those scattered surviving buildings was drained away. A few tall buildings and church spires still stood, and the occasional partly shattered house, tottering on remaining pilings, or tipped entirely on one side. The sky overhead was a pale, rain-washed blue, and the desolation of broken boards, bodies and wrecked houses went as far as could be seen – to the north where lay the Strand, the wharves, and the significant buildings of Galveston.

"I must see if my friends are safe," Richie said, huskily. Cousin George squinted into the distance through his telescope.

"The Tremont stands undamaged," he said. "They went there, did they not? And the Levy building remains."

"But what is that?" Sophia asked. She crunched across the glass to the south-facing window, the one looking out towards the open gulf. A tangled moraine of wreckage ran from out of sight in one direction, dropping across the center of what had been neat rows of houses and gardens … a shoal of broken planks and wreckage on the near side and a sweep of empty sand on the other. She blinked; Laura's house was gone, the bright painted yellow walls and gallery vanished as cleanly as if they had never been, as if a great broom had swept the sea-front and several blocks behind it clean. Not a scrap remained, seen save a bedraggled salt-cedar tree, which might have been at the corner of Q Street, three doors down from the cheery cottage where Laura lived with her family.

"It's is what the high sea brought last night," Cousin George's voice sounded heavy with grief. "The opposite of what happened in Indianola. There, the water rushed out from the bayou and pushed all out into the bay. Here it smashed everything to pieces and pushed it into land."

"My dear friend Laura and her husband live on Q Street, not three blocks from the sea," Sophia's chest hurt, for thinking of her friend, and her three children – Andy, just three years older than Min – and that pretty little cottage that Laura had been so proud of.

"They may have chosen to shelter in a safer place," Richie squeezed her hand, comfortingly. "We'll look for them in a while. There are plenty of buildings still standing. They are sure to have sheltered as many as were safe here last night."

He sounded convinced of that; looking out at the desolation, Sophia wondered how he could be so sure.

They set out an hour later; the wreckage even more devastating seen at close range, instead of from the top of the Richter house. Cousin George received a message. There was to be a meeting at the Tremont of notable men of town, to which he had been invited. He and his sons both wore revolvers at their belts, for the messenger had brought a warning about looting. The Richter's own house had sustained little damage, in comparison; the roof stripped of shingles, and furniture piled up at the doors of rooms on the first floor where the departing high tide had left it, but the walls still sturdy and four-square. They left Amelie and her cook trying to drain water and soggy cinders from the kitchen stove, in an attempt to light a fire in it, and sweeping out the soggy muck left on floors throughout the downstairs.

"At least we have a roof," Cousin George said, with a determinedly jaunty air. They struggled up Bath Avenue, following the same path of the day before – how much had changed! Even without water flowing in the street, the footing was perilous in the extreme. There were bodies everywhere, many of them covered in silt, half-buried, invisible under wood, broken furniture and such trash; men and women, children, often so bruised and dirty it was impossible to tell if they were white or colored. Sophia shuddered the first time she accidently stepped on human flesh, assuming it was only the remains of a straw-stuffed mattress. Ambrose and young Henry looked as green in the face as she was certain she was. Only Cousin George and Richie maintained a grim composure. As they walked, they saw other survivors, moving among the wreckage, some wandering as if in witless shock, numbed by the horror, yet others purposeful and decisive.

Two men moved in and out of a teetering cottage on Tremont Street, piling up chairs, a bedstead and a table in a space which had been the site of another cottage. Intent on their work, they were collecting up random lengths of lumber, and sheets of metal roofing. Two nuns, from the St. Mary's Infirmary were also searching – for what, Sophia could not exactly see at first. In their black gowns and white wing-headdresses, they looked like birds, picking their way among the debris cast up on a strange shore. When they passed close by, Sophia saw that both carried large baskets, filled halfway with boxes and tins of crackers and waterlogged sweet biscuits. A little way farther down, a pair of mismatched horses stood in harness to a freight wagon, heads drooping, while three colored men and two white were carrying bodies of the dead to it, and stacking them as if they were so much cordwood.

Sophia shuddered in revulsion. Richie said, very calmly, "They must do this, Auntie Soph – now before it gets too hot." He spoke to the nearest of the teamsters collecting bodies and spoke a few words. When he returned, he said, "There's a morgue being set up in a warehouse on the Strand, between 21st and 22nd – that's where they've been told to bring the dead they can find."

"So many," Sophia whispered. "So many … where can they be buried, Richie?"

"I don't know," Richie answered. "Those men were told as many as five hundred when they started, but there are now twice that many at the morgue and more discovered every hour. And it is not even mid-morning."

The Tremont Hotel stood, foursquare and five stories tall, although the outside walls to the height of fifteen or sixteen feet were marked with the stigmata of the floodwaters. Otherwise, it appeared sound, as solid as the Richter mansion. They ventured inside where it seemed the same fate had befallen the first floor. But there were people inside the tall-ceilinged-lobby, and several harassed-looking men behind the heavy hotel desk. Richie went to speak to them, taking his place at the end of a substantial line. "Boys, go with Mrs. Sophie and Mr. Brewer," Cousin George commanded. "After this meeting, I'll go to the Levy Building to see what is left of the office." and only at that moment did he look every year and more of his age. "Go with her to look for her friend. Where might she have gone with her children to seek safety?"

"Her husband was a telegraphist," Sophia replied. "His parents lived in the next street, but their house wouldn't have been any safer than their own; maybe to Union Station?"

"The Infirmary still stands, too," Cousin George nodded. "I believe that many would have taken shelter there. I hope you can find her; good luck, Mrs. Sophie – if you do and they need shelter, bring them to our house. At a time like this, we must do what we can for those who have not shared in good fortune."

"Papa, does anyone on the mainland know of how bad this is?" Ambrose asked, and his father shook his head. "No. The telegraph and telephone lines are down. The causeway, the railroad trestles … destroyed. I looked for them through my telescope at first light."

"Surely they must know," Ambrose replied, sounding like a small desperate boy in his agitation. "Someone must send help, as soon as possible!"

"Oh, they will know," Cousin George shrugged. "But the storm will have passed over the mainland. It will take hours, lads. Until then … we must manage on our own."

He nodded briskly and strode across the room to join with a number of other men – many of whom looked every bit as weary and worn as he did. Even if their own houses still standing, and their families unharmed, Sophia knew this was a hard blow, unimaginable in severity. The damage was incalculable, the numbers of dead … unimaginable. In an empty lot they had passed earlier, there were twenty corpses lying in the open where the retreating waters had left them, tumbled and half-naked.

"My friends are safe," Richie reported, the tension in his face somewhat eased, as he rejoined them. "They had not realized until this morning how much devastation this storm has spread. They heard other guests scrambling to the top floor last night, and the water filling the lobby, but they thought that this was only an ordinary storm … if such a storm can be said to be ordinary. Where to now, Auntie Soph – the station?"

"Yes," Sophia's breath caught on a half-sob. "What I wouldn't give, to purchase a ticket for Baby and Min and I, and get on a train and go home!"

Chapter 24 – The City of the Silent

The main floor of Union Station showed clear evidence – as did every other public and private building remaining on their original foundations which they passed in their journey to the Strand – of having been invaded by deep and turbulent water, up to the level of fifteen feet and more. Along the waterfront in the next block, were the masts of ships visible, canted at impossible angles, as the storm had left them. A single steamship appeared undamaged, to judge from a continuous drift of smoke rising from its stacks. So, Galveston harbor was not entirely wrecked.

No one that Sophia or the boys encountered at the station knew anything of Laura or Andrew Belton, or had seen her on the day before. Andrew Belton left the telegraph office in mid-afternoon when the connection to the mainland broke for good and all, dismissing the other operators from their post. He said that he was going home to help his wife and children go to his parents' house, as the waves were breaking at the bottom of the block, and urged other telegraphists to see to the safety of themselves and their families.

"So, if they did not come here for refuge," Richie concluded, and looked to Ambrose and Henry. "Then where would they have gone; somewhere which looked safe and close by their house? You boys know this city well. What do you think?"

"The infirmary," Ambrose replied. Henry nodded agreement. "It's a fine tall building on high ground and the nuns of St. Mary's would not have turned anyone away."

"Before we walk back to St. Mary's," Richie looked from each to each, with an expression of utmost gravity. "We should go to the morgue on the Strand, just to be certain. I fear that most everyone who took shelter in a house smashed by the water is likely dead or beyond hope. Auntie Soph, I do not relish asking so much of you –

but you are the only one acquainted with the appearance of your friend, or her family."

"It's too soon to give up hope they may be alive!" Sophia cried, stung, and Richie shook his head.

"Auntie, it is in my mind they may soon have to begin disposing of the dead, without waiting for them to be identified properly. There are just too many."

Ambrose nodded in agreement, his expression likewise sober. "Papa has stories that *Großvater* told of how there were piles of nameless dead at Karlshaven, when the family first landed, and then after the storms that wrecked it. There will be the fear of contagion soon. The dead must be buried without delay, and then you will never know for certain."

"Very well," Sophia agreed reluctantly, although every fiber of her mind and nerve screamed against it. Laura, so brave – brash, even hard-headed – could not possibly be dead. The four of them picked their way along the Strand. It was a simple matter, finding the warehouse of the dead. It was where the wagons were going, the building upon which men carrying shutters and makeshift stretchers, laden with their pitiful cargo were converging silently. One and all appeared to move under a spell; quiet, courteous even, but numbed. The body, voice, intellect functioned in an outward semblance of normality, under the command of an automaton, rather than a rational mind.

The dead lay in serried rows on the bare ground inside the warehouse, their faces uncovered, and in some cases, their bodies as well – just as they were found. There was a man sitting on a chair at the warehouse door, which had been drawn open to its' full extent … no, likely it had been carried away by high water.

"We are looking for a friend of mine," Sophia announced to him in a tremulous voice. "Mrs. Andrew Belton – a tall lady, with very fair hair done in a long braid. She lived with her family on Q Street…"

The man shook his head, jerking his thumb towards the interior of the warehouse. "Look for her, then." He sounded as if already drink-dazed. Sophia did not blame him in the least. She stepped into the warehouse. There were other people within, walking between the rows of serried bodies.

"She is not here," Sophia declared with relief, an hour and some few minutes later. She and Richie, Ambrose and Henry had walked among the rows, looking for the bodies of women, women of Sophia's age, with long fair hair. Before long, the young men had taken on the chore of searching the rows, calling for Sophia upon spotting a body which might be that of Laura, or a child which might be one of her children – all of whom had the same fair hair. "Then to the Infirmary." She went with a lighter step, although her rational mind told her she had little cause for relief, not when the ranks of still corpses were being added to every minute.

She and Richie and the Richter boys picked their way to where the sprawling grounds and buildings of the Infirmary lay; the stout brick main buildings still stood although those built of frame lumber looked to have been smashed as thoroughly as any other. Still, there were the living gathered there, moving with purpose and direction, a fire lighted in an open space with a makeshift stove-top of a length of metal grate laid on it, propped up with a stack of broken brick at each corner. Kettles and pots on the grate sent up threads of steam.

Sophia spoke to the first nun she saw, tending the kettles with a long-shanked spoon in her hand and her black skirts drawn back and tucked into the waistband of her habit.

"Sister, I am looking for a friend and her family who may have come here last night. The Belton family … their house was close to the Gulf and…"

"There are many refugees from the storm here," the nun replied, patiently. "They were even swept up to our windows in the high water."

"She was a tall woman, my age, and with fair hair, almost white," Sophia pleaded. "Do you know if any …?"

"I am sorry, but I cannot recall anyone such as that." The nun sounded as if the edge of her patience was unraveling. "But if it contents you to search in here, do as you please… but I beg you, do not approach any of the ill in our wards. They have endured enough pain on account of sickness, they need not be further distressed."

Sophia nodded to the boys and began to walk away. As she did so, the nun called after her. "Ma'am, there is a young boy with fair hair here; twelve years old, I believe. He was floating on debris; we pulled in through an upper window last night at the height of the storm. But he was alone."

"Where is he?" Sophia's spirits rose. Laura's son Andrew was that age.

"He is sheltered in our refectory," the nun replied. "We have had to make shelter for so many." She gestured with the long-handled spoon, and Sophia followed the gesture with rising hope.

She found the boy, sitting in a corner. He had nothing on but a length of black cloth, which looked suspiciously like a piece of nun's habit, wrapped towel-fashion around his waist, and bandaging around both his hands, which might once have been white and pristine. He was filthy dirty, but his hair blazed like a bright banner in the dimness of what had become a dormitory.

"Andy," she said tentatively – it didn't bode well that the boy was all alone. "Andy, do you remember me?" Silence, and then his eyes focused on her, as he came from the mind-place he had been in, and his dirty face brightened in joyful recognition.

"Miz Steinmetz!" he cried, "Mama's frien'!" And he launched himself at her, wrapping his skinny naked arms about her waist, and burying his face in the breast of her dress, a grasp as frantic as a child stubbornly holding on to some dear treasure.

"Yes, dear, your mama's dear friend," Sophia embraced him. "I have been looking for you all this morning, ever since we saw that your house was washed away in the storm. Where are your parents, your sisters? Do you know where they are?"

The small head shook from side to side, once, twice. "No," Andy replied in a small voice. "I think they are drownded. We were at Granpy's house together and it was storming so hard. The house was shaking, about to come apart. Grandpy said that when it did, we should try an' hold on to something that floated. Grampy pushed Grammy and I out through a window, and I think he went to help the girls. Poppa an' Mama, they were together by another window, but then the roof fell down on us. Grammy an' me, we were on a piece of roof together, but she slipped off when it struck on something an' I couldn't find her afterwards. I floated around a bit. Miz Steinmetz, I think I floated all the way to the Strand and back. I can't find Grammy, and Grampy, nor Mama an' Papa."

"We will go on searching for them," Sophia made her voice calm, and reassuring. "In the meantime, you should come with me."

"A good notion, young fellow," Richie added his own voice, which held a peculiar depth of feeling in it. Yes, Sophia recollected; he had been near to Andy's age, on that morning when he had been called to the headmaster's office and told that he was now an orphan. "Come with us. We are staying with Mrs. Steinmetz's kin, and they have extended their hospitality to any friends of hers."

"Will that be all right, Ma'am?" Andy gulped, and loosened his grip on Sophia so he could draw back way and look up to her face.

"Of course it will," Sophia knew how to make her voice sound confident, reassuring. "We will sort it out. You will come with us, this very minute. We will send out word we are searching for your family, but meanwhile, you will be with us, among friends."

"Yes, Ma'am," Andy replied, appearing immediately more cheerful, although inclined to cling to Sophia, until Richie sighed and swung him up into his own strong arms.

"Young fella, your feet are torn to ribbons and you have no shoes. There is filth unimaginable in the streets and all manner of sharp things to cut bare feet to the bone." Sophia recollected how Richie had carried Min from the station to the refuge of the Richter mansion. No, in honesty, she could not imagine her brother going to that effort. Richard would have called up Declan or other member of the servant class and ordered them to do it. Fred's words; *"I have known too many brothers, or sons of fathers whose character and temperament was completely dissimilar – improvident wastrels with worthy sons, and sensible men with shiftless and quarrelsome brothers – to wholly believe in inheritable character."* How correct Fred had been, in his hard-won wisdom.

They passed by the improvised cook-fire, and the nun presiding over it; the woman's face was lined with weariness and responsibility, and it looked as if the smoke was causing her eyes to water, but she immediately appeared less weary. She paused in her stirring of various pots. It looked as if she were cooking a kind of pale gruel.

"You have found one of those whom you seek!" she exclaimed. "The Holy Mother has heard your prayers, at least in part!"

"Yes," Sophia answered. There was no other possible response. "We are most grateful – that one precious life has been spared. We will continue searching, though."

"I will say a prayer for you," the nun replied, and hesitated, as if reluctant to ask. "Have you in your searching gone as far as the orphanage? I know it is distant from town, but we have heard nothing from them since Sister Elizabeth came with a wagon yesterday for groceries. She did not linger since she worried about dinner for the children."

"No, we have not gone any farther today than Union Station," Sophia replied, and to her surprise, Henry spoke up, stuttering in his earnestness. "Was there a Sister Marie Dolores still among the teachers at the orphanage? In the world, she was a cousin to my father. They grew up together and we are fond of her. Is she safe, do you know?"

"Sister Dolores was at the orphanage with the children who were her special care," the nun replied; her countenance lost that brief bit of satisfaction over seeing Andy Belton restored to those searching for him. "We have had no word from Mother Superior Camillus since last night."

They walked on in silence, those long blocks to the Richter mansion, more than ever now appearing as a fortress and shelter. Ambrose spoke at last, misery hanging in every word.

"The orphanage was a grand new place, out at the edge of town, away from contagion. For the health of the children, you see – but nearly on the beach. Low ground. I dread telling Papa. They were children together and Papa was always ready to do a favor for her and her orphans."

"They may well have survived," Henry replied, but after the morning spent in search and recalling the ranks of corpses in the makeshift morgue, none of them had cause for optimism.

The four of them with Andy, bruised, battered, and all but naked, returned to the Richter place, grateful in heart for that refuge. Cousin George had not returned, but Amelie had started a fire in the stove. They were desperately thirsty and counted it doubly fortunate that the rainwater cistern at the top of the house had not been contaminated by seawater flooding in.

"There is sufficient water to drink," Amelie fussed in the German which was her accustomed tongue, "But for bathing; nothing but sea-water, I am afraid. Poor lad, he needs a good wash! And clothing! There are trunks of the lad's out grown clothing …"

"I will see what will fit him," Sophia offered, and added a suggestion. "There will be so many people who have lost everything; shall we take what we can to the Sisters at the Infirmary, for the benefit of those so dispossessed?"

Amelie fell on that suggestion with happy relief – an energetic woman, accustomed to command a household, but in this present emergency, somewhat at a loss. That afternoon, they found a straying milk-cow, miserable with her full udder, wandering along 25th Street and looking with longing on the remains of the Richter's lawn and green plants. Amelie surprised Sophia by capably bringing out a clean bucket from the laundry and taking the cow by the halter. She led the cow into the garden and set to milking the poor creature, on the spot.

"The children will have fresh milk!" Amelie remarked in complete satisfaction as she shooed the relieved cow into what remained of the Richter's stable. "Oh, my father kept cows, *Sopherl* – are you surprised?"

"No, I have become accustomed to the west," Sophia answered, for in truth she had. She passed the rest of the day working side by side with Amelie, her cook, and several women – neighbors of the Richters', whose houses had been destroyed. It appeared that even more guests were going to pack the rooms, halls and galleries of the mansion, as one of the relative few still standing and sound. Wet bedding must be hauled outdoors to dry, muck swept from floors, upholstered furniture carried out into the open, clothing found in trunks and dressers to cloth those who had nothing but the storm-ripped garments they stood up in, or like Andy Belton, even less than that. And cooking; enough so that everyone had something to eat or drink, even if it was just coffee brewed with faintly salty water.

"I have never wished so hard in my life," Sophia remarked to Amelie's cook, as they fed bits of dry wood into the cook-stove, "to see the miracle of the loaves and fishes repeated in this modern day."

"Ain't that the truth!" the other woman answered.

Before sundown, George Richter came walking up 25th Street, weary and disheveled. He had not shaved since before the storm, and his whiskers were coming out grey. Happily, he was helping another man, a storm refugee by the look of him, pull a hand-cart loaded with sealed tins, wooden boxes, bottles, and kegs.

"From our warehouse," George reported with satisfaction. Sophia recollected belatedly that George Richter was the purchasing agent for the various general stores scattered the length and breadth of Texas, owned and operated by his brothers and family. "Not all was swept away or ruined beyond retrieving. We have brought enough for ourselves and our guests. I have set two men to guard the rest, with instructions to give out portions to those who have none."

Amelie squealed when she embraced and kissed him, and demanded that he tell the newly enlarged household what had been going on while she and Sophia, with the sometime-assistance of Mrs. Pascoe and Amelie's cook were restoring something of domestic order to the vast, flood-wrecked first floor.

"We have sent a delegation to Houston on Mr. Moody's steam launch – the only boat left floating which will make it as far." George replied, standing there in the hallway where sea-sand still crunched under foot. "They will ask for help, although I hope such assistance is already on the way to us."

"When will they arrive, do you think?" Sophia asked, wistfully.

"Tuesday, at the earliest," George replied, and he looked at Sophia. "Did you find your friend, Mrs. Sophia?"

"Just her son – but I hope that if I search again tomorrow …" Sophia began, but George cut her off with a curt shake of his head.

"There is little hope, for anyone who has not so far appeared alive," he said, blunt and hard, as if only that way could he keep sorrow at bay. "The bodies are everywhere in hundreds, floating in the channel between the waterfront and the mainland. So thick – a boat which came into harbor today from a steamship which had blown adrift had to push them out of the way. We were favored by fortune, my dearest, that our home stood strong against water or wind, and on high ground."

"We have eaten a supper, and saved …" Amelie began, but George shook his head.

"I have no appetite for it now. Perhaps later – I am sorry. For now, I would rather rest." He looked at his wife and sons, adding, "The orphanage is gone. All but three children, and all the nuns with it, so I have been informed."

Sophia recalled the two nuns, slipping into the back of the church on the day of the wedding which now seemed to have occurred years ago and how she had wished to speak with them. Too late now. "A nun at the infirmary told us that Sister Marie Delores was there last night," she said, with a deep feeling of helplessness at George's obvious grief. "I am so sorry."

"She was a brave lady," George said, his voice breaking, "To chose a path of her own. In my mind and memory, she is always the age of your little daughter. She was always solemn, just like your little maid. I need think of a way to tell *Tante* Magda." He turned and went up the stairs, stumbling, in his weariness and sorrow.

She passed a fitful night, sharing the bed with Min, Baby in her arms and Andy on a moss-filled pallet spread out on the floor. The two children passed a wakeful night. Although both were brave enough during the day and when awake, dark and sleep brought night-terrors. If baby wasn't fussing, it was Andy or Min, flailing against the covers and calling out in their sleep. It was more restful to be awake when the sky lightened in the east. Monday ... Sophia wondered how soon she could leave Galveston. She had sufficient money in her purse for a regular train fare for herself and Min, even enough for Andy, but what would have been sufficient in a normal time wouldn't be enough now.

George, in his weary conversation the night before had alluded to the reality that those in Galveston who owned boats and launches of sufficient seaworthiness to reach the mainland would ask impossibly high sums for passage to the mainland coast for just a single person, let alone a woman and two children – never mind an infant. Sophia couldn't countenance traveling in such a primitive fashion with Baby. Her mind called up visions of an open boat, of trudging long miles through a devastated countryside with an infant in her arms. Yes, woman must have done so often enough – but these were modern times!

In the morning, she and Amalie set to work again, with the boys – Ambrose, Henry and young Andy to assist: they tried to bring order to those rooms most particularly ravaged by high water and winds, after contriving breakfast for themselves, their guests, friends, and the children. Richie went with Cousin George, grim-faced and intent on business – business to do with relief of the city, of all those poor souls living and dead.

Oat porridge seasoned lightly with saltwater was the best of it, and gruel made from hard biscuit. A good bit of what George had retrieved from his warehouse proved to be stone bottles of beer, wine and strong spirits, but there was a wheel of good cheese, covered with wax-saturated cloth which had escaped contamination, canned meats, and dried fruit, whose boxes appeared to have floated, protecting their contents.

"I suppose that we can find canvas and paint enough to spread over the worst parts of the roof, until we can hire men to come and repair it," Amelie fretted. "I am afraid that it will leak most dreadfully in the next rain and put our hard work to waste. The plaster in the upstairs is ruined." They stood out in the ravaged garden at the front of the mansion facing Broadway, looking up at the roof – bare wood, scoured and stripped of every slate by the fierce wind of Saturday's storm.

"I suppose that we will have to think about …" Sophia began – she was thinking out loud, but the rest of the thought was lost when a dear, familiar voice called to her.

"*Sopherl* – thank god!"

She turned, her heart leaping with joy in her breast; Fred, dear Fred, hatless and unkempt. And that was Horrie Vining at his heels, similarly disheveled. Without hesitation she ran to his embrace, fierce and passionate. She found that she was weeping, near hysterical with relief, while he murmured endearments in German.

"I will never let you go away from me again!" she exclaimed, when she could speak again. "Not me, not the children! Oh, Fred, how did you come to be here? You were supposed to be safe in San Antonio!"

"How can I travel without a care, once it was clear you and two of my dear little ducklings were in terrible danger?" Fred demanded, with understandable indignation, as Min appeared from the house, screaming, "Papa!" and launched herself full-tilt at her father. "There, now, Minchen, have a care for my ribs … my sweet darlings!" and he swept them both into another fierce embrace. When he could speak again, he explained. "Word of the storm reached us as we were halfway back to San Antonio. Horrie and I caught the next train back to Houston, Saturday evening, on hearing that the telegraph lines were down. We feared the worst." He embraced the two once more, burying his face in Sophia's hair, pulling Min close, so close, as if he would never let them go again. "When we came to Houston last night, it was plain that the storm had been dreadful. More than dreadful; Horrie and I resolved to travel to Galveston without delay, and by whatever means presented themselves."

"Yes!" Amelie exclaimed, wringing her hands. "How did you manage, Fredi? The railway trestles between here and the mainland are carried away, and the wagon-road causeway, too. Come into the house – you must be starving!"

"Easily enough," Fred replied. He loosened his embrace sufficiently, and Sophia and Min walked beside him up the stairs, towards a front door still hanging awry on it's hinges, since the tidal surge which had broken it open on Saturday evening. "We rode on the train, until the track was so washed away and covered with wreckage it was not possible to go any farther. Did you know there was steamship dredge carried away in-land and marooned on dry land, three miles from the shore? No tall tale; I saw it at a distance myself, and young Horace can confirm it. You would not believe what has washed up, along the shore. Horace and I and a party of others also determined to return – we found a rowboat cast up on shore. A lifeboat cast adrift from a ship in harbor, we assume. No oars or sail, although a boat-hook. That we did find. We carried the boat to the shore and waded with it to the nearest railway trestle. We pulled ourselves across with the boat-hook, from post to post. Such was our urgency to assure ourselves of the safety of those we loved, there was no labor we would not have performed!"

At his side, Horrie Vining nodded assent, affirming his own concern. "I am relieved to find you safe with the children, Mrs.

Sophie. All the way here, we kept assuring ourselves of the solidity of Uncle George's house, but then once we gained land, and observed such awful destruction! I rejoice myself at finding you safe."

"My friend Laura," Sophia murmured, as they came within the Richter's house. "Her family was carried away, all but her oldest son, we fear. We looked for her but only found the boy. He is an orphan now we fear, with no kin closer than …"

"Well, never mind then," Fred replied. "Our family has a long history of taking in orphans. He will come with us. Tomorrow, I will get passage for us on whatever boat is operating between here and Houston. You and Min, and especially Baby, cannot remain here any longer. There will be pestilence soon, from filthy water, if not the bodies of the dead."

"I have been helping Amelie," Sophia protested mildly, even knowing that Amelie would not be too discommoded by the departure of a portion of those sheltering under her roof. "I have an obligation to her, if not to those others in this place whom we can still assist…" Fred was already shaking his head.

"No, dearest *Sopherl*, every child – nay, every woman taken from here is one less in danger, one less call on scarce food and water. Besides our other children are crying for you. Do not feel guilty because you cannot be in all places. Come home."

"Of course," Sophia replied, her heart suddenly as light as a feather. Because Fred was correct. And now, everything would be all right.

Two weeks later, she sat with Baby sleeping in her lap, and the twins leaning against her from one side, Andy on the other. Fred sat across from her in the Pullman, Min sleeping against his shoulder and little Fred in his lap. It was afternoon, the hills above Deming painted salmon-color by the declining sun. They had not lingered in Houston, nor with Magda and her children in San Antonio, being eager to return home. Somehow, Sophia thought to herself, once we are home, this will all seem like a horrible dream to the children … even to Andy, an orphan of the great storm. She looked across the car, to where Richie sat with Carlotta, patiently listening to her reading aloud to him from a picture book. She repressed a smile, even as she felt a lump in her throat. Another orphan of a storm, she thought … but here was their refuge.

There … just around the edge of the hill, the welcoming glint of Deming's garden of windmills, endlessly turning above the rooftops.

"Look," she whispered to Andy. "We're almost home."

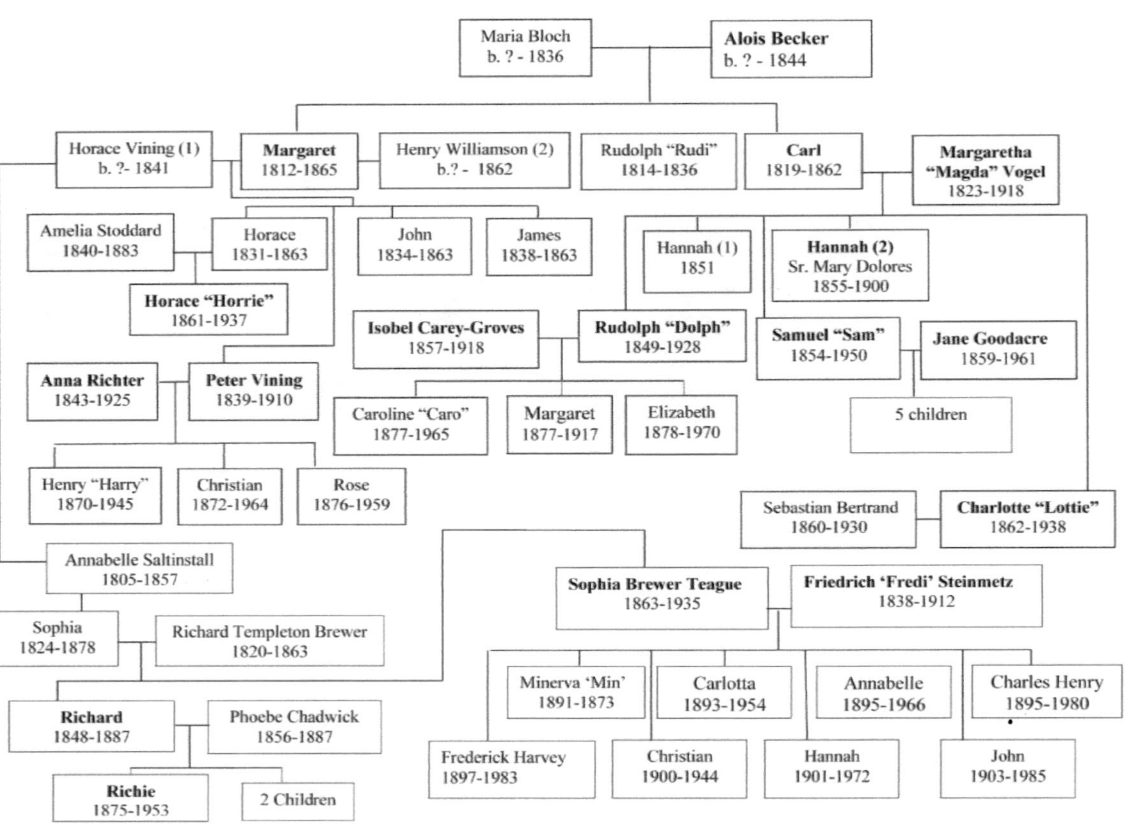
Becker – Vining Family
Maria Bloch
b. ? - 1836
Alois Becker
b. ? - 1844
Horace Vining (1)
b. ?- 1841
Margaret
1812-1865
Henry Williamson (2)
b.? - 1862
Rudolph "Rudi"
1814-1836
Carl
1819-1862
Margaretha
"Magda" Vogel
1823-1918
Amelia Stoddard
1840-1883
Horace
1831-1863
John
1834-1863
James
1838-1863
Hannah (1)
1851
Hannah (2)
Sr. Mary Dolores
1855-1900
Horace "Horrie"
1861-1937
Isobel Carey-Groves
1857-1918
Rudolph "Dolph"
1849-1928
Samuel "Sam"
1854-1950
Jane Goodacre
1859-1961
Anna Richter
1843-1925
Peter Vining
1839-1910
Caroline "Caro"
1877-1965
Margaret
1877-1917
Elizabeth
1878-1970
5 children
Henry "Harry"
1870-1945
Christian
1872-1964
Rose
1876-1959
Sebastian Bertrand
1860-1930
Charlotte "Lottie"
1862-1938
Annabelle Saltinstall
1805-1857
Sophia Brewer Teague
1863-1935
Friedrich 'Fredi' Steinmetz
1838-1912
Sophia
1824-1878
Richard Templeton Brewer
1820-1863
Minerva 'Min'
1891-1873
Carlotta
1893-1954
Annabelle
1895-1966
Charles Henry
1895-1980
Richard
1848-1887
Phoebe Chadwick
1856-1887
Frederick Harvey
1897-1983
Christian
1900-1944
Hannah
1901-1972
John
1903-1985
Richie
1875-1953
2 Children

Steinmetz – Richter Family

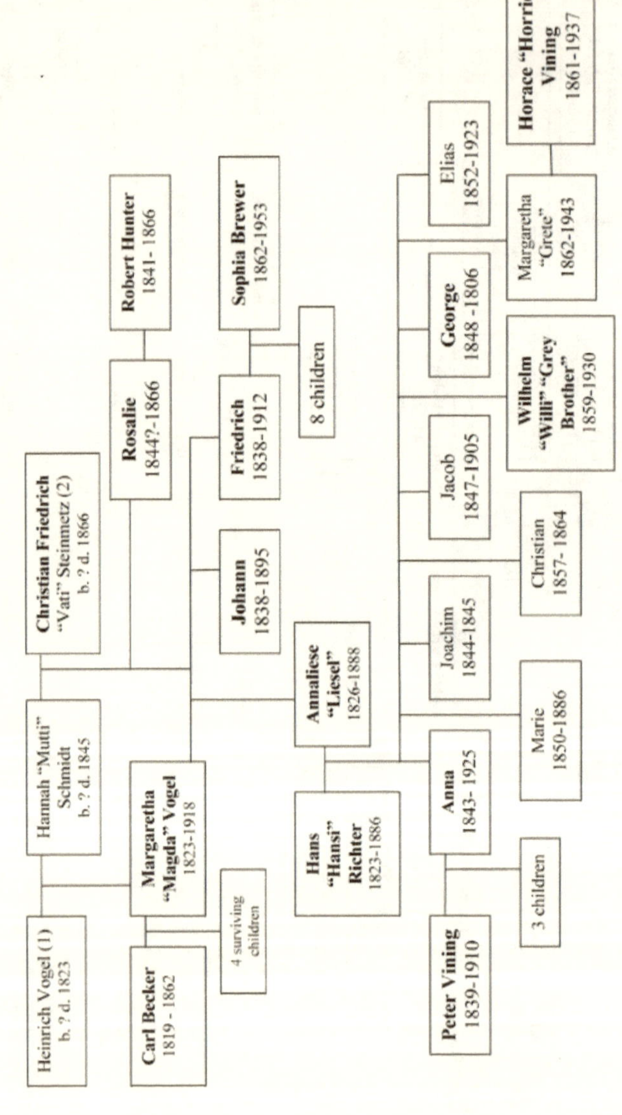

Historical Notes:
The 19th Century Internet, Fred Harvey, Lottie Deno and the Great Hurricane of 1900

Much of this story centers on a particular marvel of the 19th century; the railway, which was to Americans of that time something of what the internet is to ours. In this day and age, we have lost a certain sense of the shattering effect that technology had on that century – at least as much as the 20th. The world widened, in a way that perhaps was only duplicated by the internet, offering access to information, people, and to places – even if just vicariously. The rapidity of transport and communication was the marvel of the age, especially when compared to the century before, when nothing moved faster than a swift horse or a sailing ship in full rig, and lives were lived in candle and lamplight, and likely from cradle to grave within the space of five or ten miles. Sophia Brewer's life demonstrates something of this freedom, as well as the excitement and opportunity that the railroad offered for those who worked in some fashion for the railways, every bit as much as those those who made use of it.

The transcontinental railway and telegraph reshaped the American frontier it in a radical way, between the Civil War and the turn of the century. Life in a Western settlement no longer meant isolation, hardship and crushing boredom. A solitary rancher, mine-owner, farmer or small-town entrepreneur could now receive mail weekly or daily, rather than once a month, or whenever a ship came into port. They could order clothing, tools and furniture from a mail-order catalog (Montgomery Ward and Sears both had their beginnings in this era) and see the goods delivered in weeks, rather than years, just as Fred Steinmetz did for his ranch home in New Mexico. Diners in restaurants in Tombstone, Arizona, and Galveston, Texas, could feast on fish fresh-caught in the Great Lakes, seasonal fresh vegetables from the mid-west, and drink orange juice from California cooled on ice harvested from New England lakes, as they read the latest New York newspaper – just as Sophia served the clients of the various Harvey Houses. The working and middle classes in the west had wider horizons because through the railroad – and well-to-do easterners also had the opportunity to indulge in tourism, exploring spectacular scenery and entrancing local customs, while lapped in luxury and comfort. Entrepreneurs as diverse as Fred Harvey, Aaron Montgomery Ward, and George Pullman made fortunes in relation to railway service and inestimably improved the quality of life for westerners in general.

Fred Harvey, a Scots-English immigrant from Liverpool, developed a grand vision, that of bringing fine cooking and peerless customer service to the rowdy far West, and do so on a grand scale. In the Centennial year of 1876, he struck a handshake deal with the superintendent of the Atchison, Topeka & Santa Fe railroad to open and manage restaurants and lunch counters at AT&SF stations. The AT&SF would not charge Fred Harvey rent, or haulage for necessary supplies. Originally chartered to connect Santa Fe, New Mexico Territory, to settlements in Kansas, the AT&SF cleaned up in hauling Texas cattle to the stock yards of Chicago. They would eventually reach the Texas gulf coast, Mexico at the port of Guaymas, connect Albuquerque and El Paso, and service Los Angeles over the route which had been favored by the ante-bellum South when the prospect of a transcontinental railroad was first suggested.

Eventually there were nearly 50 Harvey House restaurants, fifteen resort hotels and thirty dining cars, attending to the needs of the traveling public. Harvey establishments were spotlessly clean, the food expertly prepared and served by staff trained to the highest standard … or else. Fred Harvey was a hands-on manager; Selina's story of him whipping out the tablecloth of a badly-set table, sending the plates and silverware crashing to the floor was one frequently repeated. The level of corporate organization didn't stop there, either. They had train conductors telegraph ahead of the next meal stop, alerting the Harvey House at the next stop how many passengers planned to dine in the restaurant and lunchroom. The company sent all restaurant and hotel laundry to be done at a single corporate facility, maintained their own dairy and ranch, provided their own brand of coffee to their Houses – as well as water, if the local wells didn't meet the standard, fresh fruit, ice and more. It was a nationwide chain long before nation-wide chains came into existence.

Fred Harvey was also passionately interested in hiring and training the best personnel available, promoting the able and the loyal, and in providing for their welfare. But his best-remembered innovation was the wait-staff force itself; all-female. This came about at the suggestion of one of his managers, sometime in the early 1880s. It seemed that many of the waiters at his location were black – and customers who were white Southern males habitually picked fights with the staff, absconded without paying for their meals and otherwise wreaking havoc – when the waiters weren't brawling with each other. This would not do; it was bad for staff morale, hell on the profit side of the ledger and hard on the furniture. Fred Harvey was an innovative thinker; the advantages to female wait-staff were immediately apparent, as were certain of the disadvantages, among them the conventional wisdom that single women who came to work in eating establishments and dance halls in Western boom towns were suspected (often with good cause) of being prostitutes or just promiscuous with their favors. Fred Harvey wanted none of that. The Harvey organization was a respectable institution, and wanted no breath of local scandal attaching to female employees, most of whom would be working in towns geographically-distant from their families; hence the fairly strict standard of dress, demeanor and chaperonage.

Fred Harvey advertised widely in the eastern and mid-western newspapers: young unmarried women between the ages of 18 and thirty, who would sign a contract to work for a set period of time (usually a year). They were required to be literate, well-spoken, accustomed to hard work, and willing to go west to wherever they were needed. Some estimates have it that over the next thirty years, 5,000 women worked as Harvey Girls, everywhere from Kansas to California. Their working uniforms were as described: plain black dresses with narrow white collars, black shoes and stockings, white aprons, and their hair tied with a white ribbon. They were not allowed to wear makeup – which likely only became a real trial in the 1920s. They were paid $17 monthly; at a time when laborers were lucky to earn $11 a month – and they kept their tips. They lived in company-provided dormitories, as described, their uniforms were often also provided, and they were entitled to perks like free transportation on the AT&SF. After a period with the company a Harvey Girl could request a specific location. Seniority in the Harvey organization could be accrued. Unless a Harvey Girl chose to marry, as so many did, she could work her way up to senior waitress or even manager. A comparison between Harvey Girls and stewardesses in the glamorous days of commercial flight has been made. Both groups were composed of relatively young, independent and adventurous women, carefully selected and working in a setting where their attractive qualities were shown at an advantage. The Fred Harvey hospitality empire not only is given popular credit for 'civilizing' the Wild West, but also for supplying that stretch of the Southwest between the Mississippi-Missouri and the Sacramento with excellent food and drink, splendid service, and a constant stream of wives – for many of the women recruited married right and left; to railroad men, coworkers in the Harvey establishments, and to customers they met in the course of their duties.

Fred Harvey's health declined precipitously in the late 1890s. He died of complications of intestinal cancer in 1901, but not before he had trained up his sons Ford and Byron in every aspect of the business. They carried on without any discernible change in focus or standards. David Benjamin was indeed in Galveston for business on the day of the horrific hurricane – arriving on the last train from Houston before rising water and a ship torn loose from its moorings carried away the railway trestles and the wagon bridge to the mainland. Coincidentally, he was also in San Francisco on the day of the 1906 earthquake … and temporarily marooned in Europe on the outbreak of World War I.

The company had one last fling during WWII, when the wartime Harvey Girls worked overtime feeding troop-trains passing through. On any number of occasions, when there was no time for the soldiers to de-train and eat, the Girls just passed sandwiches in through the windows. The Judy Garland movie, *The Harvey Girls* brought the awareness of all things Harvey to anyone who just might have escaped knowing about them … but the sixty-year run was already nearly over. Increasingly, people preferred traveling by automobile, or by airplane. The dining facilities built all along the tracks of the AT&SF were repurposed, or torn down. Some now serve as museums or city offices, or stand derelict and crumbling. A handful, like La Fonda in Santa Fe, El Tovar on the edge of the Grand Canyon and El Posada in Winslow, Arizona, are still hotels, although not operated by Fred Harvey.

As described, the Deming Harvey House was the object of a robbery, in 1904 – but by a single masked man dressed as a woman, who was not dispatched on the spot, but arrested later, when he returned without his disguise and was recognized. As for Sophia's friend in Deming, Lottie Thurmond – she was a real person, a pillar of society in Deming at the turn of the last century. Of course, this was after her first career as a professional gambler.

Lottie was short for Carlotta, the older of two daughters of an imperishably respectable and formerly well-to-do Kentucky family named Thompkins. For some reason – perhaps it amused him to have an able opponent on those evenings at home, before television and the internet – Mr. Thompkins taught his older daughter to play cards, and to play them very well. The Civil War broke out when Lottie was 17. Within a short time, her father had volunteered for service in the Confederate Army and fallen in battle. The fortunes of the family declined precipitously, along with the health of Lottie's mother. Neither Lottie, her mother, or her younger sister seemed equal to the task of running their property or the late Mr. Thompkins' business interests. The solution that Mrs. Thompkins arrived at was the logical and time-honored traditional solution: Lottie should marry a rich and able man to take care of them all. Lottie had other plans – perhaps she had fallen in love with a man her mother did not approve of – and she began working the professional gambling circuit, very profitably. At the end of the Civil War she went west to Texas. Some stories have it that she told her mother and sister she had married a wealthy cattleman. Eventually, she came to San Antonio, and worked dealing cards at a place called the University Club. She was immediately popular, even though the permitted no drinking or cursing at the poker table over which she presided – always elegantly dressed, cultured and the very soul of Southern belle-hood. Very soon she was known as the Angel of San Antonio. The University Club was owned by Frank Thurmond; When Frank got into a fight with another gambler and killed him with his Bowie knife, he had to leave town fast. Eventually, he and Lottie married, and lived the rest of their lives in quiet respectability in Deming. Frank went went into business as described here – real estate, mostly – and was vice-president of the local bank. Lottie also was an upright pillar of the community, helping to establish an Episcopal church in Deming. She died in 1934, outliving her husband by 26 years, but not a certain legend. It is assumed that she was the model for the character of Miss Kitty, in the old *Gunsmoke* radio and television series.

That 1900 hurricane which struck Galveston still stands as the single deadliest natural disaster ever to strike the United States, with a death toll equal of all later storms combined; at least 6,000 in Galveston alone – a quarter of the population at the time – and along the Texas coast. The storm surge went for miles inland, and may have carried away another 2,000, whose bodies were never found – and never reported missing, as there was no one left to do so. As hinted at in this account, there were so many dead that the overwhelmed authorities had to resort to burning them on large pyres.

There were warning, of course – the US had an active and professional weather service, but their official forecasters believed the storm was moving in a line which would take it across Florida, up the east coast and then out into the Atlantic again. They disregarded predictions by observers in Cuba who insisted that the storm system would continue westerly, impacting against the Texas Gulf coast. And residents of Galveston were, on the whole, terribly blasé regarding storms, anyway. By the time that they realized – by mid-afternoon on Saturday – that the storm coming was a particularly deadly one it was too late to even consider evacuation. The best that people could do was to take refuge in the sturdiest buildings, on the highest part of Galveston Island had always before been sufficient. Most residences were raised above the ground, in the expectation of storm tides.

The train from Houston arrived, as described, with water already so high and turbulent that they were eating away the land under the rails. One of the arriving passengers, who took shelter in the railway station itself had a pocket barometer in his luggage, and commenced to take readings, as his barometer – and that Galveston's weather station on the roof of the Levy building began to fall, and fall, and fall even farther, to the point where some observers began to think the instruments must be defective. Long afterwards, weather experts estimated the winds to have blown at 150 miles per hour with gusts reaching 200. There was no way to be certain, as the Weather Bureau's anemometer and rain gage were blown off the top of the Levy Building and destroyed early in the evening. The sky turned so dark that it seemed to some as if dusk had already fallen. The wind whipped slate tiles as if they were shrapnel. At about two in the afternoon, the wind shifted from a northerly direction to the northeast; over the next hours, the water came up and up, higher and higher, driving people into the second floor of whatever they had taken refuge in – assuming that they had a second floor. As in this story, just short of seven in the evening the water rose four feet in as many seconds. The meticulous observer Isaac Cline, of the local weather bureau office noted the rise against the dimensions of his own house, calculating that the storm surge was over fifteen feet deep and rising. He was certain that his house would withstand the storm, constructed as it was on deep-driven pilings.

Unfortunately, he and others had not considered the effect of wind and water driving an irresistible moraine of debris blocks deep into the residential areas along that part of the Island which faced the Gulf. Lumber and wreckage from other houses, reinforced with heavy timbers, iron street-car rails, and uprooted trees, all made a solid mass, which waves pounded farther and farther inland; a leviathan grinding up and adding more wreckage to the mass, until it towered almost two stories tall and stretched across the middle of town. At least 3,600 buildings were smashed, leaving those fortunate enough to survive without much shelter when Sunday morning came – a calm and mild day, considering the fury of the night before. The first train to try reaching Galveston could come no closer than six miles from shore, reporting that the coastal prairie was strewn with debris and corpses, and a large steamship stranded two miles inland. A small party of men, and one woman, resolved to reach their families on the Island did contrive to walk, wade, and raft across from the mainland as Fred and Horrie did – pulling a raft with a boat-hook along the line of pilings which had supported a causeway.

Galveston did rebuild. A seawall first suggested and rejected after the destruction of Indianola twenty-five years before was constructed; sand was dredged from the bay and used to raise the level of the island nearly twenty feet. With a great deal of trouble and effort, 2,100 of the surviving buildings were elevated. All of this proved their worth when another hurricane struck dead on in 1915, with comparatively minor casualties. However, dredging the Houston Ship Channel to accommodate ocean-going ships spelled doom for Galveston as an important player in commerce and shipping.